Also by Julia Fierro

Cutting Teeth

Advance Praise for *The Gypsy Moth Summer*

"This novel shakes and stirs family saga and summer romance upside down. The irresistible storytelling brings to life each character, and Fierro doesn't just observe, she *knows*. She gives us a particular and narrow neighborhood, and like all great novelists, she gives us the world."   —Amy Bloom, bestselling author of *Away*

"A deeply satisfying tale of family, first love, and home. It's a meditation on what makes a community and a reminder that the past is never past and home is a place that is both beautiful and heartbreaking."
—Kaitlyn Greenidge, author of *We Love You, Charlie Freeman*

"Julia Fierro's masterful second novel draws us close, makes us its confidante, and then delivers hard and violent truths about the island's legacy of denial."   —Scott Blackwood, author of *See How Small*

"Julia Fierro's marvelous *The Gypsy Moth Summer* is a novel to slowly savor, settling in with her characters as you would old friends, cherishing every sentence, every turn of plot. Rarely does one encounter a novel this entertaining, which also speaks to the complicated truths about race and class at the heart of our country's tangled history."
—Joanna Rakoff, author of *My Salinger Year*

"A luminous, urgent novel about the forces that shape us all: where we grow up; whether we are loved by our parents or understood by our peers; how class, power, and money may cast our fates. I rooted for the lovers at the thrumming heart of the book with the hungry turn of every page."   —Sophie McManus, author of *The Unfortunates*

"*The Gypsy Moth Summer* gathers all of life in its wonderfully confident reach: the buzzing energy of youth, the fraught hope of adulthood, the remorseless clarity of old age. Fierro's thoroughly entertaining storytelling doesn't prevent her from taking on weighty subjects. We are deeply invested in her characters around whom an air of tragic destiny hangs, and the pages fly by as the book hurtles toward its devastating conclusion."   —Matthew Thomas, *New York Times* bestselling author of *We Are Not Ourselves*

"*Masterpiece* is a word that often is casually tossed around, but it fits Fierro's work, which is so richly alive, so poetic, it is truly Shakespearean tragedy. I had a sense of wonder that someone could craft a novel as perfect as this one."
—Caroline Leavitt, author of the *New York Times* bestsellers *Pictures of You, Is This Tomorrow,* and *Cruel Beautiful World*

THE
GYPSY MOTH
SUMMER

❊

JULIA FIERRO

St. Martin's Press ☙ New York

THE GYPSY MOTH SUMMER. Copyright © 2017 by Julia Fierro. All rights reserved. Printed in the United States of America. For information, address St. Martin's Press, 175 Fifth Avenue, New York, N.Y. 10010.

www.stmartins.com

Illustration of gypsy moth caterpillar by Salvatore Gerardo Fierro

Library of Congress Cataloging-in-Publication Data

Names: Fierro, Julia, author.
Title: The gypsy moth summer : a novel / Julia Fierro.
Description: First Edition. | New York : St. Martin's Press, 2017.
Identifiers: LCCN 2017002670 | ISBN 9781250087515
    (hardback) | ISBN 9781250087539 (e-book)
Subjects: | BISAC: FICTION / Contemporary Women. |
    FICTION / Coming of Age.
Classification: LCC PS3606.I368 G97 2017 | DDC 813/.6—dc23
LC record available at https://lccn.loc.gov/2017002670

Our books may be purchased in bulk for promotional, educational, or business use. Please contact your local bookseller or the Macmillan Corporate and Premium Sales Department at 1-800-221-7945, extension 5442, or by e-mail at Macmillan SpecialMarkets@macmillan.com.

First Edition: June 2017

10 9 8 7 6 5 4 3 2 1

To the queen of my island,
my first and best storyteller,
the colonel's daughter,
my mother,
Patricia Irene

And to my father,
king of the gardens, beekeeper,
contadino and *carabiniere*,
WWII survivor,
Salvatore Gerardo

Contents

PART 4

An Eclipse of Moths—July–August 1992

PART 5

The Spawning—
Late August–Early September 1992

Life being what it is, one dreams of revenge.

—PAUL GAUGUIN

JUNE 15, 1992

If You Notice:

1. Extensive defoliation of your trees;

2. Caterpillars (larvae) with blue and red dots on the branches and/or leaves;

3. Egg masses.

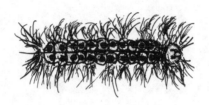

PLEASE NOTIFY:

Agricultural Commissioner's Office or
GYPSY MOTH PROJECT

2125 Old Country Road,
Suite 309

Avalon Island, NY 11743

(516) 555-2287

Thank you for your cooperation.

Prologue

Before that summer of '92, when the gypsy moths swarmed Avalon Island and Leslie Day Marshall, golden-headed prodigal daughter, returned with her black husband and brown children to claim her seat as First Lady, the island's crimes were minor. Teenagers breaking into a newly constructed mansion to throw a kegger. A maid stealing from her mistress. East High's quarterback wrapping his shiny Mustang—a graduation present from his grandfather—around the ancient oak tree on Snake Hill. And occasionally a neighbor, the investment banker, disappearing for six months, only to return lean and fit after a stay at a low-security prison.

Plenty of islanders died, of course. In peaceful slumber; a heart attack midswing on the Oyster Cove Country Club golf green; drowned out at sea and right there on shore. A few had leapt, or fallen, no one knew for sure, from the pink clay cliffs of Singing Beach. But *not one,* the eldest islanders claimed, had ever fallen at the hands of another.

Before that summer of '92, people left their front doors unlocked when they turned in for the night, and children, even those who still believed in the witches and wolves of fairy tales, fled to the woods each evening. *Be careful,* their mothers called as the children threw open screen doors and ran barelegged into the birch turned blue by the otherworldly light that blanketed the island each night. Their mothers were reminding them of the rare car on the island's snaking roads. Dusk can fool the eyes, more so on nights the island wears a crown of oyster-gray mist—those who've visited Avalon will agree. But as children do, they believed themselves unbreakable, and deaf to Mother's caution, they hurdled spicebush and witch hazel, ignoring the bite of bramble thorns. Laughing when a dewy spiderweb tore against their faces. No stories of little children lost to the woods told by well-meaning mothers could keep them from their games. Manhunt. Thieves' Den. Indians versus Settlers.

The island's teenagers, too, felt safest in the woods. Camouflaged by thickets of black cherry and pitch pine, red chokeberry and sweet pepperbush, the cool night air a balm to their sunburned shoulders. The darkness a relief after hours spent tanning on the island's beaches, their bikinied bodies slick with Johnson's Baby Oil. The trill of a wood thrush cracking the silence, they told ghost stories while a joint was passed. Stories where a single event—a full moon, an evil spell, true love's kiss—turns man into beast. Beast into man.

Not yet men and women and no longer boys and girls, they may have believed in fairy tales still but wouldn't dare confess. They played their own games in the woodland pocked with fireflies. Girls shrieked when caught by a boy. Hungry mouths found each other in the dark. Tongues twined. Hands slipped under sweatshirts. The boldest couples retreated deep into the trees to roll on a sheet someone had swiped from his or her mother's linen closet.

That summer, after the black-bristled gypsy moth caterpillars hatched and the forest throbbed with their gnashing, Avalon's youth surrendered the woods reluctantly. What more was there to fear (or was it that they feared nothing more?) than the disapproval of their parents and teachers and coaches? Worse, their grandparents' disappointment. In Grandson's too-long hair, Granddaughter's too-short skirt, the kids' *whassups* and *whatevers* and the noise they called music, and what the old men and women insisted on calling *hippie* attitudes—never mind that it was two decades since their own children had lived through the counterculture. These were the founding fathers and mothers of the island's livelihood, Grudder Aviation. The factory's four concrete stacks loomed six hundred feet tall, visible from any point on the island, and the children felt the towers following them, as constant as the moon, until the only place to hide from their elders' watch was the deep woods.

East Avalon was the upper crust—military engineers who had exchanged their navy whites and blues for suits and offices on the upper floor of Grudder Aviation, the factory all Avalonians called

Old Ironsides. West Avalon, the treeless section of the island where row houses stood shoulder-to-shoulder with gas stations and the town dump, was the meat—generations of factory workers manning the assembly floor, their fingernails ringed with the grease that kept the machines running, the fighting aircraft multiplying. The "Cats"—Hellcat, Wildcat, Tigercat, Bearcat, Panther—whose roars had shot down America's enemies and inspired the naming of every corner of the island. From East Avalon High (the Wildcats) to West High (the Panthers); to most of the shops in town—Bearcat Café, Cougar Cleaners, Hellcat Pub. Grudder was the islanders' fraternity, tribe, and church—every Avalonian had heard tales of F6F Wildcat airmen swearing they had more faith in Grudder than in God.

On an island, time can freeze, but that summer the islanders felt a change coming. East and West agreed: There was a yawning divide between old and young. Yesterday and tomorrow. The new generation of Avalonians worshipped at the altar of MTV; didn't fear the Bomb; heard the slogan "Be All You Can Be" and thought not of defending his or her country but, instead, imagined their future selves waiting to hatch like the moth eggs tucked in the crooks and bends of every tree on the island.

The new threat was impossible to ignore. *Cancer, cancer,* whispered worried mothers, as if lamenting out loud would infect their families. They commiserated in hushed voices at school bake sales; in the bleachers during a Saturday lacrosse match; and on line at the supermarket deli, paper tickets clutched in freshly manicured fingers.

East Avalonians began driving to the wholesale store on the mainland and carted cases of bottled water across the causeway. Those born factory class mocked their wealthy neighbors: *Here they come with their holy water!* But even they wrung their hands when the graffiti appeared that spring, just as the crocus broke earth. GRUDDER IS CANCER. GRUDDER KILLS.

But for now, it is June and the roses are in bloom. The tough and thorny Rugosa's apple-shaped hips thrive on the island's dunes, the bright-pink Swamp Rose in the marsh. Inland, in the leafy woods, there's the Carolina Rose, Sweetbriar, Scotch Briar, and Dog Rose. High in the east hills, the air is heady from the ladies' gardens—rows of hybrids whose names conjure Victorian women in high-collared and bustled dresses, strolling arm in arm under a parasol. La Reine, Leda, Bourbon, Starlight, Ballerina, and the aromatic American Beauty. Each bloom impeccable—a perfection that confirms the east islanders' belief that all can be cultivated. Controlled. Their children and spouses and lovers and servants; their workers and factory; their island and country. Despite that liberal governor from Arkansas slithering his way toward the White House. *Like the yellow-bellied draft dodger he is*, the Grudder executives, some navy men, grumble on the golf green. Despite the death of the Cold War, the factory's bread and butter; and the fall of the Berlin Wall and the Soviet Union; and the defense budget cuts sparking rumors of layoffs at Old Ironsides.

By summer's end, all of Avalon will have seen too much to play make believe at love and war again. So let them believe for now. Let them play. Those girls with dimpled smiles and scraped knees; those young men, lean and long but still capable of blushing; those unformed, and perhaps better, versions of the men and women they will become.

For now, they are young and beautiful, pure muscle and unblemished skin. They are in love—a faith that makes them tease death. They swing out over the sea cliffs clutching a tire tied to a tree; drop two tabs of acid and swim to the end of the ferry landing and back; drag race down the wrong side of the causeway at two in the morning; fly headfirst toward danger, deaf to their mothers' warnings—*Be careful*—all to win a bet. To prove they are what they feel. Immortal.

PART ONE

The Hatching

June 5, 1992

Egg clusters contain from 100 to 1000 eggs.

Newly hatched larvae are black with long, hairlike setae. Older larvae have five pairs of raised blue spots and six pairs of brick-red spots along their backs.

—*The Gypsy Moth: Research Toward Integrated Pest Management*, United States Department of Agriculture, 1981

The young caterpillars spin silken threads and hang down from the tree branches. Wind often breaks the threads and carries the caterpillars to nearby trees and shrubs. This is called "ballooning."

—Carolyn Klass, "Gypsy Moth," *Insect Diagnostic Laboratory*, Dept. of Entomology, Cornell University, 1981

1.

Maddie

For Maddie Pencott LaRosa, newly sweet sixteen, the East Avalon fair, first of the season, was a coming-out party.

She strode down the fairway in Bitsy Smith's pack, doubling her steps to keep up with the other girls. Bitsy, Vanessa, Gabrielle, and the newest recruits: Maddie and her best friend, Penny. Five pairs of angular hips bumping and bronzed shoulders rubbing, their long sun-lightened hair flowing behind in one stream of fiery light.

Maddie knew it was a coming-out for everyone on the eastern tip of Avalon Island, a chance to celebrate the end of a long, hard winter. The young mothers had painted their fingernails and tried out a new lip color; convinced their husbands to wear madras shorts, a Christmas gift ordered from a catalogue. Children raced down the fairway, candy apple in one hand, and in the other, a goldfish sloshing in a water-filled baggie. But Maddie felt all eyes pinned on her and the girls trailing Bitsy—the strands of her ringleader's hair like golden threads of honey tying worker bees to their queen.

Everyone at East High knew Bitsy *was* the queen. Of the sassy head tilt, condescending eye roll, the who-the-fuck-do-you-think-you-are stance, one hip jutting as Bitsy's sea-gray eyes slow-mo scanned Maddie up and down so it was crystal clear she judged every flawed bit. The new breasts Maddie had tried to hide under a sweatshirt all spring. The acne peppering her forehead, poorly concealed by uneven bangs she'd trimmed herself. Too impatient and broke—too stupid, she thought—to make an appointment at the salon in town.

Like the other girls, she'd worn white (a denim skirt and eyelet top), just as Bitsy had instructed over the phone the night before.

Maddie caught her reflection in the window of the food truck selling fried chicken wings. She liked the way her tanned skin vibrated in contrast, and as the flashing bulbs of the Tilt-A-Whirl painted her uniform red-orange-blue-red-orange-blue it was like looking through a gem-filled kaleidoscope. Proof the night was as magical as she'd hoped it would be—dreams that had carried her through the winter of '91 with its blizzards and the nor'easter turned perfect storm that had flooded the causeway, the island's only exit. As she'd trudged through the snow toward the school bus stop, Tic Tac boxes filled with hot water tucked in the pockets of her peacoat, she'd imagined the fairway stretched like a green carpet across the town square. The carnival lights burning against an inky sky. She had tasted cotton candy melting on her tongue and heard the old-timey carousel tunes. The fair had been a present waiting to be unwrapped, held under her bulky sweaters all winter long, keeping her warm.

Now the air was sweet with the pastel cotton-candy clouds of her dreams. Caramel apples sweated in the new heat. Scents mingled—Love's Baby Soft and Petite Naté for the girls and, for the ladies, perfumes with names that made virginal Maddie blush. Eternity. Obsession. Trésor.

The girls passed the dunking booth, where a toothy, smiling Tina Meyer sat. Tina was captain of the cheerleading team and president of SADD (Students Against Drunk Driving), and, Maddie had heard from bigmouth Vanessa, infamous for giving Troy Mayhew a blowjob in the back of the football bus on the drive home from an away game. A crowd of teenage boys (a few Maddie recognized) in blue-and-white varsity jackets—felted wildcats lunging across the white leather, teeth bared, claws sprung—circled the tank, their energy fanning out like the ripples in the pond behind St. John's Church.

"Soak the slut!" a boy yelled.

The buzzer brayed and Tina Meyer dropped into the water. A few cold drops hit Maddie's cheek and she wiped them away, careful not to smear her makeup. She watched as the dripping girl pulled herself from the black water streaked with colored light and back onto her perch—every curve outlined under her soaked Wildcats T-shirt. She was shivering, her lips gone purplish. Maddie barely knew Tina but wished someone would rescue her.

"For fucksake," Bitsy said so everyone could hear, including Tina, "cover the girl so we don't have to look at her mutant nipples!"

"*Tsss*, burn," Vanessa hissed, nodding in approval. "The girl is cuttin' glass!"

Gabrielle threw an I-told-you-so smirk over her shoulder, her long blond waves slicing through the air. "That twat better pray she don't get gang raped in the parking lot."

The girls giggled and Maddie felt like she was wading through a shower of shattered glass. She knew they loved nothing more than a good laugh, especially if it was the punch line to humiliating someone. Self-righteousness buoyed them so they walked on air, and Maddie felt their stride accelerate, as powerful as the engines of the Grudder Wildcats that flew in formation over the island every Fourth of July.

She tried to imagine what people saw. Girls? Women? Young ladies? Wasn't that what her grandmother's friends at the club called her? *What a fine young lady.* But there'd been rumors flying around the corridors of East High that spring—Bitsy Smith and her clique were *wild* girls. *Fun* girls. Up for a good time.

Maddie watched Bitsy prance ahead, her flawlessly straight hair swinging in time with her swiveling hips. *Swish, swish, swish.* Like the mane of Smith's Farragut, the champion horse Bitsy rode in shows, named for the first admiral in the navy, whose life story Maddie and all the island kids had memorized in grade school. Gabrielle, second in command, was the curviest, and Maddie was sure she saw Gabrielle's lacy underwear through her snug white shorts. Vanessa, Bitsy's unofficial bodyguard, was sporting newly filled-out breasts aided by a push-up bra she'd bragged about lifting from Victoria's Secret. And finally, there was Penny, Maddie's best friend, who, Maddie thought, desperately needed a bra to shape the two mounds hanging loose under her Izod button-down.

Their bodies were no longer childish. Still, Maddie needed to think of them as girls. She wasn't ready for what came next, whatever *it* was, but there was a fever in the air, hovering above the rattle of the popcorn machine and the shudder of the Zipper careening over old rails. She heard the sizzle of a sparkler; then a balloon popped with a crack and the crowd whooped and a child gasped; and, suddenly, Maddie believed in hearts leaping and swelling, breaking and exploding. Scenarios she'd come to long for after watching videos on MTV and listening to love ballads DJ Spinbad played on Z100.3. When Whitney Houston hit those yearning-filled high notes in "I Will Always Love You" (every other hour it seemed), Maddie turned up the radio, rolled her car windows down, lit a Kent King 100 she'd stolen from her grandmother's pantry, put the pedal to the metal, and sang along, free from the fear that she might embarrass herself.

As the pulsing bass of the fair's most popular ride, the Gravitron, soaked into the soles of her sandals, slithered up her calves, her thighs, and reached inside her, she believed something was on its way. How could she not? She was young and beautiful—or, at least, pretty enough, she thought—at a time in life when being young and beautiful seemed like the answer to everything.

The girls passed game after game—ringtoss and Whac-A-Mole and darts and, Maddie's favorite, the one where you shot water from a plastic pistol into a balloon that stretched and stretched, then burst with a splash. But there was no stopping without Bitsy's permission, and who wanted any of those junky prizes anyway—the sad-eyed stuffed panda bears as big as golden retrievers Maddie had longed for as a child, or the lethargic goldfish scooped from a tank. The fish never lasted more than a day.

She'd prepared for the fair. Ironed her jean skirt, double-shaved her legs, used Nair to remove the downy fur on her upper lip. She cleaned out the bottom drawer in the fridge, took the lemons her dad stuffed in his roast chicken, and, man, would he be pissed when he found out. She'd squeezed one after another over her long brown hair and lay out to tan on a faded bath towel spread over the hard asphalt of the driveway, praying the juice turned her hair buttery with highlights. Who cared that it wasn't technically summer? Or that her skin prickled in the wind gusting in from the Sound? Bitsy, miraculously, had been tan for weeks, her hair striped blond, so she glowed like the sunset that burned along shore each night.

Maddie had been tempted to buy a bottle of Sun In at Genovese Drug Store but feared the peroxide spray could turn her hair
a garish copper. Last week, Bitsy had ripped Penny a new one
when she showed up on the last day of school a freakish bronze
from one of those tan-in-a-bottle creams. The skin between her
fingers as brown as mud. Vanessa had teased Penny all week, using the few words of Spanish she knew. *Hola, Miss Penelope!*
Her fake accent and rolling *r*'s making Maddie glance around to
see if anyone had heard.

"Patience is a virtue," Bitsy had said to Penny in a motherly
tone, then added, "Think before you fucking do, dumdum, 'kay?"

Gliding through life as a member of Bitsy's pack was like riding a roller coaster for the first time—every dip and swerve thrill-
ing but also gut-flipping, so Maddie didn't know if the girls
might praise her one minute (*Oh my God, Maddie, how'd you
get your hair to shine like that?*) and knock her down the next
(*Too bad your dad, like, gave you his Eye-talian skin—have you
tried Clearasil?*).

At least, Maddie thought, she didn't worship Bitsy blindly like
Penny did. As they strode past the Captain's Ship, the screams
of its passengers rising as the ride arced into the night sky, she
spotted Penny biting into a fried zeppole ball—her mouth a
smear of frosted lip gloss and powdered sugar; the thin white-
blond hair Maddie had straightened before the fair already
crimping.

"Quit messing with your hair, Pen," Maddie whispered as they
paraded past food carts selling slick pizza slices and heroes spilling ribbons of beef.

"What?" Penny lifted her greasy fingers to her hair.

"Forget it."

Penny stuck her tongue out at Maddie before taking another
bite of the sugary dough.

That night, Penny's parents, Major and Mrs. Whittemore,
had been out of the house, knocking back martinis and manhattans at the Oyster Cove Country Club cocktail hour—their
Saturday-night ritual. So Maddie and Penny had blasted "Smells
Like Teen Spirit" on the major's stereo, screaming the chorus

until the nonsensical lyrics had felt like a prayer. A command sent out to the world to listen the fuck up. *Here we are now, entertain us/ A mulatto/ An albino/ A mosquito/ My libido/ Yeah! Yeah! Yeah!*

They had chased shots of Absolut stolen from Penny's older sisters' stash with pink cans of Mrs. Whittemore's Tab, and Penny, who pretended not to give one shit about her looks, let Maddie rub blush into her ruddy cheeks and dab shadow on her lids, so she looked more like a girl who belonged in Bitsy Smith's crew and less like the ugly duckling of the five Whittemore girls—all blond, blue-eyed, and Ivy League–bound beauties, a living ad for Avalon Island.

As she had combed through Penny's thinning hair, her Twin Turbo blow-dryer filling the room with the scent of singed scalp, strands came loose until the oriental carpet was coated in fine gold threads. She knew it was only a matter of time before Penny would have to wear a wig.

Penny had been far beyond the margins of Bitsy's clique when a seizure in sixth-period chemistry led doctors to the tumor in her brain. A status that had scored Penny overnight popularity, and an invitation to join Bitsy's crew—penned in Bitsy's own bubbly script on her personalized stationery. *Good for one official membership in the FRESHEST DOPEST gang of bitches at East High!* When Maddie had opened her own locker, the same rainbow-print envelope had fallen to the floor. She'd been sure it was a prank. Like in that TV after-school special where the fat girl is invited into the sorority only to be humiliated half-naked in front of their brother fraternity. She knew she had Penny and her cancer to thank for her place in Bitsy's clique, and reminded herself of this when Penny's klutzy jokes fell flat and Maddie felt the urge to shush her, or, worse, tell her to shut it for once.

Penny insisted her doctors were optimistic she'd be plowing across the lacrosse field in no time, carrying the East High Wildcats to another county championship. And how serious could it be, Maddie thought, when there were other sick kids, especially on the west side, where her father's side of the family—the

LaRosas—lived, near the factory and commercial streets crowded with gas stations and car washes and shops like her uncle Carmine's garage, Panther Autobody?

The fairway was packed. No surprise, she thought, the east islanders turning out big only days after graffiti—black, dripping, three-foot-tall letters—scarred the steps of City Hall, and, more shocking, the tall stone obelisk (Bitsy had a bunch of nicknames for it—"The Shaft," "Dick Tower," "Needle Dick") in the center of Town Square, a memorial to pilots killed in battle flying Grudder planes.

GRUDDER IS CANCER
GRUDDER KILLS

Maddie had seen the words herself, only a few hours before the factory sent men to blast the memorial with a power washer, drape Needle Dick with wreaths of red, white, and blue carnations, and plant like a hundred flags around the monument. A little much, she thought. Like they were asking to get tagged a second time. She guessed she wasn't alone in hoping the graffiti bandit (that's what the kids were calling him) would strike again. On Avalon, rules were rarely broken, and the thrill of such a blatant *up yours* to Grudder felt like a jump-start to the summer. Like anything was possible.

Even the old men who ran Grudder, some of them navy men like her grandfather, made an appearance that night. Sure enough, she saw they were trying extra hard—navy blues knife-edge creased, clusters of medals polished so high they flashed under the carnival lights. An FU back at the graffiti bandit shitting on Old Ironsides in her own backyard.

Bitsy led them past a group of moms Maddie recognized from the PTA, their blond helmets varnished with Aqua Net. Maddie tasted the metallic tang. A wall of humidity had rolled in from the Sound that morning and the ladies of East Avalon, Maddie included, had blown out their hair, and, in some cases, like mouthy Vanessa, who had natural corkscrew curls, used a hot iron.

Bitsy had lectured new recruits Maddie and Penny on the kind of beauty that made East girls. *Curls are too ethnic*. Leave the kinks to the Hispanic girls in Avalon Point near the ferry landing and the Jews in Rosedale on the mainland where Maddie's family ordered Chinese takeout.

Do not go ape shit with the makeup, Bitsy had preached. God forbid they look like the big-haired, gum-snapping West Avalon girls, who lined their lips with brown pencil, caked on the foundation, and hung out at the Walt Whitman shopping center on the mainland because they had nothing better to do. *Mall maggots*, Bitsy called them. Now an official East girl, Maddie learned she had a duty to mock the West High kids. Even if her cousins, the twins Vinny and Enzo, went to West High. Even if her uncle Carmine owned the busiest auto body shop on the west side.

She knew some might say she'd always been an East girl, having lived on the east side her whole life, and behind the gates of one of its grandest estates, but she felt her otherness, knew she wasn't east or west but caught between. Every month, she watched her mother sit at the kitchen table and write out a check for a single dollar in her shaky cursive—to *Colonel and Mrs. Robert Pencott*—and stuff it in an envelope addressed to her grandparents' condo in Florida. A reminder that, although, like her mother, Maddie had never known another home, they were temporary tenants in the cramped groundskeeper's cottage squatting like a forest mushroom in the shadow of her grandparents' nine-bedroom limestone Tudor, White Eagle.

She watched Penny take T. rex–size steps in her high-heeled sandals, reassurance that at least *she* wasn't most out of place in Bitsy's crew. While Penny's horsey teeth and woman-wide hips threw their herd symmetry off-kilter—she didn't even pop her zits!—it guaranteed Maddie was the good recruit, Bitsy's star pupil. But as they passed the panicked squeals of the pig race, she felt the jagged half-heart charm under her shirt and felt a prick of guilt. For her sixteenth birthday, Penny had given her one of those Best Friends Forever necklaces from Piercing Pagoda at the mall, and together they'd cracked the charm in two.

They found their brother pack at the Hoop Shoot game. The cluster of East boys Bitsy and her girls took turns dating and dumping gathered around Gerritt Driscoll, the boys' version of Bitsy, as he shot basket after basket. Yellow paper coupons spilled onto the torn grass. Enough, Maddie guessed, for a dozen sad-eyed pandas. Gerritt scored and the boys let out a roar, snapping their fingers against the canisters of mint-flavored Kodiak tobacco dip they packed between their lower lips and gums.

The boys were also in uniform—khaki shorts and striped rugby tees; sun-lightened hair buzzed military short like their fathers and grandfathers, many retired navy men turned factory suits. Soccer star/weed dealer Ricky Bell; smooth-talking Austin Drake; chubby, Grateful Dead–obsessed Cameron Rollins (Rolo); and John Anderson, who was tall and thick, a die-hard Beastie Boys fan Maddie had seen eat a live earthworm in a middle school dare a few years back.

Spencer Fox, Gerritt's second in command, nodded at Maddie before tossing his head back to clear feathered bangs. She made herself return the smile. They were supposed to be going together, although she had no clue how that had come about. Only that he'd slipped her a note in third-period social studies during a pop quiz on the Magna Carta, asking her to be his date to the Fourth of July Oyster Cove Country Club party, now less than a month away. The note said he wanted to ditch the dance and sneak out to the tennis courts behind the pool cabanas, where *I'm going to finger you till you cum*. The words in sloppy boy-scrawl had made her stomach flip, but Bitsy only laughed and said, "What *are* you bugging about? Chill, Virgin Mary. You'll be totally dope together. Unicorns and rainbows and all that shit."

Spencer walked toward her in that bowlegged saunter all the soccer-team guys had. She knew he was going to touch her and that she'd let him. She knew all the cues by now and smiled when she was supposed to; laughed along; spoke up when it was her turn, shut up when it wasn't; took a drag, a swig; let Spencer feel her up even though it made her gut clench like she was getting her period.

"Hey, Mads."

His hand was on her back, his fingers low. When they slipped under her skirt waistband, she let them stay. She counted *one, two, three*. She'd wait until ten to shift away, not wanting to look like a prude.

"You're looking superfly," he said.

"What up, Spence?" Maddie said. "You're looking pretty fine yourself."

She knew she didn't sound like herself. Feared she was trying too hard. A prickly heat spread across her chest and she prayed it wouldn't rise above her collar.

Four, five, six.

Spencer spat a stream of brown tobacco juice into the grass.

"We're chilling at Gerritt's later," he said. "Pulling bong hits. He scored some choice nugs. Believe me, you want to be there."

His pupils were two black marbles. He was already stoned. Or rolling on E. Or maybe he'd eaten some of the shrooms Gerritt and his boys had been taste-testing all week—according to Gabrielle, who was anxious to get her hands on some.

As "Pop Goes the Weasel" warbled over the carousel speakers, Spencer's damp fingers slipped under her underwear elastic—*seven, eight*—

The caterpillar inched across the top of her hand. It wore a coat of fine black bristles. She'd seen a few on the silvery birch trees edging the woods around her family's cottage, and that spring, everyone had been obsessed with the hatching of the gypsy moth eggs that had lain in wait all winter long in the woods—from Mr. Skolnick, her science teacher (*Repeat after me*, he'd said, *Lymantria dispar dispar*) to the newscasters on Channel 12 Island News, and even her younger brother, Dominic. They used words like "plague" and "infestation," and soon the kids talked about the caterpillars as if it were an impending war. Or, Maddie thought, a horror film scheduled to roll at the Avalon Cinema. *The caterpillars are coming. They're coming.* As they passed a blunt rolled with marijuana shake around the bonfire, filled plastic cups with beer from a keg in the back of John Anderson's Bronco, snuck cigarettes at the red doors that led to the make-out woods behind school. As they waited on line at the cafeteria for pizza and Tater Tots, warmed up during choral practice, and changed for gym in the locker room. Until Maddie felt something titanic rushing toward the island, gathering steam like a nor'easter barreling toward shore, and the waiting filled with a tingling urgency she knew they all felt. She felt it. Car engines revved harder, highs soared higher, buzzes and crushes burned brighter.

"Look." She lifted her palm as the insect inched across. The two lines of blue and red dots on its back glimmered like spots of blood rising after a pinprick. "They're here."

Spencer moved closer, his hand sliding up so it rested over the plastic latch of her bra.

"Killer," he said. She smelled the minty tobacco packed so thick his lower lip bulged, slurring his words. "The motherfucking caterpillar apocalypse is upon us."

"So cute!" Penny gushed.

Spencer looked at Penny with glassy-eyed disgust and Maddie knew he'd punish her enthusiasm.

"Fuck cute." He blew into Maddie's palm.

"No." She stopped, knowing she was being a baby, feeling a beat of despair for a bug.

As it floated away on an invisible thread (She got away, Maddie thought defiantly) and up into the oak branches stretched black against the plum sky, she heard Bitsy, a flame edging her voice, "Those west-side scumbags are over there."

Vanessa bounced on her toes like she did when there were fights at school, and like the time she hid a pair of panties, the crotch coated in ketchup, in Karen Lipschultz's school locker.

Gabrielle rolled her eyes. "So not cool, them showing up at our fair."

There were Maddie's cousins, Vinny and Enzo, trying to look all gangster in cowboy hats on the photo stage, a platform set up next to the bouncy house where Ms. Murphy, the mustachioed East High gym teacher, squatted, snapping Polaroid shots.

The West girls were draped two at a time on her cousins' laps and wrapped in feather boas and fringed shawls like old-fashioned saloon whores. If not for the tense silence around her, Maddie would've laughed. Vinny and Enzo were obsessed with keeping it cool, and here they were playing dress-up.

She slipped an arm around Spencer's waist. Tickled the fuzz of his earlobe with her lips, hoping it would convince him to take her faraway, fast.

"Can we go now? To Gerritt's?"

If she and Bitsy and the rest of the East crew were *girls*, Maddie thought, then the West girls were grown women. In padded bras and tight jeans—the cuffs pegged to show off every curve. She saw how they'd cropped their neon-orange and -pink tees, knotting the cotton above their navels. To show off their piercings. The cubic zirconia gems dangling from their belly buttons glimmered each time the camera flashed. She wondered if they'd done the piercing themselves. She'd heard all you needed was an ice cube, a safety pin, and a lighter, but had been too much of a wimp to try.

She recognized the girl standing at the stage edge—too cool to smile *cheese* for the camera. Carla. A sometimes girlfriend of Maddie's cousin Enzo. Her dark hair was pulled back in a dozen scalp-tight braids, and from the end of each hung a rainbow of plastic beads. When she turned to look at Bitsy's crew, the braids swayed *click-clack* like a beaded curtain. The girl puffed on a hand-rolled cigarette. As if, Maddie thought, Ms. Murphy, infamous at East High for doling out detention, wasn't a few feet away, her cheeks pressed to the camera.

She knew these were the girls her cousins bragged about after family dinners at Nonna LaRosa's house on the west side, when the boys played poker with the men and Maddie helped her aunts clear the table for pastries and espresso. Her cousins took these girls to the bowling alley on the mainland and the Avalon Cinema downtown, groped them in the backseat of the red Cougar the boys shared. Vinny had tinted the windows himself at the auto shop. Windows so dark, she'd heard Enzo boast, a girl could suck him off in broad daylight.

It wasn't the girls she feared, although the way Carla stared—her eyes feline with black liquid liner—was enough to make anyone bug. And Maddie knew she'd catch serious shit from her cousins for hanging out with the elite East girls (*rich bitches*, Enzo might say). But that wasn't it either. It was her dad. Vinny had a big mouth. If he ratted on her, she'd come home one night, tomorrow, the next week, who knew, to her dad sitting at the kitchen table. Waiting. The chair would topple back, his belt buckle jangling, the belt slithering out of his pant loops like a leather snake. And she'd get it bad.

Bitsy groaned. "Who invited these hoes to our party?"

More laughter from the East girls. An all-out guffaw from Vanessa, who always had to outdo everyone.

"Like, all of a sudden," Gabrielle said, "it smells straight-up rank." Ending with a back-of-the-throat *uck* like she was hocking a loogie.

Then, for some reason even Penny wouldn't be able to explain later when Maddie asked what the hell she'd been thinking, Penny shouted, her voice ringing above the loudspeaker announcing the start of the sack races, "All that cotton candy's gonna make your fat asses even fatter!"

The West girls came to, climbing off Maddie's cousins' laps. Straightening, stretching. Like she-lions waking in the afternoon sun. They shifted their hands to their hips and their rhinestone-studded nails flashed.

"What. The. Fuck." Gabrielle rolled her eyes hard at Penny. "You so just *asked* to get our asses kicked."

They turned to Bitsy. She was rattled. Maddie spotted the muscle in her jaw twitching. But Bitsy shifted into leader-of-the-pack mode, lifted her arm, and gave the West girls a ballsy middle finger.

Vanessa joined in, "Get lost, skanks!"

Gabrielle, her chin jutting back and forth chickenlike, imitated the West accent—the vowels stretched and doubled, as if words were saltwater taffy: "Ava-LAWN-EYE-land!"

When Penny joined in, Vanessa gave her an approving up-nod. Maddie felt a hiccup of panic. How was Penny fitting in when she wasn't?

The West girls were like a troupe of exotic dancers—rolling necks, swiveling hips, arms lifting out and up like the swans in the bay before takeoff.

Who you talking to?

Step on up and get some of this!

Gerritt and his boys turned from the basketball game to

watch. Laughing at East or West girls, Maddie couldn't tell, but she heard John Anderson say, "Crazy bitches."

She knew she should pitch in, and words like "sluts" and "trash" moved through her head, but when the carousel music started up again—this time playing "It's a Small World"—she froze. She, and Bitsy—all the East girls—no longer seemed like untouchable beauties but more like deer emerging after hibernation. Knob-kneed and awkward-footed, their noses sniffing the air for danger.

Carla stepped to the edge of the stage so the toes of her black lace-up Doc Martens hung over. She pinched her cigarette and flicked it. Maddie watched the cherry-red ember arc through the air. The butt landed with a sizzle as it bounced off Bitsy's white T-shirt.

"Shit!" Gabrielle pawed at Bitsy's chest.

Bitsy shoved her away. "I'm fine! Can everyone just shut the fuck up for a minute?"

It was the first time Maddie had seen Bitsy lose her cool.

Vanessa spoke through clamped teeth, "She did *not* just do that."

She lunged toward the stage with the same powerful advance Maddie had seen her use on the lacrosse field.

"V!" Bitsy shouted. "Take a chill pill, girl."

Vanessa did an about-face pivot. "Catch you losers later!" she sang.

Bitsy smiled. "I'm not gonna let these butt uglies kill my buzz."

She raised her hands in a W, thumbs touching, palms open. As in *whatever*. Like it was no big deal, Maddie thought.

"Let's bounce," Bitsy said, pulling at the back of Gerritt's cuffed white tee so his chest muscles stood out in relief. "I'll buy you some cheese fries at the Golden Dolphin."

When Bitsy released his shirt, he sprang toward the photo stage.

Bitsy called after him, "Don't let those welfare rats get to you, baby."

Maddie saw her lurking smile. Bitsy wanted him to avenge her.

Gerritt jogged toward the photo stage. His boys, including Spencer, followed him—a loping chain of boy-man bodies.

Her cousin Enzo—what a show-off—leapt off the stage and swaggered toward Gerritt, one arm slack behind, as if winding up to throw one of the strikes he was famous for as West High's champion pitcher. He still wore the black cowboy hat and she spotted a leather holster on his hip, the silver butt of a toy gun glinting. Her brother, Dom, had one like it when they were kids. *Bang-bang! You're dead, Maddie!*

The boys met between the photo stage and the bouncy house. The hiss of the air pump and rattle of the roller coaster made it impossible to hear but she saw Gerritt's lips moving. His boys stood at his elbows in *V* formation, collars turned up, chins cocked. One, two, three West boys showed up in black jean cut-offs and faded heavy-metal tees. Metallica, Def Leppard, Nine Inch Nails. A pack of panthers, Maddie thought. Haunches flexed and ready to lunge. East boys were wiry soccer and lacrosse players. The Wildcats football team sucked for a reason. She doubted any had thrown a real punch, one meant to bloody. But she knew the West boys had—they'd pummeled one another, drunk fathers, pervert uncles, PCP-wrecked older brothers, and God knows who else.

Gerritt and Enzo were doing the dance—bobbing foot to foot, so close their chests brushed and the cowboy hat tumbled off her cousin's head. His spiky gelled hair gleamed like black ice.

Her *cugini* had been Maddie's holiday pals all her life. Every New Year's Eve at midnight, they beat pots and pans in front of Nonna's house, and every Christmas Eve, the twins' parents, Maddie's uncle Carmine and aunt Mariana, hosted the Feast of the Seven Fishes. Four courses of sardines, squid, and octopus; and long pieces of dried baccala soaking in salty water—cod caught by her father and uncle far out in frigid sea. But her cousins were boys then. Stick-thin, squeaky-voiced, and terrified of their father's backhanded slaps. Now they'd earned muscles working at the garage—their forearms roped with green and blue veins as thick as the wires under the hoods of the cars they repaired. They smelled like cigarettes and engine grease and sex, and dared to step up to their father, who she'd seen back away.

Vinny was still onstage, glaring at the throng of boys, making a big show of tucking his cigarette pack into his shirtsleeve, rolled up to reveal the panther, eyes like emeralds, tattooed on his shoulder.

Like he was badass Dallas from *The Outsiders*, Maddie thought, and almost smiled.

"What's happening?" Penny asked.

"Nothing. They're just being meatheads."

"I don't feel so good."

Penny's pupils were even bigger than Spencer's. Black globes swimming against icy blue.

"Did you take something?"

"A little something-something," Penny slurred. "Ricky had these pills."

Penny leaned into her and Maddie felt the cold clamminess of her friend's skin.

She tried to convince herself there was no point in thinking about what came next. A fight? Penny puking all over the wedged espadrilles Maddie had begged her mother to buy? And next week, after her father heard she'd been at the fair with Bitsy Smith's crew. Or later that summer in the soupy August heat of the West Avalon fair, where her cousins expected Maddie at their side as they cruised that other fairway in the parking lot of the fire station, surrounded by families who worked down on the Grudder assembly line, not in the upper-floor offices. She knew that, by August, her white jeans would be grass-stained, her tan turned to freckle, the seat of her bikini bottoms pilled after too many swims in the salty ocean. The promise she felt tonight spent, swept away with the tide.

Enzo bumped Gerritt's chest with his own and a gasp rose from Bitsy and the girls.

"There's a smack-down coming." Vanessa jumped up and down, her breasts heaving.

Maddie felt it too. Shit was going off. Like a boxful of fireworks. She wished she had stayed at home, played her younger brother Dominic's make-believe games in the cool dark woods. She was still young enough, wasn't she?

Bitsy, Vanessa, and Gabrielle, maybe even Penny, wanted the boys to fight. Didn't they know it wasn't like in the movies where an orchestra played in the background as the camera slow-moed the punches so it looked like a ballet? Maddie had felt her dad's clumsy swings land on her back, her boobs, her butt. She'd fought back. A spastic flailing. Her chin doubling ugly. Fighting was snot and tears and breathless grunts, and once, when her dad had come after her with the broom, she'd peed herself.

Then all heads turned. The boys froze. As if a spell had been cast, Maddie thought. They looked beyond the stage to the main fairway strung with round glass bulbs.

"Cool." Penny giggled. "Black people."

"Shut up," Gabrielle hissed. "Haven't you seen *The Cosby Show*?"

As if Gabrielle had ever talked to a black person, Maddie thought. As if any of them had. The only nonwhite residents of the island were the Korean American Park family who owned Cougar Cleaners.

"Who the fuck *are* they?" Bitsy said.

All of East Avalon stared at the pretty blond woman, fair and freckled, strolling arm in arm with a light-skinned teenage boy so handsome he could've been in one of the Benetton ads Maddie had seen on the sides of buses in the city. Beautiful and happy (she'd never seen smiles so big) white-, black-, brown-, and yellow-skinned children posing in bright sweaters, arms slung around one another's shoulders.

He looked her age. Sixteen. Maybe seventeen. The apple in his throat bobbed as he spoke to the woman, who, Maddie guessed, must be his mother. But the way they strolled down the fairway, elbows linked, foreheads touching as they shared a private joke—she'd never seen a teenage boy enchanted by his own mom.

His skin was all those sugary words she'd heard East Avalon ladies, her grandmother Veronica included, call the Hispanic girls who cleaned their houses. Cocoa. Cinnamon. Café au lait. Like

they were Easter bunnies sold in the windows of Bon Bon Chocolatier downtown. And here *she* was, she thought, a hypocrite,
imagining the warmth of his skin as a spiraling heat sparked in
her belly.

A black man walked behind the white woman and brown boy,
carrying a pigtailed little girl the same shade as the handsome
boy-man. Maddie saw Principal Haskell staring at the man, and
his wife, Gloria, who sang in the St. John's choir; and Suzie
Schumacher and Joy Linden and the rest of the PTA mothers who
speed-walked in a pack around the East High track each morning, rain or shine. Even the ancient uniformed navy vets and their
corsage-pinned wives paused to look.

The man was as dark as the Africans she'd seen in the stack
of *National Geographic* magazines at the school library. His skin
was almost a purplish black. She understood, with a queasy jolt,
why her father, uncle, even Vinny and Enzo, called Troy and
Mike—the two blacks who worked at the garage and lived on
the mainland—"moolies." Behind their backs. It was Neapolitan
dialect for "eggplant." That's racist, she thought numbly. Then:
Am *I*?

The man was striking, tall and lean like one of her mom's
favorite actors—Sidney Poitier. He smiled politely at the people
his wife greeted, shifting the little girl in his arms so he could
shake hands with a line of Grudder men. Then Maddie saw the
pits of his shirt were stained with sweat; the smile he gave the
old uniformed men forced; and, suddenly, she felt like a tool having yearned for this night all winter. She saw it clearly now—the
pig races and fried dough and clueless shivering Tina Meyer and
her giant nipples.

"Oh fuck," Gabrielle said from behind.

Bitsy and the girls had formed a circle, their glossy heads tilted
toward the ground. There lay Penny, back impossibly arched, lips
pulled back, pink gums bared, trembling as if the earth beneath
her was quaking.

Maddie knelt over her, tried to catch her head pitching side
to side.

"Shhh," she cooed, pressing her hands into Penny's thinning
hair. "You're okay. You're okay!"

She looked up for help and saw them. One, two, three—too many to count. An army of caterpillars floated overhead on gossamer thread. She couldn't tell if they were rising or falling.

2.

Jules

Jules balanced his four-year-old daughter, Eva, on his hip as he searched the crowd of fair-goers. He could just make out, through the mob of islanders, his wife, Leslie, and sixteen-year-old son, Brooks, strolling arm in arm. Like two kids on a date, he thought. Leslie's golden head dipped toward the Afro his son was desperate to grow out, the ends catching the festival light so it looked like his boy wore a halo.

They had always been close, Leslie and Brooks, in a way Jules couldn't understand, more like siblings than mother and son, and they'd grown even closer since Leslie's mother died and the idea of moving from the city to Avalon Island had dominated their lives. Until it was the only thing Leslie and Brooks talked about. The island. The island. The two of them stuffing it into every conversation, no matter how trivial the topic. Until it was them and the island versus Jules, and he'd had no choice but to agree to the move, hoping the sweet dreams Leslie had spun for him, and even more for Brooks, came true. The Castle. The gardens. The good schools and hundreds of acres of untouched woods and beaches. A swing set and tree house for Eva. No more urban noise and stink, only ocean breeze.

And here Jules was, clutching Eva in his arms and trying not to panic—*Don't call too much attention to yourself when you're the only black man*, his father had lectured him so many years ago—because now Jules had lost his wife and son in a sea of white faces.

The Castle. He nearly laughed aloud each time he thought of it. How would he ever call that stunning monster a home, with its iron gate flanked by two marble eagles? Poised to swoop down, talons stretched. Leslie had forbade them from using the big house, a bona fide mansion—not until she did whatever she needed to rid the place of her dead parents' bad vibes. Burned bunches of sage, recited what she called her *positive affirmations*, hung pear-shaped crystals in the tall windows to invite good energy. Jules suspected they'd be stuck in the two-bedroom grounds-keeper's cottage for a while, and was mostly relieved. Leslie had given him a quick tour of the Castle's abandoned interior; it smelled damp and decaying—every room uninviting in its own unique way. Must watch Eva doesn't fall, he'd thought, when he first saw the entryway's cold stone walls and spiraling marble staircase, then realized the absurdity of trying to baby-proof such a place. The wall-length glass case of Admiral Marshall's gun collection, from rusty-tipped Civil War bayonets to a variety of pistols, made Jules's mouth go dry each time he tried to talk to Leslie about it, insisting they buy a new lock. How could they make a home having to pass those guns every morning and night?

He'd spotted trails of mouse pellets in the high-ceilinged kitchen (felt more like a church than a place where he'd make Eva heart-shaped flapjacks), and the droppings of some larger beast in the cobwebbed cavernous ballroom whose hand-painted ceiling—pink-edged clouds against a blue sky fit for cherubs—had made Eva gasp, then sigh, *Pretty*. He half-expected to find a family of raccoons nesting in one of the many rooms. The Castle was immense—never had he imagined such a home existing only an hour from the cramped city apartment of his childhood.

"Daddy?" Eva pawed at his cheek.

He felt the damp spot growing on the back of the white linen button-down Leslie had suggested he wear to the fair, insisting he leave the tails untucked. *No, baby, it's not messy, it's beachy. Casual.*

"Dah-dee?" Eva shouted this time and shook her head so the pom-pom bells at the ends of her pigtails jingled.

"What is it, baby girl?"

"Where's Mama? Where's Brooks?"

"Good question. I see them up there. If we hurry, we can beat them to the choo-choo ride."

"Choo-choo!"

As they passed the grandstand, a bell went off. A muffled voice barked through a loudspeaker. Pigs squealed. Feet pounded metal bleachers.

Eva had her fists up at her ears. Her lower lip quivered. He knew what that meant. Ten seconds or less to tears.

He hurried deeper into the fair.

People stared.

Only a few hours ago, he'd been looking forward to the night, almost as excited as Leslie and Brooks, who'd spent an hour trying on and then discarding outfits, until the bed was a pile of cloth—all white and off-white. And the ancient words Jules had memorized years ago in his Botanical Latin class at Harvard returned to him: *Candidus*, pure white. *Gypseeus*, *lacteus*, and *niveus*—chalk-, milk-, and snow-white. And the one he and his mostly celibate classmates (not by choice—they were a real set of nerds) had snickered over. *Virgineus*—unblemished white.

Jules was an expert on the flowers these people worshipped, ordered their maids to arrange in heirloom vases on their parlor tables, their landscapers to plant in their well-tended gardens. He had studied a variety of white lilies—the Aurelian lily, with its trumpet-shaped bloom; the Easter lily (*Lilium longiflorum*) native to the Ryukyu Islands in Japan; and the most famous, the Calla. Which wasn't a lily after all, but an aroid, and poisonous. And what did that matter now, he thought, as the thump of the Gravitron ride's techno bass set his teeth rattling.

He wished he had stayed at the house. It was way after Eva's bedtime. He imagined he and Eva floating in bubbles in the ancient claw-footed tub under the cathedral ceiling in the master bathroom.

On his very first trip out to the island, he and Leslie had left the kids in the city, watched over by their neighbor, Mrs. Umansky of the killer chocolate babka and free babysitting. It was their first night away, alone, since Eva's birth four years earlier. Leslie had teased him all through the two-hour drive—her lips nibbling at his ear, her thin cotton skirt riding higher and higher, and when they exited the causeway and entered the island, she slipped her hand between his legs. He nearly swerved into the thick woods lining the roads. *What you up to, Leslie Day?* She knew all the right things to whisper in his ear—*I'm wet*—and knew to wear a tight tank top with no bra that day so her nipples strained against the cotton. He'd learned this about her when they first met in Cambridge years ago: She was a woman who understood that men needed sex. And since they'd arrived, she'd been more worked up than ever—and their honeymoon days back at Harvard had, he thought, been busy. It was as if the island, the Castle, turned her on in a way he couldn't have on his own.

Eva was yelling, tugging on his arm something fierce. "That! That, Daddy!" She pointed to the cotton-candy machine with the domed case lit up so you could watch the tornado of fluff twist. She planted her palms against the glass.

A plump woman waddled by. She was wearing a dress that seemed too fancy for a fair, Jules thought, better suited for a wedding. An enormous orchid bloom drooped from her chest and he felt a jolt of recognition. He'd know that show-off anywhere, with its narrow calyx framing three broad fuchsia petals—two identical and the third frilled like an old-fashioned petticoat.

The woman stopped short. He saw how her makeup had smeared in the heat.

"Why, what a darling little creature you are," she said to Eva.

Creature, Jules thought. Distinct from a human being.

Before he could step forward, the woman's hand, dazzling with jeweled rings, caressed Eva's cheek.

"Daddy's getting me cotton candy," Eva said, eyeing Jules warily. Like a good city kid, he thought.

The woman looked at Jules and, startled, took a step back. As if seeing him for the first time.

"Who did your hair all pretty like that?"

The question, he knew, was meant for Eva, but the woman looked at him as she spoke.

"Mama did 'em," Eva whispered.

"It's *amazing* she was able to make braids out of . . ." She waved at Eva's head. "All that."

A bell rang out and a gravelly voice shouted, "Step up, step up! Everyone wins a prize! Get your prize!"

"There's a word for it," the woman said.

"Ma'am?" Jules asked, surprising himself. When was the

last time he'd called a woman that? At his great-aunt Eunice's eightieth birthday party maybe.

"You know," the woman continued, drawing out her words like it was a cute little trick Jules was playing, as if he were only pretending to misunderstand. "What you people call your hair when it gets all unruly? My grandson has a book about it. His mama"—she looked into Eva's face—"believes in diversity and such. Buys him books about *all* the children in the world."

He heard her say *you people*. Had she? No, he couldn't trust himself, not with the screeching brakes of the Twirling Teacups ride, and the stench of the Porta Potties, and his little girl shrieking *Look, Daddy! Look!* as the pink cotton candy spun inside the dome. And his wife so far away. Where the hell was Leslie?

He focused on the exquisite bloom pinned to the woman's dress and the sight of the orchid calmed him. Now, was it an *amethystoglossa*, the amethyst-lipped variety? Or the *porphyroglossa*, purple-lipped? He always confused the two, and who could blame him, he thought, when there were one hundred and thirteen varieties of Cattleya orchids alone. He took a step closer to get a better look.

"Aha!" he said. "I knew it. That there's *Cattleya labiate*," he pronounced slowly, pointing to the woman's heavy breast.

She took a stumbling step back and let out a hacking smoker's cough. He was pleased to see he'd ruffled this peahen's feathers.

"Beg your pardon?" she said.

"Your orchid," he said. "Its scientific name is *Cattleya labiate*. Discovered by William Swainson in Brazil, actually."

He paused, pretending to search for the date, although he knew it well. He'd taken a course in his second semester at Harvard on the hybridization of orchids.

"In 1817, I believe," he said matter-of-factly. "Translates to *crimson* for that big ruby-lipped labellum." He lifted a hand, almost reached out and stroked the frilled center petal that opened wide like a wet mouth.

"Well, well." She smiled, her chin doubling when she shook her head. As if he were a naughty boy—not fair, him surprising her like that. "You are a clever one. Aren't you, now?"

He could've gone on. Made this a night she would never forget. One she'd tell her girlfriends about at their weekly bridge game. He knew they wouldn't believe her. A black man an expert of orchids, graduated with honors from the Harvard Graduate School of Design? *Landscape architecture*, Orchid Lady would recite slowly, and the ladies' mouths would turn down, *You don't say*, simultaneously impressed and baffled. A colored man speaking Latin.

There was so much to say. Details he knew would seduce this fat, sweating woman into cherishing her orchid. Maybe even cherishing Jules. *Did you know, ma'am*, he imagined saying, *this is Colombia's national flower? Oh yes, indeed! The tissue-thin tricolor lip matches their flag—yellow for the country's gold, blue for its two bordering oceans, and red for the blood spilled by patriots.*

He would step closer, reach out and stroke the velvety lip of the flower, his fingers dark against the silvery white . . . *This was an endangered species once.* He'd transport her to the elfin forests of the highlands thick with clouds and mist and moss.

Did you know, ma'am . . . expeditions of men died so that orchid can hang off your bosom. Isn't that *something?* Together they'd ascend, he and Orchid Lady, to a place where orchids were more than mere flowers and black men were more than creatures to be ignored or feared. He heard his mother's voice now, as gentle as his father's was harsh: *Redemption, dear Julius, can be found in the most surprising of places.*

He stopped himself. He knew he played that game to give his ego a charge when it felt like a dead battery, and while it felt good to hold people's prejudices up to their faces like a mirror, he always felt shitty after. A self-righteous hangover.

The flower was doomed anyway. All that natural beauty, he thought, upstaged by curls of silver ribbon and clumps of baby's breath. The labia was torn and discolored. The whole mess of it destined to land in a trash can later that night, among coffee grounds and toast crumbs, kitty litter and used tissues. Nothing he said could save it now.

The pimpled teenager manning the cotton-candy machine handed Eva a Pepto-pink cloud as big as her head. Jules lunged, catching the paper cone before it hit the trampled grass.

"Give me!" Eva shrieked.

"Nappy!" the woman called out. She nodded vigorously, proud of herself. "That's the word."

The woman stroked Eva's hair as his little girl sunk her teeth into the pink fluff. Jules wanted her piggy fingers off his baby.

"I think my wife just calls them tangles," he lied.

He hated it when Leslie used that *other* word as she tore the fine metal comb through Eva's olive oil–slick hair, *working the naps out*. Leslie, whose hair was as fine as corn silk.

"My wife," Jules paused, "is Leslie Marshall. Maybe you knew Admiral and Mrs. Marshall?"

The woman's leaky eyes widened but his satisfaction was spoiled. He loathed using his wife as a screen but he'd seen the effect Leslie's name had on the islanders. At the DMV registering their city-battered station wagon or picking up a package at the island post office when he'd forgotten his ID. The Marshall name held a power that, as his mother used to say, turned frowns upside down.

The woman only proved his point, smiling. "Of course! Of course I know the Marshalls. Good folks. Delighted to meet you, Mr. Marshall." She hurried away on stocky legs, vanishing into the crowd.

The tang of burnt kettle corn and sweat and spilled beer rocked over him. He was tired.

He'd thought often those past few weeks of the play he'd read many years ago, the title of which was his namesake. His mother had named him Julius after the white-skinned emperor. A name that had earned him a whole lot of shit from his childhood friends in Brooklyn with their plain names—Willy, Don, Michael, John—until he'd had the sense at eleven to shorten it to Jules.

He'd finally read the play in ninth grade, sitting on the cool tile of the private-school library, the tuition for which his mother's lady, Mrs. Van der Meer, paid, against his pops's prideful protests. Once Jules had gotten used to Shakespeare's playful language, he'd savored the drama—the men's bravado, betrayal, and their longing for battle like it was a woman they wanted to fuck. The love and hate between so-called brothers had reminded him of the times he'd fought boys in his neighborhood, black boys like him who had called him *white boy* and *house nigger* because his mother worked for rich whites, and because he went to a posh private school filled with them, and because what the hell kind of name was Julius anyway. A rich-white-boy name.

He'd been disappointed by the play's final act, his newly fuzzed cheeks burning. To be named after a man fool enough to be murdered by his own men—his best boys, even. Jules had nightmares for weeks after. He dreamt he was locked in a house, a knife in his hand, knowing he'd have to kill someone, twist a blade into flesh, in order to protect his parents. He woke each time with his pulse thrumming in his ears and the metallic tang of blood on his tongue. One night he'd come to in his mother's arms, his tank top and briefs soaked with sweat. He was thirteen and spilled out of her arms. *You're safe*, she'd said, and the nightmares stopped.

He wondered if *he* was the fool now.

Someone was speaking. A voice muffled under the *brring, brring* of the strongman game where a beefy guy heaved and slammed a mallet again and again.

"Hey, man!" It was the kid behind the cotton-candy machine. He couldn't be older than Brooks. "You going to pay or what?"

"Chill out, *man*." Jules was surprised by the growl in his own voice.

He handed him three dollars. The kid's arm was inked with a black panther, jaws wide and dripping—with what? Blood? As their fingers touched, Jules thought he felt the kid pull away, flinch, and the old feeling came over him, that back-of-the-neck prickle. He lifted Eva into his arms so fast the cotton candy hit him in the face.

Eva leaned over and nibbled at the sticky mess on his cheek, laughing the hiccupping giggle he adored. He was just tired, he told himself. Adjusting to a new place and all.

He spotted Leslie ahead and a chill of relief spread over the back of his soggy shirt. They were so close—he could see the warm glow of her amber necklace, an anniversary gift they'd picked out together at an African dance festival in the city last year. He knew he looked a mess, his shirt wrinkled, his skin shiny with sweat, and that Leslie was sure to comment on it in her quiet but piercing way. *Well, someone is perspiring.*

He picked up his pace, swerving through the crowd, mumbling "excuse me, excuse me." His wife had stopped to peck cheeks with a woman as slender and blond as she was. The women on this island were beautiful, no doubt. Long-necked lilies. High-society-thin, tennis-toned, and tastefully tanned. Leslie look-alikes. Next, Leslie kissed a sallow old man in uniform, laughing at something he said with that coquettish tilt of her head. This stopped Jules for a moment and he stood there, confused, until Eva pulled him forward. "C'mon, Daddy!" Hadn't Leslie gone on and on about her hatred for the military, and especially the head honchos at Grudder Aviation, who, like Leslie's dead father, Admiral Marshall, were navy? What had Leslie called them? Squids. But here she was, practically rubbing up on some old-timer in uniform.

Leslie was like his mother, he reminded himself. Bighearted. Forgiving. Born with a gift for seeing the good in the world. Unlike his pops, who'd been an untrusting son of a bitch right up to the day he died.

Then he saw the mob of boys implode, the two in the middle bumping chests like horned animals ready to gore.

"Trouble, baby," Jules said aloud.

Eva was standing in a circle of children around the balloon-animal guy, her voice one of many, "Me! Me next! My turn!"

Jules lifted her and she screamed, "My balloon doggie!"

"We'll get you one tomorrow, sweetheart. We've got to find Brooks and Mommy and go home now, 'kay?"

"Home?" she asked. "Back to the city?"

The hopeful tilt of her chin made Jules's throat close. He wished he could say yes.

"No, silly." He nuzzled her cheek with his stubbled chin. "Back to the Castle. Remember the big beautiful castle? We can't live there without our princess."

He shouldered forward through the mob howling at two men arm wrestling on a small stage, their shirtsleeves rolled. He didn't bother with *excuse me*. He knew shit was about to blow up with those boys. He needed to get Brooks the hell out of there.

A roar rose—*Ohhhhhh*—and he turned to look back at the two gangs ready to scrap. It wasn't the preppy kids in their letter jackets that spooked him—it was the others. The darker-skinned kids (Hispanic? Italian?) all death metal in tight black tees showing off hours of manual labor and lifting at the gym. They reminded him of kids from his old 'hood, the ones his pops called "undesirables"—the PRs and blacks who sold drugs from their stoops and leeched off their mas and grandmas instead of getting jobs.

He told himself, again, *Stop. Don't let the ghosts of Leslie's parents or some orchid-pinned fat lady or a mob of bored kids ruin your new home.*

He reached Leslie, reminding himself to smile and nod as he shook the wrinkled hands of one uniformed gramps after another, Leslie saying something about the old men being on the board at Grudder. Then another roar—*Awww*—rose from the growing horde watching the kids' face-off, and he felt that familiar joint-softening fear, the best and only gift his father had left him.

"I'm taking Brooks back to the house," he whispered to Leslie.

He touched her arm. She was smooth and dry under his clammy palm. He wished they were at the cottage. In bed. The lemony scent of the star-shaped linden tree blossoms wafting over them.

"What? Why? You can't leave." Leslie looked over at Brooks, who was paying for an ice-cream cone.

"I don't want to get into it here, babe. I'm taking him."

Brooks held the cone in front of Eva. She stood on her toes to the lick the curled peak of the vanilla-chocolate swirl.

Jules leaned over to catch his breath. Leslie began rubbing circles into his back, then pulled away when she felt his soaked shirt.

"What's wrong with you?" she whispered. "Stand up, love. People will think . . ."

Her eyes darted left and right while she smiled placidly.

He saw how life on the island would play out. What a show it would be. With Leslie Marshall center stage.

She turned away and cried, "Oh my God!" her outstretched arms reaching for two women—a wispy blonde and a horsey brunette, both in white sundresses. Pamela something-or-other and Evelyn something-else. The three women double air-kissed, their spray-stiffened hair unmoving. A man in plaid shorts stepped forward and squeezed Jules's hand so his knuckles cracked, introducing himself as Captain so-and-so. Jules's slick palm slipped out of the man's grasp and he was trying to think of something to say to this man with the buzzed hair and puffed-out chest, when a cry from Eva saved him.

A bristled caterpillar crawled up her white sundress. She screeched, "Buggie! Go away, buggie!"

Then Death Metal Kid bumped Preppy Kid's chest and Jules spotted the holster around Death Metal Kid's waist, the silver steel winking—it was there, he saw it with his own eyes—and he gripped Brooks by the shoulders, the ice-cream cone falling to the grass, and dragged him down the fairway toward the parking lot. He heard his father's voice telling him to run, reminding him, as he had when Jules was a kid, that only a fool froze when his gut told him to hightail it.

It was better to stay scared, Jules thought.

Maybe if Caesar had stayed scared, he would've seen those knives coming.

PART TWO

The Feeding

Early June 1992

The gypsy moth was introduced into North America in 1869 from Europe. Étienne Léopold Trouvelot imported the moths, with the intent of interbreeding gypsy moths with silk worms to develop a silkworm industry. The moths were accidentally released from his residence in Medford, Massachusetts.

As noted in *The Gypsy Moth* (1896) by Forbush and Fernald, the gypsy moth was considered a nuisance just ten years after their release. The first major outbreak occurred in 1889, and Forbush and Fernald recount the extent of devastation: all the trees being defoliated and caterpillars covering houses and sidewalks and raining down upon residents.

—*The Gypsy Moth: Research Toward Integrated Pest Management*, United States Department of Agriculture, 1981

3.

Dom

Dom held the Dixie cup of cold water over his mom who lay on her bed snoring—her pale fleshy arms flung out to her sides like she'd washed ashore after a shipwreck.

"Go ahead," his sister, Maddie, said with an extralong sigh. "She's *so* not going to wake up on her own."

They had pulled the thick bedroom curtains open. The morning sun ignited the dusty bedroom furniture so it glittered. Still, his mom refused to wake up.

Dom had that ache in his gut. Like he needed a gulp from one of the bottles he'd stolen from the bar in his grandparents' house or he'd shit his pants.

"Just give me the cup already," Maddie huffed.

He knew, behind her pissy attitude, she was just as scared by the crap news he'd delivered that morning.

Their grandparents were coming. The Colonel and Veronica could arrive any minute.

Maddie sounded just like those girls she'd gone with to the fair. She'd stolen a bottle of gin for them, from the same bar in their grandparents' house next door. Dom had heard it sloshing around in her backpack last night and had known she'd get sick. She was a freaking lightweight, his sister. Not him. He'd been sneaking sips, then shots, and now thermoses full for a year now, since he started seventh grade at the East Avalon Junior/Senior High, an underweight kid with girlishly wide hips in a land of giant jocks searching for freaks to humiliate.

"Whatever," he said. "I heard you puking your guts up this morning. So I let you sleep. Instead of banging on your door and telling you *I told you* you'd get sick from drinking."

"Um, you just did, genius."

"Did what?"

"Told me *told you so*."

They laughed. He loved his sister's laugh. Not that fake giggle when other people were around. The real thing. He wished they could leave Mom, leave the cottage. Before their grandparents arrived. But where could they go? He'd spent a few nights in the woods after his dad chased him out the front door, belt in hand. But Maddie wouldn't want to sleep in the woods like Dom did some summer nights. Not now with the caterpillars hatching. Where did kids go when they couldn't live one more day at home waiting for shit to blow up?

A string of spit hung from his mom's parted lips. Her blond lashes were crusty with dried sleep goo. He tried not to see the dark shape of her nipples under the sheer nightgown. What would their grandmother Veronica say if she saw her only child in such a sorry-ass state? She was always reminding him and Maddie that their mother had been runner-up to Miss Avalon 1967. As if, he thought, their grandmother was reminding herself.

"Ready?" Maddie asked.

"I guess."

He let his too-long bangs curtain his eyes. His mom made him get bowl cuts at The Hair Cuttery—even though, duh, it made the teasing at school worse. He wanted his hair short on the sides, long on top, sculpted into waves like Brandon on *Beverly Hills, 90210*. Despite the extra ragging it was sure to get him at school, from MJ Bundy and Victor Hackett and all the senior douchebags who waited at Dom's locker and followed him to homeroom, calling him "faggot" and "homo," hands flopping limp-wristed as they lisped, *Do you take it up the butt, LaRosa?*

"Look." Maddie's voice was sweeter. "You know I don't want to do this. Right?"

"No shit, Sherlock," he said.

"But the Colonel's going to be here soon. Real soon. Maybe even today."

"Veronica too."

It was their grandmother he dreaded. Her relentless correction. *No slouching. No slurping.* Her use of *we* to scold him, as if she and he were pals: *We ask to be excused from the table. We don't lick ice cream off our spoon.*

The night before, when his grandmother's raspy smoker's voice followed the answering machine beep, her proper tone filling the small cottage, he hadn't picked up the phone.

"Surprise! It's Mommy and Daddy. Expect us sometime tomorrow, Ginny dear. We've stopped in North Carolina for the night. At a dreadful Howard Johnson."

She let out a phlegmy cough and he heard a voice in the background—his grandfather. The Colonel.

"Smells like mildew. And the dust! Howard was a good friend of Daddy's, as you know. It's a good thing he isn't alive to see this place. Make sure you tidy up, dear. We know how Daddy can get."

He chewed the waxy lip of an empty cup. It wasn't the first time they'd dumped cold water on their mother to bring her back to life. They'd been doing it since Dom was a third-grader, when his dad started taking extra shifts at the factory and working weekends at Uncle Carmine's garage, and Dr. Joseph, their family doctor, prescribed Mom pills for her "blues." Back then, the little cups had fit just right in Dom's hands and he'd cried when Maddie poured, turning Mom's jewel-colored nightgowns dark as blood. Now, he wondered if Mom was faking. Like girls at school who went to the nurse's office with cramps. An excuse to get out of running the mile in gym class.

He and Maddie were always waiting for Mom. To wake. Get better. Cheer up. Open the locked bedroom door after they'd pounded on it with fists. Return to them from that dream world she chose over them. Maybe, he imagined, it was carpeted with cotton balls, insulated with puffs of cloud. Like a never-ending hug.

He kicked the box spring. Mom's slack belly jiggled.

"Crap," he said. "Just do it."

Maddie poured one cup, then another, down their mother's freckled chest.

She jerked. An arm flailed like the fin of a beached fish.

"Why are you doing this to me?" she cried like a little kid, then turned pissy, spitting, "Stop it!"

"Mom," Maddie said in the voice Dom half remembered hearing when his sister soothed him out of night terrors. "You *got* to get up."

He tugged on his mother's arm crisscrossed with wrinkles matching the rumpled bed sheets. "Mom, please."

He dug into her body with his fists, kneading her damp flesh. *You fat, selfish, lazy whale.* He shoved, her body rocked side to side, and she sat up, the hem of her nightgown hitched so he smelled the fishy odor that clung to the bathroom when Maddie was on the rag.

"When your father gets home," she wheezed, "you're going to get it!"

"Dad isn't home." Tears tried to squeeze through the cracks in his voice. "He never *is*. And they're coming, Mom."

"*Who?*" His mother used a chipped fingernail to pick at the sand in her eye.

"The Colonel," Maddie said.

"And Veronica," Dom added.

His mom peeled off her wet nightgown with Maddie's help. Dom avoided her sagging breasts and looked instead at the shiny white Cesarean scar striping her belly. She'd been reminding him of it for as long as he could remember. *It almost killed me giving birth to you.*

"We made a list," Maddie said. "The stuff we need to do before they get here."

He was grateful his sister was there. She'd make sure they were ready.

Two years had passed since their grandparents had fled Avalon Island for their annual winter escape to Florida, and then, to everyone's surprise, not returned with the other snowbirds in the spring. Still, he remembered enough to expect their grandfather's inspection. The Colonel's white cotton gloves stretching tight over his thick knuckles. His golf cleats clicking across the wood floor as he neared the closet in Dom's bedroom, where a tower of dirty clothes waited to spring out like a jack-in-the-box. He knew they'd follow the Colonel from room to room and nod at his insults. Make no excuses, no matter how much they wanted to play defense. Even Dom's dad would be mute—his already swarthy complexion gone black hole with choked-back anger. His dad, the man Dom, Maddie, and their mother feared, who could, out of the blue, bug the hell out, pull his belt out of his pant loops so fast it whistled like Indiana Jones's whip in *Raiders of the Lost Ark*, was scared of only one person—the Colonel.

It seemed like the Colonel had an unending supply of white military-issue inspection gloves. Plenty for a colonel who wasn't even a colonel. Dom's dad had explained it all with a smile. How Robert Pencott had been a lieutenant in the summer of '42 (two months before he was scheduled to be deployed) when a back injury branded him 4F in the draft. He'd never fly into battle and, instead, ended up an engineer at Grudder Aviation's Plant 2, over-seeing the assembly of twenty Hellcat fighters per day. Fifty years later, he was Grudder's head honcho. *El Numero Uno*. President Pencott.

He might not be a bona fide colonel, but Dom knew his grand-father was sure as shit scary as any admiral who'd led a fleet into enemy waters. Dom only had to mention the Colonel and the kids at school backed down, nodding like Dom deserved the kind of respect his grandfather got. When he felt small and powerless, he remembered he was the only grandson of the man who'd made Old Ironsides the champion of the navy, from World War II straight through Nam. The old man had helped land American boots on the fucking moon! When Dom huddled on the cold classroom floor during duck-and-cover drills, his fingers laced at the back of his neck, he knew it was his grandfather who'd make sure the nukes they were rehearsing for never dropped on American soil.

Still, they were doomed. Destined to fail the Colonel's inspec-tion. Even if they'd had weeks to clean, there was no way to rid the cottage of all the dust, grime, and grease; Mom's used tis-sues and Bugles crumbs; Dad's wiry black body hair; and Dom's own mountain of unwashed clothes. But they had to give it a shot, he thought as he and Maddie each gripped one of Mom's arms and pulled her to stand on shaking legs. He remembered the Col-onel's maxim: *The Pencotts never quit*.

They'd have to get Mom showered, and couldn't forget de-odorant. And perfume. He imagined his grandmother sitting at the kitchen table, immaculate in one of her many cream-colored pantsuits. Smoking cigarette after cigarette with coral-painted lips. As flawless as one of those black-and-white movie stars. Not a hair out of place.

His mother stood in the doorway, readying herself to leave her cool, dark cave of a bedroom.

"Dom," she said, smiling as if seeing him for the first time, "how's my baby boy?"

4.

Veronica

She sat at her daughter's wobbling kitchen table and pretended to listen. To Ginny prattle on about trifling island gossip; her grandchildren, Maddie and Dominic, lie about their straight A's at school; as her husband, Bob, slurped down the noodles their son-in-law, Tony, had made to please him. Above it all, Veronica heard the hum of the caterpillars feeding. A sound as wet and black as the caterpillar excrement that had already begun to coat the island. She'd had to leave her open-toed sandals at the cottage door. Ruined. And it would only get worse. This was just the beginning.

She ached for a cigarette, imagined the sizzle of the paper catching, the sting at the back of her throat with the first pull, warmth spreading over her mastectomy-scarred chest.

Her granddaughter's speech felt rehearsed—honor roll, Advanced Placement this and that, blah, blah, blah—but why blame the girl? Eight decades of life had taught Veronica this: everyone is lied to for his or her own good. A mother telling a child it will be okay. A lover telling a lover I will always love you. Politicians promising a better and brighter future. Generals and admirals insisting war begets peace.

Maddie's monologue was interrupted by Ginny. "How was your trip, Mommy? We're *so* happy to see you. How's the martini, Daddy? I made it myself!"

"Fantastic, dear." She tried to match her daughter's enthusiasm. "We are *so* happy to see you too. And the children." She smiled at Maddie, then Dominic. "And Tony, of course." This was a lie.

"Daddy?" Ginny looked across the table at her father.

"Bob," Veronica said, "your daughter is speaking to you."

He was focused on twisting his spaghetti into a spool at the end of his fork with the help of a spoon, just as her son-in-law, Tony, had taught him years ago. In better days.

"Bob!" Veronica shouted. Her husband's German shepherd, Champ, sat up in the corner, ears perked.

"Thank you, sweetheart." He raised his glass toward their daughter, adding a wink.

Ginny beamed. That was all it took, Veronica thought. A smile and a wink and her daughter went over the moon. She supposed one needed only so much when used to so little.

They ate, plates overflowing with Tony's spaghetti marinara, roast chicken, and fried zucchini, prepared because the dishes were Bob's favorite, and Ginny had, Veronica guessed, begged Tony to cook. How many times had she heard Bob grumble, *At least that no-good son of a bitch can cook.*

"This is *Tony's* zucchini," Ginny said. "From his own garden behind the house."

As if, Veronica thought, Tony, an underachieving know-it-all, had performed a miracle on par with the multiplying of the fishes and loaves. The real miracle would be Tony back at school, finishing his engineering degree so he could take advantage of all the strings Bob had pulled for him at the factory.

"Daddy, did you hear? Tony's zucchini!" Ginny shouted.

Veronica stifled a laugh. She caught Dom hiding a smile behind a forkful of spaghetti. Old Champ clambered to his feet, his back legs shaking.

"Yeah, for Pete's sake," Bob said. "Tony's zucchini. Quit your hollering, Virginia. I'm not deaf yet."

He kicked Champ and the dog's legs buckled so the poor beast splayed out on the linoleum.

Ginny gave Veronica a confused look. She regretted telling her daughter that Bob refused to wear his hearing aid. Another lie. Veronica had hid the plastic flesh-toned device. Tucked it in one of her velvet jewelry pouches soft as a rabbit's ear. Drawstring double-tied. Bob was less trouble this way. She couldn't have him getting all worked up. Not when things were so unpredictable. Ignorance *is* bliss, she thought as she watched Bob stuff a slice of Wonder Bread into his mouth. A tall stack sat on a plate in the center of the table. Her son-in-law's one consolation despite his loathing for the processed bread.

The dinner plates were familiar, Royal Albert and Wedgwood patterns, chipped hand-me-downs from the big house a few hundred yards down the path past the rose garden. She had forgotten how small the cottage was. She should have stood up to Bob and had the three-room groundskeeper's quarters made over ages ago. She added *cottage renovation* to her mental list, one she'd been writing and rewriting those past few weeks since life as they knew it had been turned upside down by the call from Grudder CFO Dick Gernhardt. As soon as Veronica had heard Dick's Southern drawl on the phone, she'd known the problems at the factory had escalated to, as Bob would've joked in his more lucid days, DEFCON 1, Cocked Pistol.

The sound of Champ slobbering on the rawhide Bob insisted on giving the dog nauseated her, and she feared she might have to excuse herself. Run barefoot (the humiliation!) to the bathroom and empty her already-empty stomach. Her appetite had been absent these past six months since her double mastectomy in Tampa. Not even a chocolate éclair—her favorite indulgence—tasted right.

She'd hired a woman to cook for them, then fired her when dish after dish was filled with stringy meat that seemed to poke at Veronica's gag reflex. Pot roast, brisket, corned beef. There were too many strangers in their lives these days—distant doctors, uppity nurses, apathetic receptionists, and baby-cheeked hospital residents. She'd had to hire an aide to watch Bob during her operation, and had then paid the aide extra to make up for her husband's behavior, which the woman, unreasonably proud for someone who wiped people's behinds, had called "aggressive." True, in a moment of confused panic, he'd threatened to kill Greta, accusing her of working for the Gestapo. It had been the unluckiest week of Veronica's life—stage IV breast cancer, surgery, and having been assigned the only aide at Sunrise Home Health Care with a Germanic name, who, according to Bob, was a Kraut undercover spy.

The offended aide had been another reminder of how sensitive people were these days. So many *feelings,* Veronica thought as she watched her daughter's family, knowing they were too timid to ask the question—what on earth were she and Bob doing back on the island? She had spared her daughter the news of the cancer and the surgery; spared herself the impossible task of re-assuring her daughter. Why share the news when it would just add to Veronica's list of things to manage?

She wasn't ready to tell Ginny about Bob's situation either. She didn't trust her daughter, and definitely not Tony, to keep their lips buttoned. God forbid the Grudder men heard. Dick Gernhardt and his two flunkies, Scooter Bryden and PR-obsessed Carl Buckley. Face-to-face, they swore dedication to their Colonel, but Bob had been suspicious for years now, certain they were waiting for him to slip up. Veronica had dismissed his fears as paranoia but that was in prosperous, stable times when George Bush had just begun his term, and all of Grudder (and the island) was optimistic. The new president had been a navy man, a war hero, having flown one of Grudder's own Avengers off the USS *San Jacinto*, the bombs he dropped on the Japs hitting their mark even with his engine ablaze. Now, with the so-called *enlightened* Bill Clinton (and that pushy wife of his) making his claim for the White House, promising the whole nation a *new beginning*, Veronica imagined all hell had broken loose on the upper execu-tive floors of Old Ironsides. If they knew Bob couldn't recall the year (or his own middle name) some days, he'd be their first pick for a scapegoat.

She had tried to ward off the various Grudder men who'd called their condo in Florida every month or so. With keenly timed lies—*Bob is out on the green, practicing his swing*—when, really, he'd been slumped in his La-Z-Boy wearing boxers and his Hawaiian-print bathrobe, watching the coverage of Bill Clinton's campaign. Shouting at the television so spittle sprayed the TV guide. *You coward! You stinking draft dodger!*

Then Dick Gernhardt called again and again with one piece of bad news after another—first, the graffiti defiling the island; then the return of the Marshall girl, and her demand (who did she think she was?) that she sit on the factory board. Followed by the complaints filed by the EPA (*those tree-hugging pansies*, Bob was fond of calling them) on behalf of an anonymous complainant.

Now the darkest news of all—Tangeman Aircraft swooping in with a major offer to acquire Grudder. Over the phone, Dick had called it *a merger of equals* and Veronica had smelled BS and guessed he'd jumped ship. So when he demanded she let him talk to the Colonel (as if she were holding her own husband hostage), she knew they would have to come home.

Soon, she'd have to come clean. First, there were arrangements to be made. She had her list. Her battle plan. If she was going to check off every task on that list, she had to buy some time—make her husband look, act, and speak like the leader he was expected to be. She'd have to work a miracle, she thought, remembering her father, long-dead Elder Phelps, who had believed in miracles the way the engineers at Grudder believed in physics.

"Mommy, that cardigan is *so* cute," Ginny said.

"Yeah, Mommy," Tony said as he tore a hunk of Italian bread in two, scattering flakes of crust. "I've never seen you wear color."

Her son-in-law's island accent had always irked her, the way he murdered the ends of words so *color* came out like *col-aaaah*.

"Vibrant!" Ginny's hands took flight like two frightened birds. After marrying into Tony's flamboyant family, her daughter had adopted the irritating habit of speaking in the Italian way with big, desperate gestures.

"What do *you* think, Maddie?" Ginny nodded at the girl.

"Um," Maddie straightened her back, "I think you look lovely."

Her granddaughter was lying, but Veronica admired the girl's composure. Perhaps she hadn't inherited her mother's flaws.

"Sparkly," little Dominic chimed in, although he was no longer a boy but somewhere between. Dark like his father, his lightly furred upper lip seemed unclean.

It was a wretched sweater with sequin appliqués—hearts and stars—the kind of thing a retired preschool teacher would wear to the shopping mall. They'd left in such haste, and it was the only sweater she'd managed to pack. A mistake she'd have to suffer until she could send her girl Rosalita, head housekeeper at White Eagle for two decades, to Bloomingdale's with a list. There had only been enough time to renew prescriptions and rush through a meeting with their financial team. Old age, Veronica

had learned, was a never-ending pile of paperwork; an intermi-
nable wait in a beige-draped office, the sound of a secretary's
false nails tapping on the keyboard throwing darts of panic. But
she had kept her wits from cracking like cheap nail polish, and
now they were home. She could prepare for the end.

She had lied to everyone in Florida. From their accountant to
the girl who did her hair at the beauty parlor. Pretending the trip
north was only that, a trip. To see their grandchildren. Escape
the Southern heat. *See you soon!* Promising they'd return with
the first wave of aged snowbirds in the fall. She was prepared
to lie to everyone on Avalon Island if she must.

"That thing?" Bob stared hard at Ginny, pointing his fork in
Veronica's direction. "She hates that sweater. Complained about
it all the way through North Carolina. Called it"—his voice lifted
into a grating impersonation—"an abomination."

Someone laughed. Traitor. Tony definitely. Ginny maybe. Always eager to please her father. If only her daughter had accepted
him for the brute he was, perpetually disappointed to have no male
heir. Veronica had tried, over the years, to explain to Ginny that
people didn't change, but it had seemed cruel to dash her daughter's romantic illusions, and she had given up when Ginny, four
months pregnant, insisted on marrying Tony.

Bob continued, "You know, she tells everybody she was a
model."

He laughed and a speck of zucchini skin landed on the tablecloth. "Miss Columbia County, 1939. Or . . ."—Bob paused and
she knew he was daring himself to go on—"Miss Cow-Shit-
Between-Her-Toes, 1939!"

Perspiration sprung under her ash-blond wig.

She had warned Bob before they climbed out of the Cadillac,
Champ's paws scratching at the car door as if the dog knew he
was home. *Behave,* she'd commanded Bob, *or else.* He'd lose his
television privileges. Heavens to Betsy, she promised, there'd be
no watching the news coverage of the election, no shouting at
the set every time Clinton's ruddy face appeared—Bob's new
favorite pastime. And, she added, he'd lose the slice of Sara Lee
pound cake he ate straight from the freezer with a dollop of Cool
Whip. Once, he'd been the toast of the Pentagon, the fearless

leader of 23,000 war-machine makers. Now he was swayed by a slice of cake and CNN.

"Your grandmother," Bob said, looking at Maddie. "She's a little cuckoo. If you ask me." He winked.

Well, well, Veronica thought, someone's feeling put together all of a sudden. His spurts of lucidity would pop up like that, the neurologist had predicted. But the doctor hadn't explained how the resurfacing of her husband, the Colonel in all his contrariness, and his . . . what had the aide Greta called it?—aggression—would make Veronica feel the earth rupturing under her feet.

"Cuckoo for Cocoa Puffs?" Dom said with a big smile.

"Dominic," Tony growled. "*Basta*."

Veronica didn't have to understand Italian to know what that meant. And enough *was* enough.

"Now, Bob." She hoped he heard the warning. "I don't think anyone *did* ask you."

"*Now, Bob*," he mimicked, narrowing his damp, ice-blue eyes. "You take a Stupid Pill this morning, Nicky?"

His pet name for her made her breath catch. He hadn't called her that in years.

She felt Ginny and her family freeze, their eyes shift to the secondhand plates. They'd been expecting this, she knew, the usual abuse that accompanied Pencott family dinners like a lousy side dish. The beast had awakened.

"Shush now," she said, making sure she smiled. "Mind your manners, dear. And remember what we talked about in the car."

She would deal with him later. In the privacy of the big house.

A clear drop of snot hung from the tip of Bob's nose. She considered handing him a napkin but chose not to. Her husband was no longer a man she felt beholden to. Gone was the hot-tempered leader who'd grown used to getting his way after three decades spent in command of Old Ironsides, the womb of the navy in wartime. Gone, poof, was the man who hit her—in her belly, her side, the small of her back, places where bruises would not be visible. Replaced by a confused old man who had become more like her child. A child, she had to remind herself when the urge to hurt him, to claim her revenge, even to hit him, tumbled over her like a wave breaking against shore.

"Enough about my silly old sweater," she said, reaching for her cigarette case, then pulling away, tucking her hands in her lap. "I'm not accustomed to so much attention."

Tony served scoops of pink-and-green swirled sherbet.

"Mommy," Ginny began, and then raised her voice to shout across the table at her father, "and you too, Daddy. We have some *very* interesting news!"

Her daughter's nostrils flared as she looked to Tony, who nodded, his eyes wide with anticipation.

"Leslie Day Marshall is back," Ginny said.

"We know, dear," Veronica said. "Dick Gernhardt called."

Her daughter's face fell, disappointed, and Veronica could see, suddenly, how Ginny had aged. The new sag in her jowls. The crow's feet blooming around her eyes.

"Dick called?" Bob looked up from his plate.

"We should invite her for tea one day," Veronica said, ignoring Bob. "Wouldn't that be nice?"

"Goddammit, Veronica," Bob said, "I need to know these things. Knowledge is power. . . ."

"No," Ginny said, her cheeks reddening. "You're not listening, Mommy. There's one thing you do *not* know."

For a moment, Veronica's little girl—blond banana curls and saddle shoes—sat before her. Frustrated she wasn't being heard. Veronica had never been brave enough (or cruel enough) to tell her daughter that in this world, in man's world of war, in the din of jet engines revving and factory gears turning, a woman would never be heard.

"They're black!" Tony burst out. As if all the resentment Veronica knew he felt for her and Bob had released. "Well." He laughed huskily. "Her husband is. Black as tar. A real moolie."

"Dad!" Maddie rose from her chair.

"Sit down," Tony commanded.

"You should've seen them, Mommy," Ginny said, her eyes sparkling. "Strolling down the fairway. Acting like they owned the island."

"You weren't even there, Mom," Maddie said, rolling her eyes the way teenagers did these days.

"Well." Ginny stared at her daughter. "Peggy Brell said they . . ."

"Peggy Brell is a know-it-all gossip," Maddie said.

Veronica liked the moxie in the girl.

Bob sucked on his spoon of sherbet and said matter-of-factly, looking at Maddie, "She's a stubborn thing. If she doesn't change, no man will want her."

Maddie blinked. As if, Veronica thought, the girl was trying to wake from a bad dream. Poor thing. Veronica knew it wouldn't be the last time a man's careless comments knocked the wind from her granddaughter's sails.

"Bob, apologize."

Maddie huffed, her arms crossed over her newly grown chest. "I don't want any apology from *him*."

Tony's deep voice thundered over the table. "One more word out of you, Maddalena . . ."

The effect he had on Maddie, Dom, even Ginny—their heads bowed in fear. How had she allowed her daughter to marry a tyrant like her father? Veronica knew if she peeled back the sleeve of Ginny's flowery sundress, she'd see the same violet bruises that had bloomed there year after year.

"A colored man?" Bob looked up.

This could be good, Veronica thought. Not that they could *directly* use the Marshall girl's black husband as the reason she was ineligible to sit on the board. Heavens no. The Grudder men had always held their racist cards close to their medal-cluttered chests. But they were no liberals, Veronica was sure of that. When one lived and worked in a bubble like Grudder, within the bigger bubble of the military, and on an island with one exit, you could hold on to your prejudices, no matter how outdated and nasty they may be. This news was a weapon. Plus, there was the Marshall woman's save-the-Earth activism. A fat folder dug up by the private investigator Veronica had hired revealed Ms. Marshall had spent a night in jail after a particularly wild protest—a tree sit-in at a national park with some radical group called Earth First! who actually used an exclamation point like they were schoolchildren.

"Bob."

"What?"

"We don't call them that anymore."

"Who? What did I say?" His bulbous nose reddened.

" 'Colored,' " she said. "It's 'African American,' dear."

"African American, my ass. You know how much I did for those people?"

"Yes," she said. "I believe you've told us a million times."

Dominic giggled.

Or this news could be bad, Veronica thought, very bad. The board may want to avoid blocking a woman with a black husband. Black children. *How would it look, Mrs. Pencott?* She could already hear that public relations pansy Carl Buckley (he'd have a field day). *In this age of political correctness, we should consider the message.*

"And the children?" she asked.

Maddie answered. "A boy." She paused. "My age. And a super-cute little girl."

"What?" Bob asked. "There are children? They mulatto?"

"Biracial," Maddie said.

"What?" Bob shouted.

"You're not supposed to use that word. It's," Maddie enunciated, "bi-RAY-shul."

"Mul-AH-tow, to-MAY-tow, to-MAH-tow. I don't give a damn."

"That's enough, Bob," Veronica snapped.

Ginny dropped her fork so it pinged the china. The room was silent but for the fan whirring on the kitchen counter. Veronica drank in their shock and it revived her. Like a magic potion healing her cancer-stained organs. No one had ever dared to interrupt the Colonel.

"We're finished listening to you go on ad nauseam on the topic."

He ignored her, stared across the table at Ginny.

"You gaining weight again, Virginia?" His voice went cold as he shifted into the Colonel, the man who had drilled his only daughter, his only surviving child, on historical dates at the breakfast table each morning—the sinking of the *Lusitania*, the rise of the Third Reich, the Gettysburg Address.

Tony's chair scraped the floor. The kitchen door slammed behind him.

"Daddy." As soon as Veronica heard her daughter's meek voice she knew things would only get worse. "I'm at a relatively healthy weight. There was this doctor on *Oprah* the other day and he said . . ."

"Don't give me that nonsense," Bob said. Veronica watched his eyes, milky with cataracts, march up and down their daughter's torso. "You've put on so much weight you look like a—"

"That is quite enough, Bob," Veronica hissed through her teeth.

"It's for her own good, Veronica," he said.

"I went to those doctors you sent me to, Daddy. Dr. Atkins almost killed me with those pills."

Oh, heavens, Veronica thought, not Dr. Atkins again.

Bob licked the back of his spoon. "We burned money so you could go see that quack and do his miracle diet."

"It was speed, Bob," Tony said from the kitchen doorway, a full glass of wine in one hand. "Yeah, she wasn't eating no more. But she was passing out every day."

"Are you happy now, Bob?" Veronica sighed. "Look what you've done. You and your big mouth."

"Mommy!"

She relished her daughter's astonishment. Ginny had never heard her stand up to Bob. Or if she had, her daughter had watched the punishment that followed, a hard slap across the seat of Veronica's pants, or a pinch and twist under her arm. Reminders that only Veronica would see in the bathroom mirror when she undressed to shower.

"You're just like the rest of this island," Bob said, talking more to himself and his spoon of sherbet. "Leeches getting fat off the blood of . . ." He lost his focus, stuttered.

"Bob," she said softly. She'd give him one last chance.

"Vandals disgracing the island—*my* island—with lies! Now that we've fought their wars, they've gone and got soft and spoiled."

He was standing, his knuckles pressed into the table so it wobbled.

"They say it's the end of the Cold War." He shook his head. "They say some liberal hack from Arkansas is going to take over this country. A liar, a man who can't keep his johnson in his pants!"

"Now, Bob," Tony began.

"Mr. Healy," Dominic said, "he's my social studies teacher. He says the Cold War is over. He made us memorize the new Russian states. And gave us a pop quiz! Even though they're spelled all crazy."

"What?" Bob snapped. Veronica hoped to God he hadn't heard.

"But I was like," Dom continued, "dude, haven't you seen *The Experts* with John Travolta? And what about *Red Dawn*? The Russians are still the bad guys."

"I can't hear you, boy. Speak up!"

Maddie shouted, "The Russians are the bad guys! You are totally right, Grandpa. The Cold War is *not* over!"

"The Cold War was never a *war*," Bob said. "The young people, they don't know what war is." He laughed. "They think it's a card game!"

He fell back into his chair. "You're a good boy, Dominic."

Bob's attention made the boy's face go dreamy. Veronica had seen that look many times over the past fifty years—on the faces of seamen, even an admiral or two, and there were the boys who had begged Bob to autograph posters at countless air shows. He may have never seen battle, but he was king of the Ironworks. She had known, when she accepted his marriage proposal, she'd be second to his men, his fans, his buddies. She hadn't minded the solitude and wished those buddies, most dead or dying, were there to help her with their Colonel now.

"Ginny, sweetheart," he said tenderly, and Veronica let herself believe there was love there. "I can't be the only one who thinks you're fat." He looked at Maddie, then Dominic. "Children, be honest now. It's for your mother's own good."

"That is enough!" Veronica slammed her fist on the table so her old china rattled. "You shut your mouth. This instant."

Bob ducked his head like a disobedient child.

"Now, be a dear, and wipe that snot from your nose before it lands in your lap. Or, worse, in Tony's precious pasta."

It was hard to quit now that she had their attention.

"And we do *not*," she added, "slurp from our spoons like barbarians. Only put on your spoon what you can eat in one bite. Isn't that right, children?"

Maddie and Dom nodded.

The look on their faces—mouths open, eyes on Bob—was heaven. They waited for the Colonel to explode. *Whaddya want, a slap upside your head, Veronica?* She wished she could tell them—the Colonel has vanished. Left in his place, a man living on his own private island. She wished she could tell them—I'm preparing to vanish too—but knew they'd never understand. She herself wouldn't have, not before she became a dying woman and saw what fools they all were, her included, living as if each day wasn't a step closer to death.

A bubble bath had seemed like a nice way to die. But then she'd considered the humiliation of being found in the nude, the contents of her bowels floating in the lilac-scented bathwater. She'd been a nurse when she met Bob and knew what happened after death. The revolver was out of the question. Too much mess. She wouldn't put that burden on dear Rosalita, who'd only ever been loyal and kind. Hanging was absurd. This wasn't a nineteenth-century novel and she wasn't an inmate in a prison cell with only a pair of shoelaces to off herself, and how would she manage the rigging of a noose when she could barely pull herself up the stairs some days? The only option was pills, as many as she could find. Then a plastic shopping bag to put over her head, twine to tie it tight. She'd already decided on the translucent plastic pink sacks from the gourmet grocery in town where Rosalita bought fresh farm peaches, sweet corn, strawberry-rhubarb pie, and cardboard containers of raspberries. That would be nice—inhaling the earthy tang of fresh-picked fruit with her last breath. Her last glimpse of the world rose-colored.

She unclasped her cigarette case, a gaudy thing studded with gold beads, a Christmas present from Ginny. She shook out a Kent King 100. The lighter's hammer struck flint and the flame rose, catching the paper with a hiss. The first pull of hot smoke was divine. She released a cloud into the air above the table.

"Mommy." Ginny's eyes flitted to her father. "You know we don't smoke in the house."

"Ginny, dear, *we* don't. But I do. What was it you young'uns used to say back in the day?"

She exhaled quivering smoky O's over the table.

"Oh yes," she said: "The times they are a-changing."

"Cool," Dominic whispered.

"Well, thank you, Dominic. But let us never forget what a horribly distasteful habit it is. Yes?" She took a last drag and ground the cigarette into her bread-and-butter plate. "We must go. Bob, chop-chop! So much to do at the big house. Rosalita is coming first thing in the morning to clean."

Her daughter's family stood at the front door as they left. Ginny surprised Veronica, crushing her in a hug so sudden she let loose an "Oh!"

"Mommy, I missed you."

Veronica felt a sob rattle in her throat. Dear God, was she turning into one of those *feelings* people?

"You know how bad I am with hugs and all that. Me," she smiled, "your coldhearted mother."

"Can I stop by tomorrow? There's something I wanted to talk to you about. Just us two."

You mean, Veronica thought, *something you want me to buy*.

"We're *so* busy, dear. And exhausted! I'll need a week to acclimate. You understand."

"Of course." Ginny's fingers went to her mouth. Her daughter's cuticles were ragged, the nails chewed. "I was just thinking . . ." She paused. "A cruise would be a wonderful experience for the whole family. Don't you think?"

"Don't bite your nails, dear . . ."

"I know," Ginny said, her voice far away as she stared sleepy-eyed at the forest. "No boy wants to hold a girl's hands if her nails are all chewed."

Veronica knew she'd been a poor mother but the reminder made the scars on her chest throb.

"Oh, sweetie," Veronica began, then saw how it only relit that hopeful hunger in Ginny.

"Please? Just a quick visit?"

Veronica was sure her daughter's list was as long as her childhood Christmas letters to Santa—vacations to the Caribbean and tea at the Plaza in the city, a new Bloomies card to replace her delinquent account. Maybe even a new car.

"We'll see," Veronica whispered.

There had been a time, before Ginny dropped out of the all-women's college they'd paid a fortune for, and before she sat Veronica down in White Eagle's peach-and-gold sitting room and delivered the news she was pregnant with Tony's baby, when Bob had spoiled their daughter. He sent Ginny and her girlfriends on luxury trips across Europe; tucked a purebred cocker spaniel (a red satin bow around the pup's neck) under the Christmas tree; slipped velvet boxes with jeweled cocktail rings under her pillow every Valentine's Day. One year opal, the next sapphire, then ruby and emerald, each stone hugged by a spiraling staircase of diamonds. He had ruined their daughter, Veronica thought, because throwing money at her was the only way he knew how to love.

"I heard from Peggy Brell," a reinvigorated Ginny said, "who heard it from Elaine Lucas, that you can have lobster for every meal on the *Queen Mary*. Breakfast, lunch, and dinner!"

Ginny seemed so much like herself—pink-cheeked and giddy. And why shouldn't her daughter have what she wanted, now that Veronica was in charge, no longer forced to grovel to Bob for the most basic things like a new washing machine or a dollar raise for Rosalita. She decided right then and there—she'd book a cruise for Ginny and Tony, surprise them with it before she departed this world, checked off the final to-do on her list.

"I promise, sweetie. I'll do my best to give you everything you want."

Ginny's lips parted in surprise and then stretched into a smile. A toothy grin that reminded Veronica again of little Ginny. Pure and filled with hope.

She left a lipstick smudge on Ginny's cheek when they kissed goodbye. Her daughter smelled sweet—too much perfume hung over a sickly odor like rotten fruit. The scent filled Veronica's nose, her mouth, and she took a few stumbling steps toward the woods. Then she heard them calling. *Cah-cah-cah.*

"Listen," she said.

They all turned to the lush, dark forest, which looked cool and inviting after the cottage's stuffy heat.

"It's the caterpillars," Dom said, delighted.

Veronica strained to hear the insects' breathy whisper. What were they saying?

Champ's ears twitched and he howled before bounding off into the trees.

"Yuck," Ginny said. "They're chewing through your beautiful trees, Mommy."

"That's not chewing," Veronica said. "It's their excrement falling. Sounds like a gentle rain shower, yes?"

"You mean," Maddie paused, "their poop?"

"I'm afraid so," Veronica said. "Now we must get going. We old people need our rest. Ta-ta, all." She made herself smile at her son-in-law. "Thank you for the scrumptious lunch, Tony!"

As she and Bob walked the uneven slate path leading from the cottage to the big house (Tony could've at least fixed the path, she thought), Dominic loped behind.

"Wait!" the boy called. "He's not even going to do the inspection?"

Veronica laughed. She'd forgotten how surprising children could be.

"Would you prefer he did?" She nodded at the shabby gray cottage. "We can go back."

"No, no!" He got her joke. Smiled. She saw he needed braces and added *orthodontics for the boy* to her list.

"Bob, why don't you start home?" He was taking slow, careful steps toward White Eagle, where Champ sat at the top of the double staircase, his tail thumping against the intricately carved oak doors.

"I have a job for you, Dominic." She curled her finger playfully. She remembered how the boy had gazed admiringly at Bob as he swore and ranted on his favorite topic—war. "It's a mission actually."

She knew this was the right word to use, always the best choice for a boy (or man) desperate to prove himself.

"Top secret?" he asked, confirming her suspicion that he was like all the boys who had followed the Colonel. Looking for someone to lead them, tell them how to think, feel, and act.

"The Colonel isn't himself lately."

Dominic looked alarmed. "Is he sick?"

"No, not exactly. He'll be better soon. Don't you fret." She let her voice fall to a whisper and leaned toward the boy, who smelled tangy, like ketchup. "Can you watch your grandfather for me?"

"*Me?* Watch the Colonel?"

"Sure." She laughed. "I think you're cut out for the job. There are people on this island . . ." She paused, not used to talking to children, searching for appropriate words.

"Yeah?" His brown eyes—lovely, trusting eyes—widened, and she tried to remember the awe she'd felt when she first met Bob. When she'd misinterpreted his arrogance as courage.

"There are people out to *get* your grandfather. Prove he's not fit to run the Ironworks."

His lips parted in shock.

"Don't go worrying yourself," she said. "Just keep an eye on him. You're my new lieutenant, deal?"

She winked. All those years spent with men—seamen, engineers, cigar-chomping executives—winking at her again and again. Every wink had felt like a dismissal. Now, as her grandson winked back, she understood. To be the winker was to be the secret holder. To be powerful.

He ran off to join Bob and Champ on the lawn. Bob was clearing twigs, bending slowly as if in pain. She'd have to give him two aspirin with his evening snack. He lobbed the sticks into the woods, where they fell short, landing in the orange tiger lilies. Champ leapt into the flowers, crushing the tall blooms.

"Atta boy, Champ!" Dom shouted.

She stopped herself from telling them to watch out for the flowers. What did it matter when there was so little time left?

There, she thought, maybe she wasn't so coldhearted after all.

Kingdom: *Animalia*

Phylum: *Arthropoda*

Class: *Insecta*

Order: *Lepidoptera*

Family: *Erebidae*

Subfamily: *Lymantriinae*

Genus: *Lymantria*

Species: *L. dispar*

Subspecies: *L. d. dispar*

—Scientific Classification of gypsy moth, *Lymantria dispar dispar* (Linnaeus, 1758)

5.

Jules

He had wanted to hate the island.

When Leslie had returned from her mother's funeral with news of the inheritance, he'd been sure she was messing with him. For weeks after, at night she whispered in his ear, her hand wrapped around his dick, tugging slow, slower, up and down. *Is this good, baby? Is this how you like it?* Like she didn't know. After sex, his fingers and mouth smelling and tasting of her, they lay together, the city clamor knocking around on the street outside their apartment, and he listened as she described the Castle. She called it that—not a hint of irony—and slapped at him when he called her Princess Leslie.

She described the gardens. Acres of fern-carpeted forest (she knew he was a sucker for ferns). The fragrant salt-spray roses that blanketed the dunes of Singing Beach. It sure sounded like a fairy-tale castle, a make-believe island. Impossible to believe in, and yet he couldn't stop hoping it was real and came to want it so bad that he'd shoved her away, begged her to quit, this Scheherazade scheming, luring him away from his city, his home, to an island rotten with white conservatives. Military born and bred. *Shit, Leslie,* he'd shouted once, waking Eva, *they're natural born killers!*

He had wanted to hate Avalon, to feel the same disgust he'd reserved for her parents, who lived as if Jules were dead and his children never born. When Brooks began mentioning *the island* during family dinners, Jules had wanted to hate Leslie, who, as usual, had recruited their son to her agenda, the boy who wanted so badly to believe in something that he'd believe in anything. UFOs, God, world peace—it seemed like Brooks was obsessed with a new cause every week. Like mother, like son, Jules thought but didn't dare say aloud. It seemed a challenge these days to go a week without Leslie or Brooks getting pissed at him. Their brooding combined, forget about it. Brooks, like Leslie, had a knack for holding grudges, and could go days without speaking to him. Making Jules feel invisible.

Then he visited the island for the first time, just he and Leslie—the kids left behind in the city under the care of Mrs. Umansky. Jules fell in love the moment their city-dinged station wagon rolled onto the causeway under clouds so thick they seemed painted. The white-capped waves rocked against the boulders lining the narrow road and he felt the trembling in his chest. They drove into a forest so dense the trees joined in a lush canopy overhead, and, on each side of the paved road, reached in for a verdant hug, making it hard to see where the asphalt ended and the woods began.

He'd let the car slow to a crawl, wanting to watch the sunlight flicker through the trees, catch the birdsong, to feel the ocean breeze sifting the leaves. It was just as Leslie had promised. *Like America before the white man arrived.* Virgin land. No stoplights, no stop signs. No telephone poles—the islanders had paid through the nose to have the wires buried so as not to spoil the view.

He had no language to describe the Castle then. It took a few days for the archaic terms he had studied in required architectural courses at Harvard to return to him. Turrets and finials and gables. But studying glossy photos in a textbook was nothing like the real thing. Of course Leslie's parents had named it the Castle. It was the stuff of fairy tales, a white marble palace rising out of the trees, built to protect a royal clan from marauding villagers and pillaging hordes. From war. From the *undesirables*—what his pops had called the kids in their 'hood who spent their days slinging dope, lounging on stoops like the sun had melted them there.

It looked to Jules more like a fortress than a home with its four rounded spired towers, one at each corner of the three-story square-shaped main house. The front portico with its domed ceiling, and carriage porch (*la porte-cochère*, Jules remembered) reminded him of the White House.

The bronze French baroque front doors were as tall as the two-story city row house that had been Jules's childhood home. Leslie claimed they weighed a ton *each*. An oval medallion with ornately wrought initials decorated each door. H. M. for Hieronymus Marshall. Admiral, former Grudder president, warmonger, bigot, father to Jules's beloved.

Leslie had told him the story. The Castle was built after her father returned from a company golfing retreat to France, where he and a group of the higher-ups from the factory, most ex-military like Admiral Marshall, had stayed at a sixteenth-century castle turned luxury resort. At the souvenir shop, the admiral had bought a set of laminated place mats—the castle's stony beauty depicted in watercolor. Once stateside, he'd hired an architect and had given him orders to copy every detail, stopping short of building the moat.

If there had been a chance left for him to hate the island, to refuse Leslie's and Brooks's demands that they move, it died when Jules entered the maze that led to the Castle's gardens. Leslie, not one to keep anything under wraps, had managed to keep it a surprise, and as Jules ran into the maze, ignoring Leslie's cries, "Wait, you'll get lost! You need the directions!" there was nothing he wanted more than to lose himself in the tall (at least eight or nine feet, he guessed) fragrant corridors. It was his personal amusement park—the funny mirror glass replaced with living, breathing, oxygen-releasing walls.

He knew gardeners who hated boxwood, claimed it smelled like cat piss, but Jules inhaled deeply as he ran through the shaded lanes, reveling in the sour scent. He wished Leslie had followed him in—they could run together, until breathless, and he would tell her everything he knew about *Buxus*. Way back when, the ancient Egyptians were filling the gaps in their gardens with boxwood, just as the ladies of East Avalon did today. Pharaoh Kufu, that perfectionist, insisted the base of the Great Pyramid be lined with thousands of the trees. Imagine that—the audacity—planting hundreds of thousands of thirsty boxwoods and commanding them to rise in the desert!

He hit a dead end, almost ran face first into the evergreen. He retraced his steps, or at least he thought he had, but he ran into another dead end. He laughed aloud. Leslie's birdlike voice sounded in the distance.

"I told you, you big fool. You'll be sorry you didn't listen to me!"

"I don't care," he shouted. "I'm never coming out!"

He lay on his back in the grass. The sun blocked by the tall hedges, the sweat on his face cooled, and he thought of the city and its steel and glass skyscrapers. He'd happily trade those man-made walls for this.

The sky above the labyrinth had turned a predusk apricot by the time he emerged. Not from the entrance he'd run into like an impatient child, but from the exit, and what he saw stopped him short so he skidded across the dew-damp lawn, landing flat on his back, the wind knocked out of him.

Leslie was there, waiting, and the sight of him prone kicked her into giggles. She'd always had the humor of a ten-year-old boy, Jules thought. A sucker for physical comedy, especially if it was Jules tripping, falling, walking straight-on into a screened door.

"Oh my," Leslie gasped midlaugh, "it was just like in the cartoons! You know when they slip on the . . ."

He interrupted her, groaning as he sat up, "I know, I know. On a banana."

There it was. His garden. His second chance. They stood at the top of the wide stone stairs overlooking the gardens that unfolded like a gold and green tapestry, and, for a moment, instead of feeling grateful to Leslie, he felt only hot humiliation. He'd been so naïve. She (*Scheherazade*, he thought again) had known all along how this seduction would go down. Known he'd never be able to say no. Not to this. The garden that would replace all he'd lost last year when that nor'easter gobbled up Hurricane Grace, creating what meteorologists called the Perfect Storm (and with a manic glee that had made Jules want to throw something at the TV). A fifteen-foot storm surge had rolled over their neighborhood, the lowest point in the city, a hook-shaped peninsula sticking out in the sea. Asking for it. The community garden he and Leslie had created a decade back, named Our Garden with naïve optimism, destroyed. Even when the water had rolled back out to sea, the salt left behind strangled the few plants that had put up a good fight. His life's work, dead.

But now there was this. The Castle. The rolling lawn as wide as the city botanical gardens he had fled to as a boy, an escape from his father sitting slumped in front of the radio listening to ball games and smelling of cigarette smoke and despair, and from the kids on his block who kicked his ass every weekend for being a foo-foo private-school boy whose mama ironed his jeans so he looked spick-and-span even on Saturdays.

Beyond the lawn, the sea glittered. The view so damn perfect he had to blink away the sense that it was a painting. He'd only ever seen such perfection in the west wing galleries of the city museum, where the French Impressionists hung in gilded frames. The rosebushes were newly blooming—*They were waiting for you*—in every shade of red, white, yellow, pink, even purple. He recognized a few of his favorite hybrids. The soft pink Heritage; the fragrant Madame Plantier; and what had been his mother's favorite—he'd planted it outside her bedroom window her final spring so she could watch it unfurl—the Double Delight, with its creamy center and cherry-red edges she'd compared to a lady's painted parasol, the kind of image she'd only ever seen in movies and romance novels.

The garden was a mess, no doubt. The roses hadn't been cut back in who knows how long and the long branches had bent to the ground, most of the blooms resting on the earth, the petals brown with rot. Overgrown meandering paths had sprouted weeds as tall as Eva, encircling a pond so thick with green algae and lily pads it could've been a set for a horror film.

Jules knew he could return the garden to its glory. He buzzed with faith.

"Well," Leslie had sang cutely, her thin arm woven through his, "What do you think? Will it do?" She laughed, startling a bird from a nearby tree. A male cardinal like a spot of fresh blood against the cloudless sky. "It's your own secret garden."

And it did feel as if the garden had been made for him, plucked straight from his dreams. Circling the pond were cottage flowers elbowing one another for room—the same flowers he'd have picked himself. Bellflower. Foxglove. The regal delphinium. Ox-eyed daisies, sweet Williams, hollyhocks, peonies, and spikes of silvery-blue lavender. There were fruit trees, apple, pear, flowering cherry, and purple-leaf plum. And a long row of Cherokee Brave dogwoods, their pink blossoms so plentiful it looked like the buds perched on their thin branches. The flowerbeds, lily and iris and overgrown hydrangea in Easter-egg colors, reached into the perimeter of downy fern, and beyond it lay the woods, so it seemed as if there was no beginning or end to the greenery.

Who had created such a garden? Could Leslie's mother, a woman Jules had never met but had despised, be his kindred spirit? It was an old-fashioned country design with uneven rows and closely planted flowers. It felt authentic. Unpretentious. Of course, he knew that, just like the salon-coiffed and tennis-toned women of Avalon Island, the garden's messy irregularity was intended. He'd be careful, he promised himself (and his garden, he was already thinking of it as *his*); he wouldn't overprune, only cut back what was necessary. He wouldn't spoil the duality of its design—casual yet carefully constructed—an exquisite contradiction that had, for years, made Jules long to see the English and European gardens he'd visited only in the pages of books. Because they'd never had the money. Not since Leslie had gone to her parents seventeen years ago, told them she was carrying a black man's child, and lost her allowance, and, until her mother, in the final stages of uterine cancer had changed her will, her inheritance. Still, he reminded himself how, seventeen years ago, when Leslie had returned to their one-room city apartment after confessing to her parents, Brooks in her womb just starting to show—a miracle after so many miscarriages—she had chosen Jules (him!) over her parents. He had never loved her more.

They took her back, of course—not him, or the children—only their golden-haired daughter, whom they gave an allowance. A pittance of what she would've inherited, he'd heard Leslie explain with an eye roll to her mostly white bohemian friends—self-declared artists and writers and thespians, who, he guessed, also lived off allowances. Every few months, Leslie slipped on one of the pastel Chanel suits she kept draped in plastic at the back of the closet. She straightened her hair with a hot iron so the white-blond curtained the back of her long patrician neck. She dabbed creamy cover-up on her freckled nose. The freckles he adored. Kissed. Photographed. Her father's car picked her up and drove her to the island, where she walked through the Castle doors as if frozen in time. To collect her check. To be their Leslie. Leslie in a bottle. A lie.

Three months after his first visit to the island, he'd finally given up on resurrecting their sea-ravaged garden—*Our Garden*—it still stung to think of the name arching over the iron entrance in rainbow-colored letters he'd repainted every spring. He caved to Leslie's (and Brooks's) demands, stuffed their earthly possessions, including the kids, into a U-Haul, and made the move. Leslie had convinced him to abandon the few surviving plants—a lilac tree turned powdery white with mildew; a dozen hostas, their elephant-ear leaves cracked; and a peony bush whose blush-colored flowers looked as immaculate as before the storm. It was a fresh start, she'd promised.

It rained the morning they moved and the island air was thick with the fecund scent of damp earth, low tide and spring blossoms, and something sweet and familiar—pine needles that had sat all winter.

And so Jules rolled down the windows of the U-Haul and ordered his family to "Breathe!" gulping air until Leslie and Eva were giggling. Brooks complained, of course, calling Jules a "total dork," but soon even Brooks was laughing and Jules's head spun from all that oxygen. He knew that dizzy feeling was happiness.

When they reached the gates of the Castle, the U-Haul screeching to a halt, and Jules saw the pair of marble eagles guarding the entrance like Rottweilers, his first thought was he'd gone and brought his family—his son—to a prison. Leslie unlocked the salt-rusted chain, and from the driver's seat, with the sun behind them, he could see through her sheer skirt the *V* where her thighs met. She skipped back to the car and, once inside, the car jerking forward and onto the long graveled driveway, she'd kissed him, engulfing him in the scent that was hers alone. Almonds. Jasmine oil. The sugar that sits at the bottom of a cup of coffee. That last delicious sip.

He parked at the end of the drive. His family sat in silence, staring up at the Castle, the sun shining her brightest (like she knew they were coming) so the white marble sparkled with sugary light.

Eva poked her head between the front two seats and whispered, "Do a king and queen live there?"

Jules looked at Leslie, who gazed up at the Castle, chewing her lower lip.

"They do now," he said. "And you can be our princess."

"Barf," Brooks groaned from the backseat.

Jules turned just in time to see Leslie roll her eyes in Brooks's direction, as in *Your dad is such a cheeseball.* Jules wouldn't let their ganging up on him like usual bust his sunny mood. He was high on sea breeze, on honeysuckle.

"Um, Mom? Is that, like, an iron gate on the front door?"

His son's voice shook and Jules was grateful when Leslie spoke.

"Actually, it's bronze," she said. "Forged on this very island, in the Ironworks. Don't worry, sweetie, we'll always leave it unlocked. Cross my heart."

"Unless you miss curfew, young man," Jules added. "Psych!"

"Ha-ha, hilarious," Brooks said. Then added, "Not."

"We'll be living in the cottage next door anyway," Leslie said, turning around in her seat and chucking Brooks under his newly defined chin. "Just until I fix up the old place."

The cottage was a short walk through the hedge maze. Jules was excited, and a bit nervous, to show the kids the maze—what if little Eva got lost? He explained to Brooks how to navigate the labyrinth.

"There are two types of non-unicursal, or puzzle, mazes." Jules had spent hours researching mazes at the city library, brushing up on general info he'd absorbed way back in grad school. "Branching and island mazes. This one is a branching, which is pretty cool, since it's the older kind."

Brooks puffed out a sigh.

"Dad, can you just, like, get on with it? I don't need a plant lesson. Just the directions."

It stung, his son's rejection, even more so, Brooks's sudden loathing for anything green. Leslie had tried to comfort Jules with some psychobabble about the son having to reject his father to become his own person, but still.

"Fine," Jules said, struggling to keep calm when he wanted to shout at Brooks, call him a spoiled brat, "keep your hand—doesn't matter which one—on the same wall. When you hit a dead end, move your hand around the end of the path. You'll retrace your steps and end up where you started." He added, "That simple enough for you?"

Leslie had taught Jules the series of turns—a long combination of rights and lefts—for each route through the maze. The first path was from the front of the Castle to the cottage, and the second, the front of the Castle to the gardens. Jules had tried his best to memorize both but flubbed them each time Leslie tested him.

They made a game out of it for little Eva using the tune of "Heigh-Ho" from *Snow White and the Seven Dwarfs*. Jules and Leslie sang as their family marched through the maze. Jules played the clown—his arms pumping and legs lifting like a manic soldier. *Right, right . . . Left, right . . . Right, left, left, right . . .* Eva giggled, Brooks rolled his eyes again, and Leslie smiled. Maybe they *were* home, Jules hoped.

He had promised Leslie he would go to the party with her. An apology of sorts for what she called his *overreaction* to the fight at the fair.

"I wouldn't even call it a fight," Leslie had said. "More like a tussle."

"White boys will be white boys," he had said in the high-pitched voice of his aunt Lorraine, which he often used to tease Leslie. She'd swatted him. Pursed her lips thoughtfully, "A rumble? A spat?"

There had been a gun. He'd sworn to her he'd seen it on one of those heavy-metal kids. But Leslie had only nodded like he was little Eva complaining about the bogeyman under her bed.

He showered in the cottage's narrow bathroom stall, scrubbing the dirt from his nails with a wooden brush. God forbid he should offend any more of Avalon's blue-haired ladies, he thought.

"What are *you* laughing at?" Leslie asked.

"Just wondering if Orchid Lady will be there tonight."

"You are a troublemaker," Leslie said, smiling. "And if she is who I *think* she is, you better watch that sweet ass of yours. Mrs. Hennessey is infamous for her roving fingers. The busboys at the club can attest."

"You trying to turn me on?"

"Can you blame her?" she said. "I was watching you work in the garden. Looking all sexy out there with no shirt. All sweaty. Wood chips stuck to your muscles."

This woman, he thought. Her words alone made his soap-lathered penis grow hard.

Leslie let out a frustrated groan.

"What's the matter?" He slid the shower curtain open and it rattled on rusted rings.

She stood in front of the vanity mirror wiggling into the control-top panty hose he'd only seen her wear when visiting her parents.

"You're wearing *those*?"

He toweled himself with a raggedy thing that smelled like mildew. Leslie had yet to abandon her rule forbidding living in the Castle and so they were stuck with the portable washing machine that hooked up to the cottage kitchen sink. The clothes and towels were hung out to dry on a clothesline out back and returned with a damp, fishy odor.

"I thought you said panty hose were sexist torture devices? Invented to keep women from moving fast enough to achieve their goals. I'm just paraphrasing, of course."

"When in Rome," Leslie grumbled as she hopped up and down trying to scoot the flesh-toned elastic fabric over her pale ass. "And don't mess with a woman shoving herself into Spandex, Julius. She just might murder you."

Jules looked out the bathroom window and spotted Brooks heading down the driveway. His skateboard was tucked under an arm and his backpack hung low like it was full and heavy. Maybe with beer, Jules guessed, and reminded himself to give Brooks another talk about getting in cars with drunk teen drivers—a new concern out here in the country.

"Where's *he* going?" Jules stopped himself from running out the cottage door in his towel to tell Brooks to be careful. To watch his back. The kind of thing Jules's father would've done.

"I don't know. Out," Leslie called from the bedroom. "I put your new suit on the bed. But you'll have to wear your old loafers. Maybe we can get a pair in town tomorrow. Ooh, and I want to get my hair blown out."

Leslie had been spending money like it grew on the rosebushes he'd pruned in the garden that morning. Boxes of new clothes she brought home from town. Shiny new items that seemed to pop up daily. A red tricycle for Eva. And for Brooks, a new stereo and turntables and speakers as tall as Eva. But Leslie had promised Jules, thanks to her inheritance, there was enough money in their bank account to buy a dozen speakers. He had considered going to the bank in town himself to make sure but knew he needed to trust her.

She had made an excuse about having to replace all they'd left behind and he wanted to remind her of all the stuff still boxed up in the Castle's six-car garage, including their books—books Leslie had given him soon after they'd met. Copies of *Invisible Man* and *Native Son* and James Baldwin's collected works. The essays he had read again and again so the pages were creased and yellowed; the covers softened. He and Leslie had spent hours on snowy days way back when, in Cambridge, in bed, naked, smoking joints and sipping hot cocoa, debating what Baldwin meant when he wrote: *The really terrible thing, old buddy* (and, God, didn't Jules feel like Baldwin was talking straight at him, right up in his face), *is that **you** must accept **them** . . . For these innocent people have no other hope.* Innocent whites? How could Baldwin write with such outrage, quote God cursing Noah with utter destruction—*No more water, the fire next time!*—and blame not the bigots and lynchers but their innocence? Decades later, he was still trying to figure out what Baldwin was getting at and, sometimes, he felt close. But since they'd moved to the island, well, he figured it was time for a refresher.

He had wanted to reject Leslie's gifts. The absurdity—a rich white girl giving him a bag of books about the black experience. It should've been his pops who handed him those books tracing the history of the black man from slave to free man, but his father had been too stuffed with bitterness to find redemption on paper. Jules's teachers at Dalton, his mostly white private high school, had assigned plenty of books about struggle—*The Old Man and the Sea*, *The Great Gatsby*, *Moby-Dick*. Sure, they'd read *The Adventures of Huckleberry Finn*, but that was a whole other story. Leslie's gifts, shopping bags full of used books, had reflected Jules back at himself like a mirror. She'd given him the words to understand and explain himself.

Now they were trapped in cardboard boxes in the garage. He'd considered bringing them into the cottage, creating his own impenetrable walls with stacks of books. Along with the forgotten FREE SOUTH AFRICA and END APARTHEID posters they'd brought home from an antiwar rally two decades back—their first purchase together. The posters had traveled with them from Cambridge to New York City, had hung on the walls of half a dozen studio apartments until they were frayed at the edges.

"Who's going to watch the baby tonight?" Jules asked. "While we go to the dinner thing?"

"The Wilson girl. Completely reliable."

"We could bring Eva with us," Jules said, trying not to betray his fear of letting a stranger watch his little girl. "Ooh, lawd," he crooned in the voice he'd been using more and more since they'd moved to the island, an amalgamation of all the dialects he'd heard actors use in movies about slavery. He knew Leslie couldn't stand it. She'd even accused him of being racist, which only made him lay it on thicker. "How all the white missuses will be squealing over our sweet little pickaninny!"

"Like I said," Leslie said, "*you* are a troublemaker."

She struck a femme-fatale pose in the doorway, one naked arm stretched above her head, a hand on her hip. She wore a sheer, vanilla silk gown. It tied at the neck and clung to her like liquid. With her blond hair swept to one side, she was a bona fide bombshell and made him think of Veronica Lake. Made him want to tear the dress off.

"I decided to screw the panty hose and go au naturel."

He kissed her and let his towel fall from his waist.

"Screw me instead, baby."

"Well, that didn't take much." She wrapped her fingers around his penis. Then pushed him away. "Jules, you're all wet! I paid a fortune for this dress at Saks. Good thing it wasn't *my* fortune."

He laughed along but didn't like the way she spoke of her mother's money like it was a big joke, making it out like they were crooks.

She tiptoed to the second bedroom—they'd decided Brooks should have his own room, but Eva took her naps in there. Leslie listened, her ear pressed to the closed door.

"Come with me," she said. "I have a surprise."

He felt that familiar tugging in his abdomen when she hooked her fingers in his and he saw the quilt folded under her arm.

"But the baby."

"She's fast asleep."

"I don't know." He was worried about Eva waking, getting lost in the serpentine maze.

Leslie kissed him, the tip of her tongue pushing his lips apart and entering his mouth. Ending the conversation. He grew hard so fast it hurt. Two decades they'd been together and she could still make him feel that. What a fool he'd been to think he'd could say no to her. About moving to the island. About any-thing.

They ran through the hedge maze. The tang of fresh-trimmed wood filled the green corridors. She tugged him forward at every turn, which made the towel slip from his waist until he was using it only to shield his penis, his ass bared.

"Pop quiz!" Leslie shouted. "What's the code to get back to the cottage?"

Jules sang the "Heigh-Ho" tune, "Right, left, right, right, left, right."

"Good boy!" Leslie cheered. "But there's another code if you want to get to the secret garden tucked in the heart of the maze."

"Oooh, a secret garden," Jules teased. "I ain't no naïve little boy falling for your tricks, Ms. Leslie Marshall."

Her laugh was like coins tumbling from the blue sky.

"You'll see," she said. "Listen up. 'Cause I'm only going to tell you the code two times. You ready?"

"Yessiree, ma'am!"

She slapped his bare ass and he whooped. They ran faster.

"Left, right," she said. "Left, left, right, left."

"Left, right," he repeated. "Left, right . . ."

"No! Repeat after me, you big dummy."

"Shit, girl, it took me three tries to memorize the way to the cottage. I'm a science man, not a math man."

They chanted the code and then they were running down sun-toasty stone steps and into what Jules could only describe as a room. Made with living walls. He knew they must be close to the big garden—he smelled the grass he'd cut that morning and the tree sap oozing from the trees he'd downed. He ran his hands across the eastern wall knowing that, on the other side, his precious garden waited for him.

"I cut the grass myself," Leslie said as she unfolded the quilt, lifting it so the fabric ballooned before settling on the chopped grass.

"With what?" Jules said. "Scissors?"

"Shut up." She giggled. "It was hard. I had to use the hand mower so it would stay a surprise."

She shimmied out of her silk dress. She was naked underneath and the revelation made his breath catch. He threw his towel aside. She hung her dress by its thin straps on a twig sticking out of the wall, and then she lay on the quilt, her body still and pale as marble. His Aphrodite.

She filled her mouth with him and the square of grass became a green undulating sea. Her body shimmered in the late sunshine, the sky above striated pink and orange, and as she rode him, his hips bucking to match her time, it was as if she was made of light.

She moaned, "We're home."

The quilt grew wet under his back, with dew and come, and

after they were done, a stain the shape of his long body stretched across the quilt.

How had he gone so long, he wondered, without the scent of dew in his life?

6.

Leslie

She lost the first baby when she was nineteen. Two years before she'd meet Julius—named for a dictator, born with the soul of Saint Francis.

It was her sophomore year at Marymount, the only college her father would pay for. An all-women's teaching college with curfews, prayers twice a day, and elocution classes.

The rain in Spain stays mainly on the plain. Your father was a peer, my dear—remember who you are.

She wore spotless white gloves. Memorized the place settings of a formal dinner table. Learned to pour tea with a steady hand. This was the education of a proper young lady. Refine. Constrict. Tighten that girdle. Suck it in until you were fit to burst. Sit like a lady. Eat like a lady. Talk like a lady. Think like a lady.

The girls were kept busy. Candle-lighting ceremonies where they wore crowns of flowers and white dresses that were more like nuns' habits than party frocks. Hoop-rolling races—the winner, it was predicted, would be first to find a husband. More prayers. Before class, and vespers after dinner. God forbid they should have too much time to think. Look out their barred dorm windows and take notice of the war stealing America's poor young men.

The baby's father was a boy named Tracy she'd met at a Champagne party with their brother college, St. Thomas Aquinas. She hadn't wanted his baby, or any baby, and so when she woke six weeks after her missed period, the white sheets of her dorm bed stained brown with clotted blood, she'd been relieved. Her roommate Beverly Schneider slept deep and didn't stir as Leslie balled up her sheets, crept down to the basement, the cement floor cold under her bare feet, and tossed it all into the cafeteria dumpster.

She bled for weeks. Went through boxes of maxipads. Even had to hitch a ride to the small-town drugstore near the college to buy more. The nuns who taught the girls noticed how pale she was, arranged to have liver and onions served at her table. An extra dose of iron that made the girls wrinkle their noses in disgust. She didn't think to go to a doctor. Then there'd be all that explaining to do. And she was sure that was the end of it. What was it that her mother always said?—*When life gives you lemons . . .*

She tried to believe she was lucky. A problem had been solved. But then she'd have to run to the stark dorm bathroom with its many stalls, all without doors—Heaven forbid a girl should have an iota of privacy—and put on a fresh pad, wrap the blood-soaked one in toilet paper, and reach down into the trash so no one would find it. The nuns were militant about keeping watch and she wouldn't have been surprised to find Sister Mary Bartholomew rummaging in the wastebasket.

Like all the girls she knew, she avoided talking about the messiness of the female body. What her mother called "woman's problems." As if the ability to create life were a curse. A disease. Is that what they wanted Avalon's little girls to think, she wondered. Did they hope smearing womanhood would make the island girls less likely to drop their panties in the dunes for a Tom, Dick, or Harry?

How her mother had known about Leslie's first period, she would never figure out. She'd been dressing for bed in her pink bathroom in the Castle, the shelves lined with porcelain poodles with blue sequin eyes and fringed lashes, when she saw the dark stain on her girdle. She stuffed a wad of toilet paper between her legs and then tossed and turned all night with cramps.

The following afternoon, when she came home from a tortured day at school, hours spent fearing her blood would leak onto her desk chair, she found the kit outside her bedroom door. It was a long, rectangular cardboard box. Unmarked. Inside, a bunch of thick cotton pads to be attached to a plastic belt with a tiny silver buckle. There was a pamphlet. *What It Means to Be a Woman.*

Years later, when she carried Brooks to term, she'd know every word in the pamphlet had been a lie.

7.

Maddie

The kids started the night at Singing Beach. Gerritt and Spencer and the boys found a bunch of seaweed-stringy lobster traps washed up on shore, and Maddie and the girls watched them stomp on the weathered wood so it splintered with pops and cracks that echoed off the pink clay cliffs. The boys' faces grew sweat-slick from the effort and Maddie saw how the destruction made them buzz like it was a drug. Boys always got to do the fun stuff, it seemed, while the girls watched. Or, she thought, cheered the boys on, which is exactly what Bitsy and Vanessa and Gabrielle were doing. Hooting and applauding while lit Parliament Lights dangled from lips glossed with Kissing Potion roll-on in Orange Squeeze.

The boys stacked the wood in a towering pyramid and soon a bonfire blazed so tall and hot Maddie was sure it would keep the caterpillars away.

John Anderson drove his Bronco into the dunes and blasted Beastie Boys. "Brass Monkey" came on and everyone sang along, Rolo the loudest (and, Maddie saw, the drunkest), dancing like a spastic robot when the honking horn bleated between refrains so the rolls of fat under his snug tie-dyed Grateful Dead tee jiggled.

Brass Monkey, that funky monkey / Brass Monkey junkie / That funky monkey.

Penny joined in, playing the goofball, bumping hips with Rolo until the whole crew of kids were laughing—bitchy Vanessa the hardest, clutching her belly and yelling, "Stop! I'm gonna pee!"

Maddie had avoided Penny since the fair and was still pissed at her for taking some random pills when she knew she shouldn't, especially not with the chemo. Maddie had held back from shouting *What the hell were you thinking?* on the long ride from the fair to the ER in the back of the ambulance that had rolled onto the fairway—its flashing red-and-blue strobe and the carnival lights all mixed up so Penny's pale face seemed painted. At the ER, once the blood had returned to Penny's acne-rough cheeks, a tube pushing saline into her already bruised veins, the doctor had taken Maddie aside and asked if she'd seen Penny take anything. She had lied, knowing that was what Penny wanted. While they'd waited for Penny's more-than-tipsy parents to show up, Penny was already cracking jokes. *Good thing those black people showed up when they did—that'll give everyone something to talk about, other than me looking like a dumbass.*

Penny's MO, Maddie knew, was to laugh even the most serious fuck-ups away, but Maddie didn't laugh along this time, and made Penny promise she'd stop with the drinking, smoking, and gobbling every pill Bitsy and crew handed her. Just until she was done with her treatments.

Penny had answered, in a new, bitter tone Maddie didn't recognize, "Thanks for looking out for me, *Mom*. Uck, you're such a worrywart."

That was the last thing Maddie needed—her so-called best friend making her feel more uncool than she already felt, and so, the last few days, Maddie hadn't returned Penny's phone calls. What could she say to Penny, who insisted on pretending her seizure was "no big whoop"? Who called Maddie a nag, smiled a goofy, tooth-filled smile, and sang that damn Indigo Girls line, *And the best thing you ever done for me /Is to help me take my life less seriously / It's only life after all, yeah.*

Gerritt and Spencer dropped the ice-packed cooler into the sand. Maddie watched as Gerritt flipped the lid open with a flourish—*Ta-da!*

Bitsy squealed, "Baby, my favorite!"

She kissed Gerritt, a bottle of Bartles & Jaymes kiwi-strawberry-flavored wine cooler dripping in each of her hands. When their lips parted, Maddie saw Gerritt's were shiny with gloss. He slipped a bleached rope bracelet, a prize he'd won at the fair, over Bitsy's wrist. Maddie knew the braided rope would live on Bitsy's arm all summer, shrinking with each shower, each swim at the country-club pool and in the salty ocean, each dip into a steaming hot tub at the parties the richest kids threw when their parents were off-island. The rope would tighten until it had to be cut away.

Maddie spotted Spencer through the wind-tossed flames. His lower lip bulged with Kodiak dip and she knew if she kissed him now he'd taste awful, like tobacco and beer, but he'd done something to his hair that night, blown it out maybe, and the feathery waves caught the setting sun so the red-blond burned bright. She wanted someone to slip a rope around her wrist. Tag her. MINE. Like the message stamped on tiny heart candies for Valentine's Day. But was Spencer Fox the YOURS to her MINE? She wasn't so sure.

Ricky Bell rolled a blunt, sealing the cigar wrapping with the pointy tip of his tongue.

Gerritt yelled, "You detonating a fucking bomb, or what? Let's get this session rolling!"

The blunt made its way around the fire.

The hit Maddie took was both spicy and sweet, and a purring heat grew from a tiny speck inside her until she felt like she was made from the same stuff as the simmering gold stripe the setting sun painted from shore to horizon.

She lay on her back in the sand, not caring if it messed up her hair, and listened to Penny and Vanessa splash in the water, braving the cold June waves.

The boys raced up the wind-brushed sand dunes that had always seemed to Maddie like a mirror image of the ocean waves. Sand spit out behind their heels and they left a trail of cascading twilight-lit tracks. She and Bitsy counted the fireflies dotting the black woods as they dug their toes into the cool sand, smoked cigarettes, and sucked on the Jolly Ranchers they'd dropped into their wine coolers so the clear malt liquor turned bright pink. She felt safe with Bitsy when they were drinking and smoking, the girl's rough edges softened.

They cheered the boys doing keg stands, the muscles in their forearms twitching as they clutched the metal barrel's sides, sucking beer from a long plastic tube, white foam bubbling at the corners of their mouths. The boys chanted nicknames they'd made for one another years back—Rolo, Deuce, Snake—some in elementary school. When it was Spencer's turn his shirt fell down exposing a trail of red-blond fuzz leading from his navel to *down there* and Maddie felt as if the bonfire's flames had licked her face.

When the blunt came back around, Bitsy was standing next to her in the circle. Bitsy said, "Open wide, sweetie."

Maddie did as she was told and Bitsy's soft lips were on hers, smoke filling her mouth and nose so it streamed from her nostrils and she coughed until her sight blurred with tears. The boys around the fire nodded and mm-mm-ed like they'd tasted something delicious. Gabrielle clapped and said, "Atta girl."

It was the kind of summer night that made falling in love feel possible, more than just the plot for one of the chick flicks she and Penny had watched weekend nights before their induction into Bitsy's crew. A breeze set off the fluty song that had given the beach its name back when the Shinnecock Indians canoed its waters, harvesting oysters, before the boots of white men touched Avalon's pebbled sand. The whistling call of the wind squeezing through gaps in the craggy cliffs reminded Maddie of the stories her mother had told her and Dom, before Mom had chosen her pills, about the wailing sirens, mermaids so beautiful no sailor could resist their call. That was how Maddie wanted to feel about Spencer. A need that left no room for doubt. Impossible to pull away.

As she watched him through the flickering flames, she thought she could like him. Enough to let him do the things boys did to the girl they were "going with." His hair had a cute cowlick that made it stick up in front in a moody I-don't-give-a-shit way, like River Phoenix, her movie-star crush and the only teen heartthrob poster she'd hung on her bedroom closet door. And Spencer could be funny, and sort of sweet, especially when Gerritt wasn't around to be impressed.

He wasn't as handsome as the boy at the fair, she thought. Almost a week had gone by and all the kids talked about was *they* and *them*, meaning Leslie Day Marshall and family. While they stood on line for chicken-cutlet sandwiches at the deli and passed a joint down by the dirt parking lot near the docks, as they burned bonfires and tapped kegs, drank cases of beer on their fathers' boats in the harbor and rollerbladed to town to get more beer, and definitely, she imagined, as they whispered to one another over the phone after curfew. *They/Them* was a topic even hotter than the almost fight with the West kids, which Gerritt and Spencer and the boys had reenacted again and again until, Maddie thought, it was pure fantasy.

It wasn't just the kids. She knew the gossip mill had ground its way across the island via summer-camp carpools and chit-chat in the supermarket produce aisle. Through the housewives' call trees, their manicured fingers fiddling with plastic phone cords as that night's roast marinated. *Did you hear they . . . ? Did you see them? So-and-so said they . . .*

They and *them* were all anyone on the island talked about and Maddie had heard Sandra Weller at the bakery, Donna Rich at the Stop & Shop, and even her own parents claim that it was Leslie Day Marshall and family who had caused Penny's seizure; that it was *they* who had carried the gypsy moths to Avalon Island in unimaginable numbers. Them, them, them. Whispers slipping in and out of screen doors, joining until they formed a hue and cry thick enough to strangle the island. As loud as the drone of the caterpillars feeding on the forest. Until it seemed even the caterpillars chanted: *Them, them, them.*

Of course, Maddie knew the caterpillars (*Lymantria dispar dispar*, repeat after me) had been lying in wait all winter, cozy in their furred egg sacs tucked in the crooks of trees all over the island. Waiting patiently for their turn. But, as Dom had told her once while they played Gods versus Mortals in the woods, coincidence was kind of boring. And she too wanted to believe in a sense of order, divine providence or whatever—a sign—linking the arrival of Leslie Day Marshall's family and the metamorphosis of the island, overnight, into a nest of ravenous pests.

It wasn't like she'd never seen black people. There was the annual school trip to the city to see a musical—plenty of black people walking the crowded streets. She'd watched countless hours of hip-hop videos on MTV, and episodes of *The Fresh Prince of Bel-Air* and reruns of *The Jeffersons* and *Fat Albert*, and she'd seen *Do the Right Thing* twice when the movie came to town. Just last week, she'd climbed into Gerritt's Jeep, so crammed with kids she'd had to sit on Spencer's lap and feel his boner digging into her thigh. They had driven to the railroad station on the mainland, where double-decker trains shuttled people, mostly men in suits, to the city and back. There were liquor stores there that didn't card for cases of beer and the cashiers were always black or Hispanic.

But *they* were here in East Avalon. They would go to their schools; play on their teams; dance at their prom; and suck on the ends of joints passed at their parties. Leslie Marshall and family would share the domed dining room at the Oyster Cove Country Club, where the only blacks were valets and cleaning women and busboys. It was, after all, Maddie had heard, Admiral and Mrs. Marshall who had founded the club.

Bitsy wouldn't quit talking about what she kept calling *the fight.*

"Like," Bitsy said, "I'm going to let some lowlife from Loserville . . ."

"Screw those skanks!" Penny shouted over the popping and spitting bonfire. Maddie saw she was already drunk—her words slurring, strands of lank hair stuck to her sweaty forehead.

"Don't shoot your load yet, Penelope dear. You almost got us beat back there," Bitsy said.

Maddie was relieved to see Penny back in her place. The awkward duckling.

Then Bitsy laughed, shook her head, and said, "Damn, girl. You got some serious balls."

"*Serious* balls." Vanessa snorted. When had Maddie ever heard Vanessa give someone a compliment?

It made her feel like a monster, envying her sick friend. Her best friend. Penny was the girl she had slept head-to-toe with on sleepover nights when they filled black-and-white composition books—slam books—with their first names followed by the last names of their crushes. Curlicued script and every *i* dotted with a bubble. Even better, a heart. She had watched Penny carve the initials of her first kiss into the fleshy part of her own thigh (*RB*, Ricky Bell, behind the maintenance shed at school), rubbing Penny's back when the X-Acto knife broke through skin and blood and tears rose. She and Penny had shared plenty of firsts that year—first cigarette, first joint, and their first leg shave, passing the can of strawberry-scented foam back and forth on the deck of Penny's parents' kidney-shaped pool.

She trusted Penny, who'd been in the backseat of Maddie's father's station wagon that rainy afternoon a few months back when he'd slapped Maddie across the face. He'd caught them at the Shore Multiplex on the mainland with two Jewish boys Penny had met at a bar mitzvah in Rosedale. Penny had sworn *cross my heart, hope to die* she wouldn't tell, especially not her parents, who might get that pervy school social worker Mr. Frederick involved. Maddie's mother had warned her, and Dom, of what might happen if either told someone, anyone, about their father. That they—the school, the police . . . who exactly *they* were, Maddie didn't know—would take them away. Penny had kept her promise and Maddie owed her for that.

Pink Floyd blasted from the Bronco's subwoofers and even then the new sound, the *ca-cacking* of the caterpillars' pincers sinking into the new leaves in the forest behind the dunes, threatened to overpower the music.

"Get them off!" Bitsy screamed. "Get them *off* me!"

Gerritt peeled the bristled bugs from Bitsy's Wildcats sweatshirt and tossed them into the bonfire, where each one burst with a spark and a sizzle. Maddie couldn't tell if Bitsy wanted an excuse for Gerritt to lay his hands on her as his boys looked on hungrily, or if their fearless leader was truly scared of a few caterpillars. Maddie tried not to flinch each time she found one squirming on her but the rest of the girls, even Penny, seemed to relish the role of damsel in distress. The tiny monsters gave the girls a chance to play screeching victim. The boys, hero.

After a dozen bonfire-fried caterpillars, Gerritt announced it was time to bounce. Spencer volunteered his house—his parents, like most of the east islanders, were at the dinner party. "Getting shitfaced and eating too many pigs in a blanket," Spencer said. There was that sense of humor, Maddie thought. He walked past her, slipped a long finger into a belt loop on her jean shorts, and tugged so she twirled, her bare feet swiveling in the cool sand.

"You're the hottest girl here," he said.

"Shut up," she said, then realized she sounded like one of those dumb girls who couldn't take a compliment. "I mean, thanks, Spence."

"Psyched to show you my place," he said, linking his fingers in hers.

She was grateful for the dying bonfire and the dusk settling, because she knew a spotty blush was spreading across her collarbone.

"And my bedroom," he added.

The beach had felt safe. Even with the caterpillars. She thought of all the dark, empty rooms in the Foxes' huge colonial on Horseshoe Lane. How many times had her mother warned her? Bad things happen to girls in the dark.

8.

Jules

He'd started drinking early. Martinis, manhattans, bubbly pink sherbet punch from a crystal bowl, sacrificing his usually fickle self (he was a beer man like his pops) in the mission to blot the panic he'd felt since he and Leslie had arrived at the three-house, three-course dinner. It wasn't the whiteness of his fellow partyers that unnerved him so much but the brownness of the help. Hispanic waiters and bartenders. Honest-to-goodness butlers, straight out of his mother's period romance novels. *Don't be a self-righteous prick*, he told himself, knowing they'd chosen to be here, just like he had.

He'd never heard of a "progressive dinner" before that night, but after three decadent courses (appetizers, main course, and now dessert), three rounds of drinks, and a blur of ladies in lipstick and pearls handing him plate after plate of food, making sure their "guest of honor" was taken care of, he was as sedate as a pig led to slaughter. Caesar may have marched into his mind, that fool, but Jules was so soused he couldn't pinpoint exactly when, where, or why.

Act one of the night was held at a house shaped like a wedding cake, the pink-and-white striped awnings as pretty as icing, and the interior like a dollhouse. Frilled floral curtains that matched the ladies' sundresses, and pink-and-yellow paisley pillows propped on sofas and armchairs upholstered in plaid. How was it, he wondered boozily, that rich white people could get away with such a wild mix?

He had downed three cups of a candy-sweet drink the silver-haired hostess called a Whiskey Smash to wash away the salt coating his tongue after smoked salmon, whitefish salad, and chicken liver pâté arranged on miniature slices of brown bread and served with tiny sour pickles. There were puffs of all kind. Who knew how many varieties there were—cheese puffs, cream puffs, artichoke and sweet potato. Puffs filled with meat and fish and goat cheese and sundried tomato and pureed this and that. He popped them in his mouth one after the other (even two at a time), figuring that if he kept his mouth full, moving from one waiter's tray to the next, he might go the whole night without having to talk to anyone.

On to act two they went—a pack, a parade, there must have been a hundred of them, he guessed, walking the moonlit roads. Men in pale linen summer suits, women in strappy sandals and dresses that floated in the sea breeze. A trio of violinists led the way, young women with French braids down their backs, playing jazz with a bluegrass kick. With Leslie on his arm in her flowing flapper-esque dress, and he in the seersucker suit he knew she'd dropped big bills for, it felt as if time had stopped, wound backward. It was a Roaring Twenties starlight romp. All that was missing was the moonshine.

House number two was an enormous brick square, so stolid it reminded him of a fort. Puritanical red-brick and unadorned windows. As plain as the first wedding cake house had been decadent. Even the landscaping was stark, the only ornament a path of lean cypress trees leading from the road to the front entrance. Soldiers keeping watch, Jules thought. When he and Leslie stepped through the front door, he let loose a booming laugh and she nudged him. While the outside was as modest as a nun, the interior was lavish.

"It's like French countryside meets New Orleans boudoir," Jules whispered to Leslie. "Where are the ladies of the night?"

"Hush now, the only reason the uppity East ladies let old Mrs. Bentley host anything in this . . ." She paused.

"Den of iniquity?" Jules finished.

Leslie pinched his ass through the thin seersucker and he yelped. A trio of old men with snowy comb-overs glared his way.

"Is because," Leslie continued, "she's an officer's widow."

She explained through a wave of giggles (Jules could see his wife too was uncharacteristically tipsy), that the widow hailed from the South, and as soon as her stodgy old husband, the major, had kicked the bucket, she'd hired a flamboyant decorator from the city who had gone to town. Satin-striped wallpaper. Red-and-purple floral upholstery, and so many down-filled throw pillows Jules almost dozed off on the ornate divan. The main courses were just as sumptuous—fatty filet mignon, buttered biscuits, and gravy to die for. He ate until his chest felt tight.

He kept watch over Leslie, who flitted like a white moth from guest to guest. He wasn't going to have a repeat of the night at the fair, especially when he'd been drinking. And why had he drunk so much, he chastised himself as one after another lady smelling of talcum powder and a splash of Chanel No. 5 introduced herself—Vivian and Edith, several Elizabeths, and two women who went by Bunny. No joke. Their high-pitched delight made his head throb as they complimented him on his dashing/dapper/dandy suit and invited "you and your lovely family" to the Fourth of July party at the club next month.

They bragged about all the island had to offer, and with so much gusto it made the makeup crease around their mostly blue eyes. Like they were selling him an all-inclusive resort package. *It's a real family place.* As if, he thought, they'd forgotten there was a factory making war machines only a mile away. They asked questions—had he taken the kids to Singing Beach; down to the docks to see the sailboats; to the Whaling Museum, where you could carve your own scrimshaw keepsake out of a real oyster shell? He nodded and smiled, chitchatted until his head swam. He wasn't going to make another mistake, like the night of the fair with the orchid lady, putting himself out there by showing off.

The East Avalon boys, most past middle age, had marched straight out of a country-club pamphlet in their jewel-tone golf blazers and butterfly-collar shirts, many in outrageous prints—palm trees, golf tees. He'd seen an old guy in a poodle-print shirt walking around the appetizer party. He was relieved the men all but ignored him. He visited the periphery of a few man-heavy clusters, listened as the men took turns sharing theories on the mysterious graffiti bandit. A chap in a cherry-red golf blazer (it matched his vein-streaked nose) was convinced it was old Captain Armstrong, who, the man explained, had lost his marbles back before Nam. No, no, no, interrupted a skinny dude in plaid trousers with a Parkinsonian quiver. He had heard from so-and-so, brother-in-law to the East Avalon sheriff, that it was the west side kids. Up to no good again. The circle of men bowed their heads. As if, Jules thought, in prayer. He traveled the fringes of one group of brightly clad men (he'd never seen men wear such colors—pink, lavender, coral—not even on Easter Sunday at Calvary Baptist back home) and listened to the conspiracy theories. According to the men of the island, a variety of sources could be responsible for the graffiti—from the CIA to the *goddamn Russians* to the *goddamn hippies* to Grudder's competition, So-and-So Aircraft Company. One old guy blamed William Jefferson Clinton.

The women, in contrast to the men's vibrant attire, were ethereal in soft pastels and flowing whites that reminded him of his mother's beloved "angels"—the framed photos of turn-of-the-century society women that had hung on the kitchen walls of his childhood home. White women dressed in theatrical garb and frozen in melodramatic poses for the tableaux vivants they put on in their homes as parlor games. The photos had been handed down from his grandmother Laverne, who'd been a washerwoman for a Gilded Age debutante. *And proud of it,* his mother had reminded him.

He'd spent many nights hunched over his school textbooks trying to ignore those white women. Their long wavy hair, Cupid's-bow lips, and gossamer gowns as they played Delilah, a clump of Samson's locks clutched in a fist; or Diana the huntress, a bow and arrow pointed off-camera. Joan of Arc in a diaphanous gown, one shoulder bare, tied to a makeshift stake wrapped with silk flowers. Her Clara Bow eyes lifted toward heaven in pining adoration of her God, who young Jules had imagined as pale as those martyred women. When he'd returned home for the summer after his first year of college, having taken a history course with a radical professor whose lectures included a healthy dose of social determinism, Jules had explained to his mother that her precious photos were simply rich white women with nothing better to do than play dress-up. Who knows, he'd added, Grandma Laverne probably had to scrub those same costumes after each photo shoot. It had been the one and only time his mother had hit him, slapping him so hard his cheek had stung all through Sunday pot-roast dinner.

His mother's angels had worn crowns of flowers in their hair and crucifixes around their necks. Avalon Island's waifish apparitions wore double strands of milky pearls and each her own thumper of a diamond ring. His Leslie looked like Mother Earth incarnate with her makeup-free face and sea-tousled hair. A flower child among the Stepford Wives.

Still, it took him a head-spinning moment to pick her out of the throng of blond, willowy women, and he thought again of the FREE SOUTH AFRICA posters boxed up in the Castle's enormous garage. He tipped back the last of his drink, the sugar grainy on his tongue, and wondered if those posters would ever see the light of day.

With each progressive dinner stroll, sobriety diminished, and by the time they were making their way to the final leg of the dinner—*dessert!* the crowd cheered before piling out of the officer's widow's house—the east islanders were what his pops would've called shitfaced plastered. Stumbling, swaying, slurring and belching. Jules spotted a matronly woman barfing into the weeds on the side of the road, a sight that tipped him and Leslie into a fit of uncontrollable laughter.

"What if," he whispered, "the barfer is Orchid Lady?"

Leslie shushed him. "Stop. I can't laugh anymore. It hurts after I stuffed down all those mini eggrolls."

"It could be her. But," he paused, "they *do* all look the same to me."

"I'm going to pee." Leslie doubled over. "And I'm not wearing panties."

As the night wore on, the caterpillars' feeding swelled until it was a constant hum pulsing from the woods, threatening the parade swerving down the dark roads. Every few steps, Jules heard women screech, watched them shake their composed tresses like dogs after a swim, stomp their high heels, *Get it off me!* Bristled caterpillars inched across shoulders and bosoms, tangled in hair. He found one tucked all cozy under the collar of his suit jacket. The enchanted Roaring Twenties mood had dissipated. Not even the violinists' renditions of Big Band tunes—like "Stardust," a song his mother had played over and over on the record player—could drown out the string of curses that were straight-up 1992.

Shit! Motherfucking caterpillars!

It was a relief to make it to the final house, a four-story colonial whose six tall white pillars reminded him (predictably, he thought) of the plantation houses he'd seen in Hollywood films about slavery. Two of the house's help—an older black man in a cheap suit and a teenage white girl in a caterer's vest—stood at the front door, each holding a lint brush in one hand and a small metal tray in the other. The guests separated into two lines, men and women, and shuffled forward to be swiped at delicately so the caterpillars crawling across backs and shoulders, pants legs and skirts, fell into the metal tray.

As he and Leslie waited their turn to be combed, Jules drank in the estate grounds that looked straight out of *Garden Design*. He pointed out the snapdragons and bachelor's buttons to Leslie, explaining how the purple smokebush and arching sprays of *Sporobolus wrightii* created charming texture, but she wasn't listening, busy scanning the line ahead of and behind her.

"Who," he asked playfully, "could be more important than my botany lesson?"

"No one in particular," she said, her eyes still searching. "Everyone and no one, I suppose."

"Look at those hydrangeas! You think I could talk to the hostess? Find out who's responsible for such a sweet garden?"

"I'd skip making friends with Mrs. Gernhardt," Leslie said absentmindedly.

He was starting to wish they'd brought Eva. The little girl had become his shield. She kept him busy chasing after her, feeding her, taking her to the potty . . . all the mundane activities Jules had performed unenthusiastically back in the city had taken on a new purpose since they'd moved to the island with its neverending cocktail parties and country-club brunches. Little Eva gave him an excuse to avoid talking to people. And now he was alone. Sure, Leslie was by his side but her head was someplace else and she was making it clear he wasn't invited on whatever search she was on.

As the long line inched forward, and Jules grew nervous about being brushed by a man who reminded him of his father, he tried to focus on the cutting garden with its tall, delicate orange cosmos spiking between colossal blue hosta. He was about to turn to Leslie, tell her blue was a rare color in a garden, when he spotted the tar-faced jockey tucked among the crimson *Spigelia marilandica* blooms. A gaslight lamp held aloft in one of the statuette's black hands.

"Les," he whispered, but she was no longer at his side.

He searched the line and found her five people back, talking to a woman with hair like lemon meringue.

"This is dreadful, isn't it?" an old woman in the line opposite said. He heard decades of cigarette smoke in her voice.

He was about to step out of line, join Leslie, when he realized the old woman was speaking to him.

"Oh, yeah," he said, smiling, shrugging his shoulders. He reached through the narrow corridor between lines and held out a hand. "I'm Jules."

The woman—she was very old—held out her hand top first, like she was the Queen of England or something. He shook her long white fingers, wondering if he was supposed to kiss her knuckles so swollen they seemed ready to break through the papery skin.

"Veronica Pencott," she said in an overpronounced accent that reminded him of his mother's silver-screen movie stars. Staccato consonants and elongated vowels. "We're neighbors, you and I."

She was striking. With her silver hair piled in a high bun and her long thin neck, she could've been an aging sister to Audrey Hepburn.

"Of course," he said. "So nice to meet you."

He glanced back at the jockey statue, regretting the slip immediately because the old woman's eyes followed his.

"Oh, dear," she said. "Those pests are everywhere."

His head swam with alcohol and heavy food and the long night and he almost turned to the old lady, asked, *What did you just say?* Then he realized she meant the caterpillars crawling across the statue's shoulders, chest, face. As if the squirming larvae were hatching from the frozen black man's mouth.

She shook her head, her tongue clicking *tut-tut*. "Ah, yes, you've found Jocko. The island is littered with his plaster brethren. I wish I could apologize on behalf of the Gernhardts. Dick and Mary aren't the most progressive thinkers."

"No need," he said, smiling again. Like a goddamn fool, he thought.

He was sweating through his suit jacket, the damp spreading across his back, under his arms.

"It is quite crude." The old woman raised a penciled brow. "I've seen more elegant versions."

What she meant, Jules knew, were versions that looked less like black men and more like white men wearing blackface.

"There was," the woman drawled, "a fascinating PBS special on George Washington. Jocko was—in Washington's words—his faithful groomsman."

His boy, Jules thought.

"Of course," she continued, "he was just a child. My grandson's age, I believe. But he volunteered—or so they say—to watch Washington's horses the night he crossed the Delaware and surprised the British forces."

"How'd that turn out?" Jules asked, realizing too late how contrary he sounded.

"Quite good for Washington," the old woman said. "Poor Jocko died still tied to the horses. The reins frozen solid in his hands."

"Devoted to the end."

"Such are the ways of war," the old woman said with a sigh. "There will always be boys to sacrifice."

Colored boys, Jules thought.

"There are," she said, "some Afro-Americans" (Jules stopped himself from updating her) "who have claimed Jocko, or the lawn jockey rather, as a beacon—quite literally—for the Underground Railroad. They believe the statue represents a proud moment in United States history."

Her knobbly fingers pointed at the statuette, and he had to stop himself from telling her not to point, not to bring anyone else's attention to the grotesque thing. Leave it to white people—the lucky *innocents* (there was Mr. Baldwin again)—to spin something good out of plain bad. Putting up with racists, his father had explained, was just one of the black man's many burdens. He'd made it clear to a young Jules there wasn't anything to be done about it. No use punching a concrete wall, no use cutting the trunk of a tree when its roots run deep—his father's pockets had been deep with clichés to explain away the unexplainable. The unchangeable.

It wasn't like Jules had never spent time around rich whites. He'd attended four-course meals at his professors' homes in the toniest neighborhoods surrounding Harvard. But the liberal citizens of Cambridge would've cut off an arm before they put a caricature of a black man on their lawn, if only to save face.

There was a cheer from the front of the line near the white pillars, and the ladies' line, the old woman included, shuffled forward before Jules could respond.

Leslie took her place beside him. *Thank fucking God.*

"Sweetheart, come here for a sec?" He smiled at the lady with the lemon meringue hair. "You can have her right back."

"What's up, babe?"

"You see that?" he paused, "Over there?"

She stared into his eyes instead of at the statue, and he realized it was the first time they'd really *looked* at each other since the move.

"I knew it was here," she said, her voice flat and cold. "It's been here since I was a kid. I'm sorry. I should've taken you home after the last house."

"It's not your fault," he said. "It just caught me off guard, I guess."

"And then Mrs. Gundersen called you *boy*. I swear to God, I almost slapped her."

Her fingers plucked at her white-blond eyebrows. He wanted to pull her hand away, or, at least, tell her to stop. Those poor torn up eyebrows, he'd thought so often over the years.

"Sweetie, that's crazy," he said, "she called me a *city* boy."

"You know what she meant." Now she was angry with him. He shouldn't have used that word. *Crazy.* Not after she'd had such trouble recovering from the last miscarriage.

"*Do* we know what she meant?" He wished she hadn't said anything. Now she was making *him* paranoid.

"These fucking animals." Her face was locked in that sugary smile as she scanned the crowd, and the contrast unnerved him, made his full stomach flip.

He looked around. Had anyone heard her?

He hugged her close and kissed the top of her head, which smelled like sun and shampoo, ignoring the look they got from the old men passing around cigars by the fountain. She'd lost weight since the move and her shoulder bones poked his side.

"If you hate them so much," he whispered, "why are you working so hard to kiss their asses?"

She looked up at him with parted lips. He had surprised her. And maybe, he thought, angered her. But her sudden rage had him wondering if his sweet Leslie Day, who could be as vicious as a mother lion when wronged, had another agenda. Why had she had brought him—brought their children—to this island?

"Don't worry," she said, the serene smile renewed. "They may look happy. But their island is sinking." Her voice was heavy with disgust, like she was ready to spit a mouthful of phlegm. "Bet you one hundred big ones this place—all of it—the factory, their mansions, the whole island is underwater by October."

He felt the absurd urge to crack a joke. Standing in line waiting to have caterpillars combed off his clothes, on a strange island miles from his people—city people, colored people—and Leslie getting all fairy-tale vengeful and shit was too much.

"Big ones?" he said. "One hundred of 'em? You don't say."

She looked up at the black sky and he realized she was trying not to cry.

"Leslie, baby," he stepped out of line, escaped the boundaries of their gender, a tiny revolution that thrilled him. He turned her to face him. She tried not to smile so he knew she felt it too. "We came here to live in a castle. We don't ever have to leave its walls."

"I love you, Julius."

She kissed him. Their teeth clinked. She poked her tongue at his lips. He pulled away but she pulled his face forward like it was a mask she wanted to wear. He heard snickers. Whispering.

When she released him, he took a long breath. The cluster of old boys, unlit cigars in their mouths, stared.

Jules thought of Caesar and the kiss that preempted the massacre in the Curia of Pompey. He stopped himself from making a bad joke, whispering in her pearl-studded ear, *Et tu, Brute?*

The ladies' line crept forward. Leslie waved. "See you inside!"

The old black butler was skin and bones. As thin as Jules's pops was when he was dying. He watched the old man brush each man's shoulders and back, slow and gentle, like he was combing prized thoroughbreds. Jules was two spots away when he saw the folded bill slip from a guest's hands into the butler's hand, the exchange punctuated by a subtle nod of the old man's salt-and-pepper head. Jules had nothing. Hadn't even brought his wallet, and when it was his turn, the old man's shaky hands brushing over Jules's broad shoulders and up and down each of his arms, he couldn't bear to look the guy in the eyes. He mumbled, "Thank you, sir," and walked through the white columns and into the chandelier light.

9.

Maddie

The kids clomped down the carpeted steps and into the Foxes' AC-crisp basement, lunging for the plush sectional—*Yo, I get dibs on the end!*

Maddie took a seat on a swivel stool at the lagoon-themed bar, complete with a plastic crab-decorated net. She knew not to get too comfortable—Bitsy could announce, any minute, a game of Seven Minutes in Heaven, banishing Maddie and Spencer (or another boy) to a dark bedroom two floors above.

Spencer returned from the kitchen upstairs with a tray of food—Cool Ranch Doritos, ham and cheese Hot Pockets, mini eggrolls with dipping sauce, and a case of kiwi-strawberry Snapple iced tea. Mr. Fox owned Fox Foods, the company that supplied the factory and school cafeterias, and she'd heard about the giant freezers packed with food the Foxes had in their garage.

"Yo," Spencer said, "my mom put out a shitload of snacks."

The boys went wild grabbing food.

"Mads." Spencer threw her a package of Little Debbie oatmeal creme pies. "I know you like these."

"Thanks, Spence." He had noticed something about her. This made her want to like him even more.

"Love your mom, dude!" John Anderson said, his mouth crammed with Doritos.

"No," Rolo said as he went to town on a Hot Pocket, the bright-orange cheese dripping down his Grateful Dead shirt, "I love her more. I'd French kiss her."

"Shut up," Spencer warned, but Maddie could see he was trying not to laugh.

"Oh, Marilyn, pucker up, baby . . ." Gerritt cried and Spencer punched his shoulder.

Someone popped a tape in the VCR.

"Oh, score! This is the fourth tape. How'd you get it?" John said, high-fiving Spencer.

"I have my sources," Spencer said with a cocky nod.

As the lights dimmed, Maddie felt the boys' excitement surge as they pushed aside the girls who had clambered onto their laps to cuddle, and leaned toward the bright light of the TV, fists on knees. Dom had told her about *Faces of Death*. Not like he'd ever actually seen it. Blockbuster kept the tapes in the curtained back room with the pornographic movies, and you had to show ID proving you were over eighteen.

She promised herself she wouldn't look away. She'd show Spencer, Bitsy, all of them, she was tough, and it would make up for her acting like a terrified mute at the fair.

The volume was cranked so the video narrator's deep, mournful voice bounced off the photo-adorned basement walls—Spencer and his freckled little brothers and sisters in beachy white, his proud parents behind them, the ocean a perfect blue backdrop. Years of Spencer's elementary school photos framed side by side. Cute little Spence, she thought, but remembered how, in elementary school, he'd been the kind of boy who yanked your ponytail and ran.

In the first grainy video, a group of bare-chested brown-skinned men crowded around a leashed monkey sitting on a table. The monkey rose on its back legs and bared its fangs, its childlike screams filling the dimly lit basement.

"Oh shit!" Ricky shouted.

"Don't fuck with me, motherfuckers!" Gerritt squeaked in what Maddie guessed was an impersonation of a monkey.

The men closed in around the table. The monkey. They held sticks and knives.

Gabrielle, a professed animal lover, whimpered, "Turn it off!"

The first blow stunned the monkey. It turned in a slow circle, as if, Maddie thought, searching for help. Then the sticks and knives fell, the screen a blur of movement. Maddie did her best not to look away but then a man in a ripped T-shirt held something dripping and the camera panned in on the limp, headless body.

"Monkey brains!" Spencer shrieked, and the boys erupted in *Awwww!*

The boys jumped to stand, bumping chests, pounding fists. It reminded Maddie of lacrosse and soccer games, how the boys on the bench couldn't stop from playing out their feelings big and loud, touching one another. Tender *and* tough. Just like the night at the fair.

As the men chopped the monkey corpse into pieces, expertly severing arms and legs, Penny spoke from her seat on the sofa, "Where's the beef?"

The basement burst into laughter and Maddie wished she'd been the one to crack a joke.

They finished Side A of *Faces of Death*. A man whose bungee cord was too long smashed his legs into a concrete underpass (*Moron!* the boys shouted). An unsteady recording of cows butchered at a slaughterhouse made Maddie feel seasick. Last, some guy tweaking hard on PCP charged cars on a freeway. When he flipped over the back of a station wagon, only to get back on his feet, the boys launched off the sofa, roaring. *Dude, it's the fucking Energizer Bunny!* John Anderson yelled.

The commentary on the videos rolled out nonstop. Like the boys were watching a Super Bowl game. Penny and Vanessa were just as crude, flinging their hands, fingers shaped like guns, at the screen, moves Maddie knew they'd seen in hip-hop videos on MTV. "Bam!" "That guy's gonna make it—*not!*"

Gabrielle was close to tears and Bitsy played delicate—covering her eyes and squealing, clutching Gerritt's arm. Maddie knew *she* had to say something. Make herself part of the group. She'd barely spoken, and while some of the guys, like Austin Drake, who was so quiet it was creepy, could get away with staying mute pretty much all the time, camouflaged by their forties of Crazy Horse malt liquor and their Marlboro reds, it wasn't the same for a girl. Girls weren't allowed to be invisible.

"You know," she said, startled by heads swiveling to look at her. "That shit's not real."

"Whaaaat? You crazy, girl," Vanessa said, shaking her head.

Maddie wanted to back off, give up, but she caught Bitsy's icy stare, challenging her.

"Look," she said, "there's the same guy in three of the clips."
She pointed to the screen. "Rewind back and you'll see."

"Buzzkill," Ricky Bell said, and everyone laughed, and Maddie
remembered how her grandfather, a few days earlier, had called
her stubborn. Said no man would want her.

"You guys, she's right," Penny said. "I totally saw it too."

Instead of feeling relieved to have Penny back her up, she knew
it only made her look worse. Weak. Even more than Penny, who
was supposed to be the weakest link in the crew.

They watched Side B as a crumpled baggie filled with the
much-anticipated magic mushrooms (Gabrielle yipped with delight) was passed around. Maddie almost gagged from the smell.
Like something left to rot in the woods. When she was sure no
one was looking, she passed it on. She'd taken a bong hit halfway through Side A and was already more stoned than she could
handle. Not the warm, mellow high she'd felt on the beach but a
shaky buzz—her heart thwacking so she could hear it. Her fingertips tingled. Her chest tightened. Was she bugging out? Normally, she'd call Vinny and beg for a ride home, but not after the
fair. Who knew what he'd say to her? She felt herself teetering
on the edge of a full-blown bug-out—her pulse like the rhythm
of a dance song (*badum, badum, badumbadumbadum*), sweat
popping above her brows—and she refused to look like a wuss
in front of her cousins.

A montage played on the screen—clips of people killing themselves by hanging, shooting, jumping off bridges. A triumphant
symphonic score played in the background, reminding her of the
John Philip Sousa Memorial Band, who played on the town green
every Friday summer night. Staccato drumbeats punctuated every
impact. *Oh! Ow! Ooh!* The boys, and now the girls too, echoed
each moment like they were missed goals in a soccer match. So
much death after death that Maddie felt nothing when she knew
she should feel horror.

A parachutist fell into a pond of snapping alligators; a cult
in a desert ate gray chunks of human flesh; and, finally, a black
guy—he couldn't have been more than eighteen—was shot in the
head at his own wedding ceremony, his bride's puff-sleeved white
dress splattered red.

"Aw, shit!" Gerritt cried. "There goes that Marshall kid."

The boys high-fived. Like they were geniuses, Maddie thought with a silent eye roll.

As the credits rolled, the kids revisited the facts that had arrived piece by piece that week—from eavesdropping on their parents, mostly. The story they'd strung together was this: when Helen Marshall, the admiral's wife, had died, Leslie Day Marshall, once exiled from the island for marrying a black man, became the richest in all of Avalon. And, Maddie thought, the fairest.

Vanessa whispered, "My mom said she's a grave robber. Didn't even show for her own mother's funeral."

"My dad's flipping out," Penny said, "because she might take over the factory or something."

Bitsy laughed. "Like they'd *ever* let a woman run Grudder?"

"Dude," Gerritt said as he tucked a wisp of blond hair behind Bitsy's ear, a gesture that made Maddie give Spencer a quick glance. "Think of all those fighter jets that would get deployed every time she went on the rag."

"Ha-ha," Bitsy mocked. "So funny I forgot to laugh."

They kissed, their lips locking for ages and Bitsy caught her staring. She smiled and Maddie was sure she was about to announce a game of Spin the Bottle. Bitsy leapt off the couch and skipped toward her—a shift so fast, Maddie had to stop herself from flinching.

"Bitsy," Maddie said. "Hi?"

"Sweetie." Bitsy's breath was fruity from berry wine coolers. "Did Spence tell you about his surprise?"

"Um, no."

Spencer popped another tape into the VCR, the machine whirring as it rewound.

"And for our next feature film, ladies and gents," he announced as he dimmed the lights so there was only the blue glow of the screen.

"You'll see," Bitsy sang, and ran back to the couch on tiptoes so the watery light reflected off her smooth legs.

The boys burrowed into the sectional—the girls took their

places, one on each boy's lap. Bitsy and Gerritt, Vanessa and
Austin, Gabrielle and John, and, finally, Penny hunched over on
Rolo's wide thighs. Ricky was busy rolling spliffs—a mound of
marijuana shake and rolling papers set in front of him on a TV
tray like a kid's arts-and-craft project. Maddie knew Penny
would rather be sitting on his lap.

She considered heading for the bathroom upstairs—who knew
what Spencer's plan involved—and she didn't want to have to sit
on the crowded couch with his boner poking into her butt cheek.
He pointed the remote at the TV and the movie started and she
knew it was too late to slip upstairs because it would look like
she was running away, and, then, she wanted to.

The screen filled with naked mustachioed men and their
erections. The girls giggled and the boys hollered. The porn
was shot in a basement nothing like the Foxes' with its sponge-
painted walls and decoupage knickknacks arranged on sweet
cedar shelves. In the video, sheets were tacked over the windows.
The cement floor bare. A tired-looking woman with big breasts
lay on the ground. The kind of fake boobs that didn't jiggle,
Maddie thought, only lay there like hardened mounds of clay.

"She must be cold," Penny said.

"Uh, I think that's, like, the last thing on her mind," Gabrielle said.

"Those dudes'll warm her right up," Gerritt said. The boys
laughed. Like it was an inside joke, Maddie thought, and only
they knew the punch line.

The men stood in a circle around the woman like in some
ritual sacrifice. Some of the men were short, some tall, some
black, some white, all tugging on their penises.

"Fuck," Gabrielle said, cringing so she curled into a ball on
John Anderson's wide lap. John bucked his hips and she bounced
up and down, yelling, "Quit it, John!"

As the men shuffled forward, closing in just like the circle of
men in the monkey video, Bitsy laughed and said. "Oh God, no,"
and flipped her hair so it fell in front of her eyes. But Maddie
could see Bitsy was shifting her hips, rubbing against Gerritt's
crotch.

"Aw, man," Rolo said. "Are they going to? Naw. This is hard-core."

"Spence, dude," Gerritt said, "your dad's into some kinky shit."

Maddie imagined her feet glued to the floor to stop from running up the stairs, and out the screen door. Walking home in the caterpillar-filled dark if she had to. Wasn't there someone to help this woman, pull her to her feet, wrap her in a sheet and take her home?

"Ew, I can't watch!" Gabrielle watched through her fingers, each nail a perfect half-moon French manicure.

"Don't be a pussy," Vanessa said. Adding, when she got no response. "Get it?"

Vanessa was staring straight at the screen. Maddie wished she could be more like her. Sure, the girl was a class-A bitch and none of the boys wanted her (she'd had to go to the junior prom with Rolo) but she played tough with total believability, proving again and again she was just one of the guys. Doing keg stands, racing the guys to the beer mart on rollerblades, and packing her lip with their Kodiak so she could join in the contest—who could spit the longest stream of tobacco juice.

Was *this* sex—the sex all the kids talked about, and the adults avoided talking about, the sex in the songs they blasted as they drove through the island and partied at the beach, the sex they, boys and girls, were supposed to wish for like she had dreamt of the fair all winter? She looked at Penny, still sitting on Rolo's lap, her smile big so her teeth gleamed blue. What if Penny wasn't just pretending to enjoy this?

The men tugged their penises so hard she was sure it must hurt. They ejaculated in unison, splattering the woman's face and breasts with milky goo. The woman played dead—her eyes closed as the camera panned in, and Maddie spotted an angry zit, and realized this was a real person who had sat in front of a mirror and dabbed cover-up on her skin just as Maddie had earlier that night before leaving the cottage. The woman opened her mouth and licked at the come that had landed on her cheeks, her chin, her lips.

The basement erupted.

"Damn! She lapped that up good."

"Uck, I think I'm going to vomit."

"Best circle jerk I've seen."

Vanessa shook her head. "Is this supposed to make us want to fuck you guys? As if!" She seemed so calm, like she was already wise to this, and Maddie wondered why *she* felt like she'd be scarred for life. Stay a virgin forever.

"Don't you have something, like, I don't know, hotter?" Vanessa said. "Less cummy?"

"I hear sperm's got a lot of protein in it," Penny said straight-faced. "So, basically, she just got her daily dose."

Once again, Penny's witty one-liner won the room.

"A protein shake!" Bitsy shouted.

"*Daily* dose?" one of the boys said. "How 'bout *monthly* dose!"

Before she could add a barely clever one-liner—*how 'bout annual dose!*—Maddie felt Spencer's hot breath on the back of her neck.

"This shit is sick," he whispered. "I'm sorry you had to see that."

She wanted to hug him, kiss him even, right then and there.

"It's okay," she lied.

"Let's get out of here," he said, taking her hand and tugging her toward the stairs so she had no choice but to hop off the stool and follow him.

"Um, wait."

"For what?" he said, not bothering to look back at her. "You want to watch more?" He laughed. "I sure as hell don't."

"No."

She tried to think of an excuse. She should stay by Penny. What if she had another seizure? But Penny was laughing as she bounced on Rolo's lap, throwing her head back and giggling. "That tickles!"

On the TV screen, one of the black guys stuffed his penis into the woman as she yelled, like she was angry, "Do it! Fuck me!"

"Yo, it's the Marshall kid," someone said.

She decided to let Spencer save her. Take her far from the woman's fake moans and the men's animal grunts. Wasn't that what she'd wanted, she thought, back on the beach as she watched Gerritt slip the rope bracelet over Bitsy's wrist? BE MINE.

She followed Spencer up the stairs.

10.

Jules

He searched for Leslie, moving past one circle of chatter after another, catching the same three topics he'd heard all night—the caterpillars, the vandal tagging up the island, and Governor Bill Clinton from Arkansas. Pest. Plague. Parasite. The same language used to describe all three.

He filled his plate with red velvet cake, strawberry-rhubarb pie, and a block of coffee cake that was *to die for,* according to the wine-flushed lady in line at the dessert table. He found Leslie. She was in a circle of women her age (but who could ever tell, he thought, when it came to these women with their private trainers and plastic surgeons). Leslie nibbled on a solitary pastry—bites so small that when she set her plate down, the food seemed intact. One of the things he'd loved about her first was her appetite. She never apologized for it the way other white women did, like it was a sin to feed your body. She'd sit on a packed subway car, stuffed between a Wall Street suit and a Korean grandma, and eat an apple, core and all, spitting the seeds into her hand and tucking them in her pocket—to add them to her tray of seeds drying in the apartment windowsill. A future garden for their someday dream home. Back when they had only dreams and the Marshalls, the Castle, the island, had no place in their fantasies.

Leslie air-kissed one waifish woman after another—*mwah, mwah,* like a satirical skit on *Saturday Night Live,* he thought, wishing Leslie was by his side to get the joke. The women were draped in floor-length strappy silk dresses that seemed more like slips meant to be worn underneath a gown. Sheer silver and gold and soft pastels, they matched the desserts. Vanilla cream puffs, ladyfingers dunked in tiramisu, and mint-green petit fours. Even he was fooled by the look of enthused surprise on Leslie's face. *Oh my God, how long has it been? You look absolutely the same, darling—the same!* The women had multisyllabic names like the heroines in his mother's paperback romances. Jacqueline. Genevra. Names that sounded like a million dollars.

He wondered what that heavenly afternoon fuck in the garden had meant. What was *its* worth? He'd known, since he was a sixteen-year-old messing around with Tammy Roberts in the bathroom at Dalton, that sex was never just sex. And knowing Leslie, that dew-scented romp may have been a reward for his surrender, for moving to the island. Or had it been a threat? *Leave this island,* baby*, and this beauty—the gardens, the castle, and even the queen—will be lost to you.*

He decided he wouldn't move from his spot next to the table spread with trays of brownies and blondies and éclairs oozing whipped cream. What if he lost Leslie in this room filled with women as indistinguishable as the stalks of lillies in his garden? He saw himself, at midnight, rushing from one woman to the next, peering into each face to find his wife's.

Leslie spotted him and waved. He motioned toward the front door. She nodded enthusiastically, then held up a finger. He knew what that meant. Stuck for at least another hour. This would be the pattern of their lives now. Looking for Leslie. Waiting for Leslie. Praying for Leslie to end the schmoozing she seemed to crave since they'd moved there—and to what end, he still hadn't figured out.

He was on his third éclair, his stomach objecting, when he spotted the old guy he'd seen earlier in the poodle-print shirt, now topped by a blazer as bright as the cherry-red roses Jules had cut back that morning. And the woman at the old man's side— well, it was the elegant old lady he'd met on line. The lawn-jockey expert. Their ancient heads bowed together. They were arguing. Thin, wrinkled lips moving fast. He was sure they were talking about him. Whispering. Staring. The old man shook his head, and the lady snapped back, the tendons in her birdlike neck flexing. The old man reached forward, and Jules watched as the man pinched his companion's arm. The woman flinched, looked around, and rearranged her white shawl. She saw Jules. He looked away. Busied himself with wiping the chocolaty mess from his fingers on a white cloth napkin.

Should he do something? Get Leslie. Or even better, leave. He *had* called Social Services back in the city once, to report their neighbors, whom he and Leslie had suspected of neglecting their elderly mother. But these people were strangers.

A spasm blocked his throat and he swallowed hard. Wasn't this exactly what Leslie had chastised him for after his *overreaction* (her word) at the fair? She'd explained, in what he called her "Zen voice," that he was allowing his fears to ruin his—and their children's—chance of a happy life on the island. It was his choice, she'd said. As the mess of food and drink and heavy cream gurgled in his gut, he heard the advice of his long-dead father (anything but Zen) buzzing at his ear like one of those goddamn no-see-um bugs that had been eating him alive since they'd come to the island.

Better to be afraid than dead, son.

The old woman was making her way toward him, her face transformed into a mask of delight.

"You again!" he said. "And so soon. Unfortunately, I'm on my way out. Have to find my wife. We've got a new babysitter waiting at home. You know how it is."

He bowed his head, hoping it made up for his abrupt departure, but the woman stepped right in his path. She smelled like cigarettes and perfume. White Linen. His mother had worn it. He would've guessed a rich lady might pick a fancier perfume. Not one anybody could buy off a drugstore shelf.

"Oh, she's perfectly happy over at the dessert table. Catching up with old school friends and such. So darling to see our Leslie all grown up."

"You know Leslie?" The surprise unsettled him. *Our Leslie.*

"Since she was a wee thing. We're neighbors. Remember?" An emerald-bedecked finger pointed toward the front doors. "We Pencotts and Marshalls go way, *way* back."

"Mrs. Pencott," he began.

"Call me Veronica, yes?"

She had a habit of turning statements into questions, as if his opinion helped determine true and false.

"But of course," he said. What did ten more minutes of charades matter?

Although he wouldn't have been able to explain why, he knew she had more in common with him than with the island aristocracy. Her stiff pronunciation betrayed her—those exaggerated o's and a's that vibrated a note too long. It was as if she'd copied the speech patterns and gestures of classic movie stars. Grace Kelly. Vivien Leigh. He'd heard Leslie put on the same contrived accent when she made fun of the mandatory elocution lessons at the women's college her father insisted she attend before she dropped out and paid her own way through Harvard.

"Do you"—he paused—"watch a lot of PBS specials?"

She laughed, throwing her head back so her silver fillings caught the lamplight.

"I'm not a fan of the television programs. I do read. Which is"—her voice dropped into a whisper—"more than I can say for most of the bored old ladies on this island. Unless you call romance novels and self-help books *literature*."

She had a sense of humor, this odd old bird.

"The gossipy Gertrudes at the club," she said, "tell me you are quite the expert when it comes to floral design."

He was about to protest, play coy, remembering Orchid Lady at the fair, when the old woman waved a hand toward the lavish floral arrangements, "And what do you think of this, Julius? Is it all right if I call you that? I have no patience for nicknames."

"Well," he stuttered, "yes, of course. You can call me anything you like. And the flowers? They're lovely?"

"Are you asking? Or telling?" She pursed her wrinkled lips. "Just teasing you. I understand how difficult it is for one to be honest about *anything* on this island. Personally, I'd have taken things down a notch. I was taught less is always more." She pointed to the entryway, where a spiral staircase gleamed under a crystal chandelier. "However, when it comes to refreshments, one can never be too bold. A Champagne fountain is needed, over there, right in front of the entrance."

She fluttered her fingers and stared hard at the front door. As if, he thought, she could will the bubbling pyramid of glasses to appear. "When guests enter, it is the first sight they see. A promise of all that awaits inside."

"I like that," he said. "A little risky. But what is a party without a decorative gamble?"

She lifted her painted eyebrows and Jules knew she was pleased with his approval.

"And those flowers." She nodded at the overstuffed arrangements fighting for room among the desserts, then cringed dramatically, her droopy eyelids fluttering.

He had to laugh. She was an actor, this one. Quirky.

"I have to agree with you there, ma'am. I can *not* get behind the lily. In the garden, she is divine. But in a vase? No way. The poor flower was ruined by the mortuary business. Can't look at a lily and not see dead bodies."

"Too true, sir. I will be sure to make a note. No stinking lilies at my funeral."

She laid a hand on his forearm. Her parchment-thin skin was mottled with liver spots and purple bruises.

"Are you hurt?"

"Beg your pardon?" She looked, he was sure of it, scared.

"Your arm."

She swung her thick ivory shawl, shielding herself. The fear replaced with leading-lady poise.

"Just an old gal with sensitive skin. Now, I want to hear all about your favorite flowers. One is always in need of an expert."

"I did talk to a woman at the fair the other night." He felt like a kid, coming clean about a failed test to his mom. "She was wearing a beautiful orchid. I'm ashamed to say I didn't even think to ask her name."

"No bother. She's of very little consequence actually. Just a dull woman with the unfortunate name of Lorna."

"Um, I guess you heard." How to react to this woman whose wit was so sharp he feared he'd be cut.

"On an island with one exit," she said, "everything is *heard*." She sounded tired. Bitter. "*Seen* is another matter. You could say that Avalon is a magical place. Girls don't get pregnant. Boys don't drive drunk. The money what's-her-name stole from the PTA account is replenished as if it never happened."

She nodded at the emptied dessert table, where the old man stood on watch, a pastry in one hand, martini glass in the other. "That is my husband. Robert Pencott. Most people around here call him the Colonel."

The old man glowered. As if, Jules thought, *he* were the enemy.

She wagged a finger circled by a diamond he guessed was at least three carats.

"Teach me something," she commanded. "About the art of floral design."

He didn't correct her—explain he was a landscape architect. His grad-school professors at Harvard had warned that those in the nonplant world would label them everything from florists to botanists to landscapers. He wondered if she were testing him, if, tomorrow, she'd return to the ladies at the club with juicy bits from their conversation. If so, he better choose something good.

"Here's something you can tell those Gerties at the club."

"Oh, do tell. I'd heard you were a charmer, Julius. I'm pleasantly surprised you have *not* disappointed."

She laughed, reminding him of Leslie and the music in her voice. He imagined a classroom of white women being taught how to laugh—and there she was, Leslie, staring at him from across the room. She had a look he'd only seen a few times. Like when Brooks broke his arm skateboarding and when Eva choked on a pencil eraser and when Leslie returned home to him that night so many years ago after telling her parents she would marry Jules even if it meant them disowning her.

"My apologies, Veronica," he said, "I see my wife trying to get my attention. But I'll leave you with one fun factoid: The art of flower arranging goes way, *way* back. The Egyptians even placed them in vases just like we do today. Mostly at funerals." He laughed. "They liked lilies too. Worshipped them even. But a different kind. We know it as the water lily. The only flower that bloomed year-round in Egypt."

The old woman stared out the long front window into the

darkness he knew was the sea, but found it hard to believe—ebbing and flowing, vast—until he spotted the lights of the oil freighters in the distance, like jewels on a necklace. Maybe she'd stopped listening, or drifted off the way old people do.

"They worshipped two kinds," he continued. "The white lotus—*Nymphaea lotus*—and that blooms at night. So it was used in lunar ceremonies. And there was also *Nymphaea caerulea*. The blue lotus. And some have this gorgeous hot-orange center. Which makes sense because it was a symbol for the sun in a ton of Egyptian art." He knew he was rambling and didn't care or think to stop. He'd only had Leslie to talk to since they'd moved. Brooks wanted nothing to do with what the boy called *plant* talk. Jules missed the daily conversations he'd had with the neighborhood folk at Our Garden. Mrs. Kaminsky stopping by with her granny cart full of beer cans to redeem, checking on the pink peonies he'd helped her plant. Sal Buono lugging a stinking bag of manure through the gate for his row of tomatoes. Jules and Leslie had a dozen theories on how the old Italian procured the stuff.

"You see," he said, "those Egyptians believed the blue lotus was a magical thing. The way it closed up at night and disappeared underwater. Only for the same bloom to rise, miraculously, each morning with the sun. But if you ask a botanist, they'll tell you the truth—the new buds form *underwater*. How about that?"

She turned away from the window. Her milky eyes were shining.

"How *about* that?" There was a gravity in her voice—was it sadness? He was relieved when Leslie hooked her arm in his.

"Leslie!" The old woman transformed. As if she'd been reunited with a long-lost relative.

"Mrs. Pencott," Leslie said. "So lovely to see you."

The two women brushed cheeks, left and right, and it amazed him how much they resembled each other. Like two photographs taken of the same woman thirty years apart.

Something was off. That look Leslie had given him. And now, as he watched the women he saw the tension in Leslie's long neck. The women chattered about how it had been *ages*, how much the island had or had not changed, Veronica expressing her condolences for Leslie's mother's death, Leslie asking after Ginny, who, he guessed, was the old woman's daughter. His wife's fingers smoothed her brow and he knew she was itching to tug at a hair. *Don't do it, babe,* he rooted for her. He hadn't seen her this nervous since her mother was alive. On the mornings of her visits to her parents on the island, what she called "payday," she was her usual sunny self—reading books to Eva, teasing Brooks about the hour he spent in the bathroom styling his hair, swatting Jules's ass with a dishcloth as she stirred the pot of jambalaya that would feed him and the kids until she returned. By noon, when her father's driver was due to pick her up, she was plucking one hair after another, so she'd had to dab concealer on the inflamed skin above and below her thinned brows. He'd never told her how, the nights before those visits, he lay awake listening to her jaw click as she ground her teeth.

"What on earth will we do about these caterpillars?" Veronica said. "The visitation of this pestilence." She stared straight-on at Leslie, who, he saw, stared right back. An unflinching contest. "One might claim it a sign."

"We should really get going," he said. "So we can let the sitter go."

The old woman was smoking. One of those long, thin cigarettes—100s.

"There's no smoking in here." Leslie went ice-cold. He knew she was pissed.

"It was so nice meeting you, Veronica." He tugged Leslie toward the front door.

Veronica laughed loudly, "Oh, that's right, I wouldn't want to pollute the environment."

She took a step forward, bared her teeth, and he saw where her dentures met pink gums.

"Heaven forbid," she added, "someone call the EPA and file a complaint."

The old woman hadn't finished speaking when Leslie walked away, leaving him behind.

"I'm sorry," he said. "I mean, good night."

He pushed through the mob to catch up with Leslie, his eyes tearing from the sudden haze of cigar and cigarette smoke hanging gray and heavy, like the smoke he'd seen cloud above the factory towers in the west.

11.

Maddie

Spencer's tongue filled her mouth. They were on Mr. and Mrs. Fox's bed and the satiny comforter smelled like talcum powder and those air fresheners you plug into the wall.

They slid farther up the bed, his hips grinding into her, the buckle of his belt poking, her head surrounded by plush pillows—so many pillows. Fringed with tassels and tiny gold pompoms, backed with black velvet and wine-red silk. He'd told her to take her top off as soon as they'd walked into the room. Your bra too, he'd said. Her small breasts jiggled with each thrust and she stopped herself from covering her chest with crossed arms.

Spencer was grunting. How could he be feeling good when it sounded like he was in pain? Then she remembered those nasty dudes in the porno and how hard they'd tugged on their dicks.

She tried to get her head out from under the pillows but he launched into her again, his cold hands sliding up over her breasts, her nipples tingling, his tongue wriggling back into her mouth.

He was sweating. A soapy scent slipped off his skin. She wanted to enjoy that, and the hard knots of his back muscles under her hands. If this were one of those late-night movies, she thought, the camera would pan in on her hands sliding over his back, fingertips gripping.

A tassel fell into her mouth. The wet thread stuck to her lips and she had to spit it out. He was too busy to notice. "Dry humping," Bitsy had called it—how guys could come just by rubbing up on a girl. She was supposed to lie there and pretend that she liked it. She let out a little moan. He must have thought it an invitation because he yanked down her jeans and she sat up, knees clamped together, one hand pulling up the waistband of her panties. He was on his knees, his erection tenting out the front of his plaid boxers.

Music rose from the basement below—a heavy bass throbbing—she couldn't name the song but knew it was make-out music. The porno was over, the lights dimmed, and the couples messing around. She thought of Penny and hoped she wasn't too wasted.

He said, "Lie down." She did.

Most nights, in her own bed, she lay on her stomach, her blanket pulled up high over her shoulders, one hand tucked between her legs. At first she only touched over her underwear, but then she'd let her fingers slip past the elastic. She'd learned how to make herself feel so good she'd wished she could let out a moan, wished she lived in a house with real walls, not thin Sheetrock her dad and Uncle Carmine had used to make one bedroom into two—one half for her, the other for Dom.

Spencer's head ducked between her legs and she heard herself mumble, "Okay. Um. Okay." Almost a question. Her stomach muscles clenched.

"Relax," Spencer said lifting his head, looking at her over the pale field of her belly.

"Okay," she said again.

She felt his saliva pooling, his hot breath, his tentative tongue. His lips smacking. She tried to imagine *she* was touching herself. Safe in her own bed. Now her moan sounded more like pleasure.

A rustling sound came from outside the bedroom door. What if Bitsy and the others were hiding behind the bedroom door, listening, about to burst in and yell *Surprise!* What if they heard her—she'd be mocked forever, the humiliation impossible to live with. Because she already wanted to forget tonight and it wasn't even over.

"Did you lock the door?" she asked.

Her legs were quivering, an involuntary spasm.

"Yeah, it's locked," he said. "Chill out."

"Can I do you?"

He lifted his head from between her legs—was he smiling, she couldn't tell—wiped his mouth with a hand, and crawled up next to her.

Should she kiss him after he'd had his mouth, his lips, his tongue down there? It seemed gross, but then his mouth was covering hers. *God,* she thought, *you suck at this, Maddie.*

She tugged his boxers down his legs, which wasn't easy. She laughed. He laughed. This made her feel better. She knew he was nervous too—when her mouth closed over his penis, he shuddered and said, "Sorry."

She held her breath so she didn't have to taste him or smell the scent, like unwashed scalp, of the coarse hair around his penis. She sucked until she felt like her eyes might pop out, took a quick breath, and sucked some more.

She felt a little sorry for him. He was shaking too. His legs trembled over Mr. and Mrs. Fox's burgundy sateen comforter, reminding her of Penny's seizure at the fair. She knew it wasn't the kind of thing you were supposed to think about during a sexy make-out session.

She also felt a little sorry for herself. Why didn't this feel like it looked in the movies, in the music videos on MTV? All those couples entwined and rolling around on a sandy beach. Like Chris Isaak and that model, Helena something, in one of her favorite videos. "Wicked Game." She wanted to feel *that.*

Spencer's hand cupped the back of her head. He pulled down and she gagged. It gave her a chance to look away, wipe her teary eyes, before putting him back in her mouth. Her neck ached. It wasn't working. His penis was soft like those balloon toys filled with water she'd played with as a kid. Wigglies.

She must be doing it wrong. Should she suck harder? She didn't want to hurt him. Maybe she should stroke up and down with her hand while she sucked. She couldn't ask him for advice, could she?

"Can't you do something hot?" Like he was annoyed. Like it was her job to know what to do. She was pretty enough (wasn't she?) and sitting there half-naked seemed the definition of hot. The muscle in his jaw wriggled as he yanked his penis harder. Like he wanted to tear himself apart. She saw she was an idiot for thinking those gross dudes in the porno would get hurt tugging so hard.

She was an idiot. *Idiot, idiot, idiot.* Thinking he'd wanted to save her downstairs, take her away from—what had he called the porno? *Sick.*

"Maybe," she said, wanting to solve this, make it end, "I can dance for you?"

She'd watched a scene in one of the after-dark movies they got on their new cable box. Movies she watched when her mom was zonked on pills and her dad out who knows where. Some nights, she and Dom watched together, faces flushed, hands clamped over mouths to silence giggles. Other nights, she double-checked the TV den curtains to make sure they weren't open even a crack, and lay on her stomach on the brown couch, touching herself, the fake leather creaking and cracking.

She stood in front of Mr. and Mrs. Fox's bed, her feet planted on the plush carpet. She was cold. Goose-bumped all over, even on her nipples. She swayed from foot to foot. Rocked her hips side to side. She lifted her hair into a pile on her head and let it tumble to her shoulders. She held a hand out to Spencer. Isn't that what the women in sexy movies did—an invitation, *Join me*—and Spencer (was it harder now, she couldn't see and hoped to God it was so they could get on with it) climbed off the bed. He *was* beautiful—she saw that now. Tall and strong like the photos of Michelangelo's *David* in her history textbook. She rubbed her butt against his muscled thigh and let her fingers slide down his chest.

"Is this good?"

"Yeah," he said. "Hell yeah. Let's get on the bed."

He told her to sit on him, and it was her turn to grind but everything under her felt soft and mushy. He grabbed her breasts and twisted. She winced.

"Does this feel good now?" she asked.

"Stop fucking asking me that."

He flipped her on her back and a velvet pillow fell over her face and she felt trapped, like she was underwater, and something sharp was inside her. His fingers jabbed in and out with a wet *thwock-thwock* sound. It hurt. Like when she tried those no-applicator tampons you had to stick up inside you using your fingers.

"Shit," he said. "You're too dry."

He jumped off the bed and before she could ask, "What should I do?" he turned on the lamp. She was blind and naked and stubbed a toe looking for her clothes. She followed him out the bedroom door still buttoning her shorts.

She needed to stop him, get a sense of where they stood, before he went downstairs and told the kids—what? She wasn't sexy enough. She was a prude. Worse, he'd lie and tell them she'd been a slut when nothing had really happened. Had it?

She reached the bottom of the stairs and heard the screen door click shut.

He was leaning against his car—a black BMW convertible with seats that heated at a touch of a button—a sixteenth-birthday gift from his grandfather even though he'd only just got his learner's permit.

He lit a cigarette and as she walked through the grass, wet under her bare feet, she asked, "Can I bum one?"

They smoked. She asked him a dozen questions in her head. *Is there something wrong with me? Can I make it better? Will anyone ever love me?*

He flicked his cigarette into the azalea bushes and then he was backing her up against his car, the moisture on the black metal seeping into her T-shirt as he bucked into her, harder and harder. She dropped her cigarette when he kicked her legs open, first the left, then the right, so she was off balance, her legs far apart. He ground into her, his knees bent. He kissed her once, sloppily, exhaling into her mouth so she tasted tobacco. He lifted her off the ground with the last thrust, followed by a groan, and fell forward, his forehead pressed against the car door, trapping her between his heaving chest and the car.

She was pretty sure he'd gotten off, but he didn't look like the guys in the pornos *afterward*—sleepy and sex-drunk. Satisfied.

A sound came from the road. The wheels of a bike, maybe. Spencer backed off like he'd been caught breaking a law. He jogged back to the house in his loping soccer stride and she followed. "Spence?"

The screen door snapped shut.

She hurt. Stung between her legs. Hip bones aching. She couldn't go back in. She'd sit and wait for Penny. Even if she'd wanted to walk home in the dark—the moon was just a sliver, like a flashlight running out—the caterpillars were out there. Her feet were wet and streaked with bits of grass. Damn it— she'd left her shoes inside.

She felt like she'd failed an important test. One she couldn't retake. Boys were like that. Spencer had made her like him, trust him, then kicked her feet out from under her, made her a fool, and she knew if she tried to fight back and opened her mouth, the trap would only tighten. She couldn't win.

The sound on the road again. Wheels moving over the asphalt on Horseshoe Lane. Maybe, she hoped, it was Dom, come to rescue her on his bike. He'd been an expert spy lately, popping up outside parties. Her mini guardian angel. Like his favorite Greek god, Hermes, he was a chronic eavesdropper.

She walked up the gravel driveway, the sharp stones pricking her feet. Her soles were soft after a long winter in socks. It would take weeks of walking on the pebbled beach and the barnacled rocks in the shallows before her feet toughened.

"Dom?" she called toward the dark street.

Metal clanged. A whirr of wheels. Then a figure glided out of the dark, stopping at the top of the driveway, a skateboard flipping up to stand as he braked. She let out a strangled *Oh!* and clamped a hand over her swollen lips. To cover a smile.

"Shit, sorry," he said. "Didn't mean to scare you."

It was the Marshall boy. He hadn't scared her so much as excited her. This cute boy materializing from out of the dark. Like in one of Dom's myths. Gods and demigods dropping to Earth to rescue beautiful virgins. Like poor Laurel, transformed into a tree to escape the rape by Apollo. She imagined the boy, on his skateboard, riding a streak of silver lining from the heavens down to Avalon Island.

Of course, she wasn't going to tell him all of this, and just said, "Hey."

"What's up?"

"I'm Maddie."

"Brooks." He held out a hand and she shook it, giggling, immediately hating the way it made her sound like a ditz. She'd never shaken a boy's hand. Never known a boy who had held his hand out like she was as important as any man.

"I saw you," she said. "And your family. At the fair."

"Oh yeah." She heard the eye roll in his voice. It was too dark to see his face and he had his hoodie on. "That was mental. My dad bugged when he saw those kids making like they were going to brawl."

"It was lame. Things aren't usually so"—she paused— "disorganized here. It's a pretty uptight place. Lots of rules and stuff. Military vibe, you know?"

"Totally."

She liked his laugh. A little gruff. A man's laugh. She looked back at the house—the bottom floor's windows lit gold. Her shoes were trapped in there.

"You look cold," he said.

"I left my shoes and jacket inside. But"—she thought quickly—"I'm locked out."

"Can't you just ring the bell?"

"I can't."

She tried to make up a lie to explain why she was here— shoeless, arms bare in the cool sea breeze, but her thoughts were jumbled; all the places Spencer had humped, poked, and pinched were sore, and she was coming down from her high. She wished she could curl up on the dewy lawn and close her eyes.

"I just can't." She hoped he wouldn't ask questions. "Now I'm stuck with no way home."

"Can't you call your parents?"

"Nope."

"I get it." She didn't hear any sarcasm. He wasn't mocking her like another boy would've. "Shit can be complicated." He sounded sad. She imagined how very complicated his life must be on the island.

"Here." He handed her his black hoodie. His white tee soaked up the moonlight and she could see his face now. His smile. His fringed lashes.

"No, I can't," she said. "You'll freeze."

"Not taking no for an answer."

"Thanks." She slipped her arms into the soft sweatshirt. It smelled of him, like cinnamon and something smoky she couldn't name. "Oh, that's good."

He stepped forward, his board tucked under an arm. Was he going to kiss her? Did she unknowingly enter into an agreement by accepting his sweatshirt? She didn't want that. She'd been touched enough for one night. His hands moved over her crotch and then the sweatshirt zipped with a hiss. He flipped the hood over her head and pulled the drawstring tight.

"There," he said.

He'd been close. She'd felt his warmth. Then he was on his board, rolling away. "Catch you later."

"Wait!" She jogged into the dark night, the asphalt still warm from the day.

The board scraped as he braked.

"I'm your neighbor." She was out of breath. "We live next door. To the Castle." She corrected herself, "*Your* castle."

"You call it that too, huh?"

"Yeah," she said, feeling shy, not ready to confess how the mysterious Marshall castle had been a fixture in all the childhood games she and Dom had played in the woods. "Can I walk with you?"

"Sure," he said. "But I have a better idea."

He held her hand as he helped her onto the skateboard. He spread her feet apart, his fingers tickling the tops of her toes.

"Make sure you grip with your toes, 'kay?"

He kept her hand in his and pulled her forward on the dark road.

He towed her down Horseshoe Lane and onto East Neck Road, the artery that looped the eastern tip of the island. The back of his tee darkened with sweat, and she tried to give him a break, begged to walk for a bit—plus, he was carrying something heavy in his backpack, which hung low, bumping against his back—but he insisted on pulling her all the way up steep Snake Hill Road. When their hands grew slick with sweat, he switched. They laughed—at him grunting up the hills, her squealing as the skateboard raced down the other side, at the caterpillars dropping on them from the low branches arched over the road. Her cheeks ached from smiling. She hadn't laughed like this maybe since ever.

She taught him about the island as they made their slow journey, pointing out the Oyster Cove Country Club, and the dirt parking lot by the docked boats where kids went to smoke up. His curiosity tickled her. He asked her to name every bloom they passed—the heart-shaped nocturnal moonvine on the cement walls around the Gundersens' estate and the twining trumpet creeper's orange blooms drooping over the gates of Penny's house.

"I thought your dad was, like, a plant expert."

"I'm more like my mom. People over plants. I *do* know that one over there." He pointed to the airy white wisteria cascading over the stone walls of Mrs. Whiteside's house. "My dad calls it the *grande dame* of vines. It's kind of like a waterfall made of flowers."

"Or flower fireworks?"

"*Totally*. Damn, this island smells like the perfume counter at a department store!" He gulped air like a fish out of water.

She liked how he could be a clown, then straighten up and get serious, like when she explained military rank as they passed gate after gate of Grudder executives' estates, some retired navy.

"Wait," he said, "it goes lieutenant, major, captain . . . ?"

"No! It's captain and *then* major. Look, just don't go calling a colonel a captain, okay?" She smiled to show she was teasing.

"So I'll be cool if I call every dude on the island Admiral yessir, yeah?" He stood tall and saluted.

"They won't complain," she said. "But how can you not know this stuff when your own grandpa was an admiral?"

"It's complicated," he said. She wished she'd kept her mouth shut.

They stopped for a break at the wrought-iron gates of St. John's. The steeple glowed a heavenly white under the almost-full moon. The gates were wrapped with overgrown honeysuckle vines, and he made her laugh by falling back against the golden, syrupy spread like he was falling into a bed plump with goose down.

She plucked a pair of the two-tone flowers, deep pink inside with a yellow lip, and held one out to him. He stared.

"This doesn't look like any honeysuckle I ever seen," he said.

"It's special. They call it Goldflame."

"Ooh, I like that."

"Don't worry, it's not poisonous."

"You better not be messing." That wide grin was back in his voice.

"Now, use your front teeth to snip off the end. Ready?"

"Not sure I'll ever be *ready* to eat a flower."

"Trust me," she said. "Now, spit it out."

"Shit! I swallowed it. Tell me I'm not gonna die."

She laughed deep from her belly so it felt like something loosened inside her and when she stopped, he was watching her, a look of—what was it?—on his face. It was how she'd wanted Spencer to look at her.

"Okay," she said, wiping tears away, not caring if her mascara smudged. "Now, take a sip. Suck the end."

Her face burned when the image of her sucking not on the flower, but on his lower lip popped into her head.

"Mmm," he said. "They named this one right-on. Honey. Suckle."

"Yeah," she said. How had *she* never thought of that?

"There's a ton of good plant names. My dad taught me some stuff."

"Like what?"

"Well, nightshade for one. Belladonna. Lady's slipper."

"Those are beautiful."

She reached forward and touched his fingers. They were splattered with black paint.

"Are you an artist or something?"

He laughed. "Or something."

Maybe it was the city in him, but he knew different ways of saying the same thing, more than *awesome, cool, killer,* the words she'd heard Avalon boys use day after day. She wanted him to teach her to talk like that.

"Yeah," she said. "There's *not* enough words. Somebody

should make more." She looked away and sighed. "Sorry, that's a dumb thing to say."

"No." He reached for her, found her arm in the darkness. "That's a dope idea. Let's do it. Make our own language."

She didn't pull away, despite the way it made her feel—like she might explode, like everything she worked day in and day out to keep hidden (her mom reminding her not to talk about her dad's fits of anger at school) might stream out and strike her dead.

"Shut up," she said. "You fucking with me?"

"You ever read *Cat's Cradle*? By Kurt Vonnegut. They make up their own language. And then they make religion. And propaganda. And all these wild things happen because words are the start of every revolution."

Brooks's voice leapt as he explained more, and although Maddie had no idea what he was saying, talking about rebellion and social justice and change and equality, she wanted him to keep talking. Until the horizon pinked with dawn. She'd stand here on the dark road surrounded by shitting caterpillars all night.

The call of a great horned owl vibrated around them. Five hoots, two long and three short—*hoooo-hoooo-hoo-hoo-hoo*— and she knew it was a sign. Something good was happening.

"What the hell was that?" He turned in a slow circle.

"A great horned," she said. "The owl of fairy tales and storybooks." She wiggled her fingers at him and widened her eyes. "Whoooo."

"Hot damn." He drew out the *damn* like the last note in a song.

"You never heard an owl before?"

"No owls in the city." He paused. "Only night owls that sit on the curb in front of the bodega bumming for booze money."

"My brother, Dom, he thinks the owls are decoys Grudder uses to spy on the islanders."

"Whoa. That's some *Twilight Zone*–level conspiracy shit."

"They do have cameras all over the island."

He stopped short and she slipped off the skateboard.

"Sorry," he said. "For real, cameras?" He looked a little freaked out.

"Well," she said, "with Grudder and everything. National security and stuff."

"Ha, yeah I get it." He nodded at the skateboard. "Now, my lady, hop back on your chariot."

A car passed, its headlights swinging across his face so she saw his nose spattered with freckles, his broad forehead and the Afro (was she allowed to use that word?) that rose into an upside-down triangle. With her hand in his, she felt one step away from fingering his shoulders, his tapered waist. His shirt lifted as they made the last hill, coming onto their own street—Ring Neck Ridge—and his side was exposed. That part of guys she'd always thought the most elegant, ever since her tenth-grade art class trip to the museum in the city, where she'd sketched the statues of Greek and Roman boys, spending hours on that one detail, the place where abdomen meets hip bone, creating a smooth slide down.

They walked up the gravel driveway of White Eagle, past the white marble birds with their hooked beaks and talons. She stopped at the uneven slate path that led from the circular drive of the big house to the cottage.

"All of this"—he waved at the tall, arched windows of the big house's bottom floor, the peach drapes lit with lamplight—"is yours?"

"It's complicated. My grandparents own the big house. Me and my family, we live in the cottage."

He laughed.

"What's so funny?" She was ready to defend herself.

"Me and *my* family, we're living in the cottage too. The Castle"—he wobbled his head as if mocking the name—"is as empty as a haunted house."

She liked imagining him in the same cramped layout—maybe they even slept in the same bedroom, against the same wall, saw the same view of the woods when they woke each morning.

"This summer's going to suck," she said, picking a caterpillar off her arm and flicking it into the woods. "These things. We can't even hang outside."

"It's biblical, for sure," he said. "But wait. I got an idea."

She hoped he was going to ask her on a walk. Where they'd find a caterpillar-free spot and keep talking. Being together.

"You want to come over Friday night?"

"Sure!" Embarrassed at how obviously delighted she was.

"Bring your friends."

"Um, okay," she said. "I'm not sure what they've got planned."

She didn't want to sound like a bitch turning him down, but how could she tell him they weren't really her friends and she'd rather it just be him and her?

"My mom says I can use the ballroom," he said. "It'll be fresh. Think of it as a refuge from the caterpillar plague."

"Okay." She wanted to see him again and knew Bitsy would go nuts at the chance to hang out in the Castle ballroom. "We'll be there. Like, nine?"

They stood looking up at the big house and she wondered if she should kiss him. Or just say good night and walk to the cottage. She didn't want to make another mistake that night like she had by trusting Spencer.

A curtain moved in one of the windows—Veronica's pale face appeared and disappeared.

Brooks whispered, "Busted."

He hopped on his board and rolled toward the driveway.

He was a few feet away when he turned and she thought he was going to come back, and they would fall into each other and kiss, like in all the chick flicks she and Penny had watched on the party-less weekends before Bitsy had recruited them. But he just stood there, his board standing on two wheels.

"What's your favorite color?" he asked.

"Why?" She played stubborn.

"No real reason." He stuffed his hands into the pockets of his hoodie and seemed shy suddenly. "I just want to know more about you. Thought maybe that was a good place to start."

More about you. She turned the phrase over in her head. *More about you.*

"Me?"

"Yeah, weirdo." He laughed his warm, buttery *ha*. "You." He paused. Then walked forward, reached out, and pulled the zipper of his sweatshirt up so his knuckles brushed her chin. "Maddie."

Her name sounded different on his lips. Better.

"Forget I asked," he said. "It *was* kind of dumb."

"It's red," she blurted out. "And turquoise. Together." Something small scampered in the woods. Twigs cracked.

"How come?"

"God, you're nosy." But she wanted him to ask her more questions. Wanted to answer them all and let him know her.

They continued walking toward the cottage, listening to the *cack-cacking* of the caterpillars feeding and the patter of chewed-up leaves spat thousands at a time onto the forest floor.

"I like it 'cause"—she paused—"red for passion. Sea-blue for . . . I'm not sure what, but the water makes me feel safe."

She didn't think she was making any sense.

"Yeah," he said. "I get that. Totally." He nodded as if he really, truly did. "I thought maybe . . ." He stopped.

"What?"

"That guy. He was hurting you."

It took Maddie a moment to remember. Spencer. Shit. How much had Brooks seen? She wished she could explode now, burst into a million pieces. Die. She was humiliated. And angry. Why hadn't he told her he'd seen right from the start? Instead of making her trust him, feel safe, show herself to him, when it was all a waste of time because he'd seen her ugly and used, and here she was hoping, like a moron, he'd step forward and kiss her.

"I'm fine." She started for the cottage door.

"You know," he said, "it's not supposed to be like that."

She stared at the screen door covered in crawling caterpillars.

"That guy," Brooks said, "he—"

"Please," she interrupted him. "Stop. You should've told me you saw. Then we wouldn't have had to . . ."

"Yeah, okay. You're right."

He reached past her and wiped the caterpillars off the screen door handle, opening it, nodding at the doorway.

"Go on in."

He was on his board, the wheels skipping across the slate path, when he called, "Hey!" and she looked through the screen spotted with squirming bristled gypsies.

"Yeah?"

"You deserve better than that."

What could she say? She knew he was right and wasn't sure if knowing made her weak—for letting Spencer use her like that—or strong because she knew she'd never let it happen again.

"I'm really happy you came by when you did," she said. "Thanks."

"Bring some words Friday night," he said, his voice fading into the night. "We got a lot of work to do."

12.

Jules

Leslie was in a foul mood. Jules suspected it had everything to do with that awkward exchange at the party with Queen Veronica. Of course, Leslie had put on a good show until the very end, all smiles as they left, raising her flute of Champagne and slamming it against others amid a roar (*Hear, hear!*) punctuating one final toast. He suspected those people had enough money to replace a thousand shattered crystal glasses. She had kissed ladies goodbye—*mwah! mwah!*—but as soon as they'd stepped through the white pillars and into the hum of the caterpillars' feast, she'd fallen silent. Refused to hold his hand on the long, dark walk home.

He stood behind the cottage smoking a clumsy joint he'd rolled in the dark with weed so old it burned fast and went to his head. He counted the trees edging the woods. Twelve. Sixteen. Twenty. Too many to count. And all *his,* he thought, knowing he was acting like a spoiled kid on Christmas morning.

Something rustled in the woods. Louder. Leaves and sticks crunching underfoot. He was sure it was some beast. They were everywhere. He'd caught a trio of bushy-tailed raccoons busting into the garbage cans even after he'd weighted the lids with bricks. He'd been surprised by a scaly-tailed opossum in the garden last week at dusk. *Didelphimorphia.* Now, there was a nasty creature with its pointy snout and beady black eyes. It had hissed at him, baring its sharp canines, and he'd shouted so loud it had carried all the way to the cottage. Leslie was still making fun of him for it. He lifted the heavy-duty flashlight, which could double as an opossum-skull-bashing weapon if need be.

Brooks walked out of the woods, backpack heavy and clanging. His skateboard under his arm.

Jules's laughter startled the boy, who took a step back. Like he was ready to run the way he came.

"I thought you were a goddamn possum, son! What're you doing in the woods?"

"Nothing," Brooks said. His head was down and he tried to skirt past Jules toward the cottage front door.

"Whoa there. Hang out a bit. Talk to me."

"I met a girl."

"Yeah?" He didn't want to push too much, make Brooks clam up.

"Yeah."

"She must be a special girl. You going in there"—he waved at the woods—"with all those creeping critters. And the caterpillars." He groaned. "Listen to them binge-eat my leaves."

"She's cool."

Jules knew he was losing him. Right here and now. But also a little more every day. The chasm between father and son widening.

"Look up."

Brooks started to protest.

"Just do it. For your old dad."

"Wow."

"Yeah," Jules said.

They kept their heads tipped back and stared at the stars.

"I've never seen stardust before," Brooks said.

"Me neither. Listen to us city boys gone all country."

His son's laugh suddenly sounded more like a man's.

"What do you like about her?"

Just when Jules had given up on getting an answer, his neck starting to ache from looking up, Brooks spoke.

"She thinks I'm funny."

He heard the smile in Brooks's voice. His son, who, even as a toddler had wanted to be liked, waddling over to neighbors sitting on stoops, peering up into their faces with his wide grin.

"She like the way you smell?" He stuck his nose close to Brooks's T-shirt, feeling his son's new, solid chest. When did that happen? "'Cause you smell like an ashtray's asshole."

Brooks lunged back, his backpack falling to the ground with a clatter.

"Yo," Brooks said. "You *must* be drunk. Mom would kill you if she heard you talk . . ."

"Mom isn't here. You got a smoke?"

Brooks lit Jules's cigarette. The boy's hand shook.

"Camels no filter. No wonder you stink. You don't want one?"

"I'm good," Brooks said. "I only smoke 'em at parties and stuff so I got something to do."

"Get yourself some breath mints if you want that girl to keep liking you."

"Shut up," Brooks said, then looked quickly at Jules to check if he was mad.

"Just sayin' . . . Girls like it when you smell nice."

"Yeah, well, Mom says your sweat smells like Parmesan cheese."

"Oh, does she?"

More laughter. Maybe, Jules thought, this night wasn't such a bust after all.

"You be careful with that girl. With *all* the girls on this island."

Brooks yanked his backpack off the ground, mumbled, " 'Night," then headed around the cottage.

"Hold on there, buddy."

"This isn't the sixties, Dad," Brooks said without looking back. "Things have changed." He stopped for a moment and Jules hoped he'd turn around, come back to him. "And I'm not you." He disappeared around the corner of the little white-shingled house and Jules heard the screen door click closed.

Well, he thought, at least the two of them had laughed together. Like they had before *the island*.

He remembered the lawn jockey. Should he warn Brooks? He'd leave it be, for now. Last thing he wanted was to become his father, his son's only inheritance a fear that keeps him from living life, taking risks, seeing the world in all its spectrum, not just black and white. That line from his favorite Baldwin essay was in his head: *You can only be destroyed by believing that you really are what the white world calls a* nigger. Let's hope James

B was right about that, Jules thought as he walked through the maze, whispering the code—left, right, right, left. His chant in time with the thrumming *haaa-haaa-haaa* of the caterpillars.

An owl called from the woods and Jules smiled, hoping the horned bird was munching on a dozen squirming gypsies captured in one swoop. He was in fairy-tale land, thick with nocturnal sylvan beasts he'd only read about in textbooks and seen in documentaries on PBS. Horned owls and blind shrews. Bats circling the patio lamps. Last night, he'd heard the humanlike wail of a red fox.

He kept the heavy flashlight in hand and it knocked against his thigh, throwing tall shadows against the maze walls. The owl had made him lose count of the turns and he was starting to think he was lost, sweat needling his forehead. *Who do you think you are, city boy?* He heard his father's voice. You got me there, Pops. Touché.

He found his way—left, left, right—and was startled as he turned the last corner. It was his own shadow stretched across the stone path to the garden. He called himself a coward as he shone the beam on the hawthorn and beech and red oak. The short apple trees whose blossoms were just turning to fruit (he was still trying to figure out if they were Gala or Jonagold and would know for sure midsummer); the tall hermaphroditic linden trees, whose perfect flowers had both male and female parts, each beloved by the bees for their honeydew nectar; and the paper birch whose white bark he and Eva had peeled away that morning, covering the thin strips in magic marker hearts and stars and rainbows. He'd told her it was the wood used to make Popsicle sticks, and she had loved that.

He almost dropped the flashlight. The bark of the trees quivered, a blur of movement that made him wonder if there'd been a small earthquake, wonder if he was more than just a little drunk. He stepped closer. The caterpillars shimmied up and down the tree skin. Too many to count. The blue and red dots on their bristled backs like a thousand eyes winking at him in the flashlight's beam. He ran from one tree to another to another, tripping over roots, vines slapping his face. They were everywhere.

His knees buckled and he sat, slumped, into the ferns that circled one of his favorites—the full American chestnut. Its slim flowered catkins drooped overhead like Christmas ornaments. It had felt like a miracle spotting that chestnut on his first trip to the Castle. It was a survivor among few, of the blight that had destroyed its kind at the turn of the century. He and Eva had spent hours watching the happy squirrels scramble up and down the tree. He'd even taken photos of it, had them developed at the drugstore in town, and mailed them to Dr. Seth Feinstein, his old Harvard botany prof. Proof, and validation—how could it be that *he*, Jules, had lucked upon this rare discovery?

He remembered, years ago, telling his parents about his acceptance into Harvard. His father had urged him to pick a more practical profession.

Plumbers, electricians—these are the men people can't live without, his pops had said.

As if being the first black man to enter the Graduate Program for Landscape Architecture meant second tier.

He'd come to understand, only after his father's death, what the old man had hated most about Jules's ambitions—his son worshipping the beautiful things that belonged to white people. A beauty, he knew, his father felt they both had no right to.

So, he loved beauty. Who doesn't? Why should he be like his father and hate what he desired? Why wouldn't he want a castle and garden and queen of his own?

During those weeks in between the trips to the Castle, before he'd given in to Leslie's demands to leave the city, he'd lain awake planning the renovation of his garden, his acres of blank canvas, trying to ignore the noise of the taxicabs and buses and stoop bums outside their window. He had wanted that beauty more fiercely than anything (almost as much as he'd wanted young Leslie back in Cambridge). He hungered for it. He fell asleep walking the land that had belonged to the racist motherfuckers he'd never met, who had refused the existence of him and his incontestably beautiful children. He surveyed it from above like a hawk circling. He dreamt of digging his naked fingers into the soil, black and arable, and, when he woke, his muscles were sore, as if he'd been working the land all night.

He stood, found his pail, and set the flashlight beam on the chestnut. He picked caterpillars off one by one until they were three inches thick on the bottom of the pail. He shined the light on them and watched them squirm blindly. He grabbed handfuls and squeezed. Mashed his open palm into the bucket bottom the way he'd seen his mother make fruit preserves when he was a boy.

As his hands grew slick with their gummy remains, he promised he'd be nothing like his father. His father would surrender the garden—see these invaders as a sign of his unworthiness to possess such beauty. Jules would fight.

Various reports indicate that gypsy moth larvae can feed on at least 500 species of plants that include trees, shrubs, and vines.

In the East, the gypsy moth's favorite trees include apple, speckled alder, basswood, gray and river birch, hawthorne, oak, poplar, and willow. Less desired but still attacked are black, yellow, and paper birch, cherry, cottonwood, elm, blackgum, hickory, hornbeam, larch, maple, and sassafras.

—"The Homeowner and the Gypsy Moth: Guidelines for Control," United States Department of Agriculture, *Home and Garden Bulletin*, No. 227 (1979)

13.

Dom

It was the first hot day of the summer and Dom woke sweaty in tangled sheets. He poured vodka and OJ into his old *He-Man, Masters of the Universe* thermos, packed two bologna sandwiches, and headed for Singing Beach.

He used handfuls of sea-chilled pink clay to paint stripes across his chest, and symbols up and down his arms—circles slashed by an X, an infinity loop sitting on its side. Half-moons cupped his eyes, just like one of his favorite WWF wrestlers, the Indian warrior Tatanka.

He was Tatanka all morning, chasing an enemy tribe. His mission, a rite of passage for a brave young Indian chief in training, was to return with the scalp of the enemy chief. As he leapt over storm-felled branches furred with moss, the fern fronds he'd tucked in the waist of his swim shorts whispered. He attacked his enemy with Tatanka's signature moves—a high knee to the kidney, a battering-ram head butt to the gut, and then he'd climbed to the top of a tree downed in the last storm to deliver a crucial, match-winning, diving cross-body Tomahawk Chop combo.

He hacked at tangles of bramble and vine with his father's machete, the caterpillars flying. The murmur of their feeding—*caaa-caaa-caaa*—was the voice of the spirit gods urging him on his mission. *Thwack*, his blade buried into a tree. The white meat underneath, he imagined, was the flesh of his enemy.

He ate his soggy bologna sandwiches and swallowed the last of the warm OJ and vodka in the shade of a black walnut tree, his sweaty back against the furrowed bark. The caterpillars didn't like the walnut—he spotted only a few scooting through the bark's narrow grooves.

He flipped through the pages of *D'Aulaires' Book of Greek Myths*. It had been Maddie's favorite first, and she'd warned him not to bring it to the beach because water would ruin the awesome illustrations depicting gods and goddesses in all their immortal glory. But he carried it in his backpack every day and felt safer when it was close, so when the crummy thoughts came, he could lose himself in stories of death and birth, war and love. Love so potent it set the Furies, those wild-haired she-devils, on mortals' heels. Drove them to suicide—by drowning, self-immolation, hemlock. Only the Fates could save them, or a generous god or goddess take pity, turning the mortal into a swan, a flower, a porpoise. A spider, like vain Arachne. In the world of the gods, Dom learned, mortals shifted into animals every darn day. Transformation could be a lifesaver or a punch line. A reward or a punishment.

He had memorized the myths. Filled his mind with fearless warriors, goddesses scheming for revenge, and wailing nymphs. Last summer, he and Maddie had created the raddest game ever: Gods versus Mortals.

They took turns retelling the myths, each making a case for why their pick should be reenacted, dramatized with a chase. Their own private Manhunt redux in the thick forest between White Eagle and the then abandoned Castle.

"Look," he'd whisper to Maddie, pointing to the smoke from the four factory towers smudging the sky like a bruise. "It's Icarus's wax wings burning."

Maddie one-upped him, "Or the sparks of Hephaestus's mighty anvil. Forging Achilles's armor!"

His soft, girly voice, which only egged on the ogres at school, sounded deeper bouncing off the tree canopy. "It's Prometheus's stolen fire!"

He transformed into the mischievous Titan thief, a stick held above his head like a torch as he leapt through the fern that rose from the forest floor like the whiskers of a giant green beast. Maddie played an enraged Zeus, puffing out her chest, forgetting about the new boobs that, Dom knew, had humiliated her all spring, racing after Dom/Prometheus, bellowing, "Stop! Or I'll behead you with one of my lightning bolts!"

His stomach still flip-flopped when he remembered the look of awe on his big sister's face, and he wished she were there with him now on this perfect summer day to look at him like that. Make him feel invincible.

But Maddie had decided she was too grown-up for storytime. Now she slept in every morning after staying out all night with those girls. Now she cared more about her hair and makeup and watched the kitchen phone like she could make it ring with some supernatural ESP ability. Dom was always waiting for her to emerge from the bathroom, where she was holed up like her own prisoner—squeezing stuff from her pores, shaving the few blond hairs from her legs, staring at herself as if she believed the more she looked, the prettier she'd become. Didn't she know she was pretty enough? He'd give anything to be as beautiful as his sister. Maddalena. Had there ever been a name more goddesslike? That spring, when she'd decided she wanted everyone to call her Maddie, he'd pleaded with her to make him the one exception. She'd refused. *Boring*, he'd said, rolling his eyes just as she'd taught him.

He and Sean Waldinger had played Gods versus Mortals a few times but Dom doubted Sean would play with him again. Or talk to him the next time they passed in the school hallways. Not since that day in the woods with Victor and MJ.

He hated himself for hoping there was someone else out there who could appreciate the fantastic world inside his head. If he could find a way to show them, maybe they'd respect him. Admire him. Or, at the very least, like him.

The sun dropped, and the canopy of leaves above his head turned amber. The clay mask was cracking, tickling the corners of his mouth. He peered through the feathery fern circling the Castle gardens and watched the man. Listened to his animal grunts, each followed by the thwack of an ax-head biting into wood.

The man was beautiful, Dom thought, understanding this was the first time he knew what that word meant. The man's sweat-slick black skin glowed in the afternoon light. His muscles rippled with each heave of the ax. Like the flanks of the horses Dom had seen gallop across the green in the Fourth of July polo games at the club last summer. He had wanted to leave his seat, climb over the rope that sectioned off the spectators, walk out onto the field, and stroke the horses' quivering sides, velvet smooth but for the thick cords of veins that wriggled like eels underwater.

He moved closer, pushing aside the low bush blueberries, crouching until his knees ached, camouflaged by the waist-high fern. He held his breath and watched the man's thick back muscles hump up and down as he hacked at the pitch pine. Dom grew hard, his penis straining against his snug swim shorts.

His face was burning. His cheeks stung and itched, like they had when he'd gotten chickenpox last year. He raked his fingernails across his skin. That made it itch more, and now his neck too. He spit on his hands and tried to wipe away the red clay.

"You okay, buddy?" the man asked.

Dom stumbled over a raw stump, catching his balance before he fell onto his dad's machete.

The man was smiling and Dom could see he was trying not to laugh, and this made Dom's face burn hotter.

"Do you have a hose I can use?" he stuttered.

He knew he looked like some weirdo with the branches sticking out of his ratty shorts and his body coated in sea sludge. And what if the man had seen him watching? The secret mission Veronica had entrusted to Dom—the Colonel's protection—would be aborted before it had begun.

"Right over here." The man pointed to a long green hose that ran up the slate walkway. "You get that clay down by the beach?"

Dom splashed the frigid water on his face, not caring if it went up his nose. Still, a thousand needles pricked his cheeks and forehead and chin.

"Here." The man pulled a red bandana from his back pocket, and he was close all of a sudden, Dom could smell his sweat and the scent of soil, and he was touching Dom, wiping at his face. Dom knew his dad would have been rough, scouring his cheeks, telling him how stupid he was. *Use your brain!* The man was gentle.

He could've stood there forever, the cool water pooling at their feet, the man's large hand swabbing his skin. What if he got hard again? He sucked in his stomach and leaned over, his hands on his knees, hiding his crotch.

"I'm good," he said, grabbing the cloth.

The man shrugged, lifting his hands, as if surrendering.

"You can take that," the man said. "Soak it in cold water. Might help some."

"I don't want to take your stuff."

"Keep it." The man waved Dom's protests away. "We got plenty of rags around here."

"I'll bring it back, like, tomorrow."

"You should know that beach is polluted," the man said, and although Dom knew he meant to be helpful, his advice felt pushy. How long had this guy lived here anyway?

"I've been swimming in that water my whole life."

"My wife," the man looked toward the massive marble house, "she said the runoff from the factory pools down there. By the cliffs. That's where you got your warrior face paint, yeah?" He smiled like he was teasing and it made Dom want to hurt him.

"It's against the law to cut down trees on the island," Dom said in the know-it-all voice Maddie used to boss him around. He pointed at the fresh stumps oozing sap.

The man looked up at the Castle's tall windows. The Colonel had been right, Dom thought. Fear was power.

"For real?" the man asked. He was back to joking.

"For real," Dom said. "You've got to, like, submit a request. Do all this paperwork and stuff. It's a megabig fine."

The man sighed and Dom regretted saying anything.

"Don't worry," Dom said. "I won't tell." He lifted his hand and wiggled a pinky streaked with the clay. "Pinky swear."

"What's your name, son?" he said, reminding Dom of the fathers he'd seen on TV shows. The kind that give advice.

"Dominic?" It came out like a question. "Dom for short. I live over there." He pointed to the leaf-laid path lit by the falling sun.

"Well, Dominic Dom for Short, I'm Jules."

The man offered his hand, the palm of which, Dom saw, was the same shade as his own skin. They shook hands and Dom felt the callused ridges of hard work. Even rougher than his father's hands. The very opposite of the Colonel's silk-smooth palms. His dad had told Dom about the Colonel's monthly manicures at the beauty parlor, shaking his head and calling him "one manicure away from turning into a faggot."

"Glad to finally meet my new neighbors," the man named Jules said. "You live in that big house on the other side of the woods?"

"Yeah," Dom said. "Well, it's my grandfather's house. It's called White Eagle."

"White Eagle." He nodded. As if impressed.

"Your house is much bigger," Dom said, pointing to the Castle, and both he and the man shielded their eyes so they could look all the way up to the bell tower. "Is there a real bell up there? I mean, like, does it work?"

"You should come back for another visit and we'll try it out."

Dom wondered if this guy was one of those pervs with the white vans the school health teacher, Mrs. Whitehead, had warned them about that spring in the "Knowing Your Body" seminar.

"It's not *really* my house," Jules sighed. "I'm just trying to save the garden."

Dom and Maddie had tried to play Gods versus Mortals in the Castle garden last summer. A perfect setting for the myth of the golden apple, handsome Paris falling so hard for Helen that he didn't care one shit about inciting the Trojan War. But the garden had gone wild and not even their father's sharpened machete had been able to clear a path through the tangle. Now it was transformed. The hedges, once uneven and choked with ivy, were sculpted into perfect spheres and other whimsical shapes that reminded Dom of Christmas ornaments; the rows of rose-bushes were cut back and no longer looked like Sleeping Beau-ty's thorn-ravaged kingdom. The garden was still wild around the edges, but Dom could see that Jules was working from the center out.

"Holy shit!" Dom said. "It looks awesome." His hand flew to his mouth but it was too late. "Sorry, mister, I didn't mean to curse."

"Well, if there's one thing I think A-O-K to curse about, it's plants. Thanks, man. I'm glad you like it." Jules was beaming, but then he dragged his fingers through his short dark hair. Like he wanted to tear it out. "But these goddamn caterpillars."

He leaned over a rosebush and plucked off a fat, bristled gypsy.

"Don't touch it!" Dom yelled as Jules let the caterpillar scuttle across his palm, turning his hand slowly until it was inching its way up his wrist. "Some kid at school said they're poisonous."

"Can't be as bad as the clay though, right?"

"Yeah," Dom said. "That was dumb."

Jules squeezed the caterpillar between his fingers and yellow gunk oozed from its crushed body.

"Kind of looks like boogers," Dom said.

"The kind of boogers that eat a tree's worth of leaves a day," Jules said. "It might be a fantasy. Saving the garden. But I got to try. My wife thinks I'm nuts. I'm hoping cutting the trees back helps some."

"But the webs," Dom said, then wished he'd kept his mouth shut. He didn't want to be the one to kill this guy's hope.

"What do you mean?"

"They sort of, like, swing from tree to tree," Dom explained. "My grandfather says"—his voice cracked—"he says it's hopeless. They're sure to eat half the island's trees before it's over. They've done it before."

"That's crazy talk," Jules said. "There *must* be something we can do." He turned in a slow circle, his long arms open at his sides. Like, Dom thought, he wished he could hug his gardens close.

"What about those sprays?" Dom said hopefully, wanting to ease the man's worries. "My grandfather said that, last time, they sent up a few old planes. Doused the whole island in chemicals to kill the gypsies."

"They named 'em right," Jules said. "The critters set up their tents wherever they like."

"He—my grandfather—he said the last big plague was summer of '84. They ate the whole island naked. Not a leaf left." He felt his face burn hotter at the thought of anything naked. "I was only two years old, but I . . ."

"Your granddad got all his marbles?" He cut Dom off with a sarcastic laugh. " 'Cause that sounds like some fairy tale he told to keep you out of the woods."

Dom's mouth went dry. He remembered his promise to Veronica. The oath he'd sworn to protect the Colonel. This guy, as nice as he seemed, could be one of those *people* she said was gunning for the Colonel.

"My grandfather is the Colonel," Dom said solemnly. He thought of Zeus, Poseidon, Hades, all the big dogs in the Greek myths with their long white beards and weapons—lightning bolts, tridents, and deadly staffs.

"Oh, *the* Colonel? You don't say." Jules winked. "I met your Colonel last night at the dinner party. Your grandma too."

The man was mocking him again, and when he mentioned Veronica, Dom's stomach flip-flopped and some of the vodka and OJ launched back up his throat. He swallowed, let his hand wander to his father's machete, and imagined he was about to unleash his wrath like Indiana Jones's long leather whip, when the man spoke.

"Hey, Dom. I'm just messing with you. You want to come in for a glass of lemonade?" He nodded to an open wooden gate snug in the trimmed hedge. "Your face is all red still." He pointed at his own face to show Dom where—his cheeks, chin, and forehead. "And we got calamine lotion back at the cottage."

Dom wanted to go with the man. To have his face, now prickling with heat, touched again by this beautiful man's gentle hands. Maybe he could lay down and the man would bend over him, his breath warm, the rough pads of his fingers tracing Dom's forehead, brows, down the sides of his face, across his lips, into his mouth, Dom sucking his long fingers, the darkest brown on top and pale yellow underneath, Dom's tongue flickering, his mouth filling, in and in and in, and then the man's voice was behind him, shouting, "Hey, Dom! Come back!"

He ran into the woods, leaping over a pile of fresh-cut wood. He ran fast and hard, away from the Castle, not bothering to use his father's machete to hack away the branches that lashed his face. He knew he deserved it, the hot stripe of pain on top of pain. He was dirty and bad and sick. Just like his father had known all along. What Dom knew only now. He wasn't sure what sickened him more, that those asswipes Victor and MJ had known he'd wanted it when Dom himself had not, or the act itself—Dom leaning over Sean Waldinger's limp dick in the woods behind the school, Sean screaming so loud that MJ had clapped a fat hand over Sean's mouth while Victor held him down. They'd promised Dom that if he didn't do it, they'd beat him bloody, break his nose, his ribs, *crush his balls with their boots till they went POP!* If he didn't lick Waldinger. Just a lick. But when his open lips touched the silky-soft head of his friend's penis, and he tasted salt, and something else, yeasty like fresh bread, MJ had slammed a hand down on the back of Dom's head, forcing his mouth down and open, and MJ's hot breath whispered in Dom's ear. *Suck it. Open your mouth. There you go.*

A few days after the thing that happened in the woods behind school, Dom had the first of the dreams that would wake him with a jolt most mornings, his shorts wet and stuck to his thigh. He dreamt of faceless bodies rubbing, bucking, and sucking.

Now he knew. They were men. And he wanted them.

He stretched out the wrong way on his bed, muddy sneakers up by his pillow, not caring if he scuzzed up his Pac-Man bedspread. He stared at the posters Scotch-taped above the headboard. They'd been a gift from his dad on Dom's twelfth birthday. When Dom had seen the posters, he knew his dad had guessed about the teasing at school. Sure, they'd been a gift—tied with curled ribbon—but Dom knew they were a reminder of the kind of boy he was supposed to be.

They were the same glossy posters Uncle Carmine had plastered to the concrete walls of the office at the auto body shop. The same taped to his cousins Vinny and Enzo's bedroom walls. Swimsuit models coated in oil, naked but for a string bikini stretched over hardened nipples, a thong tucked between glistening ass cheeks. Puckered lips parted. Cindy Crawford, kernels of sand scattered across her curved butt, a trail leading you-know-where. Alyssa Milano in a strategically soaked tank top. Kathy Ireland rolling her tongue around a cherry lollipop.

At night, when Dom jerked off, letting his jizz spray on his sheets and harden—proof to his dad, he hoped, that his dick worked fine, that he wasn't all those names the meatheads at school called him—he felt Cindy, Kathy, and Alyssa staring at him. Spies sent by his father.

"Uh-oh." Maddie's voice made him jolt upright, swivel around. "Someone's in a mood."

"Fuck off."

"Whoa," she said with a laugh. "A real shit storm of a mood."

She stood by his headboard, hands on hips, squinting at the wall behind his bed. She'd caught him, he thought, and his throat flushed hot, itched like he had poison ivy, as he imagined what Maddie would think. Him staring up at the posters getting all turned on, when nothing could be further from the truth.

"It's not what you think," he said.

"What're you talking out of your butt about? *What's* not what I think?"

"Never mind," he said. "I just . . ." He paused. "I hate those posters."

She climbed onto his bed, tucked her bare feet under her smooth legs. He thought about telling her to get lost, but he wanted her there. Who else did he have? His Maddie-cake, he remembered the name he'd given her years ago.

She lifted her chin and said, in an impersonation of their mother's high-pitched, bubbly voice, "Daddy says that's normal boy stuff."

He laughed but remembering his mother's words he wanted to scream. What did she think went on at school every freaking day? *Too late, Mom! I'm already anything but normal.* The freak who follows dickwads like Victor Hackett and MJ Bundy, follows like a dumb trusting baby, into the woods behind school. Who does what they tell him to avoid a beating. A few gut punches he could've survived, he knows now. Bruises fade. Blood wipes away. But what he did—that would never fucking ever wash out.

Maddie was touching him, her hands on his shoulders, turning him so he had to look into her sad eyes.

"Hey," she said. "I hate these posters too."

It felt even better than a hug.

She jumped up to stand on the bed, the springs groaning. She slipped her fingers between the slick paper and the wall and before Dom could shout *No!* or *Dad will kill me!* she tore Cindy Crawford in half, slicing sand-dusted buttocks from the rest of her body. The hiss of the paper tearing made Dom's throat catch. Because he knew Dad would go after Maddie when he found out. Maddie had risked *that* for *him*.

He'd be okay. As long as he had Maddie.

"Dad." He knew he didn't have to say more. She was just as scared of him as Dom was.

"Here's what we say," Maddie said, her eyes crinkling with a plan, her voice lifting in mock humility: "But Daddy, we *had* to take them down! If the Colonel and Veronica saw those posters, they would majorly bug out. You can kiss your club membership goodbye."

"Dad will understand," Dom said, hoping it was true.

"Your turn," Maddie said.

He tore the posters until his ears rang with the cry of paper rending, a whimper that built to a wail, and he was ripping Victor Hackett and MJ Bundy limb from limb, and every dickhead at East Avalon Junior-Senior High that had called him a *cocksucker faggot homo buttmuncher*. He was hacking his father into pieces. And Veronica too. The carnage—dewy pink flesh and glistening lips and meaty thighs and breasts and ass—piled at his feet.

They laughed. Deep from the gut and contagious so that when his or Maddie's giggles tapered off, the other started in again, and they'd both be at it, laughing so hard Maddie pressed her knees together so as not to pee. With Maddie near he felt ready for whatever came next.

Four species of parasitic flies prey on gypsy moth larva. *Parasetigana silvestris* and *Exorista larvarum* lay an egg on the gypsy moth larva. If that egg hatches before the gypsy moth larva molts, the fly larva will penetrate the host. *Compsilura concinnata* pierces the gypsy moth larva and deposits its own larva inside. *Blepharipa pratensis* lays its eggs on leaves—the gypsy moth larva will consume the egg and the fly larva will hatch inside its gut.

—*The Gypsy Moth: Research Toward Integrated Pest Management*, United States Department of Agriculture, 1981

14.

Veronica

The girl arrived for tea in what, Veronica imagined, passed for dressed up these days. A pink-and-yellow floral pleated skirt, a white T-shirt, and a yellow cardigan. A suitable outfit even if so much of her granddaughter's smooth, sun-bronzed flesh was exposed. But those shoes. Veronica could hardly contain the cringe that rose inside her. They were something a gladiator would wear—sandals with wedge heels and canvas straps that wound up the girl's legs. Like the serpent in the Garden of Eden.

"Those shoes," she said when Maddie wobbled into the sun-room. "They're so . . ."

"Amazing, right? My friend Bitsy wears them and I convinced Mom to get me a pair for my birthday."

Bitsy Smith, Veronica guessed. If she was anything like her gin-guzzling mother and womanizing father, oh Lord.

"Your sixteenth birthday?"

"Uh-huh. I mean, yes."

Sweet sixteen, Veronica thought. The bridge between girl and woman. Heaven help her.

"Sit, dear!" She patted the cushion of the high-backed wicker chair next to her own. She'd had Rosalita rearrange the potted palms and ficus so the sunroom felt like a greenhouse. "I've planned a feast for us."

She had spent two days preparing for tea with her grand-daughter—her need to make everything *just right* surprising her. She'd never been a Suzy Homemaker.

"Take a sandwich, please."

Tea sandwiches—cucumber and mayo, curried chicken, and egg salad with almond slivers—were stacked on a three-tier glass platter. She'd insisted the crusts be cut to make them extradainty—a request that had Rosalita rolling her eyes like a teenager.

Veronica had come close to confiding in Rosalita how essential this seemingly frivolous tea party was—the first step in enlisting Maddie to spy on Leslie Marshall. Whether the girl would be aware of her role was a detail Veronica anticipated knowing by the time the first cup of tea had cooled. She had watched the adoring glances Maddie and the Marshall boy had shared a few nights back, right out front on White Eagle's lawn, seen the hunger trembling between them, sure it would pull them together. As she'd spied from behind the living room's peach curtains, she'd understood what had to be done.

"I'm sorry if this visit feels required," Veronica said, waving dismissively at the table perfectly set. The pastel petit fours from Reinwald's Bakery; the sticks of rock candy to swirl in their tea; and chocolate-covered marshmallows, strawberries, and sliced banana from Bon Bon's Chocolatier.

"I'm sorry. I don't get what you're saying," Maddie said with a sweet shake of her head.

"Having tea with your lonely grandmother, of course." She wobbled her head a bit, mocking herself.

"I wanted to come see you," Maddie said. "You've always been so busy. You and . . ."

"The Colonel." She finished for her granddaughter. "Is it funny to call him that? You can call him what you like. Grandfather? His mother called him Bobby. I insist you call *me* Veronica. To help us become fast friends."

"If you're sure," Maddie said. "I mean, about calling you Veronica. I'm *absolutely* sure I want to be friends."

Veronica remembered her own fear at that age of misinterpreting, saying the wrong thing, failing at being perfect. She sensed a note of need in the girl's voice.

Maddie lifted her chin, closed her eyes, and recited, "*Surround yourself only with people who are going to lift you higher.*"

It was the kind of aspirational language Veronica had heard growing up among the Latter-Day Saints. She remembered her devout stepmother Virgie's advice: *Surround yourself with people who are a reflection of your best self.*

"Is that something you heard in church?"

"No." Maddie paused. "Unless you count the church of Oprah."

The girl's straight-faced delivery reminded Veronica of her sister Bess, whom she hadn't seen since she'd left Palmyra a few months before her wedding to Bob. Shunned by the temple and her family.

Veronica let loose a "Ha!" and it felt good to laugh loudly, and a bit vulgar. The opposite of the hand-over-mouth tittering the women at the club did over lobster bisque and stiff whiskey sours. As if, she thought, the very idea of laughing was unladylike. She liked to laugh and she liked this girl's wit that seemed to pirouette so she could hardly keep up.

"I watch Oprah every day after school," Maddie said. "She's kind of life-changing."

"So I've heard."

"You've *never* seen it?"

"It's on my list," Veronica said.

"You're really missing out."

"I promise you," Veronica said, her hand pressed against her scarred chest, "on my mother's grave" (not that she knew where it was) "I will watch."

"Maybe"—Maddie clapped her child-sized hands—"we could watch it together."

"I'd love that." She was surprised at how true this was. She'd been prepared to lie throughout tea. Or, at least, perform. But she wanted to spend more time with the girl. Even if watching a show that sounded like a religious cult.

"I can come over tomorrow. It's on at four every afternoon."

So soon? Veronica had much to do. Meetings with the Grudder board to discuss the EPA complaint threatening to shut down Plant 2. She knew that troublemaker Marshall girl was responsible. She had her possessions to give away—so she could leave this world unencumbered. She wouldn't allow Ginny and Tony to organize some gauche tag sale after her death, where strangers (or, worse, nosy islanders she'd detested in real life like Binnie Mueller and Jessamyn Clancy) fingered her crystal and silver and Bob's mother's collection of Limoges china. Priced at a fraction of their worth. The thought of her life tagged at a discount almost—*almost*—made her second-guess her exit plan. She'd begun the arduous task of separating what to donate to Goodwill, the Salvation Army, and St. Vincent de Paul; and what to pass on. But to whom? Ginny, who slept like a cursed princess in her dark cave of a bedroom? Maddie, who was just a girl? She thought of her and Bob's lost heirs, the babies she'd miscarried. Three in the first trimester and one stillborn (her last pregnancy—she'd seen to that by having her tubes tied). A boy whose blue face had detonated Bob's spirit. Shortly after, his affairs with the various Grudder secretaries had begun.

Her granddaughter was jittery with excitement. "Yes? Tomorrow?"

How could Veronica say no?

"I'd adore that."

"I usually watch it with my best friend, Penny. But she's been busy lately." The girl's eyes wandered and Veronica suspected this wasn't the whole truth.

"The Whittemore girl? I heard what happened at the fair. How dreadful."

"She's sick." Maddie's voice dropped to a whisper. "Cancer. In her brain." She laughed, but as quickly as her giggle escaped, her hand clapped over her mouth.

"Oh God," she said. "I shouldn't laugh. It's just that everyone always *whispers* the word. Like cancer's a curse word. And now I'm doing it."

Veronica wanted to confess right there and then. Tell the girl she too had found the whispering absurd. From her primary-care doctor who'd felt the first lump to the specialist who'd diagnosed her, and all the well-meaning hushed voices in between—oncology nurses and med students and the pushy postsurgery social worker who'd insisted she consider a breast prosthesis. Imagine that, fake ninnies at eighty!

It wouldn't be right to burden the girl with news of death and disease. Maddie was special—Veronica could see that plain as day. Yes, the girl was a bundle of nerves, her nails chewed to the quick. But she wore an elusive composure like a second skin, the very thing Veronica had struggled to mimic in her study of the ladies of East Avalon when she'd first moved to the island so many decades back as the Colonel's young and mysterious bride. Perhaps (wishful thinking, she feared), Maddie could be their heir. If, by the time she and Bob made their exit, there was anything left to inherit.

"I regret not getting to know you better before we left for Florida. Things are, you see . . ."

What to say? *Your grandfather has lost his mind. The factory is being bought out. The island is sinking. I'm dying.*

"Oh, God. Don't worry," Maddie said. "I know you have a lot of important things to do. Mom's told me all about your charity work. How you helped get those poor kids on the west side money for their chemo. That's so awesome."

"Did she?" Veronica had feared Ginny resented her too much for praise. "I'm not sure about me being *awesome*. I was only the secretary on the charity board. Minnie Charlston was the president, and—"

"*You get in life what you have the courage to ask for.*" Her granddaughter spoke with that same earnest expression— eyes closed, chin up. Then she broke into a tinkling laugh. "That's Oprah too. She has *endless* sayings that help when you're feeling . . ."

"Under the weather?"

"Totally!"

"I will *totally* do my best to be courageous." Veronica pumped a fist in the air. She'd seen audiences do that on the few TV talk shows she'd peeked at. Shows spotlighting people talking about their *feelings* until they cried in front of God knows how many American viewers.

"Yeah, that's it!" Maddie cheered. "It *really* helps if you repeat the sayings a few times a day. She calls them affirmations."

"She? Oprah?"

Maddie nodded. "We can recite them together if you like."

"First, why don't we have some tea," Veronica said. She couldn't chant priestess Oprah's creed without a nibble of cake first. She felt her blood sugar dropping. "You do like cake, I hope."

"Does anybody *not* like cake?"

"You are my kind of gal."

Veronica rang the tiny sterling bell, newly polished so it gleamed just as it had on her and Bob's wedding day—a present from Admiral Hieronymus (Harry) Marshall himself, Bob's predecessor at Grudder Aviation and the father of that Leslie Day.

"My girl Rosalita did a marvelous job on our tea. With my suggestions, of course." She winked. Then imagined all the winks Maddie must've received in her short lifetime on Avalon from lecherous old men. "Did I just wink? It's like an infectious disease here on the island."

The girl's laugh reminded her of chimes in the wind.

Rosalita stepped into the sunroom carrying the heavy platter with the sterling teapot set some ancient Pencott great-aunt had gifted Veronica on her wedding day. And didn't Rosalita look fine? In her starched black-and-white maid's uniform and shiny patent-leather heels as she stepped across the polished floor and into the light spilling through the apricot shantung curtains. Rosalita had balked when she'd asked her to wear the uniform, and Veronica had almost rescinded her request, then Rosalita had said, "I do this for you, Mrs. Pencott. Because I know you want to make special teatime for your granddaughter."

Tears had pushed from behind Veronica's eyes when this woman, possibly her only friend, had known what Veronica needed before she knew herself. To make Maddie like her. It was true. She saw that now. The day before, if someone had asked her why on earth was she taking such care for a tea party with a girl— her swollen fingers fumbling with the garden shears as she clipped yellow roses and snowy hydrangeas from the garden for the center of the table—she'd have struggled for an answer. She had even asked Rosalita to unpack the good silver so the house would smell, pleasingly, of polish.

"Oh, Rosalita! What a marvelous job you've done."

"Thank you, Mrs. Pencott." Veronica heard the wink-wink in her voice.

"A-may-zing!" Maddie said. "Do you have tea like this every day?"

"No, sweetheart." She patted her granddaughter's naked knee. "This is all for you."

The girl's face changed. Confusion. A hint of fear. As if, Veronica thought, Maddie assumed there were strings attached. That, with the good, came the bad. She saw how neglected her granddaughter was. How dire her daughter's addiction. Her son-in-law's philandering.

Veronica waved toward the tray of cakes and steaming pot of tea.

"I had your grandfather's man Ray go all the way to a specialty shop on the mainland to procure us the finest tea. Harrods oolong. And our cake has arrived." She pointed to the plate of pastel petit fours decorated with iced flowers. "Please, dear, serve yourself."

Maddie studied the cakes with intense focus, and with delicate fingers picked what Veronica had decided was the prettiest—a robin's-egg-blue cake topped with a coral poppy. She took a tiny bite (so ladylike) and her brows lifted in pleasure. Veronica couldn't stop smiling. So much so that her top dentures were chafing her gums. She hadn't anticipated enjoying witnessing her granddaughter's pleasure.

"Good choice. That was my favorite too."

"Oh," Maddie said. "I'm sorry. I would've given it to you."

"No, no! And aren't you a sweet thing? I only meant I'm delighted we share the same good taste. Kindred spirits we are." Veronica sighed. "I've been eating sweets all day lately. Spent so many years watching what I ate. Denying myself. And now, I can't keep the weight on."

"Let us eat cake then," Maddie said.

Veronica added, "Every day."

Her granddaughter took another nibble of cake. Like Alice on the other side of the looking glass. Now, what will this cake do, make her grow big or small?

Veronica chose a mint-green cake with a lavender iced flower. The fondant melted on her tongue and she hummed with pleasure. Sharing with the girl made it oodles more delicious. When had she last, truly, enjoyed a bite of food?

She lifted the heavy pot of tea. Rosalita's eyes widened when she saw the delicate 24K-gold-rimmed saucer in Veronica's shaky hand.

"Please, Veronica . . ." Rosalita paused. "Mrs. Pencott. Let me serve."

How could she tell Rosalita that she yearned to hold the seashell-thin bone china once more before she died? The same cups she'd sipped from at her first formal tea with Bob's mother almost sixty years ago. That tiny bluebird rising from its nest, off the porcelain and into the clouds.

"Thank you, Rosalita. Please do."

When Rosalita left the sunroom, Maddie glanced around to be sure they were alone. "Why do you call Rosalita a *girl*?"

"Beg your pardon?"

The girl's face went as pale as the milk in Bob's great-aunt's heirloom creamer. "I'm sorry. My dad's always telling me to think before I speak."

"Yes," Veronica said. "That sounds just like the kind of advice men like to give women. Especially *young* women."

Maddie smiled.

"And you haven't offended me. Not at all. It is, however, a thought-provoking question."

"Well, it's just that . . ." Maddie began, and Veronica was pleased to see her granddaughter hadn't backed away. With change marching toward the island like a horde of enemy troops, Veronica knew those too timid to stand their ground would be trampled.

"Ray," Maddie continued, "gets to be called a *man*. And Rosalita—who is totally, like, ten years older than Ray—is called a *girl*. Weird, right?"

"Totally weird," Veronica said with a straight face, enjoying the giggle it provoked from Maddie. "You're spot-on. Women can be called girls and it barely seems an insult. But to call a man *a boy* . . . well, I'm sure wars have been waged over less."

The girl looked pleased with herself in this new role as teacher.

"This is why I like you, Maddalena," she said before sipping the oolong tea. "You've got—what is it they say these days? Balls?"

Maddie laughed, her hand flying to her mouth, too late to capture the lovely sound. She bumped the table and cream flooded the tray.

"Oh God, I am *so* sorry."

The girl was on her hands and knees, using her napkin (Veronica had chosen an Irish set embroidered with periwinkle forget-me-nots) to soak up milk streaking the oriental rug. One Veronica had traveled all the way to Turkey to purchase.

"I *knew* I was going to do something like this. That I'd break something, or spill, or . . ."

Veronica silenced her by placing a hand between her narrow shoulder blades.

"Sit down, please," she said softly. "Now, what would Oprah say?"

Maddie took her seat, smoothing her skirt.

"Life's too short to cry over spilled milk?"

"Yes!" Veronica cheered. "And we shall call our new game What Would Oprah Say?"

"I love it!"

I think I love you, sweet girl.

Maddie's hand hovered over another cake. She looked to Veronica, her feathery brows lifted.

"Eat them all! I can't have your grandfather stuffing his face. Falling into a diabetic coma. Do you watch this Oprah show with your mother?"

Maddie turned the silver band on her finger. It took Veronica a moment to see the pattern—five to the right, five to the left.

"She's been busy."

"Doing?"

"Well, she wants to open a doll shop. Like, fancy dolls you stick on stands. In fancy outfits." She thought for a moment. "Like Scarlett O'Hara in *Gone With the Wind*."

Just like Ginny, Veronica thought, to have such a romantic, and absurd, idea.

"She's been talking to investors. There's *a lot* of interest." Maddie nodded vigorously. As if she was trying to convince them both.

"I know she's gone through a hard time."

Maddie chewed her bottom lip. Veronica knew she was weighing the consequences of telling the truth.

"Anything you tell me in this sunroom"—Veronica waved at

the trails of pachysandra and spider plants dangling above—"stays in this room. You *can* trust me."

"Mom has . . . depression. She's been seeing Dr. Murray in town."

"The ex-tap-dancing chiropractor?"

"He's also a social worker and they do, like, talk therapy."

Oh the terrible things Ginny has surely said about her to that quack, Veronica thought. But she wanted the girl to continue. She needed Maddie to trust her, or her plan could not move forward. She was just about ready to mention the Marshall boy.

"You are compassionate. Other girls might feel—I don't know—resentful?"

Maddie searched her face. Wary. As if the girl suspected a trap, and this made Veronica admire her. Was there anything more detestable than gullibility?

"And your father, well . . ."

She was interrupted by a sharp crack outside—so loud and seemingly close that she was sure a bird had flown into the sunroom window.

"That's got to be Dom and the Colonel," Maddie said. "Dom said they were having target practice today, but I didn't believe him."

"Your grandfather. He's taking his anger out on those poor stewed-tomato cans. There's been more vandalism. This time, God forbid, at the American Legion."

"I heard. The post office too."

"Believe me," Veronica said. "When it comes to boys and their guns . . ."

"Dom's a big sweetie," Maddie said. "He wouldn't hurt anyone."

"I shouldn't poison your heart against men just yet," Veronica said. "They'll do that all on their own. It's amazing how much patience a girl can have with boys. And how little a woman has for men."

She dabbed at her sweating upper lip with the Irish linen. "Never mind the bitter ramblings of an old lady. I *did* meet the most remarkable man the other night. At the dinner party. Believe it or not, he's named after Caesar."

Three more gunshots rattled the window and Veronica realized she was clenching her fist over the lump of scar tissue where her left breast had been.

"This man . . ." She struggled to continue but knew she couldn't stop now. "He's a connoisseur of the orchid. Of all things. And a Harvard man to boot."

Recognition lit her granddaughter's face.

"The Marshall man. The . . ." Maddie paused.

"It's okay, dear. You can say it. He is black. We—and the rest of this island—are white. It is what it is."

"I met his son. Brooks."

"Did you?" She pretended she hadn't watched them in the moonlight, certain they'd be pulled together. Kiss. It had made her blush. Imagine that, at eighty, blushing like a girl? Peeping at young lovers from behind a curtain. She had accepted she was like the rest of the island's platinum-bobbed grandmothers—their girlhoods as debutantes, beauty queens, army nurses, and war brides, and, in her case, farm girl, so distant they all had forgotten the desire of youth. Watching her granddaughter and the boy, she'd felt a stirring of desire, a bittersweet loss, and, for the span of an owl's call, it had cracked open her precise military life as fixed as the tick of a metronome.

Maddie watched the caterpillars crawling across the window glass, and, beyond, the trees swaying in the sea wind. Veronica knew the girl had returned to the lawn on that dewy summer night.

"What is the boy like?"

"He is"—she took a deep, dreamy breath—"wonderful."

Veronica wasn't surprised. She too had fallen for the handsome black man she'd talked with at the dessert party who spoke of floral arrangements with a religious focus (a bit of a poof, Bob might call him). He had made her laugh. And had spoken as if he knew her. Knew the secrets she was keeping.

The Mormons had taught her to be "in the world but not of the world," and that is how she had lived those decades on the island. She had wanted to tell Julius that she too was an outsider. But what a thing to say to a black man—a true outsider, alone on an island of warmongering white men. On an island where every child—East and West—went on annual field trips to the Whaling Museum to learn about the first white men to settle Avalon in the 1700s. They were Dutch whalers and their crude harpoons and lances hung on the museum's walls. Veronica had visited the museum many times, volunteered at their annual benefit, seen the centerpiece of the exhibit—a treasured artifact, a rusted black cauldron once filled with bubbling whale blubber. What they weren't taught, Veronica knew, was that, first, before they set upon the whales, the Dutch men of Avalon—killers by trade from day one—had slaughtered thousands of brown-skinned natives.

Maddie sat up, patting her knees. "I'm going to the Castle," she whispered. "Tonight."

The girl knew it was a visit her parents would object to. And here she was, Veronica thought, trusting *her* with this news. Veronica wouldn't have to find a circuitous way of bringing up Leslie Day Marshall after all. Maddie had done just that.

"Brooks invited me. All the kids, actually."

"What fun," Veronica said, thinking fast. "If you see his mother—Leslie—please do tell her hello from me. Leslie's mother and I, we were old friends."

"Sure."

"And one other thing. When you come back tomorrow—we are watching the Oprah show, I hope—I want to hear *all* the details. About the Castle and Brooks." She added, "And his parents. Especially his mother."

Maddie nodded happily. Mission accomplished, Veronica thought.

They kissed on both cheeks when Maddie left (European-style, Maddie said), and she promised to be at the big house the next day in time for *Oprah*. Veronica promised in return—she'd have popcorn ready.

She stood at the picture window watching Maddie sashay across the lawn toward the cottage. Just like a young girl in love. Veronica drew circles around the caterpillars with a finger, but they seemed not to know she was there, on the other side of the glass. They charged forward like tiny bristled trains on an erratic schedule.

She'd have to find a way to use Maddie's proximity to Leslie Marshall to gain knowledge of that woman's plans. Leslie was scheming, Veronica was certain. The timing was impossible— all these problems raining down on the island like it was holy hell's target. She had learned in her eighty years that what seemed like coincidence rarely was. The pollutant complaint from the EPA. The buyout offer. The graffiti soiling the island. The Marshall girl had a hand in some—or, possibly, she thought, all—of it. And now the woman was luring in the island's children, maybe even using them in her twisted agenda. Leslie Marshall, Veronica thought, the pied piper of Avalon.

15.

Dom

The pistol, black and hard, looked out of place in his grandfather's pale and soft hands. Like bags filled with pudding, Dom thought as he watched the old man aim at the empty tomato cans propped on the salt-weathered fence in the clearing behind White Eagle. They were the cans Dom's dad had used to make the spaghetti sauce his grandfather sucked down at lunch the other day.

Dom didn't know much about him—only bits and pieces he'd stitched together to create the character that was the Colonel. What he did know was this: the islanders were scared of his grandfather. Mentioning the Colonel flicked a switch in people who usually treated Dom like he was invisible, or worse, looked him up and down with a dismissive head shake. Like the old geezers in the club dining room who played bridge all day so they could stay nice and drunk—one mention of the Colonel and *poof,* they transformed into cheek-pinching (the old ladies), back-slapping (the old men) doters who pressed folded twenty-dollar bills into his hand. "Buy yourself a soda, kid!" and "I hear they have gummy worms down at the Wildcat Sweet Shoppe!"

The rest he'd had to intel (that was a military word he'd picked up watching spy movies) from his brief experiences with the Colonel before he and Veronica took off to Florida. The Colonel was a relentless backseat driver. He rolled down the Cadillac's window when someone cut him off and yelled, "You stupid ass!" The Colonel's favorite afternoon snack was a beer and chunk of Limburger cheese, which made the fridge at the big house smell like diarrhea farts. The Colonel was always ragging on Dom's mom—calling her fat, telling her she was too *fresh* and opinionated, even saying (in front of his dad!) that she'd made a mistake marrying an uneducated man. Dom wasn't sure if all this made the Colonel plain honest. Mean. Crazy. Or all of the above.

But he was different since he'd come back to the island—Dom was sure of it. He'd studied the Colonel at lunch the other day, and again, only a half hour ago in the big kitchen of White Eagle, as the old guy slurped down root-beer floats he'd made for them. He'd chugged it like a hungry little kid, holding the frosted mug with two hands, his pinky finger pointing, its rock of a diamond ring glinting. The foamy mix spilled down his chin as he guzzled.

Now as his grandfather lifted the pistol, one eye squinting, his hands shaking, he shouted, "Shit!"

Dom pretended not to notice but he did glance back toward the path that led through the woods to White Eagle, where he knew Veronica and his sister were doing some girl thing like having tea. He'd rather be nibbling muffins and tiny sandwiches but the Colonel had given him an order to follow, and when he gave an order, you obeyed.

Champ, his thick brown coat spotted with leaves, leapt in and out of the woods.

"Champ, you knucklehead!" his grandfather shouted. "Get out of the goddamn way."

"Um, excuse me, Grandpa," Dom said. "Are you supposed to hold it so close to your face? What about the kickback?"

His grandfather dropped his arm and the gun smacked against his bright-red golf slacks. He turned to Dom and his features, already set close in the center of his face, scrunched in disgust. His left eye, frozen in a perpetual squint, had always reminded Dom of Popeye.

"Somebody's been watching too many cop shows on the television," he said. "And when you talk to me, you show some respect and call me Colonel."

"Yessir," Dom said, wondering if he should salute, bow, click his heels, scrambling for the right choice as clips from classic war films he'd watched on cable reeled through his mind.

The Colonel struck a limp-wristed pose—just like those

assholes at school—mocking Dom in a babyish voice. "*Yessir*? Say it with some testes, man. Yes, sir!"

"Yes, sir!" Dom barked, mimicking the tone he'd heard in movies like *Taps* and *Full Metal Jacket*. "I'm sorry, sir!"

"Don't apologize, boy. It makes you look weak."

"I'm sorry," Dom said before he caught himself and lifted his chin. "I mean I'm *not* sorry, *sir*!"

His grandfather laughed—a *heh-heh* that reminded Dom of a gangster. As in, *I'm laughing, but what I'm really doing is thinking of pumping you full of metal.*

The Colonel pointed a finger at the sky. "The history of free men," he announced, "is not written by chance, but by choice!"

"Free will," Dom said, nodding.

"You know who said that?" the Colonel asked. And before Dom could confess ignorance, he continued, "Of course you don't. They teach you nothing in schools today. Ike said that. The president of the US of A? Now, let me translate."

He wrapped a cold hand around the back of Dom's neck and pulled him forward so their foreheads were almost touching. Dom resisted the urge to pull away. His grandfather smelled unwashed. Like he'd just woken from a nightmare. "In other words, you got to grab the beast by its balls, boy. Before its horns tear your throat out. You hear me?"

Dom saw the red starbursts of blood vessels on the old man's nose. There was a spot of dried ice cream stuck in his silver stubble and Dom wished they could go back to White Eagle. Maybe they could watch the ball game. Anything but C-SPAN. The Colonel turned into a raving madman when news of the election, and especially Bill Clinton, came on.

"Loud and clear, Colonel," Dom said, relieved when his grandfather released him.

"Now, you got to imagine your enemy's face on the front of those cans," the Colonel said as he squinted down the nose of the gun. "Like right now, I'm seeing those vandals. Dirtying my island with their cockamamie slurs!"

He squeezed off a few more shots. He hit just one can.

"Goddamn," he shouted. "Horsefeathers!"

Dom held his breath so as not to laugh and then the cold metal was being pressed into his hands and he was holding the gun with his pinchy fingers.

"Don't dangle it like a shit-filled diaper."

It was heavier than Dom had expected and while the metal barrel was cool, the wooden grip was warm from the Colonel's hands.

"How does it feel?"

"Real good," Dom said.

The Colonel mocked him again, using that same sissy voice, wobbling his bald head. "*Real good?* What. Does. It. Feel like?" He spat out the words like each was a bullet.

Dom wished he'd had more than a nip from his thermos of OJ and Smirnoff vodka, because his hands were shaking even worse than the Colonel's and he was starting to feel majorly pissed off. He took a long, deep breath that made his chest burn and steadied his hands, wrapping his fingers tight around the gun. He thought of his Greek gods and imagined the gun was one of the totems that gave mortals transformative power. Wasn't it the power to kill without consequences that separated man from god? Via thunderbolts, poison-tipped arrows, tridents, spears, and swords.

"Fan-tastic!" Dom shouted. His hands had stopped shaking.

It was the first time he'd seen the Colonel smile.

"You're my boy, Dominic," he said, and the way he nodded slowly, approving of Dom—would he, could he, Dom thought, ever know how much that meant to him?

"Thank you, Colonel." It was all he could squeak out. What he wanted to say was *I love you. Please take care of me. Let me follow you.* He wanted to confess the terrible thing that he'd done in the woods behind the school while that psycho MJ Bundy whispered hot threats in his ear.

"I want to make you, Dominic Pencott, my second in command. My lieutenant."

Dom was too excited to correct the Colonel—his last name was LaRosa not Pencott.

"Yes, sir!"

He would be Hermes, the winged messenger, worshipped by generals, merchants, travelers, and great athletes like the WWF wrestlers. Hermes to the Colonel's Zeus.

"But . . ." Dom began, realizing how incapable he was. He *was* all those things the dipshits at school called him. A wimp. A loser. "What if I . . . choke?"

There was kindness in his grandfather's eyes when he stepped close and clamped a hand on Dom's shoulder.

"I understand, Dom. I've seen many men question their worth. Even at the most decisive moments in battle."

Dom remembered how his father had seemed to enjoy telling him about the Colonel never having seen combat—he'd been hurt, his back broken in a factory accident months before he was scheduled to be deployed as a navy pilot in the new war. His father, Dom decided, must have been wrong, or, more likely, lying to make the Colonel look bad.

"I promise you, Lieutenant Pencott, you spend enough time with the lion, and roaring becomes more and more reasonable."

It was like something straight out of Zeus's own mouth and it made sense to Dom when so little these past few months had.

"Yes, sir!"

"Now, repeat after me," the Colonel commanded as he squeezed Dom's shoulder, his eyes closing solemnly as if in prayer, "I, Dominic Pencott . . ."

"I, Dominic Pencott."

"Do solemnly swear . . ."

"Do solemnly swear."

"That I will defend the Constitution of the United States against *all* enemies, foreign and domestic . . ."

Dom repeated all the important-sounding words—enemies, faith, allegiance—and he felt himself grow stronger. Invincible. Until the world was blocked out. Just him and the Colonel in a halo of light. Gone were the birdcalls and twigs cracking and the relentless drone of the caterpillars. *Poof!* MJ, Victor—all the dickheads at school . . . Gone.

"I will well and faithfully discharge the duties of the office upon which I am about to enter," Dom repeated.

"So help me God," the Colonel said.

"So help me God."

The Colonel was squeezing his arm hard now, until Dom thought he'd either laugh or cry out.

"In wartime, drastic measures are necessary."

"Are we at war?" Dom asked. It was a mistake. The Colonel closed his eyes as if exhausted and let out a long root beer–scented belch.

He looked around suspiciously before whispering, "We *are* in a war, son. The crusade to make America great again. There are those naysayers who will tell you different. They'll say we are in a golden age. Ha! But they're liars. Or they're cowards. Content to live a cushiony life with their big TVs and their shrink appointments and their goddamn *feelings*."

Dom nodded, repeating, "Yes, sir. Yes, sir." And it seemed to work because the Colonel released his throbbing shoulder and turned Dom to face the tomato-can targets. Dom lifted the gun.

"Hold your horses there," the Colonel said, and wrapped his arms around Dom from behind so he covered Dom's hands with his own. "You're a righty, so you grip it high on the back strap. That'll help you deal with recoil better."

"Yes, sir," Dom said. The Colonel's round belly pressed into his back and he tried not to think about how close they were, and what if he couldn't control his body like in the woods outside the Castle the other day, and then the Colonel was yelling in his ear, "Pay attention, boy!"

"Yes, sir!"

"All four fingers under the trigger guard. Yeah, you got it. I'm going to tell you a little story while we get you ready to shoot. I think it'll illuminate (the Colonel drew out every syllable like it was a joke) why this island—the whole US of A—is at war."

He showed Dom how to keep his trigger finger on the outside of the guard, his thumb pointing forward where the slide met the frame, so his hands fit together—*Like a puzzle*.

"Once upon a time," the Colonel sang, like it was storytime at nursery school, "there was a boy named Willie. A Southern boy who thought he was a real big cheese. But was, in fact, a flat tire through and through. His girl was named Hillie. And whoa was she a number. Queen of the man-eating feminists!"

Dom was concentrating on the gun so it was hard to listen to the story and the instructions at once. He nodded, said "Uh-huh," and the Colonel continued.

"They were a greedy couple of kids. Wanted money *and* power. But without the cost. Wanted it handed to them on a silver platter."

Dom's arms were beginning to ache.

"Instead of fighting for his country, Willie whined and whined until he was allowed to dodge the draft."

"That's messed up."

"That's not all." The Colonel showed Dom how to stand, moving Dom's hips roughly with his hands. Feet and shoulders apart, knees bent slightly. "Willie can't keep his willy in his pants!" That laugh again. *Heh-heh-heh.* "He's screwing some broad, and get this, her name is Flowers. No lie."

Dom aimed at the middle can so the top of the front sight lined up with the top of the rear sight. His arms trembled and sweat trickled past his temple toward his chin but he didn't dare move.

"Now, Willie and Hillie want to live in the White House. If you can imagine that! And the people of America, especially the young—with their video games and MTV music shows—they don't know what it means to fear war. Oh no, they're content. Numb. They don't know what it feels like to have your son head overseas and come home in a pine box—his skull shattered by shrapnel so you can see bits of his brain. No open casket."

Dom set what the Colonel called the "sight picture" so the front and rear sights were sharp in focus and the target, the can, blurry. When, he wondered, was he going to be allowed to pull the trigger?

"They think war is something that happens in faraway countries. In history books and Hollywood movies." Dom heard the teeth-clenching bitterness in the Colonel's voice. "When they watched Desert Storm on the TV set, it looked like a game at the goddamn arcade!"

The Colonel pressed into him from behind and Dom worried he'd topple forward.

"You ready to shoot, lieutenant?"

"Yes, sir!"

"Now, when I say, you squeeze the trigger. You squeeze until you feel it resist. Got that?"

"Yes, sir."

"When violence does enter your life," the Colonel continued, "it marks you like tar. It stains you good. It devours you until you don't know how you can go on living, and you sure as hell aren't griping about your *feelings*."

"Yes, sir."

"Now, the key is to let the gun fire on its own. Don't try to trick yourself into thinking you'll know when it fires. The gun likes to surprise you."

Dom heard a smile in the Colonel's voice.

"The goddamn liberals. The EPA and their environment BS. Bush, that nitwit, cutting the defense budget. The Berlin Wall came down and hippies are still writing songs about it. They weren't alive to remember why it went up in the first place!"

"Can I shoot?" Sweat was dripping down both sides of Dom's face.

"You know what's going to happen if Slick Willie gets into the White House?"

Dom shook his head.

"The dawn of destruction! Why, in Christ's name, should we lay down arms when we are winning? When we are at the top of the game?"

"I don't know, sir."

The Colonel stepped back so his voice felt far away. "Let's see you shoot those motherfucking Krauts full of holes."

Dom had imagined shooting would be hard. That he'd be scared of the blast and the reverberating *thwang* that moved up his arm, into his shoulder, spread through his chest. But he was good. His hands steady, his aim decent. He hit one can and then another, missing the last. When he turned to see if the Colonel was pleased or disappointed, the old man was whooping and dancing a frolicky jig that made Dom think of Rumpelstiltskin.

The Colonel hobbled over to the fence to replace the cans

and Dom knew he had death in his hands. He *was* death. Like Hades, the god of the underworld with his two-pronged fork that shattered anything, anyone, not to his liking. How easy it would be, to lift and fire. Claim it was an accident. It was his first time, after all. No more stomach-clenching tense family dinners. No more nights listening to his mother cry because her father had called her a fat pig. Or, maybe, it was his mother who needed the peace of death more. How different could it be from death—that dark silent space she escaped to with her pills?

As he squeezed off round after round, the stewed-tomato cans flying off the fence, he realized he could make an excuse for the death of everyone. He gave each can a name; MJ Bundy; Mr. Brenner, that sadistic shit of a gym teacher; the Colonel and his mom and dad; and Jules, the new neighbor who had laughed at him. The only one he left out was Maddie. When he hit the can he'd named Dom, it spun in the air like a flying saucer.

"You're good, boy." The Colonel squeezed his shoulder again, even harder this time, and he fought against the pain, willed himself not to pull away. He imagined he was a knight being blessed before a mission, his grandfather's hand a king's sword. "In times like this, there are few who can be counted on."

"Watch yourself out there." The Colonel pointed to the shadowy woods where the caterpillars chewed and shat so it sounded, Dom thought, like rain falling despite the sun overhead. "There's more to fear than the witches and wolves your mama told you 'bout in those fairy tales." The Colonel smiled and it reminded Dom of those same fabled villains. "Those are just stories mommies tell to scare little kids. To make them eat their vegetables and say their prayers and stay out of the woods."

He pointed a squat finger at Dom.

"It's up to you to figure out what the real danger is, lieutenant. When you find it, you'll know. And then you'll destroy it."

Champ growled. Then bounded off into the woods, barking.

"Leave it, boy!"

The Colonel marched to where Champ dug, dirt spitting out from behind the dog's crooked back legs.

"I said, cut it out!" He kicked the dog in the ribs. Champ

yelped and ran back toward the house, his head hung low, looking back at his master. Dom's hand rose to cover his mouth, to stuff in the cry that had almost escaped. His fingers smelled like the fireworks he set off every Fourth of July.

The small larvae of the gypsy moth take to the air and are carried by the wind. The larvae spin silken threads and hang from them, waiting for the wind to blow.

—*The Gypsy Moth: Research Toward Integrated Pest Management*, United States Department of Agriculture, 1981

According to the United States Department of Agriculture, without intervention, this pest spreads about 13 miles per year. Typically, short distances can be traversed by larva, but there is suspicion that long distance flights are possible. It has been hypothesized that storms carried the larva across Lake Michigan to the western shore, a span of dozens of miles.

—KL Frank, *Interpretation of gypsy moth frontal advance using meteorology in a conditional algorithm*

16.

Maddie

She was determined to be the first to arrive at the Castle and had made Penny promise to have her mom drop her at the cottage with an hour to spare. So they could pick out outfits and do their hair and makeup. Now that Penny had suffered two seizures, there was no way her parents would let her drive—a rule that made sense to Maddie but outraged Penny.

"I mean, if I'm going to die, I should at least be able to use my learner's permit!"

They primped in the upstairs bathroom, straightening their hair (Penny's was noticeably thinner), lining their lips and coating them in Dr Pepper–flavored Lip Smacker. Even plumping out their eyelashes with Maybelline Color Shine! mascara in aquamarine. Maddie remembered Bitsy's lecture on the kind of subtle beauty that made East girls, but tonight she wanted to stand out. For Brooks.

She was so nervous or excited, or a mix of both, that she wiped her face clean with makeup remover pads and started again.

"Shit!" she slapped her hands on the bathroom counter. "I'm all blotchy."

"What's your deal tonight?" Penny said, smiling, because she knew.

She'd told Penny about her skateboard ride home with Brooks. How he'd held her hand. Even pulled her up Snake Hill Road. She hadn't told Penny about the feeling she got watching Brooks snip off the tip of the honeysuckle flower with his front teeth. How could she explain the unexplainable? Brooks had been right—there just weren't enough words.

She'd also decided to keep quiet the details about her and

Spencer's botched sex. God, how she wished she could pretend it had never happened. When Spencer hadn't called her house the day after, and then still hadn't called three days later, she'd been both relieved and worried. She was dreading seeing him tonight, and had considered keeping Brooks's invitation to herself. But she'd called Bitsy the night before, using the kitchen phone—the longest cord in the cottage and if she pulled it straight, she could sit on the step outside the front door. Guaranteed privacy. There was no telling what her father would do if he knew she was hanging out with the Marshall boy. The black boy.

In some ways, he was cool, her dad. Didn't care about curfew. Bought her a pack of maxipads without flinching. But he wanted her to be with someone like him. No Jews. No Hispanics. It was weird, him wanting that, she thought. Him being her dad and all and the last person on earth she could be with. Like that. In *that* way.

When Bitsy had finally got on the phone, after a whole minute of Captain Smith yelling for her, Maddie had said, "Guess where we'll be partying tomorrow night."

"Uck, please tell me it's not in some basement with a bunch of tools watching porn."

"Guess again."

"The beach with the caterpillars?"

"At the Castle!"

Bitsy screamed into the phone so Maddie had to pull the receiver away from her ear.

"Oh. My. Fucking. God. I underestimated you, Mads. Bigtime."

Now she and Penny stood in front of the bathroom mirror surrounded by round, bright lights Maddie's mom claimed were Hollywood-style.

"You're beautiful," Penny said, arranging Maddie's long hair so it hung over her shoulders, tumbling down her white T-shirt.

She wanted to ask how a girl even knows she's beautiful. Would a time come when she knew, for sure, either way?

"Thanks, Pen." She touched her friend's hand, the one bruised purple and yellow by the IV. Feeling like an ass for complaining about her looks when they both knew Penny's mom had made an appointment for a fitting at the wig shop in Rosedale.

Dom slammed a fist against the bathroom door. "I got to go!"

"Jeez, all right! Don't have a cow!" Maddie yelled back.

"*Hasta la vista*, Dom," Penny sang as she and Maddie hurried through the front door and into the dusky light.

They stood at the entrance to the path leading through the woods between White Eagle and the Castle. It seemed the pulsing of the caterpillars—*ca-caaaah, ca-caaaah*—grew louder every day.

"You ready?" Maddie asked. "On the count of three, we run."

"It's like the end times," Penny said. "A pox upon your heads!"

"One, two . . ."

Before she could finish, Penny took off in the long-legged stride she used to outrun girls on the lacrosse field.

"Woo-hoo!" she screamed.

Maddie joined in, "Cowabunga!"

They booked it, leaping over branches, catching themselves when they slipped on the black goo coating the ground. She remembered Veronica's posh tone—*caterpillar excrement*.

"Caterpillar excrement!" she yelled, and their laughter bounced off the trees and, for a moment, drowned out the zombie drone of the gypsies that had already become the soundtrack of the summer.

By the time they reached the Castle's front doors, the cuffs of their jeans were splattered with black slime and their makeup smudged. They stood on the rolling lawn in front of the Castle and picked caterpillars out of each other's hair. The day had alternated between sunny and gray, a late-afternoon squall had rolled in from the sea, but still the Castle's marble shone a pearly white.

Maddie found a caterpillar tucked between her sock and sneaker. Penny found one in her sports bra and shrieked. They wheezed with laughter. Maddie was relieved to be dirty. She was sick of trying to look perfect.

"Are you sure we're allowed to just, like, walk in?" She touched the initials—H. M.—in the center of the wrought-iron doors, which stood open. And looked, she thought, more like the gates of a nineteenth-century asylum than a front entrance.

"I don't know," Penny said. "He's *your* boyfriend. . . ."

"Zip it," Maddie said. She knocked on her head quickly so Penny wouldn't see, wishing it were true.

She was buzzing with anticipation. Not only would she see Brooks, she was visiting the Castle, the most extravagant home on the island, rumored to have thirty rooms and an indoor salt-water pool. In the winter months when the trees were bare, from the guest room window in White Eagle, she could spot the top of the castle's stone turrets. Veronica swore that the Marshall Castle had been in the running for Robert Redford's mansion in *The Great Gatsby* but that pious Mrs. Marshall refused to have her home turned into a movie set and definitely not for, in Veronica's words, "a film that celebrated wanton debauchery." Maddie knew it had been *her* model for all the towers in the fairy tales her mother had told her and Dom. Her mother had only to speak the word—"castle"—and an image of the Marshall place sprung into Maddie's mind, as if from one of Jack's magic seeds. She and Dom had spent many weekend hours walking the woods around the Marshall gate, its marble eagles staring at them hungrily as they listened for the cries of a trapped princess.

Then Brooks was there, framed in the massive doorway, greeting them with a quiet *hey*. His eyes met hers and she was sure they paused for a beat.

"Welcome to the Castle," he said and took her hand, pulling her into the airy blue light of the entryway.

They walked through a cavernous hall, the gray stone walls hung with the stuffed heads of huge beasts—deer, moose, and even a bear—whose glass eyes shone under the iron chandelier's light. A tall glass case held guns of all kinds—silver antiques (was that a bayonet?) and the more recent matte-black steel.

"Holy shit," Penny whispered as they walked under the arched doorway of the ballroom.

It was like walking into a dream. Maddie felt a shiver of recognition. A zap of déjà vu. Like she'd been there. Or dreamt of it.

She stood in the center of the room and looked up, turning in a slow circle.

The sun came out (just for them, she thought) and streamed through the stained-glass windows, painting the enormous domed room with wet brilliant light, making Maddie think again, like she had at the fair, of a kaleidoscope.

She looked up and saw pink-tinged clouds against a blue sky so real it was like the ceiling didn't exist. Only the edging gave it away. Filigree like icing on a solid-gold cake.

Gray rocks rose up the walls, their craggy tips piercing the rosy sky.

"It's the sunset at Singing Beach," she said. "It's beautiful."

Brooks was next to her. Her eyes were on the ceiling, tracing the silver lining in each cloud, but she smelled his cinnamon scent. Felt his heat.

"We can't hang at the beach," he said. " 'Cause of the caterpillars. So I brought the beach to you."

You, Maddie thought. *Me*. And it felt as if it *were* just she and him and he'd conjured the beach from thin air. Like a magician or one of Dom's gods. All for her. And all hers.

"I hang in here sometimes," he said. "When the sun is setting. Light a joint and lay on my back."

Please, she thought, *let me do that with you*.

"There's this moment—when the light outside and the light up there is like a perfect match." He pointed to the stained-glass windows lining the ballroom, alternating with tall white columns draped with spiderwebs. "I guess it's maybe what heaven looks like."

"Totally." Maddie sighed.

She ignored Penny's eye roll.

"If heaven exists." He winked.

"Are you an atheist or something?" Penny said. "My mom says your parents are radicals. Got any cool stories about them blowing up colleges or banks and stuff?"

"Pen," Maddie said. "Quit it with the third degree, 'kay?"

She knew Penny was just being Penny, but what if Brooks had been offended?

"Dude," Penny said, holding her hands up, "I'm just curious. I'm not going to turn them in to the pigs."

"I've seen the cops on this island," he said. "Don't think they've ever had to do anything but eat doughnuts and get old ladies' kitties out of trees."

"Not," Penny said. "They'd have a coronary climbing a ladder."

"That station looks like it was built for some Disney movie," Brooks added. "Like it's got gnomes and fairies and shit living in it."

They were laughing, all three of them, just as Maddie had hoped, and then he gave her fingers a gentle squeeze.

"I'm really happy you're here."

"Adorable," Penny said as she fell into one of the giant black beanbags with a whoosh of air and a cloud of dust.

He was still holding Maddie's hand and she dared to step forward. She made herself look into his eyes. The lids were heavy, thickly lashed, like a young Sylvester Stallone, and she wondered if this was what people meant by "bedroom eyes" in the old black-and-white movies her mom watched on the weekends. She didn't want to look away but felt a tickle knocking around in her belly. She couldn't understand why she felt so nervous when she knew she liked him. *A lot* a lot.

"Cool!" Penny pointed to the back of the room, where an opera house–style balcony hung like a cozy shelf, draped in thick red and gold velvet tied off with tassels. Penny let out a trilling impersonation of an opera singer, her mouth stretched into a clownish O. Echoes of echoes ricocheted off the tall walls and curved ceiling.

There was a burst of sound from the entryway and Maddie heard Bitsy, "Oh my God! This place is bitchin'!" and the whisper of feet shuffling over the stone grew louder until the whole gang was flooding into the ballroom. Bitsy, Vanessa, and Gabrielle. Gerritt, Ricky, John, Austin, and Rolo. And Spencer, one hand in the pocket of his cargo shorts, the other smacking a tin of tobacco dip against his thigh. *Thwack, thwack.* He had a baseball cap on—YALE—the brim shaped into a tight arch so Maddie couldn't see his eyes.

They'd brought treats. Each waited their turn to offer up their goodies to Brooks, along with a fist bump, an up-nod, a hug if you were Bitsy—and the way she pressed her boobs up against Brooks made Maddie squint. Gerritt brought an eighth of kind bud. Ricky a block of tar-black hashish he'd scored at a Grateful Dead concert, wrapped in tinfoil. There was a plastic baggie of shake left over from the shrooms, and John, Austin, and Rolo had gone in on a beer keg.

"Dude." Gerritt flicked his chin at Brooks. "Your parents are, like, cool with us being here? Drinking, smoking, and whatnot?"

"They're cool," Brooks said. "Already half asleep in the cottage. And you gotta go through a maze to get from here to there. I'm pretty sure my dad's stoned. So he ain't making it through any maze. Having ex-hippies for parents isn't half bad."

He delivered this info in one shot, played it straight, didn't even crack a smile, and there was a pause before the crew burst into laughter, the ceiling catching it so it seemed to Maddie as if the laughter went on too long.

So that's how it was going to be. There was *her* Brooks—the honeysuckle-tasting, making-up-words, sweet-and-chivalrous Brooks. And there was the cool and aloof Brooks he showed to others. He *was* hers though, she was suddenly sure of that, and the thought ignited a spiral, like the shooting-star fireworks Dom set off every Fourth of July, from her belly to her throat.

Brooks had hooked up his stereo next to a set of turntables. There were at least six black binders, the plastic sleeves filled with CDs to satisfy everyone's craving. Rolo, always jonesing for classic rock, had his Led Zeppelin and Pink Floyd. John Anderson, Beastie Boys and A Tribe Called Quest. The perfect accompaniment, Maddie thought, for his habit of crushing beer cans under his Timberland boots. There were home-burned CDs she guessed were dance music. But sounded like new drug fads. Mojo. Trance. Acid House. Thick 3D block letters in red and black Sharpie. That's his handwriting, she thought. He *must* be an artist.

After a ton of negotiation, which involved Ricky threatening to leave (and take his hash with him) if they didn't play *Dark Side of the Moon*, Brooks dropped six discs in the CD changer. Music filled the ballroom from rounded ceiling to parquet floor. The vast space seemed to devour the sound and spit it back out twice as loud, reminding Maddie of how, on foggy days, the sound of the barges offshore warped so they seemed next door even though they were really miles away.

They got to work getting their buzz on. She knew now, after a month of partying with the East kids, that they took getting wasted seriously.

Bitsy pulled a blue plastic bong out of her purse and called, "Who wants a taste?" and some of the kids—Maddie, Brooks, and Penny included—sat in a circle on the cool dirt-streaked floor and passed the bong.

Rolo and Austin tapped the keg and Vanessa was the first to do a keg stand—her shirt falling down so her lacy black bra showed. John Anderson started to reach for her breast, ready to give it a squeeze, when Bitsy lifted her face from the bong and said, breath held, "Don't you even fucking think about it, John," right before she let out a stream of thick smoke and fell into a fit of coughing.

An hour later, when Tribe's "Scenario" blasted from the tall speakers, all the girls, even Penny, were in the middle of the ball-room dancing and singing the stuttering lyrics, pointing at the boys with their lips pressed in pouts. Bitsy trotted out of the circle and grabbed Brooks, pulling him into the crowd of girls, and Maddie felt Penny shoot her a look but pretended not to notice, kept singing, *Here we go yo / here we go yo / So what so what so what's the scenario.* But when the song reached *Gots to get the loot so I can bring home the bacon,* and the usually shy Rolo was dancing, his belly jiggling under his threadbare Grateful Dead tee, Maddie saw Bitsy gyrating her lithe body around Brooks. Spencer was watching Maddie watch Brooks and his eyes narrowed in disgust before he turned away.

Maddie searched for Gerritt, knowing he'd be good for busting up Bitsy making moves on Brooks. Then the music went dead. Her ears rang in the sudden silence.

The kids groaned, *What the fuck?* and there was Bitsy standing by the stereo, clapping her hands. "Chop-chop!" she sang, "That's enough whirling-dervish shit for now. It's game time."

"Chop-chop?" Brooks whispered, his breath tickling Maddie's ear.

She knew what "game time" meant and prayed it was Spin the Bottle, not Seven Minutes in Heaven. Not much happened in seven minutes locked in a closet with a boy—cold hands slipping under her shirt, over her bra, as she massaged some guy's hard-on over his khaki shorts while the rest of the kids whispered on the other side of the door. But there was that awful moment when time was up and the door opened, light blinding the couple as they returned to the world, faces flushed, hair mussed, lips raw. Like Adam and Eve after the snake (or was it God, she couldn't remember which) told them off. Seven minutes with Brooks she'd do times ten, but odds were high she'd pick another boy's name out of the smelly Mets cap Bitsy would pass around.

What a relief to hear from Brooks that there were no closets in the ballroom, and the players settled in a circle around a few thick candles that smelled like pine trees. It was dark out now and the arched windows above were an underwater blue.

Not everyone participated. She'd spotted John and Vanessa sneaking off to make out in a dark corner after swallowing two pills of E. Rolo and Spencer were also rolling hard and had left for the woods to climb trees. She'd been able to avoid Spencer all night so far, which, she thought, probably meant he was also avoiding her, and that was just fine by her.

That left six. An even split of boys and girls.

"Lucky six!" Bitsy sang. She coordinated the events with a bossiness that reminded Maddie of PTA moms overseeing school bake sales. At first, Maddie had guessed it was the thrill of sex that excited Bitsy, but she'd come to understand that Bitsy was like the vampires in the Stephen King novel she'd read late at night under her bedsheets with a flashlight. Bitsy fed on humiliation.

Like now, as Penny locked lips with twitchy Ricky, Penny grabbing the collar of his Izod shirt with both hands, Bitsy called out, "Too much tongue, girl! I give that kiss a five, tops." As if, Maddie thought, she were judging an Olympic ice-skating competition.

"That was some *Deep Throat* shit," Ricky said with a shaky sigh before making a big show of using his shirt to wipe his mouth.

While everyone laughed (but Maddie), Penny stared at the shadows flickering across the floor. Poor thing had a major crush on dickhead Ricky.

They spun the bottle as Alice in Chains hummed from the

speakers, telling a story about a man in a box buried in his own shit. Maddie got Gerritt and gave Bitsy a quick shrug (asking if it was cool) before leaning over and giving him a quick peck on the lips.

"Thanks, babycakes," Gerritt said.

The circle laughed and Maddie found Brooks's eyes. He winked and she was relieved.

It was Gabrielle's turn and she spun the bottle the way she did everything—slow and lazy. She got Bitsy, pouted, and said, slyly, "Well, it ain't the first time."

Maddie had heard boys talk shamelessly about their johnsons and jerking off and how their hand was their best girlfriend. Ha-ha-ha. But she hadn't heard girls talk that way, not until she starting hanging with Bitsy, Vanessa, and Gabrielle, who talked openly, loudly, in front of the boys, about "stirring the soup" and "getting off." Making Maddie blush. Driving the boys wild. So when Bitsy mediated Spin the Bottle, she enforced one rule: Girls had to kiss who the bottle told them to kiss. An excuse for her and Gabrielle and Vanessa to tangle their tongues in front of the boys. Of course, if a boy landed on a boy, they spun again. The rules weren't the same for girls and guys.

Bitsy's and Gabrielle's glossed lips met. Their tongues flickered around O-shaped mouths. Gabrielle nipped at Bitsy's lower lip and Bitsy pinched one of Gabrielle's plump breasts. Gabrielle flinched, smacking Bitsy's hand and saying, without meaning it, "Bitch."

"Fuuuuck," Ricky drawled.

Bitsy looked straight at Brooks and said, "Future jerk-off material. You're welcome."

"Screw this," Gerritt said, and stomped out of the ballroom, his heavy steps echoing.

Bitsy ran after him.

"Sore loser?" Gabrielle said.

It was Brooks's turn.

Please, Maddie thought, if there is a God, he will make the bottle land on me. She knew it was a ridiculous thing to pray for. Nonna LaRosa would call it sacrilege.

He spun the bottle fast and it seemed to make a thousand rotations before stopping.

The bottle's brown snout pointed at her.

Her.

Time slowed as he made his way around the outside of the circle. A breeze blew through one of the open windows and two candles snuffed out.

"How poetic," Penny said. Gabrielle snickered.

He dropped to his knees in front of her. The candlelight made the silhouette of his hair glow like he was on fire. He tucked his hands under her jawbone and she felt his pulse twitch in the wrist on her cheek. Quick gentle kisses settled into slow and deep sucking. Until then, sex, even just kissing, had felt like something being taken away, a draining, but now she filled. Her hands were on his chest, reaching around his neck, when she heard Penny's voice, joking, "Cool your jets, kids. Get a room already."

"Shit," Gabrielle said. "That was so hot, I creamed my shorts."

For once, Maddie was grateful for the distraction the girl's crassness provided.

But Brooks was staring at the back of the ballroom. Looking worried. Most of the boys were there in one big clump.

Brooks jogged past Maddie, mumbling, "I told my mom this was crazy. That it would never work."

Before she could ask him what *it* was, he was hurrying over to the entrance, shouting, "It's cool! It's cool. I invited them."

The pack of East boys—Spencer, Austin, Rolo, and Gerritt—parted. Enzo and Vinny strutted into the ballroom, two of their buddies behind them, and, finally, Carla, her beaded braids swinging *click-clack, click-clack*.

"Holy shit," Penny whispered.

Maddie wiped her mouth. Licked her lips. Had they seen her and Brooks kissing? That's all she needed. Her cousins telling her dad.

"That bitch!" Bitsy was yelling even as she ran across the ballroom floor.

"Cool it, pretty lady," Enzo said, smooth as ever, gripping Bitsy's arms when she tried to push past him, get to Carla.

Vinny and the two West boys chimed in, "Oooh," and John called, "Cat fight!"

Bitsy glared at Enzo, and Maddie saw there was more there, and it looked like sex.

"Whatever," Bitsy said, "Rico Suave."

Penny snorted behind Maddie.

"Carla," Enzo called.

The petite girl dressed in black head to toe, from Metallica tee to scuffed, steel-toe Doc Martens, stepped forward, arms crossed.

"I'm sorry."

"What? I can't hear you," Bitsy sang, rolling her head with extra sass.

There was fire in Carla's thickly lined eyes.

"I AM SORRY," she said, loud and silly, so everyone had to know she was really saying fuck you.

Enzo applauded. A slow clap that doubled with the echo.

"Okay then," he said. "Let's party."

He pulled a plastic baggie from his pocket and tossed it to Bitsy, who almost dropped it. It must've been a quarter of weed. Even from where Maddie stood, hiding behind Penny's wide body, she could see the fat buds furred with red hair. Bitsy opened the bag, stuck her perfect nose inside, and inhaled.

"Fuck yeah. They can stay."

Everyone laughed. Brooks jogged back to the stereo. The tunes restarted. Red Hot Chili Peppers urging them to "*give it away, give it away, give it away now*," repeating the lyric until it sounded to Maddie like half manifesto, half tongue twister.

She grabbed Penny's hand and pulled her friend toward her cousins.

"What? Wait," Penny whispered. "They're kind of scary."

"*Cugina!*" Vinny cried with open arms when he saw her, giving her a tight hug so she knew she'd smell like his musky Drakkar Noir cologne all night.

"Cuz," Enzo said, and kissed her once on each cheek. "You old enough to be out partying?" His face was dead serious before it cracked open in a smile.

"The question is," she teased, "how'd you guys get here? You know Brooks?"

"Oh, yeah," Vinny said, lighting a cigarette, taking a long pull, and exhaling with the cigarette still between his lips. "We know Brooks. Been doing some work for his mom. Like cleaning up some of the rooms in this joint." He held his arms out at his sides as if, Maddie thought, he were saying *Check this place out.* "She invited us. Leslie did. You think your buddies will have a problem with that?"

He peered over her head at the crowd of East kids gathered by the stereo. Lots of looks being passed back and forth.

"You stay cool, they'll stay cool," she said. Surprised at how well she was faking calm.

"What we should be asking," Enzo said, like he was interrogating her, "is how come ol' Brooks knows so much about you? He told us about your walk home the other night."

"Yeah," Vinny said. "Sounded like it was a *long* walk."

Her stomach flip-flopped. She thought of her father. His belt.

"Just kidding, cuz," Enzo said.

Vinny laughed so hard the cigarette fell out of his mouth. "You should've seen your face. So serious. What was it old Nonno said about you that one time?"

She sighed. "That I was too serious and had the face of a nun."

Her cousins laughed. "Yeah, that's it," Vinny said. "I miss the old guy."

Maddie didn't. Both her grandfathers had told her she wasn't good enough. Too somber. Too opinionated.

"Seriously," she said, making sure she whispered, "You guys know how my dad would flip if you told him anything, like, weird. Yeah? Even if you were kidding."

"We know you don't have nothing going with this guy," Enzo said, his arm, heavy with muscle, slung around her shoulders.

"And what if I did?" She was testing them. And trying to convince herself she wouldn't care if her dad beat her black and blue.

"He's all right," Vinny said.

"For a moolie," Enzo added.

They laughed. Slapped each other's backs. High-fived. Like it was a bit they'd rehearsed on their way over.

"What's a moolie?" Penny asked innocently.

All the West boys were laughing now, Carla too. Maddie was about to tell them to fuck off when the music changed. Brooks slipped in a few discs for the West kids. Metallica's "One" came on and her cousins and their two friends roared, charging into the center of the ballroom, whipping their heads around, knocking shoulders. Rolo, who was blitzed on ecstasy, catapulted into the whole lot. John joined in, and Ricky and Gerritt, and even Brooks, until all the boys were headbanging, sweat spraying, jerking their heads back and forth so hard that by the time the lyrics cut out and the guitar started pounding in time with the drums, like the *rat-a-tat-tat* of a machine gun, Maddie was scared they'd hurt themselves.

When the song ended, the floor under the pack of sweat-drenched boys was slick. First Rolo went down, then Vinny, and then one after another, the boys started falling on purpose. Like little kids on a Slip'n Slide in the sprinklers. Except, Maddie thought, this one was made of sweat and spilled beer and ciga-rette ash.

It was after midnight when Brooks took his place behind the turntables and the electronic beat pumped out of the speakers, filled the ballroom with a rhythm that felt more reliable than any-thing she'd ever known. The ballroom became a temple. Brooks's tables an altar. The steady throb—*pa-da-boom, pa-da-boom*—filled Maddie, and she danced. There was so much room. She stretched out her arms and whirled in a circle. She let her head loll side to side, her long hair whipping at her face. She arched her back so her shoulder blades touched and her chest opened. She imagined she was wearing a glittering diamond necklace, just as her old ballet teacher Ms. Posey had instructed.

This was when summer started. She was free. From the cat-erpillars and her mother's snoring, her father's slaps, even Dom's sad face. She stopped dancing only to take a hit off a joint pass-ing around. She wished she could stay, never go home. What was the point? No one cared where she was. Her mom was in another universe, high on her pills. Her dad, who knew where he was—either working at her uncle's garage or, if her hunch was right-on, screwing Rosemary Dutton, who waited tables at Sonny's Diner on the west side.

She felt Enzo's dark eyes watching. Who did he think he was? Her brother? Her father? She already had one of each, and they were plenty useless. Penny was making out with her cousins' silent friend on one of the beanbags in a dark corner of the ballroom. Gabrielle was in full rave mode after downing the rest of the mushrooms, even licking the inside of the plastic baggie. Maddie had watched her dance in front of the speakers, her breasts bouncing under a tight tee, and then she'd stomped over to a sulking Spencer and led him to the antique sofa where they were now sucking face. Maddie wanted to cheer, thank Gabrielle, forget everything that had happened with Spencer.

She wished she could crawl inside Brooks's head as he spun records. His eyes were trained on the spinning discs, his head bobbing as he mixed hip-hop and house, a little riff here and there of something surprising, all of it seamless so the beats matched like the two records were dancing arm in arm. A velvet voice broke apart a manic techno beat, slowing and smoothing out time as it pleaded *Cupid, draw back your bow*, and Brooks found her eyes and she knew she was the most sober person in that room and also the happiest.

Then Brooks's expression changed. Grew serious, maybe even annoyed, and she followed his eyes to the ballroom door. It was his mother standing under the archway, and the sight of the golden-headed woman, whom her grandmother had made her promise to watch, made Maddie take a step toward the door. But Vinny and Enzo were talking to her, their heads bowed so they could hear over the music. Her delicate arms were crossed over a baggy sweatshirt. Even in sweats, Maddie thought she looked elegant. When her lips stopped moving, the boys nodded and she shook each of their hands. Like they'd made a deal.

Maddie had to pull Penny away from the mute West boy—Paulie—when it was time to go.

"But he's my lover," Penny slurred.

"Okay," Maddie said trying to be patient. "You can hang with your lover another time."

Brooks helped her get Penny through the woods, although it was hard work. Maddie's ankles were torn up by prickers and mosquitos and they arrived on the lawn of White Eagle covered in caterpillars and spattered with black goo, but none of that mattered. Because she was with Brooks. She put Penny on the couch in the cottage and left a trash can nearby in case she had to barf. She hurried back to the front door. Finally, they would be alone.

He was gone.

A small square of paper rested on the welcome mat.

She unfolded it. It was his list of words. For her. He had nice handwriting. For a boy. Her boy.

Wildinger—a feeling so strong it makes you want to tear your hair out

Grateship—the symbiotic friendship between two people grateful for each other

17.

Veronica

She looked past the caterpillars slithering across the window and spotted Bob trudging across the wide sea of lawn. Champ loped at his side, Bob's hand absentmindedly stroking the dog's thick brown coat. It comforted her, knowing Bob wasn't alone. His binoculars bounced against his paunch and she tried to remember a younger version of him, all muscle and bone and a full head of hair. The dog tags Admiral Marshall had specially made for him tangled on his naked chest when they'd made love for the first time after a long business trip. Veronica had known right away he hadn't been faithful to her while away—there just wasn't enough desperation in the act. The knowledge had stung and she'd made fun of herself—*you naïve little twit*—for believing he'd have chosen solitude. For her.

He was up at the seawall almost every night since they had returned. There was a new crack in the foundation and he had commanded her to *get on the goddamn horn* and call the engineers. Order a ton of boulders to be shipped on a barge. Fortification. She had nodded and said, *Yes, Bob*, but hadn't called anyone, and knew she never would. There was no room on her to-do list.

She lit a cigarette and resisted the urge to scratch the phantom itch where her left breast had once been. She tried to imagine what he saw when he looked out over the sea. It was as if he was waiting. For something. Or someone. Gripping the cement with his feet, like he could will the crumbling seawall to remain solid, root it into the earth, brace it against the surge sucking at the foundation. It was just like him, she thought, to pick an unwinnable battle with the sea, the merciless ebb and flow that would remain long after the seawall crumbled, long after he, and she, were dead and gone. Most likely, she thought, he was dreaming of revenge. Like some mad sea captain at the water-whipped helm of his ship.

It would rain soon—dark storm clouds swarmed over the sea. What would happen to the caterpillars, she wondered, realizing they didn't repulse her as they did the rest of the islanders. Perhaps a plague was just what the island needed.

Common names: Asian gypsy moth (English), erdei gyapjaslepke (Hungarian), gubar (Romanian), gypsy moth (English), lagarta peluda (Spanish), limantria (Italian), løVstraesnonne (Danish), maimai-ga (Japanese), mniska vel'kohlava (Slovak), neparnyy shelkopryad (Russian), Schwammspinner (German), spongieuse (French)

—National Biological Information Infrastructure
& Invasive Species Specialist Group

18.

Jules

He was in the garden day and night. Watching over his trees. Brushing the bristled beasts off bark with his naked fingers.

He wasn't bonkers, which was what Leslie had called him that afternoon when he'd refused to come in and take a break. He was obsessed—he admitted it. But as his pops had said to him many times: what *was* a man without an obsession? Sure, his father's obsession had been listening to ball games on that valve radio—Dodgers games, even after they'd shattered the old man's heart, abandoning Brooklyn. Jules came home from school every day to his father twisting knobs, cussing up a storm. He worked construction and was laid off more days than not, and Jules had suspected his father preferred it that way, despite his mother's housekeeping job barely keeping them afloat. His pops had memorized players and stats like Dustin Hoffman in *Rain Man,* and there was no doubt baseball was as close to a life's passion as he ever got.

His father's voice in his head grew louder each night Jules spent in the garden. Just as the hum of the caterpillars' feeding swelled. His father's visits surprised him every time. That honeyed bass that could fill a room. He'd had the gift of a voice and had sung in the Calvary Baptist Church choir. When he sang "Oh to Be Kept by Jesus," women wept in the pews. A few had to be propped up by their neighbors to keep from swooning.

At first, Jules had kept his promise to Leslie and wore his heavy-duty work gloves as he plucked one caterpillar after another off the trees, but it was tough to grab those squirming suckers. He'd been doing it glove-free for a few days. So far, so good. No rash. He was beginning to think the stories he'd heard—first from

Dom Short for Dominic—about gypsy-moth larvae being poisonous, causing rashes on human skin (and even under the fur of animals) was an island legend, spun to keep little kids from getting lost in the woods.

He'd worked on the trees late that night, long after dusk, long after the forest's night music began, and was outside the kitchen door soaking his hands in a pail of cold water—maybe they *were* starting to sting a bit—when he heard Leslie's voice. He decided to surprise her and opened the screen door slowly, careful not to let it slam shut. He toed off his dirt-caked Carhartt boots and padded toward the ballroom. Brooks had been blasting music all night for his new friends. Jules wasn't thrilled about a gang of kids partying hard in what he wasn't even ready to call his home. But Leslie had persuaded him in that way only she could. A nibble at his ear. A silent promise of a fuck in the not-so-distant future. And she was right—Brooks needed to make friends. And the Castle was far enough from other houses that the music wouldn't carry. "But what if someone gets hurt?" he'd asked, and Leslie had called him a party pooper and he'd chased her, caught her, and their lips were together, their tongues twisting, and, well, that was that.

The music had died down and now there was that whining, pleading stuff the kids called *alternative,* and he heard girls giggling. Leslie was standing outside the arched entryway of the ballroom, talking to a few kids. Boys. She saw him and he knew something was wrong. Her smile was plastic, put on like a mask, and then one of the boys turned, saw Jules, lifted a hand and said, "Hello, sir."

It was the boy from the fair. The one Jules had been goddamn sure was wearing a gun. If he closed his eyes, he could still see the silver pistol in a holster slapping against the kid's black-denim-covered thigh.

"Hi, babe," Leslie said.

He gripped her arm, the bulky sweatshirt—his old Harvard rag—bunching under his fingers. The three boys, all dark-haired and wearing heavy-metal tees, just like at the fair, backed away, and one—not the gun-toter, another with a mullet and long side-

burns, called to Leslie, "Thanks, Mrs. Marshall. We'll be by tomorrow. At noon."

"See ya," said the gun-toter, and there was slime in his voice,
mocking.

"What the fuck, Leslie?" Jules was growling. Felt the vibration in his chest.

"Relax, baby," she began, smoothing the hair on his forearm
dusted with dirt.

"Do *not* tell me to relax. Don't you know who those kids are?
From the fair. The kid with the gun!"

"You are overreacting," she said. "Again. You wouldn't let
Brooks go out. So I brought the kids to him."

She was walking away, a hand raised without looking back.
A dismissal that made the pulse in his neck throb.

"You know, I'm not going to talk to you when you turn into
this . . . this . . ."

"What?" He jogged to catch up with her, stepped in front of
her as she entered the maze so her chin bumped his chest.

"Beast!" she yelled, droplets of her spittle hitting his cheek.

She skirted around him and was running. He knew he had to
keep up or he'd be lost in the maze. Why hadn't he memorized
the turns? He'd tried, but like everything he attempted on this
goddamn island, he'd failed, Leslie's code slipping through his
fingers.

"Leslie, stop!"

She whipped around each turn, and the tall maze walls, black
against the near-full-moon sky, seemed to throb. The tang of
pine stuck in his nose—the scent he had worshipped when they'd
first arrived now seemed noxious and he felt his throat close. He
was heaving when he reached the cottage lawn. Leslie was gone.
The cottage screen door thwacked shut.

He found her in the bedroom. She was crying. Her ice-blue
eyes shot with red.

"What is wrong with you?" she whispered, and he knew, if
Eva wasn't asleep, she'd be screaming. "You scared me, Jules. You
scared me."

"You should be scared of *them*"—he leaned over to catch his breath and then stood, pointing back toward the Castle—"of those boys."

"They're just kids, Jules. Poor kids. From the other side of the tracks. You remember what that means?" She was mocking him, her hands on her hips.

"Don't you talk to *me* about what it means to be poor, Mrs. *Marshall*," he spat. "Born with a silver fucking spoon up your ass."

She coughed up a laugh, more like a huff. *Don't you dare laugh too, Julius,* he heard his father say. But he knew it was ridiculous what he'd said and then Leslie was explaining.

"Those boys," she said, "their dad has cancer. And you think they're paying him disability? Hell no. They're claiming *preexisting condition.*"

He sat on the bed and the coils squeaked.

"Shit," he whispered.

"Yeah, total bullshit is what it is," Leslie said. "So I'm paying them ten bucks an hour to clean out the Castle. You cool with that?"

"Yeah," he said. "Whatever."

He was ashamed. What had gotten into him?

She stood in front of him, pressed her belly into the top of his bowed head. The belly that had carried their children—the ones who lived and the ones who died before they could be born.

"I'm sorry," he said.

"What was that?"

"I'm sorry."

"Wait," she said, "I can't hear you."

He grabbed her so they were rolling on the bed, the coils screeching.

He was still in his dirt-splattered work clothes, but who cared? He pulled her underwear down and the thin material ripped and this filled him with that hunger he lived for, like he hadn't eaten in months, like he'd die if he didn't fuck the woman he loved right there and then. The woman who could make him go from gut-shot rage to lust, just like that.

"Wait," she said, and rolled onto her stomach, arching her back so her ass lifted, inviting him. "I'm ovulating."

"So?" he said, his belt buckle jangling as he fumbled. "Let's make a baby."

Her face turned hard for a moment, and he thought he'd screwed it all up, but she said, "I want you to do me like this, baby," and he felt his dick jump.

She'd taught him these things—ways to have sex without having sex. She even had names for them, like "a pearl neck-lace," where she lay on her back, her breasts squeezed together, a perfect cushion for him to glide up and down until he came on her chest. He'd been embarrassed years ago when he'd realized it wasn't something she had made up, but something another guy must have taught her.

Now he placed himself snug in the warm cleft and she reached back and pushed her cheeks together while he slid back and forth, back and forth, one hand planted against her lower back, the other gripping the headboard so it rocked, bumping the wall, and he came while she giggled, whispering, "Shush, you'll wake the baby."

There was the sound of twigs cracking outside their bedroom window.

"What the?" He jumped off the bed, leaving a trail of semen from Leslie's back across the bedspread.

Something—no, a two-legged *someone*—ran into the forest toward the path that led to their neighbors' house.

"What was it?" she asked sleepily.

"Just a raccoon," he said.

A creepy little fucker of a raccoon, guessed Jules. Named Dom Short for Dominic.

19.

Leslie

She lost the second baby on a bright spring day while working in Our Garden. Concetta Monteleone had come by as she did every Tuesday afternoon, lugging her granny cart. On this day, she'd brought a fig tree, the roots wrapped in burlap. She'd grown it herself from a cutting her father had brought back from the motherland. *May the Madonna care for his soul*, she whispered, and kissed the crucifix hung around her neck.

The tree was not heavy. No more than the plants Leslie lugged and hoisted every day at the garden. Not wanting to bother Jules, and, also, wanting to show she could do the work. She was no prima donna.

She heave-hoed the little tree out of the cart, the sticky three-pronged leaves slapping her chin. She felt the twinge low in her belly. She let out an *Oh!* and Concetta's withered face twisted in concern. Like she knew the baby was doomed. In the way that old Italian grandmas, real-life white witches, know.

The bleeding started that night. Trickled down her thigh in the shower so it diluted pink. She was numb. She knew it was coming. The cramps had come in waves (the way the midwife had described labor) all evening. She could only eat half the home-made ice cream Jules had made for her cravings. She'd devoured bowl after bowl of his mint chocolate chip all through the first trimester.

She waited to tell Jules. Because then she'd have to tell him about the first baby. From college. The baby she hadn't wanted but whose loss had hurt so she had stayed in bed for three days. Until Sister Mary Bartholomew threatened to call her parents. Worse, she'd have to tell Jules that *his* baby, *their* baby, was dead. The baby they'd wanted so bad they'd spent three years trying, making lists of names, imagining his or her future (Astronaut? Artist? Accountant?) and how they'd decorate the "nursery"—the bedroom closet Jules would dismantle, tearing down the shelves to make a cozy space Leslie would paint marigold.

PART THREE

The Molting

Late June 1992

Larvae develop into adults by going through a series of progressive molts through which they increase in size. Instars are the stages between each molt. Male larvae go through five instars (females, through six) before entering the pupal stage.

When population numbers are dense, larvae feed continuously day and night until the foliage of the host tree is stripped. Then they crawl in search of new sources of food.

—"Gypsy Moth," *Forest Insect & Disease Leaflet 162*, US Department of Agriculture Forest Service, 1989

20.

The Colonel

He jogged through the woods, Champ lunging ahead and leaping on and off the trail leading to the Castle.

"Quiet, dummy. You'll give us away."

He hadn't wanted to bring the shepherd, but he'd been half-way through the woods when he'd heard Champ's collar jingling and the dog had bounded out from the trees. There wasn't time to turn back. He had to warn the island.

There'd also been no time to change, and he was wearing his Hawaiian robe over his pajamas, clutching the opening at his crotch closed with one hand.

His slippers came off a few times. Sticks and sharp pebbles sliced at the soft meat of his soles. He had to stop where the trail climbed a steep hill, and when he bent over to catch his breath, his stomach convulsed and the ice-cream cake he'd had after dinner splattered on the leaf-covered ground. Champ hopped over and licked at the mess.

He'd been on watch since sundown, glassing the horizon as he sat on the upper balcony of White Eagle, waiting for something, what he wasn't sure, but he had that feeling in his gut he remembered from many years ago, when he was just a kid pilot hungry for action. Before the accident had labeled him a god-damn cripple and he'd missed the war.

It was that woman's fault. That self-righteous blonde return-ing to the island. She'd rattled Veronica at the dinner party last month. He didn't know what she'd said, but his Nicky hadn't been the same since. It was like Nicky was on watch too, waiting for the Krauts to show up on their shores. Who did the Marshall girl think she was? Slinking back with her mulatto family so she—she!—could teach a lesson or two to the decorated veterans and devoted engineers who'd sacrificed their lives for Old Ironsides. For the country.

There was no room left for heroes these days. The young people filling the space between their ears with information sucked up from TV and their music discs, turning that shit into opinions and *feelings* they worshipped like they were the priests of their own cockamamie religion.

They'd survived that peanut farmer's son and his cowardice. What a nightmare that had been—a naval officer turned namby-pamby in the White House. Admiral Marshall had thrown a lavish party the night Reagan was elected and Carter booted—Grudder's naval production plants safe after fears of closure had loomed over the factory for four long years, turning many a Grudder man's hair silver, Bob's included.

He could still taste the brine of the oysters served in the Castle ballroom to celebrate Carter's return to his peanut farm. Washed down with glass after glass of Veuve Clicquot. Nicky had looked like heaven in a silk gown as red as spilled blood, and Bob had wanted her that night, watched her glide across the Castle ballroom, thought about taking her into the admiral's study and having her right then and there. His cock had been hard with victory. The White House reclaimed. Reagan spouting insults at the Soviet Union like a petulant schoolboy, and the Grudder boys at the party were giddy, placing bets on how long it would be until that actor with the big mouth started World War III.

The admiral had brought Bob up to the Castle's bell tower, the highest point on the island, and as they looked out over the glittering sea, Bob felt it his duty to watch over the entire world. The admiral snapped open his lucky lighter and the flame rose to meet their cigars. A storm had been threatening all day and the clouds over the water hung low and heavy. Thunder made the sky tremble, reminding Bob of the F-14 engines as they prepared for takeoff, and he closed his eyes for a moment, imagining the rows of Tomcats preparing to fly the nest—he thought of them as *his* babies even if he was just VP—destined to intercept Libyan jets over Syria, protect carriers out at sea, dominate dogfights over the Gulf of Sidra. They were his life's work, his beauties.

He had known the glory days were close again—he'd smelled it like rain in the air. Only a matter of time, before island boys, East and West, started wearing their jean jackets sporting the Tomcat badge—a cocky cartoon cat and the motto "Anytime, Baby"—passed on by the boy's father or grandfather, who, just like the famous Maverick of *Top Gun*, had tested the fighter's legendary swing-wing action.

Then, as the thick cigar smoke rose into his eyes, he'd remembered Grudder's debt. How the company had almost folded when the navy had refused to pay its bill—Admiral Marshall locking himself in his office overlooking Plant 2 for days, raging about the "crooks at the Pentagon," taking out full-page ads in the *Times* and *The Washington Post*, trying to shame the government into paying, when everyone, even Bob, knew it only made Grudder look like a sore loser. If it hadn't been for the Defense Department paying off the bill, well, who knew if they'd be standing there watching the sheets of rain approach from miles away.

A moment alone with the admiral was rare, and so he tried, again, to urge the admiral to expand, even if it meant merging.

"Look at Nordrom and McDougal busting into the commercial airplane biz, boss," he pleaded with the old man. "That's some nice security."

The admiral only slapped him on the back and said, "Bobby-o, I like your ambition. But we're war-makers, not cruise-ship directors. Let the others make planes with cushioned seats and Muzak piped overhead."

He stopped himself from reminding the admiral what a shitty year it had been. What with Grudder barely surviving a hostile takeover from that slimy Texas conglomerate—who knew who the admiral had paid off in the Court of Appeals to make that fiasco blow away. It had been a close shave.

He tried one more time: "Sir, what about a merger with someone we trust? That way, when a bunch of goons come round threatening to take over, we've got some choices."

The admiral sighed. Bob had heard that sigh before. Last year, when what he'd thought had been a bright idea, breaking into city-bus manufacturing, had produced a bunch of buses with cracked undercarriages and they'd had to pull the whole damn project. Another close shave the admiral had only just forgiven Bob for.

"If survival means marriage," the admiral said, his eyes sweeping the water like he was searching, "with McDougal or Nordrom, or Dick or Harry, hell, I'd rather go down with the ship."

"We could talk to NASA again. . . ."

The admiral interrupted him, "You see that spot over there? Between the dunes?" He pointed to the shore, a streak of moonlit silver where the water met sand. "That's where the spies landed. Dirty Germans."

"Pastorius? Here?" In his excitement, and after all that Champagne, Bob leaned so far over the balcony he almost fell. The admiral grabbed the collar of his tuxedo jacket and pulled him back. Like a mother cat would a kitten, he would think again and again over the years.

"Watch it, Colonel. I can't have my best engineer, *and* my heir apparent, falling to his death."

And with that, the Colonel was born. In a moment, Bob rose through the ranks. Within the boundaries of Avalon Island, at least.

"They came on shore in the middle of the night," the admiral said. "Dressed like Americans but with one piece of their Kraut uniform. A hat. A scarf. Those clever bastards."

"But why? Wouldn't that give them away?" he asked.

"Because they were cowards! They knew if they got caught wearing their uniform, we couldn't have shot 'em dead. Or, better, tortured them. Our hands were tied by those Geneva laws."

In the light of the moon, he saw the old man's eyes were wet.

"What kind of world are we living in, Bobby? Where the enemy has laws to protect him?"

He decided to try one last time. If there were ever a time, it was this, now, the normally stoic admiral moved to feeling. Vulnerable, he hoped.

"Sir, it *is* a new world. The rules have changed." He took a steadying breath. "Which is why I think we need to reconsider—"

The admiral squeezed his shoulder and he felt the bones crunch.

"Bobby-o, don't fret. We thought we were doomed after the Big One. But then Korea happened. And after that, Nam. This country won't stop needing us. There'll always be another war. Another reason to make killing machines. You can count on it. In fact"—he looked out over the sea—"it's the one goddamn thing we *can* count on."

The Castle gate had been left open. A sign from the admiral, he thought as he launched himself up the spiraling stairs leading to the bell tower, his old knees creaking with every step. The sound of Champ running ahead, the dog's toenails clicking on the stone steps, echoing in the narrow stairwell, urged him on.

There was no stopping now. If he, the island's watchman, didn't warn them, who would?

21.

Jules

He had bought six five-foot-tall, twin-head, thousand-watt tripod work lights at Home Depot. Each cost one hundred dollars, but if what Leslie said was true—that they were swimming in her parents' money—what the hell.

As he placed each lamp around the garden perimeter, connecting them with hundred-foot-long extension cords, he surprised himself by wishing his father were there with him. He'd show Pops the fruit trees, their branches heavy with apple and cherry blossoms. The rows of roses fit for a queen's bouquet. He'd cut the best blooms and wrap the stems in damp paper towel and a layer of aluminum foil. He'd slice off the thorns so his mother didn't stick herself.

But they were both dead. He could only show them his garden if he laid the blooms at their graves.

His father had been visiting more often. Like Pops's ghost had hatched with the caterpillar eggs, and as the trees grew naked, the verdant canopy thinned, his father was there, in the garden, more and more, witness to the battle of Jules versus the caterpillars.

He needed some advice. About the caterpillars, hell yeah. But there were his old profs from Harvard he could call about that. Tonight, he wanted to talk to his father about Leslie. He'd been worrying over her since the dinner party. The change he'd seen in her after just a few weeks on the island. At the party, she'd seemed like one pretty white woman in a group of many, chitchatting, air-kissing, throwing her head back and letting loose a stage-worthy laugh. He'd hardly been able to distinguish her from the rest.

Son, don't you know people don't change? His father's voice was back. *You would've known if you'd listened. Just one goddamn time. Instead of fighting me. Always fighting me.*

"Pops." Jules felt he should apologize. Now that his father was dead and gone, he wished he'd let him win a few battles. He could've faked it. Just like he'd been doing on Avalon for the past two months. "She's the mother of my kids."

That girl, his father said, and Jules could hear his head shaking, *she could talk a pig into eating its own tail.*

He was too tired to argue. He had one more extension cord to attach before he could plug in the contraption. It was starting to look like a madman's experiment. Julius Frankenstein.

And you know, his father went on, *you can't trust a person*—a woman—*who changes as fast as that girl did. One day, white. The next, trying to pass like she was born and raised in the 'hood.*

"Hold on," Jules thought, but it felt like he was talking aloud.

She's spending a lot of time with those white boys, his father said, and Jules could see his furry brows lifting. Judging.

"She's doing her social-worker thing," Jules said. "She's got a big heart. Just like Mama."

He tried to play it cool, but Pops was right. She was with those boys—the heavy-metal kids with the gel-slicked hair and the smirks—most of every day now. Cleaning out the Castle, she claimed. But what if?

What if, his mama used to say, *Grandma had balls; she'd be Grandpa.* He smiled.

Leslie had been unlike any woman he'd met, and definitely different from all the white girls he'd known, and there had been many interested in the sole black man at Harvard Graduate School of Design. Bored girls he'd met at protests and clandestine meetings of the Students for a Democratic Society. Girls looking for an "experience," Jules used to joke with his boys back home when he visited on holidays. Girls looking to piss off their bigoted daddies, and prove they were different, better maybe, than their friends. Those girls talked the big talk but most preferred to "stay in," which turned into stay in bed and fuck all night, and that was fine for Jules back then. The sex trumped the nagging awareness that threatened to cloud his youthful rose-colored glasses—they didn't want to be seen with him. After a few dates spent smoking weed and screwing in his one-room apartment overlooking Harvard Square, they'd stop returning his calls, realizing, he'd guessed, how very *not* different they were.

Not Leslie Day. She wanted to be looked at. With him. She had wanted him to *see* her that snowy night in '68 at the Golden Pig Chinese restaurant/bar/comedy club in Cambridge, where so many warm, turtleneck-clad bodies had gone after an SDS meeting planning a sit-in at University Hall in protest of Vietnam. To share dragon cocktails served in giant bowls with four or five straws as the windows fogged up with all that body heat, hiding the blizzard outside. They were young and giddy for the future and couldn't know that, in just a few months, Dr. King would be shot down on his motel balcony in Memphis.

He'd spent years averting his gaze when white women walked by on the street. If they were his classmates, he might strike up a cordial conversation, nothing too intimate—unless, of course, they were one of those girls looking for an *experience*. All black men, he'd learned young, seemed equally dangerous in the eyes of a white woman. The woman who would become *his* Leslie had walked across the Golden Pig that snowy night, and, without a word, wrapped her lips around his dragon bowl straw, her eyes on his like she was scared he'd look away.

He connected the extension cord to the last lamp tripod, and as he pulled the long cord toward the steps leading up to the patio, careful not to whack the newly bloomed mophead hydrangeas, he felt excited. What would his garden look like illuminated in the darkest hours of night? He could work out there all night if it came to it, picking the caterpillars off the leaves of the surrounding trees. The trees were everything. If he couldn't save them, he was worth nothing. It had been the trees, in Prospect Park and Central Park and the Bronx Botanical Gardens that had first helped him believe that art began in nature.

He sucked in a deep, steadying breath, his swollen finger on the switch connecting the lamps. The garden was awash in light. As if illuminated from above by a massive beam. He had to squint to see. It wasn't what he'd expected. In the artificial blaze, the leaves of the lilac trees and dogwood looked sickly. Unnatural. Alien. The caterpillars stood out like tiny black wounds. Hundreds of punctures. The enormity of the trauma socked him hard. His poor trees.

He pulled the plug and was about to make his way back to the cottage, already singing the code softly—*Left, right, right, left*—when the deafening sound came from above. He bent his knees, shielded his head with his arms, thinking it must be an airplane falling from the sky, the end of the world, an asteroid racing toward earth, and then he knew it was the bell in the tower. In his tower. *BONG. BONG. BONG.* The ground shook under his feet and he feared it was enough to make his damaged trees give up their last bit of life.

He took the stone steps two at a time. *BONG. BONG.* His teeth rattled.

Halfway up, the bell, mercifully, stopped.

Coming out of the stairwell and into the star-pocked sky, he had a moment of vertigo. It was his first time in the tower at night and the sea and sky seemed like one vast canvas, as if he had floated up into the Milky Way.

He saw him. A hunched figure standing at the lip of the wall, leaning over the edge.

"Stop!" Jules shouted. He leapt forward, grabbed the thing's jacket, and yanked it to the ground.

It was an old man. Wearing a ridiculous jacket . . . no, a robe. In a gaudy Hawaiian print—orange hibiscus blooming on turquoise. He almost laughed aloud when he recognized the old man from the dessert party. The Colonel. Veronica's Colonel, and Dom's.

"We're in the belly of the whale," the old man whispered, clutching at the collar of Jules's dirt-streaked tee. "It's swallowed us whole."

"You're okay," Jules said, catching his breath, trying to slow his heart—not sure if he was reassuring the old man or himself.

"Where is the admiral?"

"Um, I don't know any admirals," Jules said. "Can I help you down the stairs? Take you back home?"

Jules hooked his hands under the old man's flabby arms.

"Let's stand up now, sir. It's cold up here. We'll go downstairs," Jules spoke as if it were little Eva sitting there, her arms crossed midtantrum. "I'll make us some coffee."

"I'm not here for a goddamn tea party, son. Admiral Marshall! Wake him immediately."

Jesus, the man was out of his mind, and here Jules was, once again, alone. He considered shouting over the wall for Leslie, but she was asleep in the cottage and there was no way she'd hear him, and the last thing he wanted to do was lean over the edge. Who knew—this crazy old goat might try to push him.

"The admiral . . ." Jules began, ready to state the obvious, that Leslie's father was dead, had been dead for more than ten years, but he decided to play along, guessing that would be a more efficient way to calm this guy down, get him back downstairs, so he could figure out how to get him home. "I'll see if I can wake the admiral, okay? But first, we need to get you down the stairs."

"I can't!" the old man cried. "Please," he held his hands out, palms up. "Don't make me leave the watch. The Germans will be here any minute. I promised him I'd keep watch."

"Promised who?" Jules said.

He heard the slow shuffling of steps coming up the stairs and almost groaned with relief. Leslie was coming to his rescue, at last.

"The admiral, you fool!"

The man had shifted from whimpering, cowering child into bullheaded raging adult.

"Who the hell *are* you anyway?" he bellowed. "Are you his man?"

"Man?" Jules took a step toward the dimly lit stairway. What was taking Leslie so goddamned long?

"His man. His servant." The old man shook his head.

"Now, *you* listen to me," Jules said, straightening to his full height, his hands fisted at his sides. "I'm trying to be civil. But you are trespassing on my property."

"Bob?" A soft, creaking voice came from the stairwell.

It was Veronica. She wore what looked like a pink bathrobe, dotted here and there with crawling caterpillars. Her pink-slippered feet were stained black.

"Nicky!" the old man cried, reaching for her. "Wake Admiral Marshall. Tell him to call Bobby Kennedy and Admiral McCain. And"—he was wheezing and Jules feared he was having a heart attack—"Frank. We need Frank over at Plant 2. Tell the admiral to call Jack and say—you listening, Nicky? Say the watch is over. He'll know what I mean. Tell him the Krauts are here. But wait . . ." He paused, his fingers picking at his bottom lip. Like a scared child, Jules thought. The old man's voice dropped to a whisper: "We don't know who could be listening in. Tell him, Pastorius. Operation Pastorius. You want me to spell it for you? P-A- . . ."

The old woman sat down next to her husband. Jules wondered if he should run to get Leslie now, bring up some blankets. The stone floor under his feet was chilled. The sea wind fierce. They could catch pneumonia. Veronica was trying to calm the man down, shushing him the way Leslie did Eva after the little girl had cried so hard and long she could only hiccup and gasp for breath.

"Nicky!" the man cried. "Why aren't you writing this down? P-A-S-"

"Yes, sweetheart," she said tenderly, nodding slowly as she spelled out the rest, "T-O-R-I-U-S. I know. But that was a long time ago. It's 1992, Bob . . . 1992."

Jules knew only that the word was Latin. But not the Latin he'd studied his whole adult life. That was a peaceful Latin. The genus and species and kingdoms of plants.

"Ma'am?"

"Veronica," she said, and smiled at him. He could see how beautiful she must have been once. "I'm so very sorry for this. He hasn't been himself."

"What can I do to help?"

The old man wept. His head cradled in the bony nook between the woman's collarbone and chin. He shuddered as she stroked his back over his thin pajama shirt. "Shhh," the woman cooed, "shhh," and with her hands naked of all those jeweled rings, her thin white hair mussed, her face makeup-free, Jules was transported into a fairy tale. Where on earth was he? At the top of a castle tower by the shining silver sea with a fallen king and queen. As if he'd been dropped into one of the tragedies penned by old Willy, from whom Jules's mother had borrowed his name.

"I'd be so grateful," the old woman said, "if you could help us down the stairs, Julius."

He took off his robe—the burgundy chenille Brooks had given him for Father's Day last year, bought with the boy's own money earned selling kitchen-knife sets door to door. Jules and the old lady wrapped the man who called himself the Colonel. They walked side by side down the first few steps, into the warm light of the spiraling stairway, but Jules's robe was a foot too long and snagged under the old man's feet.

"I'm going to carry him," Jules said, and Veronica nodded yes, her eyes closing for a moment in what Jules knew was sad acceptance.

He lifted the man, now quiet, unblinking, lost. Jules feared he may have had a stroke. He was as light as Leslie had been that first visit to the Castle, when she and Jules had run through the maze, laughing all the way to the secret garden, where Jules had lifted her into his arms and they'd been as happy as an old-fashioned bride and groom on their wedding day.

22.

Dom

Dom was crouched on his stomach in the ferns, the fronds tickling his nose. He'd brought a Whatchamacallit bar the Colonel had given him last week, but it was tucked deep in the pocket of his cargo pants and he was worried the crackling wrapper might give his position away.

As soon as he'd heard the unmistakable *bong, bong, bong* of a mighty bell—not the sound of a bell through a loudspeaker like the effect on his Casio keyboard, but a *real* bell—he knew it had to be the Castle. He'd dressed so quickly in his stealth outfit that he'd forgotten to put on underwear and he could feel his balls chafing in the canvas pants. He'd worn black head to toe—winter turtleneck, long pants, rolling up his black dress socks over the pants cuffs, and he'd borrowed Maddie's Doc Martens, hoping he didn't get them scuffed 'cause they were kind of brand-new. He was already sweating, his hair a damp, itching mess under his black winter ski mask/hat. But it was worth it. For the camouflage and to keep the creepy-crawly caterpillars off his skin.

What they said about those things being poisonous was true. The Colonel had been rubbing lotion into Champ's fur all week after taking him to the vet for a wicked rash. Now Champ had to be tied up when he was outside, poor boy.

Dom missed the summer woods of last year. Laying in the cool, damp pachysandra, the only thing crawling over him an ant, a ladybug, a daddy longlegs. This summer sucked. There was nothing to do. No one to hang out with. He had to entertain himself with spying on the new neighbors. And what he saw the other night, outside Mr. and Mrs. Marshall's bedroom window . . . well, he wasn't sure if it could be called entertainment but it was one hell of a show. And it wasn't really spying, he told himself. He'd been given a mission to keep his eye on these so-called neighbors, by not one but two VIPs of Avalon Island, the Colonel and Veronica.

Dom had watched the man put his thing in his wife. From behind, so the man's thick butt muscles had flexed as he pumped away. Dom had heard from Patrick Hanover that people did it like that—the man behind the woman—so they wouldn't make a baby. Dom had wanted to look away, knew it was just as dirty as the stories he thought up at night in his own bed, but he couldn't. It was part of his mission. He didn't want to give the Colonel a false report.

Now, from where he lay, approximately sixty feet from the ballroom windows, the stained glass glowing like in St. John's church, he had a decent view of what the Marshalls were up to tonight. The door leading from the ballroom to the stone patio was propped open, and if he looked through the heavy military binoculars he'd found in the Colonel's closet, he could just make out the figures sitting on something. A sofa? He turned the knobs on the specs slowly until one was in focus, and then the other. He almost dropped them in the sprays of fern.

The Colonel was curled up on the sofa. His hands tucked under his chin like a little kid all cozied up in his bed on Christmas Eve. Those hands that were never still, that were always reaching out and grabbing Dom's arm tight around the biceps to make sure Dom was listening. Flying up to the sky to ask God to help him make some point. Jabbing in Dom's face so Dom knew he was in trouble because *you are on my list, buddy*, so you better get in shape. *Shape up or ship out, pal.* And poking, they were always poking into Dom's chest, harder and harder, until Dom had to take a step back, surrender, and let the Colonel know he was in charge.

But here he was, the Colonel sleeping like a baby. His head in a woman's lap. Dom had to refocus the binoculars and there it was, clearer, clearer. It was Veronica. A smile on her face as she talked to *him*. Mr. Marshall.

He had to find Maddie. Tell her the Colonel had finally gone bananas, just as the black man had guessed, mocking Dom that first humiliating meeting the day Dom had painted his face with clay. *Your granddad got all his marbles?* And Veronica, well, what if she was fraternizing with the enemy? The very ones she'd warned Dom about when she'd given him his mission. *There are people who are out to get your grandfather.*

Maddie might be in that castle right now, Dom thought. Doing *it* with Brooks. Maybe they were a whole family of sex addicts, and who could Dom trust now? Not his mom all doped up in la-la land. Not his dad. He knew what his dad would say. *Use your brain, Dom! Is Dom short for Dummy?*

He should've listened better when the Colonel had given him his orders. Stupid, stupid, stupid, he told himself. He'd been so nervous and excited, his hands shaking with the weight of the gun, and he hadn't focused on the Colonel's words. Something about witches and wolves in the woods, and some guy named Slick Willie, and a wall that had come tumbling down. You should've written them down, Dom. Dumb Dom. Because, now, the two missions—the Colonel's and Veronica's—were all mixed up in his head and how was he going to save the Colonel, the island, the country, when he couldn't even remember the instructions?

After molting to the fourth stage, larval behavior changes dramatically. Larvae feed during the night, then descend the trees at dawn in search of protective locations where they rest for the remainder of the day.

At dusk they climb the trees again to feed.

—"The Homeowner and the Gypsy Moth: Guidelines for Control," United States Department of Agriculture, *Home and Garden Bulletin*, No. 227 (1979)

23.

Maddie

She had dubbed the ballroom "Neverland." When the kids left the Castle every morning near dawn, knowing it was just a matter of hours until they were back, they said, "See you back in Neverland." The name—*her* name—stuck. It was, for Maddie, a land between lands. Between childhood and whatever came next. A land between consciousness and coma, or, as Vinny liked to say, *fucked up into oblivion!* which sounded right to Maddie, because it was like they climbed through a secret door into another world—far from the caterpillars, their parents, the shitty things that had happened to them, and, maybe, she hoped, the even shittier things that *would* happen.

It was the twenty-first of June and Bitsy announced a Summer Solstice party. The girls were to be nymphs, sprites, and fairies, so Maddie wore her middle-school graduation dress—long white silk meant to look wrinkled. She bobby-pinned two tiger lily blooms into her hair and dug through her mom's makeup bag for lipstick. Revlon's Toast of New York—a perfect brown-red she knew Bitsy would approve of.

She waited until her dad left the cottage for her uncle's garage (or so he said) before painting her lips in the bathroom.

She puckered. Pouted. Parted her lips and leaned forward so her little bit of cleavage was visible, squeezing her elbows to double it. She looked like a woman in a painting. Like a woman going to a Summer Solstice ball at a castle. Dating the guy who lived in that castle. Well, really, he lived in the cottage next door to the castle, and she wasn't sure if they were officially going together, but she knew she liked him.

As Penny had said, and she was the only one who knew, "You like him a lot, Mads. *A lot* a lot."

She left her sneakers outside the ballroom, and the hem of her dress kissed her naked toes. She stood in the archway. The ballroom was flooded with chemical light. She saw herself in one of the gold-framed mirrors. Her white dress lit an alien blue by the black light. A demigoddess meant to haunt the woods. She wanted Brooks to see her.

Neverland was a home away from home for her and the kids. Who could blame them when the island was crawling with caterpillars, when their parents and grandparents, and every islander over the age of eighteen, it seemed, were obsessed with the graffiti that turned up every few days or so, in black paint and now a new vibrant blood-red. GRUDDER KILLS. GRUDDER IS CANCER. Across the automatic doors at the Stop & Shop. Down the walkways of the post office and the public library, and, in a bold move that rattled even the oldest war-hardened vets, sprayed across the front door of the VFW on Main Street.

At least once a week, the memorial got tagged in Town Square—Bitsy's "Needle Dick." The Grudder janitorial team showed up and powerwashed the tall gray stone spotless. The East Avalon police station had all ten officers on back-to-back duty and the vandals were, Maddie had heard the Colonel say, "making them look like goddamned fools!" It was impossible to avoid listening in on the islanders' worried talk. *Why is this happening?* In line for cones at Baskin-Robbins and at the box office to see *Batman Returns*. As if, she thought, they were asking *Why us? Why me?*

How could they be so clueless, when she, all the kids, knew people from east to west were filling the oncology wards at St. Isaac's Hospital on the mainland? Rows of them, Penny and Maddie's uncle Carmine included, sitting side by side with chemo tubes stuck in their arms. The supermarket sold out of bottled water daily. There was something on the island making people sick. Even back in grade school, she and Dom had flicked lit matches at the oil slicks floating on Lake Makamah. The water lit with a *swoosh,* the flame blue-hot and unwavering even in the sea breeze.

So they escaped to Neverland each night. They played kids'

games. Tag; Red Light, Green Light; Mother May I?; and
Chicken—the girls on the strongest boys' shoulders, swatting
at one another until someone screamed *Uncle!* Every night—
from dusk to near dawn—they danced, drank, smoked, swallowed E, and laid paper tabs of acid in the shape of suns on
their tongues; they made out and smoked and danced even
more as Brooks spun record after record, matching beats so
perfectly Maddie couldn't tell where one record ended and the
next began.

They made the ballroom their home. East *and* West kids. Gerritt and his boys were now pals with her cousins, and Bitsy quit
threatening to claw Carla's eyes out. Enzo and Vinny turned into
valuable members of their community, scoring enough ecstasy to
keep the kids rolling all summer. With Ricky's supply of kind
bud, the acid Gabrielle got from an ex off at college upstate, John
Anderson's fake ID bringing in cases of beer, and Brooks DJing,
the ballroom turned into their own private rave.

Everyone had donated something for what Bitsy named *the
renovation.* Which made it sound, Maddie thought, just how it
felt—a revolution. Vanessa, two neon inflatable chairs snatched
from her parents' pool deck. Penny dragged in a dusty shag carpet she'd found in the shed behind her dad's golf clubs. Rolo's
Grateful Dead tapestries hung behind the turntables and when
the black light switched on (the treasured glass tube had come
from Ricky's pool cabana, a.k.a., "the drug den"), the smiling
kerchief-wearing Deadhead bears danced amid psychedelic swirls.
There was a tent Bitsy dubbed the "make-out room," lit by
two tall halogen lamps saved from the garbage dump, and Maddie contributed velvet sofa pillows she'd found in White Eagle's
garage, and a soft chenille bedspread with a pom-pom hem they
stretched out on the floor, so a stoned Maddie felt like Hera on
Mount Olympus lounging on a tiger pelt in front of an ever-
burning hearth. Plus three lava lamps, two round rattan chairs,
a pile of faded quilts, and enough pipes, bowls, and bongs for a
hundred ravers, including a water bong Ricky had made from a
plastic office cooler. Even Vinny and Enzo pitched in—sacks of
stolen coconuts slung over their shoulders like Santa Claus (Vinny

worked part-time as a bag boy at Stop & Shop). They used somebody's dad's machete to crack open the furred fruit, pieces scattering across the ballroom floor, and drank straight from the
shell so milk dribbled down their chins. After all the meat was
eaten, Vinny scooped the shells clean with his bowie knife and
they became ashtrays.

"Mads!" Penny crushed her in a hug. She had a joint clamped
between her teeth and it fit with her gypsy costume. Puffy para-
chute pants and big gold hoops on loan from Carla. The costume
had been Maddie's idea. A silk paisley scarf (borrowed from
Mrs. Whittemore) kept Penny's new blond wig in place. Carla
had taught Penny how to draw a cat eye with eyeliner and two
pieces of Scotch tape, and Maddie thought she looked pretty in
an *I Dream of Jeannie* kind of way.

In the cold blue light, she saw how thin Penny had grown, her
cheekbones like steep hills. Her teeth a ghostly blue. She thought
of asking how she felt but knew that would just piss Penny off.
She'd made it clear she wanted to be treated like everyone else,
like she wasn't sick.

Brooks was behind the turntables, weaving a slippery electronic pulse into a thumping house beat that tickled deep in
Maddie's chest, urged her to rush to the dance floor. She made
her way to Brooks, who saw her and nodded, a hand pressing his
headphones close, the other sliding the cross-fader as he looped
one record into the next. She passed a trashed Bitsy lying on the
floor, rocking back and forth in one of her mom's strapless ivory
gowns. She was rolling on E, Maddie could tell from her clenched
jaw. A choker of diamonds winked on Bitsy's neck and Maddie
guessed she'd hacked into Captain and Mrs. Smith's house safe
to borrow it.

The East boys had wussed out and worn their usual—khaki
shorts and rugby tees, except for Rolo who had stuffed his thick
waist into a pleated cummerbund that looked decades old. A tall
felt purple-and-white striped Cat in the Hat topper he'd bought
at a Dead show covered his long greasy hair.

Enzo had called Maddie the night before, adorably nervous
about what he should or shouldn't wear. "Think Mad Max meets
the Lost Boys," she suggested, and now she saw that he, Vinny,

and their two buddies, Paulie and Tim, had gone all out in tight jeans and muscle tanks, topped by leather jackets and vests, their hair gelled in spikes or slicked back. Black on black.

"Damn, that's hot," Gabrielle said as she strutted past, then pulled Vinny away by his leather bolo tie toward some dark corner where they were sure to get hot and heavy.

Maddie had seen plenty of fooling around that month—kids partnering off in the dimly lit ballroom or slipping into a car for a clambake, smoking a joint with the windows shut so the car filled with thick, weed-sweet smoke. Making out on E, she'd learned, from watching Bitsy and Gerritt, Gabrielle and Tim, Vanessa and Enzo (the combos changed every night it seemed), was more than *making out*. She understood why they called it ecstasy, the lovers' faces twisting in anguish one minute; euphoria the next. They sniffed and licked each other, ran fingertips up and down each other's arms, backs, necks, thighs. Like that game they'd all played as kids. Round and Round the Garden, fingers stroking circles into a kid's palm, walking up to the elbow, the shoulder, the armpit. But no game she'd played as a child looked as delicious as the ones played in the ballroom. She wanted to feel that. With Brooks. But she was too nervous to do anything more than smoke pot, despite the way both Penny and Bitsy were always pushing her, calling her a prude.

Enzo was in the middle of the dance floor, the diamond of blondwood in the center of the ballroom. Every night, her cousin danced until his dark hair was sleek with sweat. Enzo danced like he *was* the music, shifting moves as seamlessly as Brooks shifted records. He spun on his back and then hopped up to stand, the motion graceful and liquid so he reminded her of a ballet dancer. He was an acrobat too, and most nights, the kids cheered as he threw back handsprings stretching from one corner of the ballroom to the next. Gerritt called him Ninja and it stuck.

She caught Enzo's eye now and gave him a thumbs-up before he did some footwork so fast it seemed to blur. Rolo was impressed enough to take a break from his Deadhead jig to howl at the gold-trimmed ceiling. Vinny and Enzo were at the Castle day and night—days working for Leslie Marshall doing odd jobs, like cleaning out the dusty rooms so Brooks's family

could move in. Her cousins had a lot to hide from that summer—
a sick Uncle Carmine meant an angry Uncle Carmine, and she
knew he was home most days instead of at the garage, too weak
from the chemo to work on cars. And Aunt Mariana had a hot
temper she expressed with a wooden spoon.

She watched Brooks's long fingers glide the cross-fader left to
right on the turntables. She had found a pack of glow-in-the-dark
star decals in the back of her closet and used Krazy Glue to stick
them to the edge of the table. With the Stop sign Spencer and
Austin had liberated from the entrance of East High nailed to
the wall behind Brooks's head—stars and sign lit a spectral
blue—it was like looking up at an altar, Brooks their priest. Ce-
lestial. That was how the music he spun made her feel, and she
knew she wasn't alone. All the kids, even shy Austin, spent half
the night dancing, until the stained-glass windows fogged with
the heat of their sweat.

She hadn't known music like that existed. It wasn't like the
pop music she listened to on the radio—songs with a tune and
lyrics so you had to listen and think hard to decode the message.
Brooks's music was about the beat and nothing else. Like the
sounds Maddie tapped her foot to without thinking—the steady
clunk-clunk of the clothes dryer, the even *pachum-pachump* of
a car's tire skimming the grooves in the highway on a road trip,
and the unmistakable sound of the caterpillars feeding, *ca-cack,
ca-cack*. The beat was as necessary as her heartbeat—*boom
badam bap, boom badam bap*—and the rhythm melted into the
air she breathed in and out, the damp heat her arms and legs
sliced through, and she learned a vital skill. How to turn her
brain off and let her body lead. She danced and danced. Sweat
sprayed from the ends of her hair. The thin silk stuck to her back
and chest and belly and when she felt Brooks's eyes on her, she
felt a rush more potent and altering than any drug she'd tasted
or smoked or snorted. In Neverland, entranced by Brooks's beats,
she was transformed. Like a lucky (or cursed) mortal in Dom's
myths.

Her pulse matching the kicking groove of a new record, she
slipped the piece of paper from her pack of Parliaments. She'd
folded it into a small square, worried if Enzo spotted her pass-

ing it to Brooks, he'd tell her dad. She dropped it on the table next to the turntables and Brooks slipped it into his palm, without looking up from the records, without skipping a beat.

She had scribbled "meet me in the garden in 10" (signing it with a heart) on the folded paper, and was making her way to the ballroom entrance when she saw Bitsy and Penny staring up at the balcony.

Bitsy said, "Yo, someone's going to die forever young tonight."

"Boys are stupid," Penny slurred.

The guys had found a coil of thick boat rope washed up on the beach, and had spent three nights trying to lasso the wrought-iron chandelier. Three nights filled with the boys' tantrums each time they missed hooking the chandelier. Maddie and the girls—Carla too—laughing until their cheeks ached. She saw now the boys had finally hit gold. Austin, junior captain in the yachting club, had tied a knot he swore was secure.

"I am not," Vanessa said, "driving those morons to the ER when they fall."

Maddie looked back at the dance floor, where Brooks was busy spinning.

"You know you want to try it," Bitsy teased.

"You're damn right I do," Vanessa said.

"What if . . ." Maddie began.

"Puh-lease don't start with your what-ifs, Maddie," Bitsy said. "Carpe diem, bitches!"

Bitsy, Vanessa, and Penny high-fived. Maddie knew she'd have no chance getting a word in now.

"Dude!" Spencer yelled from the floor, his hands cupped round his mouth. "You ready?"

Austin volunteered to go first. Or, Maddie guessed, had been nominated by Gerritt to go first. He held the rope taut so the chandelier lifted with a creak loud enough to be heard over the music. The crowd of kids under the balcony groaned as Austin climbed onto the lip of the balcony, the tips of his Teva sandals peeking over the edge.

The music stopped. It was the first time, in all the nights at Neverland, that the beat had stopped short, and it left a hollow ache in Maddie's chest.

"Ready?" Austin shouted.

He swayed back and forth and the kids' *oooohhhh* sounded like the roar of a crowd's wave at a ball game.

Brooks yelled, "Get the fuck down!"

Austin jumped, locked his legs around the rope, and swung out over their heads like a swashbuckling pirate. The kids screamed as Austin lurched above, and then Brooks's hands were pulling her away from the center of the room, and she heard him curse, "Jesus fucking Christ." Austin let go in time to fall into the beanbag chairs someone had tossed under the chandelier. His legs buckled but he bounced up to stand, lifting his arms in the air and letting loose a roar like he was one of Dom's WWF wrestlers.

Brooks ran toward Austin, one arm slack behind him like he was ready to throw a punch, but Enzo caught him just in time. Locked an arm around Brooks's neck to hold him back. Her cousin whispered into Brooks's ear and, slowly, that hot rage warping his handsome face vanished. Vinny gripped Austin's forearm and pulled him toward the ballroom entrance.

"Me and Austin are going to have a smoke outside. Everybody chill." He winked at Maddie and she mouthed *thank you*.

"Oh. My. God," Bitsy said as she slid a cardboard box out from one of the shadowed corners. "Has this been here the *whole* time? Or did I just find a real live treasure box?"

"Yo," Enzo said, shoving Bitsy aside and hoisting the box, his forearms flexing. "What the hell is that doing here?"

Her cousin looked at Brooks and the two boys exchanged a look Maddie didn't understand. But she knew something was wrong.

"What's in it?" Penny asked.

A few kids shuffled forward to investigate.

Enzo, still holding the box, elbowed the circle away.

"Back the fuck up," he said.

The room fell silent and Maddie felt her pulse in her ears.

She saw Brooks was focused on the cardboard box. Like it was something he didn't want them to see.

"Dude," Brooks said. "I don't know how that got there." He stopped when he saw Enzo's face.

Her cousin was scaring her. He'd looked like that last Christmas when he and Vinny, drunk on bottles of Uncle Carmine's homemade wine, argued over a poker game and ended up on the floor next to Nonna's dining-room table, slugging it out. Vinny had lunged for a steak knife before Maddie's dad had knocked his hand away from the table and dragged him, still swinging, out into the cold, dark night.

"Screw this." Enzo set the box on the floor.

"Oooh!" Gabrielle pulled something out.

It was a can of spray paint. The kind Maddie had used last fall to help decorate the Homecoming Day float.

"It's arts-and-crafts time, kiddies!" Bitsy said.

"Can we?" Penny asked Brooks. Like a little kid, Maddie thought, begging for a cookie. "Can we paint the walls?"

"No way," Maddie began. Not the exquisitely painted walls she'd fallen in love with on her first visit to the Castle. The craggy rocks of Singing Beach rising. The rosy clouds with their silver linings.

"It's fine," Brooks said. He sounded tired. "We'll be painting in here next week. My mom wants to cover up this old stuff."

"Seriously?" Rolo asked.

Maddie saw Rolo too had a can in his hands. Everyone did. Poised and ready.

"Have at it," Brooks said, waving at the walls. He didn't sound like himself. She wondered if she should try to stop them.

Bitsy was the first to skip over to the western wall, where the tangerine sun sank into the painted sea. Maddie wanted to yell *No!* as the paint sprayed with a hiss. Vanessa grabbed a can and then Gerritt and Ricky, and even Penny. Last, Enzo, with a pissed-off shrug. Maddie and Brooks stood in the middle of the ballroom, listening to the *shhhh* as the kids covered the walls with their names, and the names of their crushes; with hearts and skulls and rainbows; with peace signs and anarchy signs; and swearwords and smiley faces. Black paint on black paint until it seemed to Maddie that the ballroom grew midnight-dark.

Brooks took Maddie's hand and she didn't pull away. She didn't care if her cousins told her dad—what was a beating compared to this? This feeling. He handed her a can of paint with a sad smile and they joined in. Someone turned the CD player on and Rage Against the Machine blasted from the speakers—*Killing in the name of! / Some of those that work forces, are the same that burn crosses*—raw and angry, and the black light went on, set to strobe mode so a blinding white light pulsed with the music, and the walls came to life like animals, the shapes of the words throbbing— FUCK YOU. I HATE YOU. LOVE ME. She turned in a slow circle, searching for Brooks, wading through the oily fumes. She couldn't tell one person from the next. SAVE ME. DIE AVALON. CARPE DIEM.

There were bodies on the dance floor, thrashing, flying at one another like winged monsters in fairy tales. Elbowing, kneeing, shoving, and stomping.

OBLIVION. HOPE. GRUDDER KILLS. GRUDDER IS CANCER.

The vandal. He, she, was there. In their ballroom. Those were the words sprayed across the island. Here, in their Neverland. A hand found hers and pulled her out of the chemical cloud, out the side door. She gulped air, coughed and spat to clear her lungs. But the poison was in her nose, coating her tongue. She dropped to her knees in the damp grass and rubbed her hands through it, used the moisture to wipe at her lips.

"You okay?" Brooks was talking but she was too dizzy to lift her head, sure she would puke.

Her head spun. From the fumes, the strobe, what she saw on the ballroom walls. The vandal was inside.

She took a deep steadying breath.

"Let's go down here," she said, standing, pointing to the rows of red roses that looked black in the moonlight. "Where it's quieter."

How could she tell him the truth? That she was worried her cousins would see them and tattle to her dad, who'd beat her. Because he was a racist. Because we all are, she thought. She had made a promise to herself, that she would stop hiding her feelings for Brooks, but that was before she saw those words dripping on the wall.

"That was so fucked up in there." He paced up and down the rows of roses, talking more to himself than to her. "What is happening? I don't get how this could've happened."

"What?" she said. "I don't understand."

"Shit! I pricked my finger on a thorn."

She laughed.

"You think that's funny?" She heard a smile in his voice.

"Sorry. I didn't mean to." She was nervous.

"You better hope I'm no Sleeping Beauty."

The moon was only a quarter full. She heard the paper unfolding before she saw the white square—her list—in his hand.

"This is really cool," he said.

"It's dumb." She meant it. Everything felt dumb now. She was dumb. An outsider to whatever dangerous game was being played. Someone she knew, maybe a bunch of someones, had tagged up the island for weeks while she partied alongside him (or her), clueless.

She wanted to listen to Brooks read her made-up words—she'd worked hard on them, chewed the erasers off two pencils—but the words looping across the ballroom wall were still there burned on the back of her eyelids like the flash of the strobe. Could it be Gerritt or Spencer? But they both had a stake in the island—their fathers were Grudder higher-ups. And it couldn't be her cousins—their families relied on the money they made working extra summer shifts at the factory, especially since Uncle Carmine got sick.

" 'Wishwatcher,' " he read. " 'Someone always looking for a sign.' " He sighed. "Damn, that's a good one."

"Thanks."

" 'Doomdreamer.' " He hummed thoughtfully. "You seem more like a glass-half-full kind of girl."

She laughed, as if he'd gotten her all wrong. Praying he was correct because right now, she felt hopeless.

"I guess things could always be worse," she said.

"Things can *always* be worse," he said. "Next word. 'Skin-seeker'? Sounds kind of dirty."

She slapped him playfully. Let her hand linger on his arm, giggled when she felt him flex. Just like a boy.

"Sometimes," she said, "I don't want to be me. I want a different skin.'

He was quiet.

Maybe, she thought, she'd offended him talking about skin. She was about to apologize, explain that's not what she meant.

"I like your skin."

She knew she should say thank you, but he was back to reading the list.

"What's this one? 'Second-balcony scream.'"

"It's dorky." She grabbed at the paper and the corner tore.

He pulled back. "No," he said, like he was annoyed. "I don't like it when you're mean to yourself."

She tried to forget the faceless vandal who might be sitting next to her. Or, she hoped, moshing to Metallica in the ballroom.

"Now," he said, sweeter, "explain this 'second-balcony scream' to me. Please."

"Have you ever seen a play in a big theater?"

"Yeah," he said. "My mom used to take me. In the city."

"And you know how, when you're up in the balcony, and it's like a really dramatic moment, and the audience is *super* quiet. The hero or heroine is onstage delivering their lines. And it's like you're scared to breathe, 'cause you might break the spell."

"Yeah," he said. "It's magic."

His fingers crawled into her palm, tracing little circles, and she remembered the childhood game. Round and Round the Garden. She didn't want him to stop.

"And you get that crazy urge," she said, "to stand up and scream. Scream so loud that every head turns away from the stage. To look at you. It's not like you want to. But like you *need* to."

"It's the last thing you want," he said. "It'd be so fucking embarrassing. Like walking into school naked. But still, you've got to."

"Yeah." She laughed, amazed he understood.

He turned to face her. So close. If she lifted his shirt, she could stroke whatever was underneath. She wondered if he was hairy like a man, like his father, who she'd seen working shirtless in the garden. Or if his stomach was smooth like a boy's.

"I get that feeling," he said, glancing at the ballroom windows, vibrating with a new song. The thrashing bass guitar just as dark and angry. "Standing on the balcony in there. Sometimes,

I lean as far over the edge as I can. The same balcony," he laughed, "where that jerkoff almost killed himself."

"Hey," she said, touching his chest, feeling hard muscle under soft cotton.

"It's not like I want to die," he said. His warm hand was covering hers. He trembled. "You know . . ."

She was sure he was about to admit something. It couldn't be him. Not Brooks. Sweet, gentle Brooks.

"This island," he said. "It's making people sick."

Was that a confession? He couldn't be the criminal every east islander feared, searched for, dreamt of locking up?

"Like Penny," she said.

"And lots of other people. My mom . . . The doctors told her she couldn't have kids. Because the island made her sick."

"But she had you. And Eva."

He was silent and she wanted to fill the humming space between them and a story came to mind.

"You know that lake behind the factory?"

"Yeah," he said. "It's got some weird-ass Indian name."

She laughed. "Lake Makamah."

"Yeah, it was on the tip of my tongue."

"It's supposed to be haunted. By the Lady of the Lake."

He was listening. She felt his eyes on her lips.

"She was in love with a Dutch settler and they'd meet in the middle of the lake. Each of them rowing out. But then her parents found out. Her dad was like some big-deal chief."

"I don't like where this is going."

"He forbade her to see her lover. And so . . ."

He finished the story. "She threw herself in the lake."

"How did you know?"

"Star-crossed lovers," he said. "It's an old story."

He jerked his head toward the woods. "You hear that?"

"I don't hear anything," she said. "Except the caterpillars. . . ."

"Listen." His breath brushed the back of her neck as he looped his long arms around her, under her breasts. She let herself soften.

"I thought I heard one of those fairy-tale owls," he said.

She looked into his face. There was soft fur on his upper lip. The spatter of freckles on his nose she'd first seen on their walk home—that first night of her new life—looked like a constellation.

He said, "I get other urges too."

"Oh yeah, like what?" She knew this was the right thing to say.

"Like right now." He drew his fingers down her neck, chest, over the space between her breasts so she had to suck in a breath. "There's something I need to do."

He showed her his fingers, the tips gold from the pollen of the lilies she'd bobby-pinned in her hair.

"Your dress is covered in it," he said.

He brushed a powdery line under each of her eyes—left and then right.

"Now," he said, "you are Princess Makamah."

He kissed her. Or maybe she kissed him, she'd wonder later, and understand it didn't matter. All that did was how beautiful she felt. *I am beautiful. It is true.* She almost said the thing she knew a girl should never say after a first kiss. *I love you.*

One must see an episode of severe defoliation by the gypsy moth to appreciate fully the dramatic impact this insect can have. Most noticeable, of course, is the great change in appearance of yards and gardens when autumn appears to have arrived months ahead of time.

—"The Homeowner and the Gypsy Moth: Guidelines for Control," United States Department of Agriculture, *Home and Garden Bulletin*, No. 227 (1979)

Tree trunks may be encircled with a 14–18 inch piece of burlap or similar material. Place it at about chest height and arrange so it hangs apronlike around the tree trunk. The apron must be checked daily, and all "trapped" larvae and pupae should be destroyed.

—"Gypsy Moth" *Fact Sheet*, Dept. of Entomology, Penn State College of Agricultural Sciences

24.

Jules

He put in a call to Dr. Feinstein, the old goofball who had talked about "our green neighbors" at Harvard as if they were humanity's saving grace. And what if they were, Jules thought. Then they were doomed.

He ordered three cases of sticky tape from a natural pest-control company per Dr. Feinstein's suggestion. He waited five days for the package to arrive, aware he was checking the mailbox a little too frequently for a grown man.

Most days he spent hovering over shrubs in the garden, or up on a ladder in the tree canopy, using his fingers (he worked faster glove-free) to pick caterpillars off his oaks, speckled alder, willows, blackgum, paper birch, and poplar. The apple trees in the back were the pest's favorite—the bright-green leaves Swiss-cheesed and the underside of the leaves, which he'd always thought so lovely with that hint of silver and velvety touch, were coated with newly hatched larvae. He picked until his bucket was full and then he dumped the mess of beasts into an old cooler filled with soapy water. He enjoyed watching the caterpillars wriggle around in the bubbles before falling still. He caught himself staring as time passed—the sun traveling across the now visible sky—without his realizing it.

When the box of sticky bands finally arrived, he did a dance in the driveway, gravel spitting out behind his heels. The triumph was short-lived. Sure, these bands were great if you had a small lawn with a few trees to protect but there were a thousand trees around the Castle. His trees.

He called Dr. Feinstein again, trying to explain the scope of the infestation but it was like the old man, who was pretty Looney Tunes himself, thought Jules was crazy. Don't worry, the professor said, the leaves will grow back next year. Trees, he reminded Jules, are far more resilient than we, their lesser, weaker neighbors.

Jules had decided to screw the all-natural crap. He drove over the causeway to Home Depot on the mainland and demanded they point him toward the poison. A salesman in a canvas apron covered in inspirational pins—HANG IN THERE and DON'T WORRY, BE HAPPY—tried to talk Jules into burlap sacks you tied around the trunk to catch the caterpillars. Like little caterpillar hammocks. And safe for the environment! Reminding Jules (as if *he* had to be reminded) about the dying bees. Instead, Jules had purchased a dozen pints of Btk, *Bacillus thuringiensis*—a nasty bacterial spore he knew Dr. Feinstein would never have condoned.

Back at the Castle, Leslie and the kids safe in the cottage with the doors and windows shut, he'd diluted the clear liquid with water (one and a half tablespoons per gallon of water), hooked his spray can to the hose, donned his safety goggles (Leslie insisted), and blasted those parasites out of the trees. It rained caterpillars and he whooped and hollered. *Take that, you fuckers!* Bacillus thuringiensis *subspecies* kurstaki *spores gonna kick your hairy asses!* He was the hero in every action flick he'd ever watched. Sylvester Stallone as John Rambo holding a rattling M60 machine gun. Kurt Russell in *Backdraft* saving a little boy trapped in a burning building. Hell, he was even Ernie Hudson aiming his proton pack at a green hot dog–gobbling blob in *Ghostbusters.*

The tangerine, late-afternoon sun caught the droplets and a rainbow arced overhead, and although he knew the science behind the optical illusion—he'd studied Snell's law of refraction in physics his junior year, the bending of a light wave's path as it passes between two medias—*this* felt like a miracle. An occurrence beyond science. Proof he'd made the right choice. Hope his trees, his garden, would survive. He sprayed until the bark of his precious trees darkened and his jaw ached from smiling. He sprayed until his goggles fogged over and the can was empty.

The next morning, he took a closer look at the layer of cater-pillars blanketing the ground around his phenomenal chestnut tree. The smaller ones were dead. The bigger ones, who had al-ready molted two or three times, shedding their casing and re-appearing longer and wider with bristles so long they reminded him of the hair on his great-aunt Ida's chin—they were squirm-ing. Alive.

Back to square one. He ordered more green sticky bands.

Now the bands Jules and Brooks had wrapped around the trees were covered in big fat bristled caterpillars. Most looked dead but a bunch were alive and flailing and when the sun caught the red and blue dots along their backs, they winked like eyes.

"Ha!" he shouted, driving a finger at the tree. "I got your number. You going down."

He slung an arm around his son's widening shoulders and crushed him in a hug.

"We did it, buddy," Jules said.

Brooks rolled his eyes and faked a weak smile. Since they'd moved to the island, his son was like one of those bobblehead dolls with googly eyes you stuck to your car dashboard. Eyes roll-ing, head shaking. Like every word coming out of Jules's mouth Brooks heard in a foreign language. When had his son grown to despise him?

"Why can't we just leave them alone?" Brooks said. His work-gloved hands were on his hips, and his body shouted bored and tired and fed up. "Maddie says they'll be gone in a few weeks. The leaves *will* grow back, Dad."

His son punctuated this last part with a comically loud sigh, and it made Jules see, just for a moment, how crazy he might seem. A madman on a doomed mission. The leaves around the garden had thinned so the roses were thriving, blooms upon blooms, from extra sun. Why, Jules thought, couldn't he see that silver lining, take it to heart, wrap it around his aching back and shoulders?

No, this consumption of his land—it was *his* land now—was bigger than some cyclical disturbance of nature, even bigger than bad luck. It was goddamn unfair. To be given his dream, his fantasy garden, only to have it ransacked by pestilence.

He wouldn't relent. He would stop those squirming freeloaders. Still, he had to save face. Especially in front of his son.

"You're right about that, Brooks." He made sure he sounded calm, even indifferent. "The leaves will grow back next year. *But* some of these trees will die. The defoliation . . ." He saw Brooks's eyes glaze over as they did these days when Jules *talked plants*, which is what Brooks called it. "Listen to me, son."

"I *am* listening." Jules heard the rising indignation and realized he shouldn't have pushed. "I've been listening all day. But I got to meet Maddie. You're making me late."

Maddie. Maddie. Who was this Maddie? Jules guessed she was one of the girls who partied in the ballroom each night. He heard his father's voice—so loud, it felt as if three generations of Simmons men were standing in the garden surrounded by twitching half-dead caterpillars. *Keep away from those white girls, boy. Is it really worth the risk?* He heard his father's honeyed laugh. *Plenty of dark girls happy to get you off.*

But that wasn't true on this island, and he wasn't his father, and he swallowed the impulse to warn his son, and instead asked, "Tell me more about Maddie." He stooped to look into his son's face, smiled when he saw Brooks's mouth twitch.

"Just a girl."

"Oh no, she ain't *just*," Jules said, and slapped his son on the back.

"Quit it, Dad," Brooks grumbled but Jules could see him smiling. Finally.

"All right then, you get lost. Go find your Maddie."

"Dad!" But the boy was tugging off the work gloves and running up the patio steps. With a new bounce in his step, for sure. Jules felt a prick of envy as he tried to remember what it felt like—young love—how it filled you so one touch from that little hottie and you burst like the freaking Hindenburg.

He called after Brooks, whose long legs took the steps two at a time. "Clean up the ballroom first! It smells like a saloon in there."

Brooks stopped at the top step and turned. Sass returned, hands on hips. "What? No way! Mom said it doesn't matter. Vinny and Enzo are getting ready to tear the room apart anyway."

Jesus, Jules thought, he had no idea what plans were multiplying in his wife's mind. She had those dark-haired boys in the heavy-metal tees busting holes in the walls with sledgehammers, tearing down wallpaper in long, ragged strips. Leslie watching it all with her arms crossed and a smug smile on her face. Reveling in her revenge. He wondered if she heard her father's voice, her mother's, as she watched the destruction of their castle, just like he heard his father's in the garden.

He didn't want Brooks hanging out with those boys, he thought as he unwrapped the band hugging the scaly trunk of an old sugar maple. Brooks was hardly ever at the cottage, spending all his time in that ballroom, which stank of spilled beer and cigarette smoke. Leslie only laughed Jules's concerns away. *He's just a boy. He's just having fun. He's just making friends.* Yeah, Jules thought, not wanting to get into it with Leslie for the hundredth time that month—our boy is *just* making friends with the enemy. With those meatheads who brawled at the fair. He imagined his son racing through the maze, his fingers grazing the hedged walls, toward the cottage where he'd primp and pick at his hair, make himself handsome for this Maddie. It all stank of danger.

"Brooks!" His voice was his father's, the booming bass ricocheted off the trees, "You clean that ballroom. And," he felt the thrum of his pulse in his throat, "you quit talking back."

His son's voice was faint, far away. "It's Mom's house. And she says I don't have to."

"Fuck!" Jules shouted.

He grabbed the spade, lifted it over his head, and brought the flat rusted metal down on the caterpillars stuck to the pile of green bands. Again and again. Still, the mashed pieces squirmed.

He dropped the spade only when his hands began to ache. His fingers were covered in a coarse red rash that itched so badly he wore his winter gloves to sleep so he wouldn't scratch himself raw, or worse, make the sores ooze.

Leslie had tried to get him to swallow a Valium to help him sleep. Spend his nights in bed, not in the garden. But Jules had important work to do. He wasn't ready to surrender. Not yet.

25.

Veronica

She had fallen in love with the girl. There were even moments, during their teatime (and Oprah time), where Veronica wondered if she did want to live after all.

"Call me Nicky," she urged Maddie. "Please."

When was the last time she'd asked someone to call her that? It must have been Bob when they first met at Pilgrim State Hospital after the accident at the factory had broken his back. Veronica had been a nurse-in-training. Starched white uniform and pantyhose with seams up the backs of her legs.

Maddie had arrived at White Eagle at four on the dot every afternoon since their first tea. Veronica made sure the popcorn was popped and buttered, the TV set programmed to *Oprah*. Even the day after Bob's *episode* at the Castle bell tower, when she'd been up half the night. Her body had felt bruised and she'd found a gash on her foot where a branch had torn through her slipper. But still, she wouldn't miss her afternoon with Maddie. Not for anything.

It had been like pulling teeth to get Bob out of the TV room and away from the coverage of the presidential election. She set him up in his study with the portable television and a Sara Lee pound cake. His eyes widened like a child's when she told him he could eat the whole cake *if* he didn't leave the room or disturb her special time with Maddie. She knew it was cruel to bribe a confused old man, but it was worth it. The things she learned from Oprah! Who knows, she thought, what different choices she'd have made if she'd tuned in earlier and had Oprah's affirmations in her life?

What a brave woman. A few days ago, she and Maddie had watched a rerun where Oprah confronted a group of skinheads.

Honest-to-goodness neo-Nazis with shaved heads and black boots and swastika tattoos. How could this woman—this *black* woman—forgive such monsters, especially when, as she and Maddie watched, transfixed (Veronica grateful for the commercial breaks), those scalped boys in their red-suspender-hiked trousers shouted slurs in Oprah's face, called an audience member a *monkey,* even used the *N* word. She had heard the nasty word come out of Bob's mouth, and the mouths of countless Grudder men. As well as Veronica's own father. Even the pious saints in Palmyra were not free from hatred. But that Oprah— she was one cool customer—she didn't so much as flinch. By the end of the episode, she was holding hands with the biggest and meanest boy, and they were crying together, and Maddie was crying too (without shame, Veronica saw, amazed) and she too felt the tears pushing through and wanted to let them loose, she truly did.

After each Oprah episode, she was depleted. To have eighty years of preconceived notions shattered, and then rearranged, in just forty-five minutes. But she also felt a new calm as she and Maddie sat in the wicker butterfly chairs in the sunroom surrounded by the ficus and palm trees. Together, they summarized (*recapped,* Maddie called it) that day's episode, sharing their favorite moments. Her granddaughter, the naïve thing, loved when Oprah cried, her faux lash–fringed eyes sparkling in the studio lights as she bit her lower lip. As if, Veronica thought, the woman had ever held back a single tear!

Today's topic had focused on young girls and their increasingly mature sexuality, and Veronica saw how it had made Maddie squirm. Oprah had invited a sexual psychologist—was that really a job a person could have?—to talk about girls today having sex earlier than ever.

As she and Maddie sipped their cooling tea and nibbled at carrot cake Rosalita had frosted with cream cheese, the forest's denuded leaves framed by the picture window, Veronica knew she should say something. It was her responsibility, after all. But Oprah's open, and even chatty, talk of birth control and orgasms and masturbation (a topic Veronica thought would've been censored) had made her want to turn the TV off. Eighty years old, she thought, and still a prude. Terrified to talk about what had been unnamable in her father's house back in Palmyra. Her stepmother Virgie had called the act of sexual intercourse "coupling," which had felt two steps shy of the mating the cows and sheep did in the barn.

As Maddie shifted in her chair, sighing dreamily—a girl in love, Veronica thought—the sun caught the red in her hair so it glowed coppery. Veronica saw that the girl would, someday, be beautiful. As Ginny had been. Veronica wanted, badly, to summon the right words—the *talk* she'd avoided with Ginny, assuming, stupidly, she thought, that Ginny would learn about sex from her girlfriends, not some grease monkey from West Avalon who got her pregnant a few weeks shy of her nineteenth birthday.

She tucked a cigarette between her lips and struck her lighter. It wouldn't catch.

The cigarette fell, rolling under her chair.

"Goddammit." She threw the lighter across the table so it clanked into the sterling sugar bowl. "Oh my, it seems as if I'm having a tantrum."

"Here," Maddie said. "Let me help."

Her little charade had worked, Veronica saw. The girl was paying attention now.

She watched her granddaughter's face, focused and serious, as she held the lighter under Veronica's cigarette, the paper catching with a sizzle.

"Thank you, dear," Veronica said. "I've realized, that in old age, one's most gallant saviors are other women."

She offered her granddaughter the pack. Then pulled it back.

"Silly me. I've forgotten how healthy you kids are these days. Say no to this and that, et cetera. All those public service commercials."

"No, it's okay," Maddie said, peering over her shoulder as if her parents might walk through White Eagle's doors any moment. "I do like a cigarette. Just once in a while."

"Here." Veronica slid the pack across the table. "I won't tell."

The girl lit the cigarette, took a deep breath, and exhaled. She was transformed—a little further from girlhood and a step closer to womanhood. Relaxed and poised. This, Veronica thought, is what they call bonding—a phrase she'd learned from Oprah.

"You're almost a woman now."

Her granddaughter paused, and with teacup in one hand, cigarette in the other, she reminded Veronica of Ginny. Hadn't she had tea with her daughter and shared cigarettes? If she had, it was so long ago, she couldn't remember. She hoped they had.

"I wish my parents—especially my dad—would stop treating me like a kid."

"He's a tough cookie, your father."

Maddie laughed.

"What is it?" Veronica asked.

"You sound just like Mom. She says that all the time. 'Tough cookie.'"

"You remind me, very much, of your mother."

"Is that"—Maddie paused—"a good thing?"

The question surprised Veronica. "Of course."

The ash at the end of Maddie's cigarette fell into the dainty porcelain saucer. For today's tea, Veronica had chosen a Shelley fine bone china set decorated with a lovely pink thistle.

"Oops, I just ashed in your fancy dish."

Veronica stubbed her cigarette out in her own saucer, not caring if the delicate hand-painted flower burned away.

"Well," she said, "it's a good thing your crabby great-grandmother Pencott isn't here to make a fuss. She could be such a bitch."

Maddie's mouth fell open. That feeling of surprising someone, it filled Veronica.

"When I was young, they had a saying for those girls on the show. We called them 'broken-blossomed.'"

Maddie's face shifted. It had taken Veronica a few weeks to read her granddaughter—not just what lay on the composed surface, but what wriggled underneath like the minnows that darted across the sandbar when the tide was out. Now she saw fear.

"Were you," Maddie paused, "one of those girls?"

"No," Veronica said, "but maybe I wish I had been? There are things much worse."

"Like what?" Her granddaughter was almost whispering.

"Like knowing nothing. Like waiting for your husband of just a few hours in a room in an inn. Wearing the long white nightgown you've worn your whole life." Veronica laughed. "It even had a high collar. Tiny pearl buttons all the way up the back. A terror to undo."

The girl looked grateful. "It can be kind of scary," she said. "Even when you do, sort of, know what to expect. But how could you know *nothing*? Nothing—really?"

"Nothing," Veronica said. It was almost impossible for her to believe it herself. "That whole first year, I thought *it* was something people did with their clothes on. I was too scared to take my nightgown off."

There was a new look on her granddaughter's face. Pity.

"And your grandfather, well he'd had it with those buttons. Swore a blue streak."

They laughed and Veronica was relieved to return to their lighthearted banter. She used the tongs to place two chocolate-dipped macaroons on her granddaughter's plate, her hands shaking so they barely made the journey from platter to plate.

Maddie nibbled on a macaroon and then let out a long sigh.

"So many sighs today, *ma petite amie*," Veronica said as she sipped from her steaming cup of oolong.

"I'm just . . ." The girl paused. Another sigh as she shifted sideways in the chair so her smooth muscled calves bounced over the wicker arm. Normally, Veronica would protest, but she'd learned to stop herself from critiquing Maddie. She would treat her, she thought, with more kindness than Ginny, whom she'd felt a duty to straighten, enhance, polish. And look how that had turned out.

"Is it that boy from the Castle?"

Maddie looked surprised. Concerned even. She glanced at the hallway and Veronica knew she was imagining the front door, the slate path to the cottage, her father.

"I may have one foot in the grave," Veronica said. "But I'm still a woman."

"It's just that . . ." Another pause. Maddie twirled her ring. The silver band that read LUCKY. Probably, Veronica thought, a dime-store purchase. She reminded herself to leave her jeweled rings to Maddie. The star sapphire matched the girl's eyes.

"You can trust me," Veronica said. "I wouldn't dream of telling your father." That creep, she thought. That bully.

Maddie swung her legs around and leaned forward so Veronica saw the swell of her small breasts. Just a hint of the cleavage that was to come, sure to catch the attention of many men. To make her as bright and visible as the star on a Christmas tree.

"And don't tell Mom, okay? 'Cause," she paused. "She still loves him."

"Who?"

"Dad, silly. She tells him everything."

Poor girl, Veronica thought. Not a soul to trust, knowing *she* wanted to be that soul.

"Well . . . spill the beans!"

"It sounds stupid," Maddie said. "Like I'm one of those ditzy girls that falls for a boy and walks around like a zombie."

Veronica nodded. "But . . ."

"But Brooks . . ." She paused. "He makes me feel . . ."

"Yes?" She needed to hear it. To remember what it felt like.

"Important. Beautiful." Maddie looked away. The girl was ashamed. "I almost told him that I, well, that I loved him, after the first time we'd . . ."

"Go on. First time you what?"

"Kissed." She stared at the crumbles of macaroon in her palm. "I shouldn't be telling you all of this."

"No!" Veronica surprised herself.

Rosalita called from the kitchen. "Mrs. Pencott, you needing something?"

"No, Rosa, we're doing wonderfully. Thank you!"

"How did it feel?" Veronica was whispering. As if, she thought, she and Maddie were two schoolgirls.

Another sigh. But this one, Veronica could tell, was full of satisfaction.

"It was like," Maddie said. "I felt comfortable. Like, for the first time ever."

"Yes?"

"Like I could say and do anything and not feel worried he'd think I was dumb. Or weird. Or ugly."

"You *are* beautiful. Don't you see that?"

"No," Maddie said. "I never did. But I think I do now." She smiled. "I think, maybe, I really do."

They ended the visit with their little ritual. There was nothing Veronica looked forward to more than she and Maddie sitting together as the sun sank, making a list of their favorite Oprah sayings. Not that this was something she'd have admitted to the old Veronica, the jaded woman before the visit to the oncologist.

Maddie began, reciting in what Veronica guessed the girl considered a grown-up voice, solemn, her chin tilted toward the ceiling, "Lots of people want to ride with you in the limo, but what you want is someone who will take the bus with you when the limo breaks down."

Veronica had felt as if she and Bob had ridden that damn bus all year, and the rest of the Grudder men, and their wives too (hadn't Mary Gernhardt given her a dirty look at the beauty parlor last week?), were sipping Cristal in the limo, whose exhaust was blowing back in her and Bob's faces. She thought of the night at the top of the Castle's bell tower. Thank heavens Julius had been there. On their proverbial bus.

"Amen to that!" Veronica said. Oprah was always amen-ing.

June 30, 1992
Dear Diary,

Hi!

It feels silly talking to you like you are a real person but I guess it's just like Kurt Vonnegut would say, "and so it goes."

B gave me some Vonnegut novels and they are AMAZING. Like perspective shattering but then reorganizing and it's like I'm seeing the world (and me in the world) in a whole new way. Sounds kind of cheesy I know. But it's true. I'm changing.

It was also B's idea that I start writing to you (in you?). A place where I can stick all the crap I'm always worrying about. The dark slimy stuff (caterpillar poop!) that keeps me so busy being scared (B told me this and he's super super smart) so it's like I don't really have time to live. You know? B keeps a diary too. And though I'd NEVER EVER read it, I really hope my name covers its pages.

So it goes. Today's worries:

1. Penny might die

2. Penny might get so popular she won't like me anymore

3. B will stop liking me

4. Dad will find out about me and B

5. I'll get kidnapped and sold into a sex-slave cult like in that video we watched in sex ed

6. My mom is going to take too many sleeping pills and die in her sleep

7. Nuclear war

8. Chemistry next year with psycho grader Mr. Lomansky

9. Dom will never cheer up and kill himself

10. Dad is having an affair with that skank Rosemary Dutton

11. Something bad (so bad I can't even imagine it) is going to happen

Well . . . I guess I feel a little better. Thanks for listening! See you later, alligator.

Love,
Maddie Pencott LaRosa

26.

Leslie

She lost the third baby a few weeks before her twenty-fifth birthday. Number five at thirty-one on the subway returning from the farmers' market in Union Square. She felt the warm blood leak out of her as she leaned against the subway car pole, hugging a paper sack filled with oxalis seeds. A gift for Jules, who loved the purple shamrock despite its reputation as a weed.

By then, she and Jules had baby number four, alive and well. A miracle baby, or just a stubborn little thing, who knew or cared? The round-cheeked boy had stuck it out through forty weeks, the last six she'd spent flat on her back on bed rest, a fetal monitor strapped to her beautifully swollen belly. The baby's heartbeat a constant rhythm she heard even in her dreams.

They named the little survivor Brooks after her cousin who'd died flying a Grudder A-6 Intruder over Vietnam.

At least you have your little boy, the hospital nurse said, three years later, over the purr of the vacuum used to suck baby number five from Leslie's womb. She began to think it cruel—making a life and knowing all along it would perish. Could those itty-bitty beings *feel*? Suffer?

Her obstetrician urged them to keep trying. Jules wanted another baby. A playmate for Brooks. The tests had been done. So much blood pulled from her veins that the inside of her elbows seemed perpetually black and blue. No immune system hiccups. No hypo- or hyperthyroid disease. Cyst-free, diabetes-free. Hormones balanced. Cervix intact. Uterus shaped just as nature intended. It was a mystery to every doctor and midwife and specialist. A mystery that felt anything but mysterious when she saw the blood on her panties. Red like her mother's prizewinning American Beauties. She remembered a poem she'd read in college. When reading poetry at night under her covers, hiding from Sister Mary Bartholomew had felt like a rebellion. *The blood flood is the flood of love.*

She walked into her high school's twentieth reunion with Jules in a wide-lapel Armani suit she'd splurged on (thanks to the Amex card her mother let her use, a secret she kept from Jules), and armed with a wallet stuffed with photos of baby Brooks. Her dress a size 2, she'd never looked better. The scraping of her uterus only a few weeks prior had made her lose her appetite. She was happy to be there. To see old friends. But also to be seen. Leslie Day Marshall, transformed into a woman so different from the rest of the island girls, with her city life, her black husband, her social work making the world a better place. Her longtime suspicions confirmed—she *was* better than the island. She listened to the tipsy chatter of her former classmates—their Lilly Pulitzer sleeveless shifts traded for shoulder pads and snakeskin pumps. As the night wore on, the chatter turned to tears and she squeezed their acrylic-nail-tipped fingers as they talked of the babies they'd lost. Sheila McCafferty. Loreen Brice. Genevieve Smith. Ginny Pencott. On and on. An island's worth of mourning mothers.

She had a friend who worked at the CDC. A shy brainy biologist she and Jules had met through meetings with Earth First! and who she suspected was sweet on her, and so she called him and invited him to dinner. Asked him to tell her everything he knew about biomonitoring and if it was possible to measure the toxic chemicals in a person's body. What if, she asked, those poisons had been in her blood and bones and tissue from the very beginning, when she was just a baby herself, sucking her thumb in her own mother's polluted womb?

27.

Dom

He walked the perimeter of the woods around the Castle—there was a real rager in the ballroom tonight; he'd heard the thumping bass all the way from the cottage. He was on his second loop. The caterpillars were loud. Like they were competing with the music pouring from the Castle ballroom. He'd sworn an oath to the Colonel that he'd keep an eye out and "report back anything cockamamie" and so he would do one more loop.

He heard the voices—one high and bright, the other low and lazy. He hid behind a massive oak covered with caterpillars. Big fat fuzzy ones that looked as if they had molted at least three or four times. He was fascinated with the little beasts' transformation—they could go from one inch and lightly bristled to three inches long and so hairy he couldn't figure out how, crawling all over one another in a big caterpillar orgy, their bristles didn't get tangled.

The leaves were so thinned out, there weren't that many places a secret spy could hide these days in the woods of Avalon Island. He hustled forward a few feet and ducked behind a paper birch. Someone had wrapped the trunk in burlap to catch the gypsies and the sack was slung low like there were hundreds trapped inside.

He was at the edge of the forest, where the trees turned to a cloud of fern and bramble and vines, when he heard the girl's voice again and knew it was Maddie. He stopped himself, just barely, from launching out of the woods and scaring the shit out of them. He watched for a moment—she and Brooks so close it was as if they were wearing the same zipped sweatshirt, and when he stepped out into the light of the Castle's driveway, the old-school gas lamps lit and flickering, he saw they really were wearing the same sweatshirt, the zipper pulled all the way to the top so it glinted at the top of Maddie's back.

"Hi guys," he said, not wanting to startle them but he did and they stumbled and almost fell on the grass. They laughed— Brooks reaching his arms around Maddie to unzip the sweat- shirt, she looking up at Brooks all lovey-eyed the whole time.

Hello? Dom wanted to say. *Remember me? Your brother? Who you haven't spoken to in days?* But he knew that would only make him sound pathetic, so he said the first thing that popped into his head, "Want to play?" He thumbed behind him at the woods.

Maddie lifted herself on her toes and bit her bottom lip and Dom knew she wanted to.

"Play what?" Brooks said, lifting his brows and looking down at Maddie.

"We'll show you!" Maddie said, and grabbed his hand and pulled him toward the woods.

"In there?" Brooks said, stopping short so the soles of his Converse skidded across the driveway, scattering stones. "With those *things*?"

"It's cool," Dom said, desperate to make this guy believe him. It had been ages since he played the game, and ages upon ages since Maddie had played. "We'll be moving around the whole time. And they're starting to retreat. Into their cocoons."

"Yeah?" Brooks said. "Sounds to me like they're louder than ever. Like the caterpillar troops have multiplied."

Dom laughed, but Maddie stepped forward, hands on her hips. "You scared, tough guy?" Then she took off into the woods, her arms pumping, leaping over the ferns.

"Shit," Brooks said and jogged after her.

Dom tried to talk slowly, but he was so excited and there was so much to say. How would they pick the perfect myth to reenact? He thought of famous battle scenes—the felling of Achilles by Paris in the Trojan War with a single arrow to the heel, or they could do Achilles slaying the great warrior Hec- tor, and, since they'd never played with another boy before (Maddie was awesome at fighting, but she was still a girl), they could do the battle of Zeus and the Olympians against their greedy, baby-swallowing father, Cronus, and his fellow Titans. Yes, that was so obviously the one!

"You guys," Dom called, "I have a great idea."

Maddie and Brooks were standing on a fallen log by the circle of stumps Dom liked to imagine had once been an ancient Native American meeting place.

"We already picked one," Maddie said. Even in the faint moonlight, Dom could feel she was smiling. It was good to have her back.

"How about the war of the Olympians and the Titans?" he said. "How epic is that?"

"We're going to do Orpheus and Eurydice," she said. Then, to Brooks, "It's the most tragic love story ever."

There was a beat of silence between them, filled by the drone of the caterpillars and the thump of the techno radiating from the Castle.

"Cool," Brooks said. "I guess that makes me . . ." He looked at Maddie.

"Orpheus, silly! And I'm the devastatingly beautiful and virtuous Eurydice. Dead by a snakebite while fleeing from the rapist," she paused. "I can't remember his name, but whatever."

"Aristaeus," Dom said, exaggerating his impatience, hoping she saw what happened when she took time off from the game. "The shepherd."

"Yeah, yeah," she said. "The raping shepherd."

Brooks spoke, "This is some heavy shit."

"And you," Maddie said, taking Brooks's hands and spinning him in a circle so the forest floor whispered under their feet, "You are Orpheus, son of Apollo, a great musician. When I died, you played your lyre—it's like a guitar. Sort of."

"Not really," Dom said.

"Stop interrupting, Dom," Maddie said. "You mourned with your magical guitar."

"I like the sound of that," Brooks said. "Kind of like Jimi Hendrix."

"And who am I?" Dom asked, worried they'd forget he was there.

"Hades, of course," Maddie said, and sashayed over to him, giving him a quick squeeze of a hug. "Only the most mysterious and elusive of all the gods. The keeper of the gates of hell."

Dom smiled. "Here is my pitchfork," he said, and grabbed a long stick, imagining it was the two-pronged spear of the god of hell.

Maddie directed, moving them into their places—Dom sitting on the tallest stump, his throne, and Brooks approaching from the east, strumming the thick peel of paper birch that was his lyre. Or, Dom thought, laughing to himself, his *magical guitar*. Dom used his deepest voice and demanded Orpheus tell him why he had trespassed into the Underworld, and how he had charmed Cerberus, the three-headed dog.

Brooks/Orpheus dropped to one knee and bowed his head (Dom was impressed), and then looked to Maddie and said, "For true love."

When it was time for Orpheus to return to the world above, Dom gave him his conditions, "You can take your dead beloved bride," Dom boomed, his voice battling the caterpillars and the ballroom music, "but on *one* condition!"

"Anything," Orpheus/Brooks said, "to return my love to me."

Damn, Dom thought, this kid was good. He was already scheming, thinking up ways he could get the two of them to play the game again. They'd do all the love stories, one after another.

"Do not look back at your bride before you return to the light of Earth above. Or you will lose her forever!"

Orpheus/Brooks walked in a slow circle around the stumps, Eurydice/Maddie following behind, gliding in a little waltz. She let her head fall zombie-like, her long hair whipping around her shoulders, and with her face painted an eerie blue by the moonlight, she was beautiful. As beautiful, Dom thought, as the real Eurydice.

"Now!" Dom directed. "You see the sunlight ahead. You are almost there. Almost out of hell. But you can't bear the temptation. To look back. Look back!"

Brooks looked behind him, a slow sorrowful turn of the head, and Dom jumped off his throne and looped his arm through Maddie's and pulled her away, into the woods.

He kept pulling her even though she was trying to yank her arm away.

"Dom," she said, "let me go."

"Let's go home," he begged. "We can watch a movie. *Spaceballs* is on again."

She pulled herself free and ran back to Brooks, who caught her and lifted her and it was like a movie, Dom thought, the way they looked at each other. Like they were the only two people in the world and he mourned for himself then because he knew he would never find a someone who looked at him like that. Not even if he moved far from the island, to a city maybe, where boys *like him* were tolerated. Where they fell in love and maybe even held hands as they walked down the street. He knew it as clearly as if those three old bitches, the Fates, were getting ready to cut the string of his life.

He walked away, down the path toward White Eagle.

"Dom?" Maddie called. "Come back. We'll play again."

"Yo, Dom," Brooks yelled. "That was fresh. Don't go, dude."

"Fuck off!" Dom yelled.

He heard footsteps in the dry leaves—Maddie was coming to him—and then Brooks said, "Mads, leave him. He needs to cool off."

Dom did not look back.

Since 1980, the gypsy moth has defoliated close to a million or more forested acres each year. In 1981, a record 12.9 million acres were defoliated. This is an area larger than Rhode Island, Massachusetts, and Connecticut combined.

—"Gypsy Moth," *Forest Insect & Disease Leaflet 162*, US Department of Agriculture Forest Service, 1989

28.

Maddie

He showed her the way to the secret garden. Held her hand as they walked through the maze and sang the code to the tune the seven dwarfs sang in *Snow White*.

"Left, right," he sang. "Left, left, right, left."

He was adorable, she thought.

It was their own private room, he said, made of living walls. There was a blanket spread over the grass, and that he'd thought of her, ahead of time, when she wasn't even in his line of sight—it meant everything.

The music in the ballroom sounded far away and she felt safe knowing no one could find them. Only they had the secret code.

They searched the sky for shooting stars and he saw one first, and she wasn't jealous like she'd normally be because it was his first shooting star ever. He gasped when he saw it.

They kissed some more. It had only been a few days since their first kiss but she thought she was getting better. She felt so safe with him that she almost (almost) confessed that she practiced kissing her hand each night. She wanted to be good for him.

She was used to not thinking about the words she saw on the ballroom wall. Not trying to figure it out. This was all she wanted, all she'd ever wanted. Lying next to him, their fingers twisted together, making up words for their language.

"You know how the sun slips through the leaves in the afternoon?" He paused and she closed her eyes so she could see what he was imagining, "And the shadows, they jump around. Kind of like birds, a whole lot, flapping their wings at once?"

"Yes," she said. She saw.

"I need a word for *that*."

"It's got to have 'dappled' in it somewhere," she said. "Or is that too predictable?"

"'Dappled' is good. 'Flicker,' though, might be even better. It's like that golden afternoon sun is on fire, you know?"

She did.

He could take anything—a tree, a cloud, the change in light at quarter past five on a summer day, and turn it around and around until it was something beautiful. Like the caterpillars. While the rest of the island cowered, Brooks had learned the story of the gypsy moth, spending hours in the library hunched over science books.

"Okay," he said, rolling onto his side so they were face-to-face, lips to lips, "this is weird. Ready?"

"Yes."

"You're not going to like it," he sang.

"Just tell me already."

He kissed her. Nibbled her bottom lip.

"Ouch."

"Serves you right. Getting all sassy."

"Please," she said. "Tell. Me."

"The girl gypsy moths," he said, "they come out of the cocoon with working wings, but . . ."

"Yeah?"

"They don't fly. They just sit there and wait for the gypsy moth dudes to come to their pad and . . ." He trailed a finger down the front of her shirt.

"Yeah?"

"Is it okay if I touch you?"

"Uh-huh."

"Here?"

His fingers slid down her neck, across her throat, and she swallowed hard as they moved down, past the V-neck of her tee, stopping at her breast.

Two of his fingers circled her nipple over the white cotton that seemed to glow in the moonlight. He was barely touching her, but the circles grew and grew and when she closed her eyes she saw them burning. She heard a moan—was that her?—and there was a tiny sting between her legs, nothing worse than a prick from a beach cactus thorn, and a wet warmth hummed between her legs. All that, she thought, with just two fingers.

"Is this okay?"

"Yes." She laughed because it felt as if she had screamed, her voice ringing between the leafy walls of their secret garden.

He tipped his head forward so their noses touched. She could feel him smiling, the muscles around his nose and mouth stretching. She was smiling too. She couldn't help it. She couldn't unsmile, as hard as she tried. Was it okay? None of the women in the VHS tape the boys played in Spencer's basement had smiled. They gnashed their teeth. Even their ecstasy seemed angry and pained, their mouths parted as they grunted, *Do it to me! Give it to me!*

His lips were as soft as the satin lining on her childhood bedroom comforter. The one with the Holly Hobbie print. She slept with it on nights she was scared she'd done something wrong, something that would get her a beating from her dad—her mom sound asleep so there was no one to rescue her.

"More?" Brooks asked.

"Yes," she said, and sucked his lower lip, tugging at it so it slipped slowly out of her mouth.

He liked that. His penis was hard, pressing into her thigh. She was doing a good job, she thought, and dared herself to do more. She let the tip of her tongue flick into his mouth. He moaned breathily in time with a gust of wind that set the trees above swaying, the leaves whispering.

His mouth was on her nipples, hot and wet, over her T-shirt. Who knew this could feel so good with clothes on, she thought. He tugged—a pinching that made her gasp with something she'd never felt before, a feeling between pain and pleasure, and she spoke without any thought, "I'm wet."

He came alive then and she realized he'd been waiting, holding back. For her. And that was sweet. He hadn't wanted to scare her. He was on his knees, unbuckling his pants, pulling himself out of his boxers. It was dark and she couldn't see, but she smelled that doughy smell she remembered from Spencer. She lifted herself on her elbows, scrambling backward.

"I'm not," she started. "I don't know if I . . ."

"Don't worry. I'll take care of both of us."

She was ready to jump to her feet. To run. But where was the entrance to the garden? The hedged walls seemed to rise to the clouds like Jack's beanstalk.

"You don't have to do anything," he said.

"You mean . . ."

"You don't have to touch me. Come here." She heard him tap the blanket, the dead leaves underneath rustling.

She crawled back to him, the damp grass soaking her knees. Hoping she wasn't making a mistake like with Spencer.

"All you have to do is lie down. Close your eyes. I just want to make you feel good."

She wanted to believe him.

"Can I touch you?" he asked. "Under your pants?"

"Um, okay."

She heard him take a breath. His fingers fumbled with the button on her shorts.

"I can help," she said. She undid her shorts and slid them down to her knees. Her panties were white and the metallic pattern shone in the moonlight.

"Stars," he said, and she heard him smile.

"They're silly."

"They're perfect."

His hand cupped her just like she'd done herself at night lying on her stomach, rolling her hips into her hand until her pleasure broke like a wave.

He was using his fingers—those magical two fingers—pressing into her panties and she felt the wetness seep through the cotton. She grabbed his hand.

"I'm all wet," she said. "You'll get wet."

"I want that. I want that so bad."

His fingers were moving again, digging, gently, until the wet cotton was pressing against her and he was moving side to side, like when he slid the fader on his turntables to bring in a new record. He was searching and when he found it, she gasped,

"Oh," and he whispered, "There we go," and she was stuttering, "Um, um," and tried to push his hand away, but didn't try too hard, because it felt good, so good, and the swirling heat inside her rose and rose and rose as he stirred her with his two fingers. Almost at the rim of the thing holding in her pleasure. Almost spilling over.

He was touching himself too, she felt him off balance, tugging himself with one hand, stirring her with the other.

The pleasure was so big that it almost hurt and she was almost there, she could see, feel, reach toward the end like over a giant hill, and she'd never felt so *with* someone but also alone, because the pleasure, though given to her by someone else, it was hers.

His fingers were working hard now, her panties wet, the crotch stretching as she lifted her hips to meet his hand, and his fingers slipped under the cotton for a few seconds, wet flesh meeting flesh, and she moaned and apologized, *I'm sorry I'm sorry I'm sorry,* and his fingers scrambled back outside her underwear as if she'd scolded him and she wanted to grab his hand and stuff it back into her panties, but didn't know how to ask, and it didn't matter because they were both almost there, and she imagined what they looked like from above—what did the horned owls see? Their bodies connected by his magic fingers, writhing, shaking, going there together.

"I'm sorry," she whispered as she came and her hips lifted off the ground. "I'm sorry."

"No," he gasped. "Don't be."

But she couldn't help herself. Surely, to feel this good must be bad.

She rolled over and let her face fall into the sweat-warm place between his chin and chest. She'd never move again, she promised herself, she'd live and die here. Her hand swept down and she ran a finger down his naked hip. The bone sloped like one of the sand dunes at Singing Beach and she used her finger to scoop a bit of the milky semen that trailed down his thigh.

"That tickles," he said, and she wasn't sure how she knew but he was growing hungry for more.

"Is that it?"

"What?" He laughed. "You want more? I got to rest, girl."

"I mean, aren't you going to . . ." She stopped herself.

"To what?" He bent his head and she smelled coconuts in his hair, so much softer than she'd imagined it would feel as it tickled her chin.

"Put your fingers inside me? That's the only way I've ever done it before."

"You like that better?"

"No!" she said louder than she'd meant to. "I only want *that*. I mean what you just did. That *that*." Her cheeks were hot. She was making a fool of herself. "That was good. I want that." She paused. "All the time."

They laughed at her. Together. And that made it okay.

"How'd you know how to do that?" she asked. "Forget it. I don't want to know."

"My mom wasn't scared to teach me about sex. Don't you know about the clitoris?"

"The what?"

Brooks took a breath and she heard him trying to choke back another laugh. She slapped him playfully in the chest.

"Tell me."

"Oh, man." He sighed. "So, like, women have this piece of skin. Or maybe it's cartilage. Tucked in there, like." He paused.

"And . . ."

"Think of it like a magic button."

She fell back beside him and he tapped the front of her damp underwear. A streak of pleasure shot through her.

"Oh, yes. Mrs. Whitehead didn't teach us about the"—she paused, enunciating every syllable—"clit-or-is in ninth-grade sex ed."

It was only then that she felt the tickle of the caterpillars on her arm, on her thigh. Marching through her hair. They were making their slow, methodical journey across Brooks's body too, one sluicing through the milky fluid on his hip.

"There are caterpillars on us," she said.

"I know," he said dreamily.

29.

Veronica

She sat on the peach linen chaise longue in their bedroom, smoking cigarettes and watching Bob mumble in his sleep. He seemed agitated, even crying out once.

Champ lay on the carpet at the foot of the bed. His ears twitched each time his master stirred. Poor dumb dog, she thought. His loyalty was sure to kill him.

She thought of Champ's sister, Princess. Thirteen years ago, she and Bob had driven across two states to a farm known for their world-class German shepherds. Bob had insisted, claiming the dogs were sired by a stud whose great-great-great grandfather had searched for bodies in the rubble of London's bombed buildings during the war. The breeders, when hearing Bob was the head of Grudder Aviation, let them walk into the fenced-off puppy area and Veronica had been knocked on her behind when she leaned down to pet the mass of floppy-eared pups, and then they were climbing over her, licking her face with their sandpaper tongues. It had been delightful. She hadn't surrendered her body like that since Ginny was a toddler, and it made her feel like a mother. It made her laugh. When the breeders called the dogs off, she'd been sad but didn't know how to explain that she wanted the pups to paw at her, to cover her body with theirs.

They had picked out two roly-poly pups, the only bitch in the litter and one of her brothers. Princess and Champion. Princess had died of cancer two years ago. When the vet had sliced open their silver-and-black beauty for what they had hoped would be a lifesaving operation, the tumors were everywhere. Veronica had been the one to sign the euthanasia and disposal papers. Bob had been so distraught he had nearly hyperventilated in the waiting room. The receptionist had brought her a brown paper bag that smelled like luncheon meat and showed Bob how to breathe in and out, the paper bag inflating and deflating like a bellows.

The change in Bob was born in that moment, she thought now as she watched him kick away the ivory satin bedsheets—he was still murmuring in his sleep but more softly. It had taken him weeks to recover from the loss of Champ's sister. And now Champ was old, and what would happen, Veronica thought, when Champ died? His back legs were going fast, buckling when he took the long flight of stairs up to the master bedroom each night. He was almost fourteen. Why shouldn't there be euthanasia for people, she thought, lighting another cigarette off the butt of the last. Why should the sick and old have to suffer? Why should the young and healthy have to watch their onetime heroes decay?

"The show must go on," she said to the dark room, and Bob stirred, turning over, clutching his pillow like a child dreaming.

She remembered the little box. The gift Dominic—it must be him, the scribbling on the note was all boy—had left at the back door last week. *For the pain.*

Like the glass box in Wonderland that appears, magically, out of thin air, Veronica had thought as soon as she'd opened the dusty velvet box big enough for a bracelet or a brooch. But instead of a cake iced with the words EAT ME there was the note and a hand-rolled cigarette. When she lifted it to her nose and sniffed, she knew it wasn't any ordinary cigarette. She'd hid the box on the top shelf of the butler's pantry near the extra Metamucil and cans of Ensure she'd had forced Bob to drink after Princess's death when he was on his mourning fast.

Now she slipped on her quilted pink housecoat and her once plush pink slippers, now torn and stained from the walk through the woods to the Castle bell tower, and went to the pantry.

The box was still there. She had to stand on her toes to reach it and a wave of vertigo washed over her and she imagined how they'd find her. Dead in the pantry with a Mary Jane cigarette. She laughed at the image, and then laughed harder when she imagined Peggy Brell and Binnie Mueller at the club gossiping about it over drinks.

Outside on the patio overlooking the green sea of lawn, she was grateful for the cool breeze blowing west toward the factory instead of away. The night air was clear of the oily residue from the smoke that pumped out of Plants 2 and 3 day and night. As constant as the sun and the moon.

She reread her grandson's note: *For the pain.* For what pain? Wasn't there an infinite variety, she thought. Physical. Emotional. Existential. The pain of youth when it seems as if time slogs ahead like a snail stuck in the sunshine after a rainstorm. The pain of middle age when time slips through one's fingers. And the pain of old age. Well, that was one helluva list. He couldn't know—about her cancer. Could he?

She tucked the pointy tip of the gift between her lips and lit the other end. It was windy and she had to huddle in the alcove between the back door and the kitchen window, sucking hard to keep it burning. She pulled in a great gulp of smoke. Her lungs seized. Her throat burned as if she'd swallowed an ember. She remembered the unfiltered cigarettes she and her sister had choked on behind the barn in Palmyra so many years ago. She gripped a patio chair to steady herself until her lungs loosened and she could take a breath. She wiped the tears with the back of her hand, her knuckles so swollen they seemed to belong on another woman's hand. A stranger. She stubbed the damn thing out on the concrete wall, tucked it back into the box, and clamped it shut, smoothing her housecoat as she turned to the house. Then she understood why they called it a high. She was lifted. As if a great hand had reached down from the clouds and straightened her hunched back, making her feel tall. Strong. Like Alice, she had grown. The pain was gone. In her back, at the base of her neck, in her knees and shoulders and in between the seized joints of her disfigured toes.

She stepped out onto the great wide lawn turned a silvery blue by the path of moonlight shooting from the horizon, across the sea and through the grass. Like a carpet made of mercury, she thought, and hobbled forward wanting to walk across it. And the smells. It wasn't just the nearby lilacs she could smell, it was everything. The lavender and seaweed and white pine and bayberry. The sweet fern and pine needles that had lain toasting in the summer sun all day. And the sounds! It was just as her father had told her so long ago that she was only remembering it now. She on his knee on the old wicker rocking chair on the porch one summer night. Him explaining what life was like before they got electricity. He called it the music of the night. She could hear it now. The *ba-boom* of the waves breaking against the seawall. The crickets' song. The warbling call of the night herons and the croaking chirp of the spring peepers in the wetlands. And yet something was missing. All these sounds were so clear, deafeningly so, because there was one sound absent. The caterpillars had fallen silent.

She had done it, Veronica thought. Maddie had banished the pestilence. In her current state as she stood on the mercury path that seemed to lead from her lawn to heaven (she could almost believe there was such a place), it made sense to her that a young girl full of life and love, of sex and vigor, of hope, could make magic.

"You did it, my girl!" Veronica shouted toward the thick woods that led to the Castle, not caring if she woke Bob and Ginny and Dom and that jerk, Tony. Let them witness the miracle! It was a sign. She was sure of it.

She turned back to the house. She was exhausted, quite suddenly. When had she last felt such exhilaration? She patted the pocket of her housecoat and felt the small box that held her treat. She imagined her warm, soft bed. Lying next to her husband. As snug as the caterpillars tucked in their cocoons.

30.

Jules

He woke sweating and tangled in the bedsheet. He'd had a nightmare that his hands were on fire. Now that he was awake, they still burned. His fingers were so swollen, their sides touched so he looked like one of those circus freaks. Flipper Boy.

Leslie's side of the bed was empty. He sat up, too fast, his head spun. For a crazy moment, he'd imagined her cheating on him, screwing one of the boys from the ballroom. One of the dark boys.

He looked in Brooks's room, and there was Leslie and their little girl. One spoon wrapped around a tiny one. He chided himself, *Get your shit together, man. You're being paranoid is all.*

He checked the bathroom cabinet for the pink bottle of calamine lotion. He'd been using bottle after bottle on his hands, and the claylike smell of the cool lotion had an effect, instantly soothing him. It was missing. He must have left it in the Castle kitchen.

He found the bottle next to the brass-and-enamel-bedecked La Cornue stove Leslie's mother, he guessed, had insisted on. Although, from what Leslie told him, her mother could make only two dishes—pot roast and chicken and rice soup. He coated his hands in the cream. Then he heard the sound from one of the rooms at the end of the long dark corridor that ran from the kitchen, past the ballroom and ended at the admiral's study—a wood-paneled room with emerald-green upholstered wing chairs and a desk that rivaled the one in the Oval Office. It was an animal sound, a keening that rose and fell, and, goddammit, this was all he needed, a beast—a raccoon maybe—stuck in the house.

He walked past the ballroom, which seemed empty, until he spotted a few bodies slumped on the antique divan the kids had pulled into the room. He laughed quietly, imagining what Mrs. Marshall, the admiral's wife, would think if she saw her Queen Anne furniture soiled with beer and bong water and dotted with cigarette burns.

The sound was louder now, a moaning that sounded like pain, reminding him of Leslie in total agonizing glory as she pushed first Brooks out, and then, twelve years later, Eva. The door to the study was half open and Jules could see, in the green light that spilled from the banker's lamp on the desk, that there were people in the high-backed green wing chair in the center of the room. A couple. The girl sat with arms akimbo and legs apart, like a smug queen on her throne, and the dark-haired boy (Jules only guessed he was a boy because of his wide shoulders) knelt in front of the chair.

And then the sound escaped her lips. The animal moan. It was pleasure. The boy's face was buried between the girl's legs, nodding up and down. The girl lolled her head from side to side—her eyes were closed but Jules knew, from the long glossy, blond-streaked hair, that it was her, the leader of the girls. What was her name? Her limp arms came to life and she gripped the armrests of the chair and lifted her hips. Jules was hard now, his dick rising against his thin pajama pants. He was still holding the calamine lotion, but he had forgotten to put the cap back on, and as the girl's moans reached a new height, he looked down and saw the pool of opaque pink goo spreading on the dark wood floor, and the girl was laughing, biting her bottom lip and saying, "Oh, Daddy," and the boy was on his feet, his mouth wet and glistening, and charging toward Jules and he saw it was the same boy from the fight at the fair and he ran from the room like a fucking coward he told himself and the boy slipped on the lotion and Jules heard a thump and then the boy cursing and the girl—Bitsy, that was her name—giggling.

He was in the garden, leaning over to catch his breath, his swollen, poisoned hands throbbing, and he heard it. Or he didn't hear it, but it felt as if the silence was a noise unto itself. No more *ca-cacking* of pincers tearing at young leaf. No more *spit-*

spit-spit of their shit raining down on the forest floor. He fell to his knees and let his hands rake through the soft grass.

"Jules?"

He turned and saw Leslie standing at the top of the stone steps, like a sylph in her white nightgown.

"Sweetheart," she said, and he heard the fear in her voice. "Are you okay? I thought you were, maybe having a heart attack."

He laughed loud and long, his booming voice bouncing off the lush walls of his garden.

"It's over!" he cried. "Listen."

His beautiful wife tilted her golden head.

"What a relief," she said quietly.

"Relief!" he shouted. "Sweet, sweet relief!"

He lifted her into his arms and twirled her around, the skirt of her nightgown ballooning.

"Everything is going to be okay," he whispered.

PART FOUR

An Eclipse of Moths

July–August 1992

The adult moth will emerge, fully developed, by splitting the pupal skin.

The name *Lymantria dispar* is composed of two Latin-derived words. *Lymantria* means "destroyer." The word *dispar* is derived from the Latin for "unequal" and it depicts the differing characteristics between the sexes… it is noticeable that the females are bigger than the males. Another important difference between the sexes is that females possess fully formed wings but do not fly.

—*The Gypsy Moth: Research Toward Integrated Pest Management*, United States Department of Agriculture, 1981

July 4, 1992
Dear Diary,

Hi again! I went back to my last entry and scratched through #4.
I scratched it so many times the paper tore through and that just
made me even madder. It's BS that B and me have to hide our feelings
for each other. Especially when they are the MOST true pure
beautiful good feelings ever. I know if my dad finds out he'll hit me. Or
worse. Maybe he'll finally hang me on the wall by my hair like he's
always threatening to. Like that's even something he could do!!!

How could our love be so bad when it feels so good? Before him I
hated all the love stories I read about in books. Or saw in movies. AS IF.
I remember thinking when I watched Love Story and I even got mad at
Penny for blubbering like a baby when Ali MacGraw died. But it IS real.
I know that now. You can feel safe with another person. You can feel
like a better version of yourself. That's how I feel in the secret garden.

Tonight's the stupid 4th of July party at the OCCC. The only reason
I'm going is because B promised he'd go with me. And I'm going to
do it. I really am. Tonight is the night we're going to show the whole
island who we really are. They'll be blinded by how beautiful we are
together me and B. Just like the gods and goddesses and the way they
blinded mere mortals when they appeared in their heavenly form.
Avalon won't know what hit them when they see us loving each other.

B told me how the gypsy moths communicate through pheromones
(spelling??). How they let out these chemicals that show the boy moths
how to get to the girl moths. And how scientists have made that same
chemical in their labs. I wish I could spray the club with that shit tonight.
Make EVERYONE in Avalon fall in love just like me and B. It would be
peacetime forever after that. No more Wildcat jets made ever again! HA!

My dad is totally going to flip. But WHATEVER. Let him hit me.
Let him pull my hair. Let him nail me to the wall. I don't care. All that
matters is that B and me are together. Forever. Knock on wood.

See you later, alligator.

Love,
Maddie Pencott LaRosa
P.S. (So I don't forget)
Cottage to Castle: Right, right, left, right, left, left
Cottage to Secret Garden: Left, right, left, left, right, left

31.

Veronica

She stepped carefully into the green silk dress and, what do you know, it fit like a glove.

It was the dress she had worn to Admiral and Mrs. Marshall's Christmas party in 1983—her first East Avalon event after Bob's promotion to president. An A-line Dior in green crepe with a square neck and chiffon shawl. Now, because of her curved spine, the skirt brushed the tops of her gnarled toes.

She heard something and froze. There was a pinging at her closet window.

A brown speckled gypsy moth was trapped between the window screen and glass. She knew it was a he because females were a creamy white and could not fly. This summer was her fourth gypsy moth infestation on the island. By far the worst. Perhaps, she thought, the females hadn't even hatched. The males split their cocoons first, their life's purpose to fly frantic zigzagging patterns in search of a mate. Horny fools on the prowl. She opened the window. Slapped at the screen. The moth flew into the room. She scurried after him, the back of her dress unzipped, swatting the air. He landed on a pink cashmere cardigan tagged for Goodwill. She attacked. Caught him between thumb and forefinger. His furious wings tickled her fingertips before she crushed him between her palms.

She lit the leftover marijuana cigarette, squinting against the rising smoke. The burning weed clamped between her false teeth, she reached back, her shoulder bones creaking, and tried to zip the gown as green as the lawn stretching outside her window. It was useless. *She* was useless. She'd have to ask Rosalita for help.

She had worked hard to fit in with the ladies of East Avalon.

She'd had to, coming from Palmyra. Born, as Bob loved to say, "a beauty queen with cow shit between her toes." There had been many bridge parties, many ladies' luncheons, where she feared she stuck out like a lump in mashed potatoes.

She hadn't quit studying the ladies, even five decades later. Not everyone would call it "work"—she hadn't perched in her gilded cage long enough to drink that particular brand of Kool-Aid (as the kids said these days). But still, she had toiled. How could she not when so much was at stake? When Bob rose to president, he became one of the most powerful men in the country. His seat reserved, as he often reminded her, at round tables at the Pentagon and the White House. He teed off with Presidents Eisenhower through Bush.

She hadn't any formal education, but the ladies of East Avalon had taught her all she needed to know, *more* than she wanted to know, about how to be a woman of wealth. The sucking in, straightening, lacing, tightening, commanding one's own body like a drill sergeant. She had learned to wear that composure like a diamond-studded girdle, drawn tight so her ribs cracked with every step. She had a few tricks—pinching the meat between thumb and forefinger when she grew drowsy at a political dinner full of Champagne toasts and endless applause, or she'd prick her finger with one of her pearl-tipped hat pins. Her work had paid off. She had been no lump but one of the ladies. Invisible among their ranks. Was it time to surprise the ladies of East Avalon, she wondered, or too early to let the cloak drop at her feet?

Her disguise had required a pricey wardrobe, and, in the last two months, she'd bagged sixty years of it. Jumbo trash bags lined her closet floor. Naked hangers dangled above. Tens of thousands of dollars wasted on cashmere cardigans from Bergdorf's and long-trained gowns from Saks she'd worn once to galas. Enough golf shirts and slacks for ten lifetimes on the green. Eight Hefty bags of shoes alone. The soles of some unscuffed—only worn inside the store. Pantsuits and skirt suits and so many blouses in silk, linen, and all manner of synthetic fiber. Each bag labeled with its destination. *Salvation Army. Goodwill. St. Mary's Chapel by the Sea.* Six bags to be shipped back to Palmyra. An anonymous donation. Her plainest slacks and shirts because no self-respecting Mormon sister would trade eternal life ever after for a sweetheart neckline.

She thought of Maddie. Trapped on this island steered by a madman. What she wouldn't give to see the girl get away. Free to be visible, invisible, whatever and whomever the girl dared. If only she could ship Maddie off the island like her bags of clothes.

The Dior was too decadent for Goodwill. It would have to go someplace after she wore it tonight one last time. Perhaps the Ladies Auxiliary Charity shop at St. John's. She imagined the East Avalon ladies who shopped in disguise (as if privacy exists on an island with one exit!) hiding under brimmed golf hats and dark sunglasses, picking over the lost treasures of women dead, feeble, or abandoned in a nursing home by their ungrateful children.

She stood in front of the same mirror she had looked into the morning of Ginny's wedding sixteen years ago. She straightened her spine, lifted her chin. Hell would freeze over (borrowing one of her husband's favorites) before she gave this gem to those cheapskates, Bunny Templeton or Clara Friedrich, to wear when she was dead and buried. She promised herself she'd wear only the brightest colors for her remaining days.

She floated through the gold-and-cream country club dining room. Never had she *not* minded walking into that room—its mirrored walls multiplying the wealthy of East Avalon so she felt a claustrophobic panic. But today she was as cool as a cucumber. Or, as she'd heard Maddie say (and Oprah too), "whatever."

The round scoops of chicken liver pâté, a popular dining-hall appetizer, had always reminded her of cat food. Today, they seemed the most appetizing thing in the world. She whisked a plate off a table as she passed, dug the Melba toast into the creamy ball.

She spotted Ginny's long blond hair hung in looping curls down her back. She felt a swell of pride—her girl had done it, gotten out of bed and made herself up! Perhaps things weren't as dire as Veronica had feared. Then Ginny turned and she saw her daughter's blurred look. Puffy eyes. Lipstick uncertainly applied. Ginny shifted into over-the-top enthusiasm. *Mommy!* When Tony leaned forward to give Veronica a peck, she stepped back. She waved a finger at the sweater wrapped around his shoulders—tendrils of curly black hair reaching out from his collar.

"What—are you off to play a set?"

She let her laughter linger as she walked away, imagining it the tail of a scorpion, hoping her jerk of a son-in-law stung.

She felt so buoyant, she didn't even resist when Eleanor Smith, cochair of the Annual Oyster Cove Country Club Fourth of July Surf 'N' Turf Dinner, cornered her by the shrimp cocktail and insisted on pinning a ribboned corsage to Veronica's chest.

"Come now, Veronica," she slurred. "*All* the East Avalon ladies deserve a flower."

She knew what the beastly woman meant. Even the disgraced ladies. The merger was moving forward. Tangeman Aircraft had offered 2.1 billion, outbidding three other vultures. The news hadn't gone public, but she was sure it was making its way 'round the club dining room, would be all over the island by the time the first firework burst overhead.

"Pin away, Ellie!" Veronica sang, relishing the confusion scrunching up the woman's already wrinkled face.

Yes, Veronica thought, she may be dying, she may have failed in saving Old Ironsides, but at least she'd worn her sunscreen on the golf green and tennis courts. *She* wouldn't look like a dried-up mummy in her casket. As the woman's pudgy hands fumbled over her chest, she feared Eleanor might bump one of her scars or, worse, notice how the bodice sagged around the empty pockets where her breasts had been. The twit was digging into the silk again and again—silk Veronica imagined Christian Dior had reveled in after the war rations ended. All that glorious fabric hoarded for years finally free to be used in extravagant abundance! The pearl-tipped corsage pin tore tiny holes so that a wisp of thread hung loose, and Veronica used all her waning strength not to strangle the woman. At last, the trio of purple orchids were in place. Eleanor clomped away in her orthopedic flats, over to Binnie Mueller, fake smile lit, flabby arms open for a hug.

Veronica was sweating. Her heart tapping so fast she knew

she needed ice water or she'd go into full palpitations. She had to yell over the din to get a soda water from the bartender. That moron Geoffrey Norris, who ran Plant 4, was telling jokes again. Every one starring a rabbi, priest, and a pinup girl, or something equally offensive. The circle of men hee-hawing at his jokes like a bunch of asses—the kind with tails. The East Avalonians were having a grand old time doing what they did best—pretending their grip on war and peace was unshakable.

She had felt so divine when their driver, Charles, first dropped her and Bob (in a docile mood, thank heavens) at the revolving glass doors of the club. She had dumped Bob with Dominic, who had become his grandfather's nanny. Later, she spotted the boy switching Bob's rum and Coke with his own glass of soda. He was a crafty one. Getting tipsy, making eyes at that waiter—the Hispanic boy she'd always suspected was a little light in the loafers. Touché, young Master Pencott. *Touché.*

She inspected the dessert table that nearly ran the length of the hall. The chocolate-peppermint molten cake was just the right amount of runny at its center, but wasn't it so 1989? She should've known that Eleanor, who always played it safe no matter the game (bridge, tennis or golf), wouldn't have made any—what was it Julius had said?—*decorative gambles.* If it had been up to Veronica, she'd have done something classic but almost forgotten. A revival of sorts. Baked Alaska. And once, she remembered, she'd served hollow chocolate eggs filled with strawberry mousse for a White Eagle holiday party. It had been the talk of the ladies' bridge tournament the following week. She should do that again, she thought, and then remembered how her time was almost up.

She watched a cluster of women ooh and ahh over one another's dresses and diamonds and recently coiffed platinum hair. Oh how giddy they must feel, pinned with exotic blooms, the very opposite of the overpruned gardens these same women paid day workers to plant around their estates. Like beautiful prison walls. Privileged prisoners, Veronica thought, shut in their beautiful houses surrounded by beautiful things, day after day, as their menfolk made the fighting machines that kept the country safe, and the coffers full.

She had been one of them. Walked her gardens, volunteered for charity, hit golf balls, tennis balls, even captained a boating race that benefitted the Korean War Veterans Association. She had kept herself busy, trying to make from out of thin air a kind of *work*. What was life without work?

She *was* one of them. She was still there, yes? She smoothed her shaking hands down the thick silk bunched around her waist, to feel herself. Alive. She downed a mimosa—the citrus tang and bubbles heavenly as it glided down her throat. She remembered her favorite Oprah quote—she wouldn't dare admit it to Maddie. *Think like a queen. A queen is not afraid to fail. Failure is another stepping-stone to greatness.* The Champagne bubbles gone to her head, she tried to remember her mission. Exactly *what* was she trying so hard not to fail at?

She reached the end of the dessert table, passed the marbled cheesecake and etched crystal bowl filled with tiramisu, and there was Maddie. Pretty in a pink sundress. With her beau, Brooks. The two lovers were Veronica's only remaining mission. She'd make certain her granddaughter was safe and happy before the island fell to pieces.

The little Marshall girl was holding Maddie's hand, all dressed up in a flowery frock with a full skirt. A yellow satin ribbon tied around her waist.

"Darling," Veronica cooed. "You are the prettiest lady in this *entire* room."

The girl—Eva was her name, Veronica remembered—smiled, ducking her head shyly, rocking side to side so the skirt of her dress twirled.

The sight of Julius refilled her high.

"Oh! I was *so* hoping you'd be here today."

"Ms. Veronica."

He laughed quietly, the dimple in his cheek showing. Then he raised his eyebrows and checked to see if anyone had noticed. Was she being too loud? Who cared!

"There's no time for subtleties anymore, I'm afraid. The clock is ticking," She looped her arm through his and dragged him from the dessert table toward the center of the room—the laid-down dance floor where guests mingled in groups, sipping cocktails and nibbling puff pastry. Playing make believe, she thought, pretending the island wasn't on the edge of DEFCON 1. "Tick, tick, tick!" she sang brightly.

"Um," Julius began to protest, looking back at his little girl.

"Oh, nonsense. Maddie will watch her." She called over her shoulder, "Won't you dear?"

"Of course, Grandmother," Maddie said.

Julius stumbled to keep up with Veronica.

"The theme of the day is 'whatever,' dear Julius! Which reminds me. I have a message for Leslie."

She pulled him into a quiet corner, where an enormous ice sculpture in the shape of an F4F Wildcat poised ready to land on a platter piled with empty oyster shells.

"My Leslie?" He looked confused.

"Yes, silly! What other Leslie do we have in common?"

He glanced around and she realized he was searching for his wife now. Poor Julius, he felt the bad news coming.

"You tell Leslie," she paused. "*Our* Leslie, that the war is over."

"I don't understand," he said. "Mrs. Pencott . . . if you wait here, I'll go find her."

"No need. We've already flown the white flag. We've surrendered! Grudder is no longer. Now it's *Tangeman Grudder*. And my time here is finished."

She was ready, finally, to confess. Tell someone she was dead. Then she saw how scared the big man was. Understood that Leslie had kept him in the dark all this time.

"You *do* know why you're here, don't you?" she asked, speaking slowly because he seemed suddenly childlike in his confusion. "Why Leslie brought you here? Why she came back to the island?"

He shook his head. As if, she thought, he was dizzy.

"Never mind," she said. "Now, where is Clara Friedrich? That stuck-up . . . Thinks she knows all there is to know about roses. You need to teach her a thing or two."

"Um, okay," he said tentatively. Like he feared she might be mocking him, Veronica thought. "I did do a three-month research fellowship on hybrids at the Smithsonian Botanical Institute. . . ."

"Of course you did!" Veronica squeezed his arm, drawing him closer. This handsome, brilliant man. This—what was it she'd heard Maddie say—*clueless* man. She wouldn't rain on his parade. Not today, at what she knew would be her last visit to the stuffy Oyster Cove Country Club. Good riddance. "*You* are a genius and it's time we spread some of that wisdom around, don't you think? Sowed it like seeds, yes? If you can forgive the pun."

"If you say so, Mrs. Pencott."

"Please, dear. When will you ever start calling me Veronica?"

He bowed his head and whispered in her ear, "Veronica."

His warm breath made her clip-on pearl earring wobble and she knew that, in a past life, in a different body, a different time and place, she could've swooned for this man.

"Oh, there's Clara." She pointed at the table where boiled shrimp hung on the edge of a massive carved ice bowl. "She won last year's blue ribbon at the annual Avalon Flower Festival." She dropped her voice to a whisper. "Everyone knows she broke the contest rules and used some experimental fertilizer from China. Those American Beauties didn't get that way all on their own. No sirree! Let's go show her a thing or two."

She pulled Julius forward, calling, "Clara, dear! I have someone you *must* meet."

32.

Jules

He had eaten five lobster tails, using the same technique that had worked so well at the progressive dinner party. Keeping his mouth full so he only had to nod and lift his eyebrows in agreement when one after another old biddy greeted him, asked how he was enjoying his first clambake. He nodded and smiled and stuffed his face with shellfish, sausage, and corn baked in a potato sack deep in the sand under layers of seaweed and hot stones, so it was salty, like he was eating the sea itself. But he couldn't enjoy anything really, not when he was worried about Brooks. Waiting for the right moment to pull his son aside and ask what the hell was going on.

And now the old woman, Veronica, had taken him hostage. He had no idea what she was talking about. Messages for Leslie. Something about the factory. Her creepy predictions, like she was a witch crystal-gazing. *Things are about to change.*

It was her warning that had unnerved him most. *Be careful, Julius. Nothing is as it seems on the island. Especially when at war.* Now he understood—the woman was demented. The country had been at peace since the end of the Gulf War. But as she pulled him around the dining room, like a new pet she wanted to show off, her congested breath rattling, the atmosphere in the room changed. The women spooning globs of chocolate mousse and creamy tiramisu, the men dropping shots of whiskey into mugs of beer with a foamy splash, suddenly, they seemed to Jules, desperate and famished and scared.

He and Leslie had fought back at the Castle. Why *should* he go to the Fourth of July party, he'd asked, when she'd only ignore him, sashay from guest to guest, leaving him to trail after little Eva and make sure she didn't pull down a tablecloth covered in

Bellini-filled flutes. *Another Leslie Day Marshall schmooze-fest,* he'd said, and Brooks had snorted, which, Jules knew, could've meant allegiance or insult. Or both.

Leslie called him *passive-aggressive.*

He called her a *narcissist.*

Brooks called them both *downers.*

Eva cried.

In the end, he'd ironed the seersucker suit he'd worn the night of the progressive dinner party, even sprinkled baby powder over a wine stain, a trick his mom had shown him.

Ta-da! He'd announced himself with open arms, the back of the suit jacket still toasty from the iron, just as Leslie, Brooks, and Eva were climbing into the car headed to the club. His wife's smile warmed him inside out. A peace offering, he hoped, since they'd been fighting like cats and dogs for weeks.

The car was running, Eva strapped into her car seat, Brooks fiddling with the radio dials until he found what he wanted—a station blasting "Baby Got Back"—and then Leslie was laughing, dancing, wiggling her hips in the seat, even Eva waving her plump arms above her head. Jules popped the trunk. He'd left his new dress shoes back there. The price tag had made his mouth go dry but Leslie had insisted. Brooks's backpack was tucked next to the shoes and when Jules lifted the shoebox, the backpack rattled. Like it was full of metal.

He unzipped the bag—not that he needed proof. He'd grown up a city boy. He knew the jangling of spray-paint cans when he heard it.

When they had pulled up to the clubhouse, Jules busy handing the keys over to the valet, Brooks had disappeared. He must talk to his son. Then he, Brooks, and Leslie would sit down and have a long talk about what came next. Leslie would refuse, but Jules didn't see a way around going to the police. Maybe, if Brooks turned himself in . . . he stopped himself. Brooks *could* be holding on to the cans for someone else? Those ratty metalhead kids who had ruined the ballroom walls with their foul tags. SAVE ME. FUCK ME. He'd stopped there, not wanting to read any more. Who, he wondered, did they think was listening? He'd told Leslie about the sprayed walls and she'd responded with the same apathetic shrug she'd used again and again those past few months.

He managed to lose Veronica and downed his third drink, something fizzy with lime, the rim coated in red, white, and blue sugar granules. The American flag swizzler poked him in the nose. Then he heard his father's voice so loud and clear, he searched the room, turning in a slow circle. He was losing his mind, he thought, then spotted Brooks with Eva by the lemonade fountain. Brooks hand in hand with a pretty young girl who, Jules guessed, was *the* Maddie. His son was nervous, his fingers lifting to pick at his hair, his eyes moving from one corner of the room to the next like he was waiting, but for what? Each time the girl leaned close to him, to whisper in his ear, to tug on his shirtsleeve, Jules saw Brooks pull away. Something he guessed Maddie noticed too, because her smile looked put on. A mask.

You better keep watch over that boy, his father's voice grumbled. Jules finished the drink and made his way back to the bar for another. Something to silence his pops.

But after the fourth drink, and even the fifth, his tongue fuzzy from the lime, the voice remained.

Don't just stand there like some tar-faced lawn jockey, Julius.

Leslie waved to him—a wiggle of fingers from her spot at the great window overlooking the rolling hills of the golf course.

Like some damn trophy husband. A pet to keep chained up in the garden.

His stomach convulsed, and he was heading for the bathroom that smelled like aftershave and pipe tobacco, where Muzak slipped out from invisible speakers, and a Hispanic man not much younger than Jules handed out towels and received a measly quarter in a porcelain dish.

Veronica reappeared. She tugged him forward and spent the next twenty minutes introducing him—thrusting him into the middle of conversations was more like it—to one confused old lady after another. At first, he smiled meekly, shook the offered hands, every one bedecked with jeweled rings stuffed over swollen knuckles. He assumed Veronica was trying to get him gardening work, but when her sassy side took over, he saw it was a game. She was mocking the island elite, and the dumb lugs didn't even know.

"No, Dolores," Veronica said with a sweet smile, "He can't trim your rosebushes. He's not a day laborer, he's a landscape architect. He went to Harvard, for chrissakes!"

Veronica grabbed Jules's arm and pulled him away and he did his best to stifle a laugh as he glanced back at poor Dolores, her mouth hanging open over her doubled chin.

"Forget that dingbat," Veronica mumbled. "And be careful no one hands you their empty glasses. Half these people think you're a busboy."

Coming from anyone else on the island, Jules would have been offended. But Veronica had felt, ever since that night at the Castle after the mad Colonel tolled the bell, like a friend. Or a comrade, at least. Neither of them belonged on this island.

He thought, at first, she was drunk. Her eyes were glassy. Bloodshot.

"Ms. Veronica. You seem," he started, "different tonight."

"Shucks." She slapped his arm playfully. Like a teenage girl flirting in the school hallway, he thought. "An old hippie like you should be able to appreciate my *elevated* state of being. Come with me, Julius. Let us transcend together. Ooh, lookie there!"

He followed Veronica's crooked finger. Orchid Lady from the fair stood by the buffet in a shimmery blue dress that made Jules think of porpoises. A jumbo shrimp tail stuck out of her mouth and when she spotted Veronica pulling him toward her, she nearly dropped her plate.

"I don't think this is a good idea," he whispered into Veronica's poufy silver hair, tasting hairspray.

"It is indeed," she said. "Just watch me do my magic."

"Really," he said, "I don't think—"

She stopped him. "Don't think, just smile. She'll be less scared if you smile."

He heard his father's voice. *They're all scared of you. They'll always be scared of you.* Jules knew he was right. No matter how hard Veronica, in her sweet but manic Good Samaritan crusade, tried to change their minds.

She's just another Lady Van der Meer, his father's voice said. *And you're her pet project. One that has to be leashed in the garden each night. God forbid you go rabid.*

As Veronica rattled off directions to a slack-jawed Orchid Lady, who, it turned out, was named Lorna Hennessey, and the chair of the East Avalon Flower Festival that year, Jules thought of his mother's *lady,* which is what she'd always called Mrs. Van der Meer, her employer of more than four decades and, no matter how much his father had wanted to deny it, their family's benefactor.

It was, he thought, as Orchid Lady nodded—*why certainly Jules could participate in the flower festival that year*—thanks to Mrs. Van der Meer that he was standing there listening to these two ancient white ladies discuss him like he was stock to be traded. It was still a mystery to him how his sweet-natured mama had won the argument with his father, convincing him to let Jules attend the private high school paid for by Mrs. Van der Meer. Must have taken Mama all her patience, and courage, to stand up to the man who was as hard as dried cement. His pops had ranted that taking white people's money was like . . . how had his father put it?

Like forging your own chains.

But his mother had insisted, waved Jules's test scores in his pops's face, parroted her *lady,* even using the woman's hoity-toity inflection, *The boy is clearly gifted! Destined for great things.*

His mother's shining eyes had unlocked something—a kindness?—in his father, and Jules had worn those chains, rode the Van der Meer scholarship from Dalton to Columbia to Harvard, all the way to the Oyster Cove Country Club.

He wished Mama were with him now. She, like Leslie (the Leslie *before* the island), had seen the promise in people. He knew just what she'd say. *Julius, look at all these fine people!* He and his pops were always teasing her about what she called "her appreciation for finer things." His pops called it "rich-white-people shit," but who could blame her, Jules thought. She'd grown up the light-skinned daughter of a maid in the Van der Meer home on Central Park East, becoming a maid herself at sixteen. She'd come of age surrounded by beautiful things. Like a girl lost in a museum.

But his mother was dead, and wealthy whites no longer fascinated him the way they had when he'd first met Leslie almost eighteen years ago, the Twiggy look-alike who wore coveralls when they'd volunteered at an urban garden in Roxbury, far from Harvard's landscaped campus. That first year with Leslie had been filled with dizzying excitement—all the attention he'd been paid by her friends, who, like Leslie, didn't live in the dorms, but in palatial townhouses on posh Beacon Hill. They called themselves *artists* and *activists*, although it was hard to figure what medium they worked in, or what cause they were dedicated to. To Jules, it seemed they bounced from cause to cause with the same ambivalence they showed him—when he was new, they lavished him with attention, but after a few months, he was old hat.

Not his Leslie. She was a believer. In change. In good. In the power of one person to make a difference. Even after the idealism of the '60s burned out, Leslie's friends, one by one, doing an about-face, following in their mothers' and fathers' footsteps—bored housewives and paunchy investment bankers—his Leslie stayed gold.

His father's voice was just a whisper now, but, still, it buzzed at his ear like the mosquitos that swarmed the island on humid nights.

Who you trying to convince, Julius? Yourself?

He studied the corsage pinned to Orchid Lady's ample bosom, even more exotic than the bloom she'd worn the night of the fair. A trio of green-white *Brassavola novola* orchids. He had to stop himself from leaning forward and sniffing the strong, citrusy tang, and then remembered he'd read somewhere that they were only fragrant at night, in order to attract the right moth. An image of her covered in gypsy moths gave him a moment of confidence and he smiled and nodded. "So lovely to see you again."

Veronica and Orchid Lady moved on to a new topic, something about the factory, and he was relieved, ready to make his exit. He glanced out the window, past the rows of golf carts, and saw Brooks walking away from the clubhouse toward the green course. He was with that girl. They were holding hands. People were looking out the window. Did Jules see them shaking their heads?

Don't be paranoid, he told himself. *Don't be a fool,* his father said.

"Excuse me, ladies." He bowed his head. "I'm headed to the little boys' room."

"Make sure you come back, Julius dear," Veronica called after him. "I'm not finished with you just yet!"

He was out of breath when he caught up with Brooks and the girl. His new pointy-toed dress shoes squished across the damp turf.

"Brooks," he wheezed.

"Dad." He was annoyed. Like usual. "We're just taking a walk."

Jules tried a friendly tone. "You must be Maddie."

She blushed and looked up at Brooks, who stared into the hazy dusk settling over the silent green.

Something, Jules knew, was wrong. Couldn't the girl see that?

She reached out and Jules shook her hand. He could fold it inside his palm if he wanted to. Make it disappear. She was pretty. Maybe even beautiful. There was something about her face—her round cheeks and petite mouth—that reminded him of a painting. Raphael or da Vinci. A *Mona Lisa* smile. What was Brooks thinking, Jules wondered, knowing his boy, if he could read his mind, would've called Jules a hypocrite.

"Okay," Brooks said, impatience churning. "You met. Now can we go?"

"Hold your horses, kiddo," Jules said, surprising himself by sounding all Ward Cleaver. "I just need to talk to you for a sec. That cool, Maddie?"

"Sure." She smiled. Innocent.

He wondered if she had any idea what kind of trouble she might be getting his boy in. Sure, it was only a *might* at this point, but hadn't she heard stories about what happened to black boys who fell for white girls? Once those white girls got sick of them.

Jesus, he thought, he sounded just like his father who had

called him all manner of names when he'd come home from Harvard and told them about Leslie. *Fool. Dumbass. Fluffernutter for brains.* That last one had made Jules and his mom laugh but, still, it had stung and there'd been a moment, time slowing, Jules's breath loud and thick like he had cotton stuffed in his ears, where he'd been sure his father would disown him. Would declare him *no son of mine.*

"Over here," Jules said, "in private."

He walked toward the metal shed turned blue in the twilight. When Brooks didn't follow, he seized the boy's arm, pulling him around so their backs were to Maddie. To the mob at the clubhouse.

"What the—?" Brooks said.

It was near dark, the golf green stretched out before them. Like they were shipwrecked on a distant planet, Jules thought, where the sun shone an unearthly blue.

"What are you doing, Brooks?"

His son looked at Jules's hand gripping his arm. "What are *you* doing, Dad?"

"We need to go home. And talk. Not here."

People were streaming out of the clubhouse, taking seats in the white folding chairs set up for the fireworks show. The strings of round bulbs hanging from the outdoor tent reminded Jules of the fairway lights, and although it was only a little over a month ago, it felt like years, and he knew that everything that had and would happen, this surging unease, had begun that night at the fair.

"Come on," he said, and bent to whisper in his son's ear, catching that sweet scent that belonged to Brooks and Brooks only.

Had he smelled like that as a baby? Jules tried to remember. All those nights he'd spent holding him, the tip of his finger planted in the baby's mouth, Jules's head jerking forward each time he dozed off, and none of it—the exhaustion, the aching back, the pins and needles in his arms—had mattered because it was his son he was holding. His son. A survivor.

"I opened your backpack," he whispered. It came out like a hiss and he knew he'd made a mistake.

He went to put an arm around Brooks's shoulder, to show him he wasn't mad. God forbid he ran from Jules, from his protection—they'd figure it out together, like a family—but the boy pivoted out of reach so fast Jules stumbled. Almost fell. Brooks was walking away. Like Jules was a stranger.

"Get back here!" he shouted, and checked himself. The tent was full of people. He didn't want to make a scene or call attention to the very reason he was shouting. His boy was the vandal. The villain everyone—from the cross-eyed postmaster to the mad Colonel and even his one ally, Veronica—was looking to string up.

The girl's pale face looked back as she and Brooks walked away from Jules, vanishing into the inky darkness. Behind him, at the clubhouse, "God Bless America" blared from stereo speakers. The first firework launched into the sky with a hiss of air, and Jules counted one, two, three, before it burst red, white, and blue.

The crowd went *ahhh*.

When black-and-white egg-laden females emerge, they emit a pheromone that attracts the males. The female has a small gland near the tip of the abdomen which releases the pheromone, with a pumping motion, termed "calling." It can attract males from long distances, tracking the scent through its erratic flight pattern.

—*The Gypsy Moth: Research Toward Integrated Pest Management*, United States Department of Agriculture, 1981

33.

Maddie

His lips tasted like the peppermint ice cream they'd shared in the clubhouse dining room.

It had been Maddie's favorite since she was a girl, when Sunday lunches at the club with her grandparents had meant Shirley Temples with extra maraschino cherries, a club sandwich speared with frilly toothpicks, and peppermint ice cream for dessert. With a stick of chocolate-covered mint. Always served by the club's restaurant manager Mr. Hickey himself. Something special for the Colonel's granddaughter.

Lunches at the club had been safer than family meals at home. The Colonel had to play nice. He couldn't go off on her mom, calling her fat, in front of the islanders. They felt like a real family for a few hours, even if she'd known it was make believe, playing her part, sitting upright and smiling in the satin-sashed dresses her mother insisted she wear because it pleased Veronica. Her grandfather's friends, most Grudder higher-ups, stopped at their table to crouch down and shake the Colonel's hand (he never stood the way she'd seen other men do when her grandfather visited a nearby table—men jumping out of their seats to stand like toy soldiers), telling Veronica how lovely she looked, nodding curtly at Maddie's father who'd always be an outsider, and smiling at her mother, complimenting her pretty new dress. The same men pressed squares of paper into Maddie's and Dom's small hands. Crisp twenty-dollar bills folded so many times they were creased like miniature accordions.

She kissed Brooks again. To taste the peppermint, but also to make him stand still—he'd been antsy all day.

Her family was dead. In her mind, at least. They'd been that way since she first stepped into Neverland and heard Brooks's music. Sure, her dad was in the clubhouse faking fun with people he despised. Her mom was there too—all swollen from her pills and junk food and sadness, stuffed into a flowery dress that belonged on *Little House on the Prairie*. Pretenders. She and Brooks would never pretend, she promised. They'd be real.

The first firework whistled into the air. The crowd at the clubhouse said *ahhh*. Maddie remembered the look on Brooks's dad's face, his long arms hanging at his sides. Defeated. Sad.

"Maybe we should go back?" It came out like a question. "Your dad seemed super worried."

"I don't want to talk to him," Brooks said, and the hollowness she heard made her worry too.

The slow sizzle of a roman candle then the rapid *pop-pop-pop*. Brooks flinched and pulled away from her. He bumped against the wall of the tin shack, making it rumble like thunder.

She wrapped her arms around his warm middle and squeezed.

"I didn't know you were scared of firecrackers." She laughed. "Brace yourself. It's going to get real loud."

His body tensed. Almost, she thought, like he was pulling away. Something was wrong tonight. She'd felt it as soon as she'd walked into the club. As soon as he'd pulled his hand away when she'd reached for him in the main dining room.

"I got to go," he said. "I told Vinny and Enzo I'd meet them."

"For what?" she asked, although she didn't want to know. She remembered the dripping black letters on the ballroom walls. GRUDDER IS CANCER. GRUDDER KILLS.

A rocket launched with a *thwump* and a *sizzle* before lighting up the sky with a shower of gold glitter.

The crowd at the club went *ahhh* and Maddie felt a pinch of disappointment that she and Brooks were all the way over here, alone.

"Oh, those are my favorite!"

It didn't sound like her voice and she knew she was trying too hard, wanting to change the mood—his mood—make everything better. Why did it feel like something bad really *was* happening, just like the list of worries she'd written down in her diary? What if writing them down, somehow, like the dangerous magic in one of Dom's myths, had made them come true?

"I got to find my dad," he said.

She felt betrayed. "But he said those mean things. About us." She paused. "About me."

"What are you talking about?" He laughed and tucked a piece of her hair behind her ear, and for a moment, she believed everything would be okay.

And he was right. His dad had only stared at her like he was *thinking* bad things. Like, if his eyes were a meat cleaver, he'd slice Maddie and Brooks apart.

"He just worries about me," he said.

"I worry about you too."

"I know you do, baby."

He kissed her and she closed her eyes. A triple *thwump-thwump-thwump* made him pull away and then a loud *boom* sounded and three starbursts—red, white, and blue—cracked open the black sky. The crowd whooped back at the club and someone yelled, "US of A!"

"Let's go," he said, and she couldn't tell if he was mad at her or scared. Or both. But it pissed her off because this was *not* what she wanted this night to be. She wanted it to be perfect. Their coming-out party. And although she knew she sounded like a child, she said, "What is wrong with you tonight?" She twisted out of his reach. "You're being a real bummer."

His face was lit red and then purple and then gold by the fireworks that were launching one after another. *Thwump. Thwump. Thwumpthwumpthwump.* He walked back toward the club. That wasn't what she wanted either.

"Stop!" she shouted, and couldn't tell if he was ignoring her or couldn't hear. "Remember the second-balcony jump? Scream. Oh, whatever." She wished the fireworks would end and then everyone would hear them arguing, know they were *together-together*, and there would be no turning back. No more hiding. "Let's jump and scream together. So every-fucking-one hears us."

She gripped his arm with both hands and he wheeled around. He laughed. But it was the kind of laugh she didn't want.

"Why'd I think you'd understand?" He shook his head.

She had to make it better. Before they got within sight of the club. Because now she'd lost her strength, the guts that had made her think she could show her true self in front of Avalon, the version she saw reflected back at her by Brooks.

"My dad's right," he shouted over the squeal and bang of the rockets detonating behind him. "Don't you get it, Maddie? Are you really that stupid?"

She wasn't sure what he meant but knew it was the worst thing he could call her.

Someone was coming. A tall black shape moved toward them quickly from the direction of the club. It must be Brooks's dad, she thought. Come to rescue him from her bad influences.

"We're not the same, you and me," Brooks yelled over the *whirly-whirly* and *whizz* of the fireworks, the crowd's *oohs* and *ahhs*. "No one's going to beat the crap out of a preppy little white girl."

She pointed behind him, tried to warn him, but could only reach forward, wrap her arms around him, hope her body could protect him. Hope her dad would beat her instead.

He didn't slow down, walked right between Maddie and Brooks, wrenching them apart just as a couplet of hot-pink starbursts lit the sky on fire. His face was a contortion. Like a mask in some horror movie.

He was cursing in dialect. "*Porca Madonna!*"

She'd heard the words before and Vinny and Enzo had translated. *The Virgin Mary is a pig.* She knew it was the most vile thing he could say.

"Maddalena." His voice cracked like an instrument out of tune, like he was about to go off, hit Brooks, hit her, drag her across the grass by her hair like he'd always threatened.

"I'm going to make this shit boy suffer for what he did to you."

Brooks tried to stand tall, his fists balled tight at his thighs, but she saw his knees buckle. He leaned against the tin shack and another rumbling wave sounded.

"Dad," she began.

"What? What, baby girl?"

She had never seen her dad like this, not in all the years she and Dom and their mother had feared him, waiting for him to go demon-eyed, chase them with his hand raised like the blade of an ax. Never had he looked so much like a murderer. And so much in love with her. Maybe, she thought, he finally loved her, the way she'd prayed he would. Maybe, she thought, he was grateful to her for giving him someone to punish. A *BOOM* split the night and silver, fern-shaped bursts branded the sky, their fronds shimmering as they dipped down back to earth.

The crowd cheered. Someone whistled through his fingers.

"Tell me," her dad begged. "Tell me what he's done!"

The finale began. A recorded orchestra played "The Star Spangled Banner." Hundreds of drunk voices sang along as the red and gold and blue spheres lit the night sky, as the dotted peonies, and chrysanthemums trailing sparks, and silver weeping willows fell in slow motion, and, her favorite, the spiders, shimmering like bombs of fairy dust, all of it blooming behind Brooks's head so she saw he was already in mourning. The eyes and lips she loved, the prettiest thing alive she'd ever seen, looked dead.

She tried to speak, to explain to her dad she was fine. Nothing bad was happening. But the report of the works was even louder than the gunshots she'd heard during the Colonel's target practice—the whizz-hum of tubes shot into the air, the screeching whistles, the *boom-boom-boom* of one mine mortar after another launching stars and serpents. There was no hope of being heard.

She dared to step toward him. He tensed when she touched his arm, the thick black hair soft under her fingers.

"Daddy?"

"Yeah, sweetie?"

"I think that"—she paused—"I think *you* think that Brooks made me do something I didn't want to do?"

Her father's gaze lost focus. He shook his head.

"I want to be with Brooks. More than anything."

She laughed because it was silly, wasn't it, her dad thinking she was some helpless nitwit of a princess. Andromeda, kidnapped by a monster. Another damsel in distress in need of saving. She knew, instantly, what a mistake it was to let that giggle out. Knew her dad would punish her. Maybe not then at the party, but soon. Not just for loving a black boy, but for laughing at him in front of the black boy. Her dad split the world into *him* and *his,* and the rest who were out to mock him, push his face in the mud. She knew she'd just joined the ones against him. The *others.*

He stared at the ground. What was he doing? She couldn't tell if he was about to charge Brooks like a stung bull or fall to the ground weeping.

"Sir?" Brooks's voice cracked like he'd swallowed glass.

"Don't," her dad whispered, "talk to me."

He was gone. Walking back toward the white tent that glowed like a giant votive candle against the smoke-hung sky.

"Maddie," Brooks said.

They fell to their knees in the damp grass and held each other. Boys do cry, she thought, as she tasted his wet cheeks, wondering if it would've been better if her father had killed them both right there on the golf green for all of East Avalon to witness. She knew there was no hope for them on the island. There never had been.

34.

Veronica

She gave Bob one of the pink pills she'd found in Ginny's bathroom and he was asleep in no time. She could still feel the buzzing in her body but knew she'd feel even better if she finished the marijuana cigarette. First, she had to find that darn Walkman Ginny had given her a few Christmases past. She sunk to her knees to sort through the cluttered hallway closet, not caring if she dirtied her green silk dress.

Ginny, the sweet thing, had included a few cassettes—composers she knew Veronica loved. Bach's Cello Suites. Chopin's Nocturnes. Veronica couldn't remember if she'd ever thanked her daughter for such a thoughtful gift. Was she really that cold-hearted? When she found the Walkman, she released a girlish squeal.

Bach was too depressing. Chopin too erratic. But Tchaikovsky was perfect.

She used a pair of meat shears to cut through the thick casing. Why must they wrap things in plastic like every object was a time capsule meant to survive the next millennium?

The earpiece was made of a soft, cushiony foam and once she'd figured out how to put the cassette in the right way, made the mistake of rewinding and then fast forwarding—so many buttons—the music blasted into her ears and she dropped the little bit of marijuana cigarette she had left. She had to search for it in the dewy grass, and when she stood there were wet spots on the green silk. The new Veronica laughed. There was no way those cheapskate East islanders, like Binnie Mueller, would be buying her beautiful dress at the charity shop. No way, José.

She lit the short stub (what *did* they call it again?) and took a few deep inhales—the smoke thick and sweet. She pressed

Play and it was as if the music were inside her, filling the empty space where her breasts had been. The violins swelled. The cellos crooned. She sang along. *La-di-da-da-daa-da-da*. She lifted her arms and imagined handsome Captain Smith was holding her. No, Julius was there. All dapper in a tuxedo with tails. She waltzed across the grass, one-two-three, one-two-three, just as Master Marco of the Serenade Dance Company had taught her so many years ago in preparation for her wedding. Her hands sheathed in tight white elbow-length gloves as Master Marco twirled her until she was nauseated. So when she and Bob had their first dance—she hadn't chosen the song, Bob's mother had done all that—she wouldn't embarrass the Pencotts.

There had been so many lessons to learn. Elocution lessons to eliminate what Madame Bouvier, her chignon-topped vocal coach, called Veronica's regional twang ("so-der" pop instead of "so-dah"), replaced by the la-di-da transatlantic accent that was taught to actors at the time. There were hours of measurements at Bergdorf and Bonwit Teller for gowns made of silk, satin, lace, trimmed with fur, hung with capes and trains, and dotted with sequins, crystals, and beads. So outrageously formal that when she stepped onto the velvet pedestal and looked in the mirror she couldn't help but giggle. Like a girl playing dress-up. She was made over once, twice, three times—Mother Pencott sending her back to the beauty parlor to be dyed a different shade of blond so by the time she settled on a platinum a dozen shades lighter than Veronica's natural honey-gold, her hair was brittle to the touch.

She tried to remember what it felt like—to radiate the way Maddie did now. To be so visible that men, and women, couldn't tear their eyes away. She remembered missing the attention after her monthly bleed stopped and every part of her—her skin, hair, between her legs, grew dry and she became what people politely called *older*. But all she'd had to do was throw a formal party at White Eagle—festoon the marble eagles with twinkling lights (Bob had wanted German shepherds when they'd built the house but she'd talked him into a fiercer option inspired by Admiral Marshall's own pair) and have the help use a ladder to construct a Champagne fountain taller than all the Grudder men. Oysters on the half shell and lobster tails and filet mignon steaming under heat lights. A line appeared at the door as the orchestra played Big Band tunes which lent an air of buoyant nostalgia to the scene. Tall ramrod-straight officers in their crisply seamed navy blues and Grudder's head honchos in tuxedos, each wrapped in woodsy aftershave, bowing, taking her hand and giving it a soft kiss. Their wives were there, of course, but on those nights, it was the other women who were invisible, beholden to her. Mrs. Robert Pencott, the first lady of Avalon Island. Her only competitor, the newly widowed Mrs. Marshall, sat alone in her grand castle through the dark woods, refusing to attend what, in her Catholic obstinacy, she'd called *hedonism*.

Those nights, her bosom straining against the satin of her favorite gown—a teal floor-length Valentino she'd picked out at Saks on a trip to the city—flashes of color accompanied the Champagne glasses clinking, the rustle of taffeta skirts, the booming laughter of men who believed themselves invincible. Sound danced with color until her plane of vision was an exquisite canvas more lovely than any of the Old Masters' works she'd seen on her trips to the Louvre.

Perhaps, she thought now, she could have had one of those men. Or several. Hadn't they glanced longingly at her diamond-draped cleavage? Captain Gunderman certainly. And Lieutenant Colonel McCafferty. He, with the full shock of red hair and the wandering eyes. So why hadn't she? She feared her husband. The hot stripe of his palm after a party where he'd caught her talking to another man, laughing, her hand on the man's dress uniform sleeve. Bob stumbling drunk (calling her a whore—she, who'd only ever been with one man) but his aim was always spot-on, punching her in places that would not leave visible marks.

She thought of Maddie the other day in the sunroom after Oprah—the girl was blind to her own beauty. Just as Veronica hadn't been able to see her own. And now it was too late. After she'd come home from her first formal at sixteen, her dance ticket full of boys' names, scrawled in their nervous chicken-scratch, her stepmother had smelled the youthful vanity on her, had knocked her down, with phlegmy disgust, *Lookie here, it's Grace*

Kelly, but with cow manure between her toes. She must have told Bob that story, she realized now for the first time, and he'd been slinging it back in her face for decades.

As she'd entered those matronly middle years, forty-five to sixty-five, it was like she moved through life draped in a magic cloak. A vanishing act. But now, in her eighties, she'd circled back to infancy. She was *cute.* A cute old lady who received uninvited smiles from young women at the beauty parlor. As if, she imagined, they were thinking how sweet and sad it was—an old lady trying to make herself pretty.

But with Dom's magic Wonderland cigarettes, she could at least *feel* beautiful. *La-di-da-da-daaaa-da-da.* The hem of her dress grew heavy as it soaked up dew. And still she danced. She could dance all night. She closed her eyes and dared to keep them shut as the symphony swelled to its crescendo. Perhaps, she thought, she'd waltz off the edge of the lawn and into the moonlit sea. There were worse ways to go, no?

Maddie had given her a gift. A book filled with inspirational quotes from Miss Winfrey. The kind of thing people read on the toilet. She'd memorized all of Queen Oprah's words. *So go ahead. Fall down. The world looks different from the ground.*

35.

Maddie

She walked into a dark, silent house and straight into the kitchen, where she knew her father waited. She had already accepted what was about to happen.

When she flicked on the light, she couldn't stop herself from flicking it on and off—one, two, three, four, five times, her lucky number—and he was steps away by the fifth flick, hunched panther-like as he moved through the strobing light. The switch landed on off.

He yelled. She caught a phrase here and there. That black boy. If her nonna knew. *Fa schifo*. Disgusting. *Porca Madonna* again and again. Like she was the gentle Virgin, she thought. He hit her back, her thighs, her ribs, her ass. She was there and not there. On the kitchen floor smelling the garlic he'd stuffed into last night's roast chicken. Watching from far away, where scent was merely an idea. A chair toppled back with a clatter and she heard her mother's voice. She called to her—*Mom!*—then laughed aloud, knowing how useless that was. Her mother had never helped before. But she could. She could. Maddie repeated *she could, she could* and a spark flared inside her so she was back in her body feeling every slap and punch and shove. He kicked between her legs and the flame blew out. It must've been an accident, she thought, ready to look up and forgive him for hurting her *there*. He'd never hurt her *there* before.

Mercifully, she felt nothing. Something popped in her side but it was more her knowing than feeling it. She was wrapped in that gauzy place that was not anywhere.

His fingers tangled in her hair. She slid across the cold tile. He means to hang me by my hair. He's finally going to do it. *Maddalena! You watch yourself or I'll put a nail in that wall and hang you by your hair.* She had wanted to cut her hair, but her mother said no. Her father wouldn't like it. Was that so he'd have something to hang her by? She watched these thoughts pass in that distant soundless, smell-less, tasteless, touchless place as he dragged her toward her mother's room. The triangle of light meant the door was open. Where was her mom? She wanted her mommy. Her mommy could stop him. She could. She could sit on him. She could. Roll her fat body on top of him. Pin him to the floor like one of Dom's wrestlers. She could. She could. The spark flared again. It was an ember now. Her chest burned. So hot it pulled her back to that other place, the real living breathing place, and oh my fucking God she was going to puke because he smelled like a dead person, a corpse, like shit and piss and sweat and stale wine and period blood and the greasy smoke that pours out of the factory stacks and Penny's sweat after a chemo treatment and Maddie is on her feet swinging at him again and again until she feels her nails catch and now she is the panther, claws bared slashing and tearing and she won't stop, she promises, not until she's flayed his skin and he's nothing but marbled muscle and bone. She'll eat him if she has to. To make him stop.

When the light came on, she was sitting on the kitchen floor. The package of condoms she'd bought at Genovese Drugs and hid in her underwear drawer, not wanting it to be all on Brooks, lay by her feet where her father had tossed them. She should've known, she thought, he'd go through her things. *Stupid girl.*

Her arm was wet. She wiped at it and her fingers came away bloody. The skin loosed in a flap and she did her best to move it back into place. Like a torn pocket, she thought, in need of a few stitches.

Her father stood over her, his chest heaving, his nostrils flared so she saw the black nose hairs curled inside. He held the kitchen broom. Like a trident. Like he's Poseidon, king of the seas, and they are playing one of Dom's Gods versus Mortals games. And so who did that make her, she wondered. Which maiden at the peak of her youthful beauty about to be raped, beaten, killed? Who will save her? Which goddess up above will take pity on the mortal Maddalena and change her? Into a dove so she can fly far away. A dolphin leaping through the sea. Or something fierce, fanged and taloned, a half lion/half eagle griffin tearing her father's throat. Drinking his blood. Devouring him until he is a pile of greasy, tooth-scarred bones.

Her father's hand lifted to his face. He stared at his fingertips dark with blood.

"I hit you back," she said quietly.

The broom fell to the floor with a clang. The metal wrapped around the bristles was twisted and torn.

"I hit you back." Louder.

She locked the bathroom door and set to taking care of the jagged cut that ran from the crook of her thumb down her wrist. She found a roll of gauze yellowed with age. She wrapped the wound again and again but the blood seeped through. Her arm looked like one of the cocoons that turned caterpillar into moth. What if she wrapped her whole body? A cocoon like a magician's box. Step in a girl, walk out a . . . what?

She changed her pee-soaked underwear. She brushed her hair one hundred times just like her mom had taught her when she was a little girl wearing plastic heart hairclips. She dabbed a spot of Covergirl concealer over the burst blood vessel under her eye that reminded her of the pink chrysanthemum bursts she and Brooks had watched explode over the golf course that night.

Her father sat at the kitchen table. A shudder of déjà vu washed over her, but she already knew she'd been here before. As Dom liked to say, *No shit, Sherlock.*

He'd be crying. He was.

He'd ask for forgiveness. He did.

He'd tell her she was his life, his angel, his love, his baby. He did, he did, he did, he did.

She knew he wanted her to say *It's okay, Daddy. I forgive you. Don't go beating yourself up, Daddy. You did it because you love me. Because you are a good daddy. I love you, Daddy.*

Instead, she leaned in, close enough to see the flesh-colored mole sitting snug between his nostril and cheek, and she screamed so loud she tasted blood. She was sure her vocal cords snapped, sure she'd never speak or sing or hum her pleasure into Brooks's ear again, and that was okay because I HIT YOU BACK.

36.

Veronica

She watched the moths circle the blazing lampposts lining the path from yard to house. Swarms upon swarms. Darting around the glowing glass globes so they dampened the light and threw frenzied shadows across the lawn. It felt like a miracle made just for her. Halos of wings.

Maddie came running across the lawn, through the quivering moth wings that parted for the girl like a foaming sea.

Oprah must be her fairy godmother, Veronica thought. Oprah had heard her wish to have Maddie at her side.

"My girl!" Veronica opened her arms, and when Maddie fell into her, her sharp young bones jabbing Veronica's scarred chest, she swallowed the pain. She almost called her Ginny as their bodies pressed close so she felt the *thwump* of their breastbones meet and she didn't care if the girl felt the absence of her breasts. It was time to confess. Oprah would say—*share. Heal.*

Maddie was talking fast. And crying. Her face streaked with makeup. Veronica rubbed her stiffened fingers up and down the girl's naked arms. She was begging to stay with Veronica. Take her into White Eagle and lock the doors. It was a dream come true. Like the grandfather clock in the entryway had wound back and her daughter was home with her. A second chance.

She took Maddie inside and sat her at the dining table. Veronica was still wearing the sodden silk dress and it weighed heavily but there wasn't time to change. She poured a nip of brandy into a Baccarat cup and sat with Maddie, patting her shaking hand. The girl's words were a jumble. *Her father. Brooks. The broom.* Veronica saw her bandaged arm—sloppy like she'd done it herself. Blood bloomed through the white gauze. She unwrapped the bandage. Tried not to flinch when she saw the skin hanging loose.

"Let's play our game," she said, and when Maddie looked up, her eyes bloodshot, confused, Veronica said, "Our affirmations, silly girl," and what a joy it was to hear Maddie laugh. "What would dear Oprah say if she were here with us?"

Maddie smiled weakly and the proof she'd been able to comfort her granddaughter, even just a bit, revived Veronica.

"I'll start," Veronica said as she led Maddie up the stairs, toward the guest bedroom. "Remember that one about integrity?"

Maddie's voice was quiet when she spoke: "Real integrity is doing the right thing . . . Um. I can't remember the rest."

Veronica finished, "Knowing that nobody's going to know whether you did it or not."

She tucked Maddie in, pulling the covers up so the satin border tickled the girl's chin. Just like Ginny liked it.

"Your turn now. Just one. And then you can rest."

"I don't want to go back," Maddie said. "Can't I stay here? Please?"

"Of course you can!" Veronica reminded herself to tamp down her excitement. "I mean, we'll have to ask your," she paused, "mother."

"Not my dad." Veronica heard the fear, reminding her how she'd felt toward more than one man in her long life. First, her father. Later, Bob.

"No, of course not." Veronica smiled. "In fact, while you rest, I'll go over to the cottage and pick up a few of your things."

"Now?" Maddie sat up. "But it's late."

"Don't you worry your sweet little head over it. Your only job is to have pleasant dreams."

"But," she said, gripping Veronica's arm. "He's there now." She paused. "He's angry." She whispered the last part, "He might hurt you." She looked to the window that faced the cottage.

"I promise," she said as she kissed her granddaughter's forehead, "he will never hurt anyone again. Yes?"

There was a tapping against the window screen and Maddie

flinched. A pair of moths, their speckled wings quivering. A frantic dance.

"Yes?" Veronica repeated.

The girl's voice was a whisper. "Yes."

The metal lockbox in Bob's closet was unlocked. The gun was heavier than she'd imagined. The metal cold. In the faint light of the bulb overhead she could read the inscription, the Navy SEAL motto she'd heard Grudder men, navy men, recite again and again over the years. *The only easy day was yesterday.*

She kicked off her sandals halfway across the lawn leading from the big house to the cottage. The train of her green gown was soaked, pulling her off-balance. She lifted the hem and let it hang over her arm. The cool sea breeze tickled her bare legs.

He was in the kitchen. Sitting at the table, his head cradled in his arms, his shoulders slumped.

Her feet made a wet sound on the tiled floor and he looked up. First, surprise. Then, guilt. There was a long red scratch across his cheek. Atta girl, she thought.

"She got you good, did she?"

"I'm sorry," he said, ducking his head. In shame or anger, she couldn't tell.

She wondered how many times he had asked her daughter, her granddaughter, and who knows how many mistresses, for their forgiveness.

"Tony," she said.

"Yes, Mommy?"

She let the heavy black gun slap against her side, knowing it would say more than mere words. His eyes followed the movement to her crooked hip, widened when he spotted the gun.

"Don't you ever—*ever*—call me that again."

He nodded.

"You're forgiven," she said. "But only this one last time."

He nodded again, more vigorously. As if, she thought, he was a naughty little boy trying to weasel his way out of a whipping.

What would Oprah say? Then it came to her.

"Forgiveness is giving up the hope that the past could be any different."

Tony looked up at her, his eyes swollen with tears. God, he was so infuriatingly dumb.

"You understand?" she asked sweetly. "You *capisce?* Now, stop feeling sorry for yourself. It's pathetic."

She opened the door to her daughter's bedroom, and the smell of decay—sweet like rotten strawberries—hit her so she had to hold her breath.

Her eyes adjusted to the dark and she found the bed.

"Mommy? Is that you?"

Ginny propped herself on her elbows and her sheer bathrobe opened. Veronica saw her daughter's fleshy breasts fall to each side, the stretch of pale freckled skin between. She reminded herself to tell Ginny about the cancer, soon, so she could get herself checked.

"Yes, Cookie. It's me."

"I was having the strangest dream. Set in a fancy hotel. You were there. And Daddy. And Mary and Sue from college."

"Was it a good dream?"

"It was," Ginny said as if surprised. "I'm going to go to sleep now and see if I can go back. But . . ." She paused. "I need my pills. They're on the dresser. Would you mind?"

"Not at all, dear."

Veronica laid two pills in her daughter's open palm. Listened to Ginny swallow them dry.

"Finish your dream."

She shut the door, locking her daughter in like a sleeping princess. And was she, Veronica wondered, the evil queen?

She typically lays about 500 eggs. The eggs are covered with a peachy fuzz that can cause rashes if touched by bare skin or fur, especially on humans and mammals. Then the female leaves to eat, while her eggs are protected.

She does not live to see her offspring.

—*The Gypsy Moth: Research Toward Integrated Pest Management*, United States Department of Agriculture, 1981

37.

Leslie

The female moths were dying. She knelt on the patio in the faint glow of the black light leaking through the ballroom windows and watched the white moths twitch on the slate floor.

These are the mothers, she thought as the pulsing bass of her son's music made her legs tingle.

Her beautiful son, her angry boy-man son, had locked himself in the ballroom as soon as they'd returned from the fireworks at the club. Had refused to speak to her when she'd asked him what was up. Jules had been worse. He wouldn't look at her. It had been a relief when Eva had fallen fast asleep in her car seat, her face swollen from crying through the fireworks. They'd driven home through the fog in silence, their clothes stinking of gunpowder and smoke.

Last week, Brooks had told her how the female moth's one purpose was to reproduce. She waited for a male to catch her scent, make his awkward zigzag journey to where she sat on a branch. Waiting. Crippled. What kind of monster is nature, Leslie thought, to give a creature wings never to be used?

She had followed Brooks into the ballroom when they'd returned home and he'd shouted at her to go away. Jules hadn't even tried. He walked like a zombie toward his precious garden. So she'd decided to sit outside on the patio and wait. Just like the white moths. She waited for her boy, her love, her life, her firstborn after so many dead, to come to her. She'd hold him. Kiss his sweaty forehead. Beg him to tell her his sadness. Hand over his pain. She'd swallow it whole to free him.

But hours passed and still he did not leave the ballroom. At first, there had been a dozen dying moths falling from branches overhead, skittering across the stone patio, and now there were thirty. Thirty-one. Thirty-two. So many dead mothers who would never see their babies.

The music throbbed louder, harsh and raw, until he was playing only hate-filled heavy metal. What she'd always thought of as angry-white-boy music. A few East Avalon boys had come to the front door of the Castle but she had told them politely to go away. Come back tomorrow night. Their eyes were hidden under baseball caps tucked low, the brims shaped into tight arches, and she felt them glance toward the music blaring from the ballroom before they climbed back in the BMW one of their parents, surely, had bought them.

Her helpers had also shown up. Vinny and Enzo and Paulie and the quiet one whose name she could never remember. She sent them away too, but only after paying them one hundred dollars each. She spotted the black paint staining their fingernails when they reached for the crisp new bills and told them, in her mother's tone, to scrub with some turpentine. She didn't want them to get in trouble, of course not, but she had her own son to protect. Jules knew, or was on the edge of knowing, she could feel it, and there was no way out of telling him now.

She realized too late, just as their souped-up Cougar with the tinted windows peeled out of the driveway, gravel spraying, that she should've given them smaller bills. They'd have trouble breaking the hundreds at any of the stores on the west side. She imagined the owners of West Side Liquor holding the bill up to the fluorescent lights to spot the anticounterfeit strip. To make sure it was real. Another person doubting the boys' worth, telling them they were no good without having to say anything at all.

They were the kind of boys people didn't trust. That was why she'd had to pick them. When she'd seen them that night at the fair, putting on a show, flexing their muscles so the panthers inked on their arms seemed to stretch and strut, bare fangs, she knew they'd be perfect for the part. Envoys who would spread the message Brooks had already sprayed across that phallic monument in the center of town. She had counted on their anger, their frustration, their pent-up lust for power, which, she'd known, since she was a girl, burned brighter in boys than even their need for sex and money.

But Brooks, her bighearted boy who wanted to see the good in people, became too attached. Wanted to call off the plan just when they were so close. The factory near ruin. He'd been worried his new pals would get in trouble. What she hadn't foreseen was the girl. It was just like Brooks to fall in love with a broken doll. She'd witnessed Tony LaRosa's temper flare years ago when they were at school—his fists smash jaws. One look at the girl and she'd seen past the cardigans worn to hide bruises. Brooks was like Jules. A fixer. A healer. Too good for this world. And she had brought them to an island lousy with the bad.

The music slowed and a mournful voice replaced the techno beat. She was cold in her thin sundress. But she wouldn't leave him. Not until he came to her. Like he always had.

She fingered the diamond choker she'd made a big show of buying in town—parading Jules and the kids in and out of Friedman's, the same store her father had escorted her to each Valentine's Day to pick out a new charm for her bracelet. A tiny wishing well with a bucket that swung back and forth. A miniature sterling replica of a Wildcat jet. A heart that read I LOVE DADDY. She'd been wearing the choker two links too tight so she could feel it there throughout the day. It reminded her why she had returned, why she had sacrificed so much by coming back. She was there to cause them pain. The men at Grudder, and their grandfathers and great-grandfathers, who had dumped toxic chemicals in such numbers that a three-mile plume of trichloroethylene hovered under the island, poisoning the well water.

Thirty-six moth mothers. Thirty-seven. When they fell from the trees they made a soft *pip-pip* as they landed on the slate floor. She heard something. He was coming to her at last. Her boy. But it was only the whisper of the dying moths' wings fluttering against stone. A sob rose from her belly and she swallowed hard.

She had explained the plume to Vinny and Enzo. After all the time they'd spent together, the hours plotting where to spray the graffiti (the truth), they'd begun to feel like surrogate sons. Brooks had helped. He was a natural-born activist. There had been an enraged hopefulness in his voice (anger and hope *could* coexist, she'd always believed this, ever since her first antiwar rallies in Cambridge) as she'd listened to him educate the West boys—lift them up, empower them with knowledge. He explained how the toxic cocktail had started out small. A pond-sized mass that had hidden like a cancerous cell under the plant for years before beginning its southward journey, spreading out under all of West Avalon, contaminating the water supply, stretching past the Avalon Turnpike in 1982, then creeping past the border of east and west in '86, so that now the island hovered over a plume curled like a giant octopus. Its tentacles reaching up out of the ocean, gripping every corner of the island, pumping poison into the sinks and showers of every home.

The charming one, Vinny, had wept when Brooks told them how Grudder had known for decades. Held countless meetings on the upper floors of Old Ironsides. Hired teams of lawyers to hide the truth. Brooks had put an arm around Vinny, told him it was Grudder who'd made Vinny's father sick. Grudder who had killed not just the old and weak, but also the young and strong. Withered the babies in the wombs of Avalon women from east to west.

She'd bleed any day now and blamed her tears on that. After all those failed pregnancies, three before her beautiful boy was born, and two before sweet little Eva, all those months spent charting her temperature, counting days between cycles, hoping, wishing, and even silently reciting the prayers she'd memorized as a girl in the pews of St. John's, she never forgot when her body was scheduled to bleed.

She knew she had lost Julius. Named for a dictator who, like the Grudder men, seemed benevolent on the surface but who was cruel and conniving, who kept hidden any truths that didn't fit his agenda. But Jules was a man whose only ambitions were to make the world a greener and more beautiful place. Who designed community gardens for the poor. Who taught children how to feed themselves with a packet of seeds and a bag of soil. He was a magician. Not like her father, the admiral, whose magic had wrought destruction. Jules's magic created life. She hoped he would never understand how she'd become more like her father than she'd ever imagined—obsessed, in love with her plans for destruction.

July 11, 1992
Dear Diary,

Hi, it's me, the dumbest girl on Avalon Island. I thought about going back and ripping out my last entry. Tearing it to SHREDS and letting the pieces float over the cliffs of Singing Beach. But it seemed like a total drama queen thing to do. Like something Brenda Walsh would do on 90210 (gag me!) and you know how I feel about her.

The 4th of July party at the club was a total bust. It was so bad that I spent days worrying about B breaking up with me. Plus, my dad had a total freakout and if it wasn't for Nicky, sweet sweet Nicky, who knows where I'd be now. I'm living at the big house. Even staying in Mom's old room and sleeping under the same strawberry-print bedspread she used before she met my asshole dad.

But the BIG NEWS is that Nicky and me we're cooking up a plan for me and B to . . . in B's words "make like the roadrunner."

Nicky has been AMAZING in helping us plan and in a few weeks we'll be out of here. Far from the island. Far from my parents. Far from the Colonel who's gone nuts and spends all day yelling at the TV set. Far from all the crap this island tries to cram down kids' throats.

I'll miss Dom but he can visit anytime he wants! He can come and live with us even!

Sometimes, when I think about all me and B have to look forward to, my head spins and I have to pinch myself (hard) to convince myself I'm not tripping. We can hold hands and it won't matter who sees us. We can stand in the middle of the city and scream I LOVE YOU and no one will want to hurt us for just telling the truth.

I'm making a list of things I want to do when we're off the island. Here's what I've got so far:

-a weekend in a quaint bed and breakfast (the kind that serves hot biscuits with breakfast) where me and B can lie in bed all day and watch the snow fall outside

-a kiss with B at the top of the Empire State Building (so unoriginal I know but still!)

-a MAJOR haircut, like chopped off

More coming soon! This is just the beginning . . .

Love,
Maddie Pencott LaRosa

38.

Dom

He found her diary between her mattress and box spring. It was so obvious. Like she'd wanted him to read it. Wanted him to stop her from leaving the island. Leaving him.

He'd brought the diary up into his favorite climbing tree but his hands were gooey with sap and now the pages of her last entry were stuck together. He couldn't put the book back. She'd know he'd read it.

A yelp sounded from the front yard. The Colonel stood on the lawn in his slippers and palm-tree-print robe that made Dom think of that weirdo on *M*A*S*H* who dressed in ladies' clothes. The robe hung open so Dom saw his sagging briefs and the dog tags glinting against his white undershirt. There was something in his hands and he brought it down on Champ, who yelped with each blow. It was the bamboo back scratcher he kept next to his recliner.

Dom knew he should climb down and protect Champ. But instead he squirreled into the crook of the tree. The branches were nearly leafless from the caterpillars and the Colonel would only have to look up to spot him.

"That'll teach you to shit on the carpet!"

Thwack. The dog cried out. A human-sounding pain.

Why wasn't Champ running away? Then Dom heard the rattle of the chain. He's trapped, poor dumb dog. Dumb for loving the Colonel, who can't love anyone or anything but his planes.

The chain rattled again and Dom saw a brown-and-black blur run to the big house. The Colonel waddled after, yelling, "You're gonna eat that shit. Gobble it up. Or you'll get another beating."

The screen door clicked shut, the yowls muffled. Then there was silence. The dog must have surrendered. Swallowed his own stinking shit. The thought made Dom hurl and the Chef Bo-yardee ravioli he'd eaten for dinner came up with the Bud-weisers he'd snagged from his grandparents' fridge, the whole mess splashing down the trunk of the tree. Dripping so it sounded like rain.

He thought about how everyone deserves to be shot at one point in their life. Some more than once. He deserved it as much as his dad. Yeah, his dad had been the one to hit Maddie, but it had been Dom who had ratted on her at the party, when his dad asked, "Where's your sister?" and Dom had pointed him in the direction of the caddy shacks. His father had stomped off, the arms of his pastel sweater swinging, not noticing Dom was so drunk he was swaying like a sailboat in a storm.

He'd wanted his dad to catch them. To put an end to Maddie and Brooks. *Up in a tree.* K-I-S-S-I-N-G. That night in the woods, when they'd played the last game of Gods versus Mortals, he'd seen the way Maddie and Brooks looked at each other, like they were the true Orpheus and Eurydice meeting in fiery Hades, full of joy and love despite being surrounded by the dead. Dom had been invisible to them that night. What if he was one of those soulless dead?

39.

Maddie

They were in the secret garden. Lying side by side as the night breeze dried the sweat from their naked bodies. Shouting swelled from the ballroom. The parties had grown so crazy that the noise reached them there every night. Reached them in the one spot where Maddie had felt unreachable. Safe.

"It's some wild rumpus shit going on in there tonight," Brooks said.

"It scares me," she said, "a little."

"It scares me a lot," Brooks said. "Every time Rolo swings off that balcony, I want to shout, 'Motherfuckin' timber!'"

His head was in her lap and she leaned over and kissed him. Her hair fell over their faces like a curtain and, for a minute, the noise of the ballroom, the hum of the crickets, the whole world it seemed, was shut out.

"I wish I had a word for how much I love you, Maddalena Pencott LaRosa."

"How much *do* you love me?"

"From the moon and back?"

"Um, I think it's *to* the moon and back."

"No," he said, "I've heard that one before. But *from* the moon and back—that's just for you and me."

"Try again," she said.

"How about . . ." he began, and she could hear him thinking, his wonder-seeking brain buzzing. "I love you *so* much . . . that I even love your flaws."

"My flaws?" She slapped his forehead and he gave out a fake cry of pain. "Is this how you woo the woman you love?"

She'd called herself a woman, surprised at how correct it felt.

"I love the way the vein in your forehead wiggles when you get all frustrated, Maddalena Pencott LaRosa. . . ."

She rolled him off her lap and started to stand. He grabbed her and wrestled her back to the ground.

"I love your stubbornness. . . ."

"You just won't quit, huh?"

"I love your impatience. How you tear open a bag of chips not caring if it's the right or wrong end."

She stopped fighting him. He'd been watching her, studying her, *seeing* her. She felt as bright as the star at the top of White Eagle's seven-foot-tall Christmas tree.

Back in the ballroom, her calf muscles still tingling from tensing them as Brooks made her come, she avoided Enzo's stare. The where-the-fuck-have-you-two-been stare.

Vinny passed around the latest baggie of magic mushrooms he'd procured.

"Kids," he shouted, "this is a public service announcement. These babies give you a wicked trip. So, go easy over there. Don't be munching a handful."

He was looking at Penny, who dipped her fingers into the baggie and popped one and then two ear-shaped pieces of mushroom into her mouth.

Maddie hurried over and gripped Penny's arm, which was so frail she worried she'd hurt her.

"Penny," she said. "Come with me to the bathroom?"

"Fuck off," Penny said.

Maddie felt a few heads swivel in their direction. Bitsy, definitely Gabrielle, they had a nose for conflict and fed on other people's problems like it was fine food.

She crouched next to the edge of the sofa, where Penny sat grimacing as she chewed the mushrooms.

"Ugh, these taste like shit," Penny said. "And smell even worse."

She stuck her fingers under Maddie's nose and the stench of earthy decay made Maddie gag.

"What the fuck, Pen?"

"Just giving you a secondary high, buddy," Penny said, winking.

"Come with me to the bathroom. Please."

Her voice cracked and she knew she'd be in tears any minute. Maybe Penny would hear that and give in, and Maddie would lock the bathroom door and convince Penny to puke that shit up. If Penny refused, Maddie would stick her own finger down Penny's throat. She wasn't going to let her have another seizure. Not right after she'd finished another round of chemo.

She was about to remind Penny of the night of the fair, the hours they'd spent in the emergency room while Major Whittemore paced the fluorescent-lit linoleum and a tipsy Mrs. Whittemore had cried all over the IV tubes pumping saline into Penny's veins. Penny leaned close so Maddie could smell the mix of the shrooms and the chemo meds. Penny smelled like floor cleaner after each treatment at the hospital.

Penny whispered, "I'm not going anywhere with you. You fucking betrayed me."

A speck of Penny's spit landed on Maddie's cheek and she flinched. She rubbed until the skin burned, like it was poison.

She never should've told Penny about the plan for her to leave the island with Brooks. She heard her father's voice in her head, *Think before you speak, Maddalena,* and it made her want to punch herself in the face.

Brooks stood in front of the turntables, spinning a record that was upbeat and fun (Vinny had requested a shroomy vibe). With the black light aglow and the Christmas lights on, he looked like an angel. She wanted to run back to White Eagle, pick up the suitcase she and Veronica had packed, grab Brooks, and leave. Forever.

First, she had to take care of Penny. She had decided she'd pay a visit to the Whittemore house and do what she swore she'd never do—rat on her best friend. She'd tell Penny's mother everything. The drugs, the drinking. Not the sex, as far as she knew there wasn't anything dangerous about mixing sex and chemo.

And she had to say goodbye to Dom. Sweet Dom. Promise she'd send for him as soon as she and Brooks got settled.

"Damn," Ricky said. "She's going to trip balls. That's totally too much."

"Pleeease," Maddie said. "Come with me, Pen."

"You need a chaperone to go to the bathroom?" Vanessa asked. "Maybe you can get a freakin' hall pass."

Gabrielle snickered. She was holding the baggie and popping piece after piece of dried mushroom between her glossy lips.

"What you mean, Ricky," Bitsy said, "is Penster has got one huge set of balls."

Penny smiled, glowing in the light of Bitsy's approval.

"Bitsy," Maddie said. "This is totally *not* a good idea."

She was about to remind Bitsy about Penny's seizure at the fair—screw anyone who was worried the truth might kill their buzz. Then Enzo spoke and when her older cousin (seven minutes older than Vinny) spoke, everyone listened.

"Just go with Maddie already so we don't have to listen to her whine." His dark eyes widened in a message that said *do it*.

Penny whirled to face her as soon as the door to the bathroom shut behind them with a click that echoed down the hallway. She realized—too late, Penny was already shouting—that the kids in the ballroom could hear everything.

"How could you do this to me?"

"Do what, Pen? I'm not *doing* anything to you."

"You are. You're leaving. You're fucking leaving me."

"Please," Maddie said, "calm down." What she wanted to say was *Keep your voice down. Don't let Vinny and Enzo hear.* "I'm sorry, Pen. I really am. But I can't stay here. My dad. I'm scared he'll—"

Penny clutched the marble sink so her knuckles turned white.

"You okay? You don't look so good. Sit down before you fall."

"Don't touch me!" Penny shouted.

Maddie started to tug the door open, "I'm calling your mom and telling her to come pick you up."

Penny squeezed between Maddie and the door, pushed it closed hard and fast—almost crushing Maddie's hand.

She wagged a finger in Maddie's face. "You think your life is bad. I can make it even worse."

There was a knock on the bathroom door. Brooks called through the thick wood, "You okay in there?"

"We're good!" Penny yelled in a fake happy voice.

"Let me out, Penny. Please. You're scaring me."

"*You* threaten *me*?" she slurred. "I'll tell everyone—your dad, your mom, the cops—that you're running away. They don't let rich little girls run away, you know." A trickle of drool crept down her chin.

"Penny, you don't mean that."

"Oh, don't I? I'll tell Principal Haskell—I'll tell every mom in the PTA—about how your dad slapped you. I was there! I saw it with my own eyes."

Maddie wished she could leave. Let Penny choke on her own vomit. Crack her head open on the hard stone floor. But she couldn't.

"Brooks! I need you in here."

Penny splayed her body against the door, bumping it with her butt each time Brooks pushed from the other side. If it hadn't been so sad, Maddie would've laughed.

Eventually, Ricky took Penny out, arms linked. She clung to Ricky, whispering, "I like you."

Brooks shut the bathroom door and Maddie said, "Please, can we go? Now? Like *right* now? Something bad is going to happen. I know it."

He whispered, "Soon, real soon," and his warm breath on her cheek made her feel like maybe, just maybe, everything would be okay, when Bitsy pounded on the bathroom door, yelling for them to come quick.

Penny stood on the ballroom balcony, her toes gripping the smooth wood edge.

"Penny," Maddie said softly, scared she'd startle her.

"Howdy!" Penny called down.

She was holding on to the faded red velvet curtain with one hand and Maddie heard the rings jangling. The fabric was old. It would tear.

"Oh, God, Penny, please come down."

Penny used her other hand to direct Spencer's placement of the beanbags for her landing.

"A little more to the left. No, *that* left."

"That's the right," Spencer yelled back.

"Don't fucking argue with her," someone said, a girl, Gabrielle maybe, but Maddie couldn't take her eyes off Penny, who was acting as if she leapt off a balcony every day. Like she was a freaking acrobat in Ringling Bros. Like it was no big deal.

"Oh shit," Brooks whispered.

"Okey-dokey, I'm ready to fly."

Maddie ran forward where she knew she'd be in line with Penny's fall.

"Maddie," Brooks said. "Get out of the way."

"No, I got this." She stopped him with an open hand. "Penny, I'm sorry. I promise, I swear. Cross my heart and hope to—"

It was too late.

Penny leapt off the balcony with a lively "Geronimo!" but instead of swinging out over the ballroom, her hands slid down the rope as if it was coated in butter. She landed so hard Maddie felt the ballroom shake with a loud *crack*, like the wood floor had split, but it was Penny who broke, lying there, splayed out, her right leg twisted at an impossible angle.

40.

Jules

He'd been a big fucking dope. It had taken him two months and change to figure out Leslie was scheming. She *was* that Scheherazade after all. He didn't know exactly what she was up to, not all of it, but he'd find out soon. He had a feeling he couldn't ignore—they were about to lose everything.

He was in the garden. He spent all his time there now that the moths were laying eggs. He was almost grateful for the distraction—it was hard work, propping the ladder against each trunk, using the hand spade to scrape away the egg sacks covered in the mother moths' own buff-colored body hair. Climbing one rung after another. Methodical extermination.

The moon was nearly full. Lighting his way. He felt a thrill spark in his gut each time he happened upon a mother moth mid-egg secretion, the furred sac protruding from between her wings. He smashed the mother and unborn caterpillars with the flat of the spade.

The chestnut received most of his attention. If there was one thing he'd do right on this island, it was protect that tree. His discovery. He thought of Darwin and his long-necked rhea birds.

He scraped and scraped, moved up rung by rung. Repositioned the ladder until he'd completed the circle, the tree's bark free from white-winged moths and insulated sacs. Bits of gauzy webbing stuck in his hair and on his sweaty arms. He hummed his father's old spirituals. The same songs of suffering and redemption he'd sung to Leslie. To Brooks. To Eva. But now his father's bass was there, in the woods with him, singing harmony to Jules's tenor.

The pieces came together. The clues from those months on the island he hadn't wanted to see, knowing they'd spoil his family's new home. His perfect gardens. His chance at a new life.

Leslie at the fair air-kissing look-alike women. Flirting with the ancient uniformed Grudder men. Bringing those kids into the Castle so they infested the ballroom like the caterpillars did the forest. Inviting those greasy-haired headbanger kids into what she swore was *home*. Leslie huddled on the sofa with Brooks, whispering into their son's ear. Filling their starry-eyed boy with poisonous tales. The cocktail party. *These fucking animals,* she'd spat. He should have known, he told himself as he scraped away the eggs. *Should've, should've, should've* chugging like the engine of a train that was nearing and as it charged closer, so much made sense. Brooks disappearing on his skateboard with that heavy backpack. Filled with cans of spray paint, Jules knew now. And all for what? What was the damn endgame? He wouldn't be there to find out. It was time to leave. He'd pack up his and Brooks's and Eva's things that weekend and leave the island. Leslie could come or stay. He'd drug his son if he had to. Tie him up and strap him in the car. He'd do anything to get Brooks off that island after he'd seen the girl's father walk off the golf green the other night, out of the fireworks smoke like a ghost out of hell. The man's face twisted with rage.

"You married one of your mother's angels," his father's voice jolted him so he nearly fell off the ladder.

"Pops, don't start. I'm tired."

God, was that ever the truth. He imagined letting his body fall slack, falling to the egg-and-moth-carcass-covered ground below.

"That woman is putting on a play, Julius. Her own private tragedy been brewing right under your nose. Just like those bored rich white ladies dressing up in their parlors. Flowers in their hair and rings on their toes!"

He laughed. He had to. His pops (or was it him, he thought, losing sight of what was real) remembering those pretty white toes that had peeked out from under diaphanous gowns in his mother's old photographs. He'd studied those toes as he sawed into his fried pork chops and potatoes at the kitchen table so many years ago. Longed to touch them. Kiss them.

Brown male moths in search of mates fluttered around his face, batting his cheek with their soft wings. He remembered the posters—FREE AFRICA. END APARTHEID—Leslie had hung on the walls of their apartment, and the crudely carved statues of African fertility gods she'd placed on the mantel. She bought him his first dashiki made from bright purple and green kente cloth. She marched by his side in New York; Washington, D.C.; and at universities across the South, where they protested the absence of African American Studies departments. She was a believer, and he had witnessed her unquestionable faith. Or was it faith that made it impossible for her to question anything—that made her as monomaniacal as Ahab chasing his great white whale. What was Leslie chasing?

His father's voice joined the *flit-flit-flit* of the moths. "You were her open door, Jules. In walked lily-white Leslie, out walked . . ."

"Stop!" Jules shouted.

A moth flew into his eye and he swatted at the air, losing his balance, lunging toward the tree and hugging it to stop from falling. His cheek pressed against the mother moths and their egg sacs soft as velvet. They complained with a brush of wings against his cheek.

All those years, he'd feared what his father warned was true. *You can't trust that girl.* The girl who could *talk a pig into eating its own tail.* After all that had happened on the island, all that was sure to come—he felt danger churning toward them like a hurricane gathering strength as it moved across the sea—he knew she had married him because he was the farthest thing from her own past, the very opposite of what her parents wanted her to choose. And now, it seemed she was through pretending and wanted back into the white world of the island. Where did that leave him? His children? His son? He'd been terrified when Brooks was born, and too ashamed to admit that he'd prayed for a girl in secret, even after all of Leslie's miscarriages. This world, on and off the island, wasn't safe for a black boy.

He stepped onto the top rung of the ladder and began his circular scraping. A voice echoed in the woods. He shook away what he assumed was his father back for another visit. But the voice—two voices now—grew louder. Thrashing through the ferns toward him.

It was Brooks and Maddie. Both out of breath, their thin, narrow chests heaving. They stared up at him. They looked so small down below. As if, he thought, he'd climbed into the clouds.

He couldn't make out what Brooks was saying, only the shape of the boy's mouth as it stretched. Then the ladder rattled and Jules clung again to the tree. His son was shaking the ladder. As Jules climbed down, his chest tightened with anger. He was going to let that boy have it, messing with him like that.

"What the goddamn?" he said on the ground. "You could've killed me up there."

"I need you," his son said. Jules stopped himself from smiling but the words were a gift. When had his boy last needed him? "There's been an accident."

"Eva? Your mom?"

"They're fine," Brooks said.

Maddie was already running back toward the Castle, looking back, begging them, "Please! Hurry!"

Jules saw her eyes. She was terrified.

He pushed through the circle of kids standing in the middle of the ballroom. The girl lay on the floor. Her foot was pointing in the wrong direction and Jules thought he must be seeing things wrong. Maybe the race through the woods, his own exhaustion, the unnatural glow of the black light was messing with his eyes.

"Bring one of those lamps over here."

"Yessir," someone mumbled.

A girl's tinkling giggle echoed against the domed ceiling.

Jules stood, straightening so he was a head taller than most of the boys.

"You think this is a game?" he said. "Go home."

The kids were slack-jawed and slant-eyed. Wasted. It was a muggy night and the stench of the ballroom—spilled beer and bong water mixing with the girls' sugary perfume—hit him and his stomach lurched.

"Go!" He felt the vibration of his voice in his throat and it felt good.

He pressed his ear to the hurt girl's chest and heard her

heartbeat under the whispers of the kids' feet across the ball-room floor. His head rose and fell with her ragged breath.

"You called an ambulance, right?"

Brooks looked at him dumbly. Maddie clung to his son's arm. She started to speak but then one of the headbanger kids stepped forward. The one who had manners. Vinny.

"Me and Enzo . . ."—he nodded at that other kid, the one from the fair, the one Jules had caught going down on the girl in the study—"we're going to drive her. It'll save time."

Enzo nodded.

"You got to be kidding me," Jules said. "She can't be moved."

"I told you, Vinny," Maddie glared. "I'm calling an ambu-lance."

The Vinny kid stepped forward and grabbed Maddie's arm, tugging so her bare feet slid across the ash-stained floor.

"Cuz," he said in that smooth voice like he was flirting. "You know we can't have the five-oh showing up." He nodded at the ballroom walls covered in graffiti.

Jules could almost make the connection. The black letters sprayed sloppily across the ballroom walls, the vandalism on the island, the paint cans in Brooks's backpack, but the hurt girl's leg was twisted so her heel pointed toward her temple, making him lose focus.

"Get your hands off her," Brooks growled at Vinny.

"Brooks," Jules commanded, "run to the cottage. Wake your mother. Call an ambulance. Tell them it looks like she shattered her leg. Maybe her hip. Tell them what she was on. It's impor-tant."

"I think," Maddie said, "she'd eaten some mushrooms. Smoked some weed. And beer, maybe four cups? Maybe more."

Jesus, Jules thought. This was it. This was what he'd been waiting for. They would lose everything.

"Brooks," Vinny said, and Jules heard the threat in the kid's voice, "don't move."

"Fuck off," Brooks said.

That's my boy, Jules thought.

Vinny lunged toward Brooks, and Jules stood, taking a long step to block Vinny, whose chin thunked into Jules's chest.

"You don't want to test me, boy," Jules whispered.

Leslie ran into the ballroom. Her white bathrobe fluttering behind her like she was one of the mother moths. The only one with working wings who could take to the air. Thank God, he thought. She'd take care of this mess.

"What happened?" Her hand flew to her mouth. "Oh my God."

But instead of looking to Jules, her eyes turned to Brooks. Then moved to Enzo and Vinny.

"Brooks!" Jules shouted. "Go call the ambulance."

"Wait," Leslie said, raising a hand so her palm faced Jules.

"Wait for what?" Maddie cried. She was kneeling, holding one of the girl's limp hands. It was then Jules saw the hurt girl's bald head gleaming in the lamp's light. Her blond wig had fallen to the side.

"It's better," Leslie began, and Jules saw she'd slipped into pretender mode. Smile on, brows lifted. She was ready to convince someone of something, "if I drive her. Vinny and Enzo can help. Maddie can come along."

The two boys moved toward the hurt girl.

"Let's do it," one said, and Jules heard the tremor in the boy's voice.

"Are you fucking out of your mind?" he shouted at Leslie. "What's *really* going on, Leslie? Brooks, you go and call. Now!"

Brooks jogged toward the arched entrance.

"Anyone who tries to stop him," Jules said, "will be reported to the police. You hear?"

He stood guard until the flashing ambulance lights hit the stained-glass windows so colored shapes danced across the wood floor, across Leslie's and the boys' faces, across Maddie's wet cheeks, across the hurt girl's still body. He held his arms out, protecting her, until they ached. He planted his feet on the wooden floor. He was a tree, he thought, centuries old, his roots long and deep, and nothing, nothing, was going to move him.

At least he'd do one thing right. He'd save one life on this island. Maybe, he hoped, it would make up for all he could not save.

41.

Maddie

The TV set in the emergency room was mounted on the wall and covered in a mesh cage. Every channel played Bill Clinton's acceptance speech at the Democratic National Convention and Maddie wanted to scream at the nurses and doctors surrounding the sets (just like the moths flocking to porch lights across the island), beg them to do their job and refill her friend's morphine drip.

Penny had come to screaming in the back of the ambulance as the gurney rocked side to side with every swerve. Maddie hadn't known a person could make those sounds. It reminded her of the raccoon her dad had trapped in the shed behind the cottage. How it wailed as the poison it had eaten killed it slowly. A scream that had cracked Maddie open and changed her. Made her understand there was no peace in death. Only after.

Penny was awake after three hours in surgery. The doctors had pinned her right leg in three places. Her femur was shattered. Her hip broken in two places. When they'd arrived at the ER, the nurses had cut away Penny's clothes and Maddie saw the bone sticking out of Penny's torn skin. She'd rushed to the bathroom just in time to puke into the sink.

Now Penny was crying. She sounded like Dom when he was trapped in a night terror. *It hurts. It hurts so bad.* Again and again. Maddie tried to calm her. Rang the bell for the nurse until the blue light stayed lit but, still, no one came. Brooks was hunched over in a chair, dragging his fingers through his hair so it stood up straight. Maddie found herself wishing, for the first time in a long time, for a grown-up. Penny's parents were talking with the doctor who'd performed the surgery. It was bad. There'd be no more lacrosse championships.

Brooks stood, his chair slamming into the wall behind him. He walked out of the room, the curtain rattling on its rings, and Maddie heard him yelling in the hall. A pink-cheeked nurse gave Penny a shot of something.

Brooks's mom had stayed back at the Castle with Eva. His dad was waiting in the ER lobby. They'd sat together in silence during the surgery. Brooks's dad had spoken only once. Telling them they'd done the right thing calling the ambulance. Penny could've died from blood loss or infection.

Maddie watched a smiling Bill Clinton talk about growing up fatherless in a place called Hope. Listened to him play his gleaming saxophone as the crowd cheered.

Maddie knew something was wrong when she saw Brooks's mom on the white marble steps of the Castle's entrance holding a sleeping Eva in her arms.

"The police are here," Leslie said to Jules, nodding toward the house. Her voice fell to a whisper. "In the ballroom." Maddie thought she saw the woman's lower lip tremble before she bit down so hard she left a dent.

"They want to talk to us." Leslie looked at Brooks. "To *all* of us. Down at the station." She swallowed and the tendons in her long swan neck tensed.

Maddie's first thought when she walked into the ballroom was, What have they done to Neverland?

"My lights," she heard Brooks's dad whisper.

Five tall lamps on tripods lit up the paint-spattered walls so the letters glistened. As if, Maddie thought, they were still wet. Officer Hardy took photos of the wall with a Polaroid camera.

LOVE ME

FUCK ME

SAVE ME

SUMMER OF '92 4EVER

ROLO IS A ~~FOOL~~ GOD

PW + RB

GRUDDER IS CANCER

GRUDDER KILLS

Officer Hardy escorted them, one by one, to the little room at the back of the police station. Maddie had known him all her life, had been in the same class as his son Scott since kindergarten, and when he saw her he said, "Hey-ya, Maddie," and she felt a little better. Not as scared as she'd been during the long ride from the Castle to the station—Brooks and his dad squished in the back of one cop car; Maddie, Leslie, and Eva in another. Leslie had refused to look at Maddie and stared out the window as she rocked sleeping Eva in her arms. But as Maddie sat on the hard wooden bench in front of the station's front desk, waiting for her turn—first Brooks, then Jules, then Leslie, disappearing and returning—she began to panic. Would they call her father? Would he slap her in front of everyone and then take her home and . . . She tugged at the sleeve of her Wildcats sweatshirt so it covered the bandage.

She remembered she and Brooks and Penny joking about the police station that first night in the ballroom. What was it Brooks had said? That it looked like the setting for a Disney movie. A thatched cottage fit for gnomes and dwarfs and talking animals. She thought of mentioning it now and realized how dumb that was. Reached for his hand instead. He pulled away.

Leslie hummed to Eva. A song that sounded familiar. Eva woke crying, squinting in the fluorescent light. Leslie unbuttoned her shirt, pulled out a pale breast, and Eva took her mother's nipple into her mouth and settled down. Maddie couldn't look away. She'd never seen a baby nurse. Didn't know that big little kids like Eva could. Leslie caught her staring and gave Maddie a cold, hard look that made Maddie's stomach flip. Like Leslie was blaming *her* for all that had happened.

Officer Hardy led Maddie to the tiny back room that smelled like old bologna sandwiches and overheated coffee. Sheriff Stroh was sitting on one side of a table looking tired. A button over his big gut had popped open.

"Maddie LaRosa," he said with a sigh. "Surprised to see you here." And she knew he was blaming her too. He was disappointed, just like her mother and father would be, and maybe even Veronica. And what if Veronica wouldn't help her and Brooks escape the island, now that it was even more urgent they get away?

He asked her who had been partying at the Castle.

She named everyone, making sure not to miss even one kid. The more kids, she thought, the more people to blame. Less of a chance it would fall on Brooks's shoulders.

No, she said, she didn't know who brought the drugs.

No, she said, Mr. and Mrs. Marshall (Simmons, the sheriff corrected) had never ever given them any drugs or alcohol. They had no idea what was going on in the ballroom each night.

No, no one had helped Penny climb up to the balcony. She had done it herself.

Yes, they had tried to stop her.

"I did everything I could. I begged her," Maddie said as tears blurred the room.

No, she didn't know anything about the graffiti on the walls. No, she didn't know anything about the vandalism. No, no, no.

"Are we going to jail?" she asked, and a sob broke free and then she was crying so she got the hiccups.

Sheriff Stroh chuckled. "No, darling."

She asked if she could go back to the hospital. To be with Penny.

"Someone's coming to pick you up," Sheriff Stroh said. "Bring you home so you can get some rest. Then you can be at the hospital bright and early to visit your friend."

Please let it be Mom, Maddie thought. Not Dad.

Officer Hardy led her back down the corridor and she heard Enzo's loud voice protesting. "Don't even look at me, man."

Her cousins were sitting on the bench, only a small space between them and Brooks and his parents. Enzo glared at Brooks. Leaned over and whispered. Maddie saw his lips moving but couldn't make out what he said.

"No talking," Officer Hardy said in a harsh tone Maddie would never have guessed the man capable of. He'd been her soccer coach back in elementary school and had baked them cookies shaped like soccer balls. "Please," he added.

Vinny tried to catch Maddie's eyes but she looked away. "Maddalena," he said, and then spoke fast in Italian but she couldn't understand him, not with his teeth clenched like that, not with Brooks looking up at her so sad, and then Veronica was there, bursting through the front door in her white cashmere coat, her arms wide, her hair wrapped in a turban, like she'd jumped out of an old black-and-white movie.

"Oh dear," Veronica was saying. "What a night you've had!"

Maddie exhaled. The room spun and Veronica looped an arm through hers just in time to brace her.

Her grandmother winked at Officer Hardy, who bowed his head and said, "Mrs. Pencott, ma'am."

"I'll be taking this one with me now," Veronica said, smiling at Maddie.

42.

Veronica

She left Maddie in White Eagle's guest room to finish packing her things, then hurried as fast as her old legs would move across the lawn to the cottage. Thank goodness for small miracles, she thought—Tony wasn't home. Dom sat in front of the TV set watching that trashy show *Cops*.

Bad boys/ bad boys/ whatcha gonna do?/ whatcha gonna do when they come for you?

Veronica nearly laughed at the irony, then remembered the fear hanging over the bench at the police station.

Ginny's bedroom door was closed.

Dom eyed Veronica suspiciously, popping one potato chip after another into his mouth, as she grabbed brown paper grocery bags and began stuffing them with Maddie's clothes, makeup, hair gel, the stuffed animals sitting on the girl's neatly made bed.

"What's going on?" Dom asked from the bedroom doorway.

"Maddie needs some things." Veronica sat on the bed to slow her heart. Breathe in and out.

"Is something bad happening?" Dom asked.

He sounded like a child. She opened her arms and said, "Come give me a hug," and he came to her.

She heard Bob shouting at the TV as she climbed the front steps of White Eagle, out of breath. All morning, he'd been ranting at the images of Clinton and Gore departing on a bus tour of America. Maddie sat next to him on the sofa, her hands folded in her lap. The poor girl was in shock.

"I brought someone!" Veronica sang.

Dom hopped onto the sofa next to Maddie and wrapped his sun-browned arms around his sister. The girl sat still, her gaze unfocused. As if, Veronica thought, under a spell.

"Good boy," Veronica said. "You take care of your sister while I finish up the packing."

She started in her bedroom, dumping her diamond necklace, pearl and ruby ring, emerald brooch, into a velvet pouch. If only she'd had time to go to the bank and open the safety deposit box where they kept cash.

Bob yelled from the TV room. "Did you hide my pistol so I wouldn't shoot this draft-dodging piece of shit?"

The pistol. Hadn't she locked it up after her visit to Tony in the cottage?

"It's in the lockbox, dear," she yelled back. "Don't go shooting the television set!"

She found the cash she kept in the junk drawer next to the oven. Four hundred, plus change. And there was the money in her vanity. Two hundred and forty. She wrapped it in an envelope, secured it with a rubber band, then stuffed it into the inside pocket of the suitcase open on the guest-room bed. Maddie's bed. She'd enjoyed having her granddaughter with her those past few weeks. Their quiet breakfasts in the sunroom. Their daily *Oprah* viewings. She loved watching Maddie talk, think, move—the way the girl wiggled her toes while she read one of the novels Veronica had loaned her. Books by Edith Wharton and Charlotte Brontë. Tolstoy and Willa Cather. The girl devoured them. Veronica had dreamt up so many plans for them. Trips to museums in the city. A private fitting at Saks so she could buy Maddie some proper clothes to take to college someday. Movie marathons and book discussions. Painting lessons. The kinds of activities she should've done with Ginny years ago. She'd even looked into flights to Chicago so the two of them could watch *Oprah* live. Silly dreams, she thought now as she wrapped a pair of ruby earrings in black velvet and tucked it in the girl's worn leather purse.

It was nice while it lasted. A second chance to be a mother. When Maddie left the island, Veronica would kill herself. She'd call the nursing home and arrange to have Bob picked up. Then she'd gather the pills, make one last whiskey sour to down them, and with her rose-tinted plastic shopping bag, she'd, finally, complete her plan. Her mission.

"Hug your sister," she told Dom as she pushed the velvet pouches full of jewels into Maddie's hands.

"But," he started.

"No buts," Veronica said. "You'll see her soon. You and I will drive into the city next week and spend a long visit with Maddie."

She had already made the arrangements—rented a studio apartment in a nice neighborhood, within walking distance of a community college where the girl (and her boyfriend) could study for the GED.

"But," Maddie said, "I don't want to leave you."

Veronica was, all at once, relieved, amused, bereft. Her heart could still break. A jaded old woman could feel girlish pain.

"It's okay, my love. I've known so much in my eighty years. But I never knew what it felt like to feel safe. I want you to know that."

She held the girl's trembling hands. Bill Clinton's rasping voice sounded from the TV, preaching about community, compassion, and hope, about growing up without a father.

"Puh-lease," Bob shouted at the TV. "You're a crybaby sissy *and* a womanizing piece of garbage!"

"You've found the person that comforts you, Maddie," Veronica whispered, leaning close so she could smell the girl's sugary perfume. "Your salvation. You found that. Protect it." She added, "Protect *him*. Get him off this island first thing in the morning."

"Okay," Maddie sobbed. "Okay."

She didn't mean to tell Maddie the story of her own mother's abandonment. A story she'd never even told Bob. "For years, I thought my mother was wicked . . . for leaving me, and my brothers and sisters. Now I understand." She looked at Bob standing in front of the TV, his skinny legs bare under his Hawaiian-print robe, the remote control in his hand, pointed at the set like a gun.

"Life is short." She smiled at Maddie. "A girl must do what's necessary to claim . . ."—she paused—"*steal* her own bit of happiness."

43.

Dom

He'd followed her halfway to the Castle. Begged her to let him carry one of the stuffed suitcases she dragged down the dirt path. She had yelled at him, "Go home, Dom!" Like he was the Colonel's dumb dog.

Didn't she know there was no home without her?

He turned back. Choked on his tears on the walk back to White Eagle. Let snot run into his mouth.

He sat for a bit in the cool, damp pachysandra that stretched from the edge of the cottage lawn into the trail. He didn't mind the wet, or the tickle of the spiders and blind roly-poly bugs crawling along his bare legs. If he could, he'd ditch his bed and clothes, even his toys, and live in the woods. Eat berries and squirrels, whose thin skulls he'd crack with a sling and stone and roast over a pit, just like in the book he'd read about the soldiers who'd fought guerilla-style in Vietnam. Weeks, months, endured living off the jungle—eating monkey brains and centipedes.

She had to come back. Didn't she? This was just like in one of those after-school specials on TV. The girl running away from home only to realize there was nothing better in the outside world.

It was his fault. Ratting on her and Brooks to his dad at the Fourth of July party at the club. If he hadn't, she would've never moved out of the cottage and into White Eagle. The first step to leaving him behind.

He thought of all the wrongs he'd done her. Like the time he'd kneed her in the nose when she was tying a shoelace so a spurt of blood sprayed her white T-shirt. All 'cause she called him a wuss. Which he knew was the truth anyway.

The night was cool, the air soft from the breeze blowing ashore. Maybe, he thought, he could convince her to play just one game of Gods versus Mortals, a quick chase through the forest. When it was time to crawl in bed, he'd fall fast asleep. No jerking off. No dirty thoughts that he'd have to drag around guilt-heavy the next day.

"What's going on here, Lieutenant?"

Dom jumped to his feet and wiped his face with the front of his T-shirt.

"Maddie," Dom stuttered. "She's gone."

The Colonel clapped a hand on Dom's shoulder, setting him off balance.

"Loss is hard, my boy. But inevitable in times of war."

"You don't understand," Dom said, sighing. He was tired and scared and cold. He didn't want to put up with his grandfather's confused ranting that made Dom's head feel like it was stuffed with chattering crows. "There is no *war*."

The old man's Popeye eye squinted hard.

"*I* don't understand?" He laughed. *Heh-heh*. "I'm the *only* one who understands what's going on here."

Dom kicked at the damp dirt.

"You don't know how lucky you are," the Colonel said. "Got a chance to go to college. Get educated. Instead of ending up like your father."

"Dad's fine."

"You think *fine* is working on the factory floor? Or being a grease monkey in a car garage?"

The tips of Dom's ears tingled with heat.

The Colonel laughed. It was ugly. His stout body bending forward so the top of his bald head caught the moonlight and glowed.

"Your father is a *fraud*," he said. "I know you love your dad, son." He squeezed Dom's shoulder so it ached. "But he's ruined your mother's life with his lack of skills and education. Why do you think she takes those pills?"

"Because she's stuck on this crappy island filled with old clueless men like you who have no idea—"

The slap stung more than Dom had imagined it would from those soft, manicured hands.

He squeezed his eyes against the tears. He wasn't going to cry. Not now.

When he opened his eyes, he saw his grandfather was staring at his hands. They were shaking, making the old man's soft, round middle quiver. Like a bowl full of jelly, Dom thought. The Colonel lunged toward him. Dom recoiled, stepped back, tripped over a tree root, almost fell on his ass. He was ready to run through the forest. Run to the shed and grab his father's machete.

"Let me tell you what real fear is, Lieutenant Pencott," the old man said, his head bowed, his hands twisting. Like he was strangling an invisible man. "Not the numb complacency Americans are used to today. Oh no!"

Dom knew what fear was. Fear was MJ Bundy's voice in his ear. *Suck it. Open your mouth. There you go.* Fear smelled like Sean Waldinger puking up the square pizza he'd eaten for lunch. He should confess. Show the Colonel in sickening detail that afternoon in the woods behind the school. Then, he'd finally get the punishment he deserved. The Colonel wouldn't hold back.

"Some nights," the Colonel whispered, "I dream of someone attacking us. On our own soil. They think it can't happen. But oh yessirree, it can!"

Fear, Dom knew, sounded like the wet *thwock-thwock* of his mouth as he took Sean Waldinger in it, MJ's fat hand pressing down until he gagged.

"Something's got to happen," the Colonel mumbled. "To wake America up. Show them their safety is a fantasy. A lie! Then Grudder will be needed again."

He almost felt sorry for the old man. How could he not know, Dom wondered as he heard the sound of tires screeching through the woods, near the Castle, that there was no saving them now?

44.

Maddie

She dropped her bags at the front of the Castle entrance. Her hands were striped red from the suitcase handles. She felt a migraine coming, ready to wrap her in that gauzy gray that felt like both a prison and a release. She couldn't worry when in that much pain—not about abandoning Veronica and poor sweet Dom, leaving without saying goodbye to her mother. Eleven hours and she and Brooks would take the ferry across the Sound, where Veronica swore there'd be a driver waiting to take them to the apartment in the city.

The ballroom was still lit by the tall work lamps. Brooks sat in one of the beanbag chairs. His eyes closed. His headphones on, the cord dangling unplugged at his feet.

His mom and dad were there too, arguing. Maddie stepped into the shadows.

Jules's sweaty face shone under the harsh light. "What did you *think* was going to happen?"

Leslie stared at the wall of graffiti. When she spoke, her voice was quiet. As still as the calm at the eye of a hurricane, Maddie thought.

"They killed our children. Our babies."

She pointed toward the front door, as if, Maddie thought, the islanders responsible for whatever the stunned woman was talking about stood in line at the Castle's doors, waiting for their talking-to.

Jules's voice softened. "And . . . Jesus, Leslie, you used *their* children. The island's lost boys. You might as well be one of their admirals sending boys out to die. And for what? For your perverse justice."

"Poor little islanders," Leslie said, and Maddie knew Brooks's mom was mocking his dad. Her pretty mouth was ugly and warped. "They're killers. They poison the world with their bombers. The island with their garbage. They kill their own children. Brainwash them to worship at the altar of war and greed and destruction."

Jules shook his head. Laughed. "How long did it take for you to come up with that BS? You should get a job writing propaganda for the fucking Joint Chiefs of Staff."

"The people on this island," Leslie said, "don't deserve your pity." She shouted, "And they sure as hell don't have any pity for you!"

"There's something you need to hear, Leslie," he said softly. "I didn't want to be the one to tell you. *You* are no saint."

She screamed. Maddie saw Brooks flinch. He covered his head with his sweatshirt hood and she wanted to run to him but she was scared. His mom was going crazy. Digging her fingers into her hair and tugging so golden strands floated in the light-filled air. Like the caterpillar threads in the night sky at the fair.

"You think you *know* me, Julius? Then how can you not know how my dead babies have been with me? Always. I carry them in here." She punched her stomach hard. Maddie winced. "My babies! Poisoned by those monsters you feel sorry for."

"You are not better than everyone on this island," he said. "You used us. You used our children. And for what? Some revenge plot straight out of a crappy movie?"

"You'll never know," she said, "how vengeance heals the soul."

Maddie stepped out from the shadows. Her sneakers squeaked across the ballroom floor.

"Brooks?"

He stood, walked over to her, had just reached her, when tires screeched outside. She knew it was Vinny and Enzo even before the four of them—Maddie, Brooks, and his parents—made it out onto the Castle's marble front steps. The twins' red Cougar's engine revved and gravel spit out from behind the back wheels. Like in some old movie about gangs and brawls, and she looked to Brooks, almost laughed, because it was so silly, her cousins showing up like this. After everything had worked out okay. They'd all talked to the cops. No one was locked in jail. Penny would be okay. The doctors had promised. And soon, she and Brooks would be far away. Safe.

Brooks's face was gray. The muscle in his jaw flexing. The car doors swung open and Black Sabbath shattered the quiet. Sounding nothing like music, Maddie thought, but more like hard things hitting one another and breaking. Maddie felt Leslie flinch, then saw her lean close to Jules, whispering in his ear. Whatever Leslie said made Jules stare at his wife like he was confused. He disappeared into the house.

"You guys," Maddie called out. Brooks pulled her back so her hair swung into her face. "I'm *just* going to talk to them."

"Don't move," he whispered.

"Yo, Brooks," Vinny said. Sounding, Maddie thought, friendly enough. "We got to pow-wow, man."

She saw the glint of something dangling along Enzo's leg. The thick chain her uncle used at the shop to tow broken-down cars. She thought about running to the cottage, calling her father—maybe he was at the garage, maybe not—it was close to two in the morning.

"I'm going to call Sheriff Stroh," she said.

"Don't move, Maddie." There was a threat in Brooks's voice.

"You need to go," Leslie called to Vinny and Enzo. "It's late."

"Leslie," Enzo walked out of the shadows and into the lamplit drive. Maddie saw she was right about the chain. "Leslie Day."

Now that they were closer, standing between the two old-fashioned lampposts burning with gas, the white moths making them glow a foggy white, Maddie saw all four boys were there. Paulie held a bat. Mute Tim a metal bar.

"Did you rat on us, Leslie?" Vinny said. "You promised you'd protect us."

"And I will," Leslie said. "I did!"

She was begging. Maddie saw the thin white cotton of Leslie's bathrobe tremble.

"Maddie," Enzo said. "Come here." He sounded like her father. That same clipped command. Same up-nod with his sharp chin. She almost walked down the steps.

Brooks yanked her behind him.

"She's staying here."

Vinny laughed. Ugly and clownish. All that time she'd been scared of Enzo, when Vinny, she saw now, was the one to fear. Hiding under winks and buttery charm.

"You're right," he said. "We don't want her anyway. Not really. Not after you ruined her with your dirty black you-know-what."

"Vinny?" she said.

His answer came when he grabbed the baseball bat from Paulie's hands and drove it into the lamppost. An explosion of glass and white moths' wings. Brooks's arms wrapped around Maddie, shielding her. The gas flame, free, shot up and burned brighter, bluer.

Vinny hopped up and down. Excited. Giddy with his own power, Maddie thought. Enzo high-fived Paulie. Quiet Tim threw back his head and howled like a wolf.

They smashed the clay pots lining the brick path that led to the front door. The violets and geraniums and purple shamrock Maddie had seen Jules plant. Black dirt sprayed.

They shouted ugly things about busting into the Castle, tying Brooks's family up, showing Leslie what it felt like to be with a real man (*She'd wanted them,* Enzo shouted, from that first night at the fair, *don't lie, Leslie!*). They promised not to hurt them too bad, but an eye for an eye, Vinny said. Even Maddie, he explained, had to be taught a lesson. They called them liars, cowards, rats, and cheats, and the worst thing Maddie knew anyone on the island could be called. Traitors.

They were only a few strides from the front steps when Maddie heard Jules return and Brooks said, "Dad, no. No."

She smelled the hard alcohol on her cousins. The cigarette smoke. Their drugstore cologne. Enzo had the LaRosa eyes, like Dom. Like her father. Fringed with dark lashes. So big there was a slice of white that showed above and below his irises. Nonna LaRosa had told them it was good luck. A touch of God.

Vinny lunged forward. A flying leap. Just like when he stole a base, Maddie thought, his long, lean body stretched in a kind of arabesque, as graceful as a dancer onstage. She couldn't tell what came first, Brooks pushing her aside so she fell into the rosebushes next to the stairs, her face and arms and legs stung by thorns.

Or the shot.

The crack of the blast washed over her like whitecaps pounding the shore in a storm. The flash of the muzzle lit the air and she watched Vinny's back arch, his arms fly up at his sides, frozen in surrender. Like all the Jesuses on all the crosses that hung on Nonna LaRosa's walls.

A swell rose up from the dark woods. The breathy buzz of the caterpillars feeding—they were back, Maddie thought numbly—like a damning curse. But it was Enzo screaming, wailing, pounding his fists on his twin brother's bloody chest.

45.

Jules

The rifle rolled out of his hands. A woman screamed. Was it Leslie? He dropped to his knees and raked his fingers through the grass. His grass. Pulled it toward him as if he could gather it up in one wide swath, wrap it around his shoulders like a cape. Disappear.

His father was screaming too. *What have you done? What in God's name have you done?*

Jules's ears rang with the dull *thunk* of flesh hitting flesh, and over it all the music of the night—the grasshoppers chirping, the owls hooting—as if nothing extraordinary was happening.

He remembered a line from a play. Not the one he was named for. Another about a monster of a storm. *Hell is empty. And all the devils are here*. On this island. On his lawn. And he was one of them.

PART FIVE

The Spawning

Late August–Early September 1992

The female lays her eggs in July and August close to the spot where she pupated. Then, both adult gypsy moths die.

Four to six weeks later, embryos develop into larvae. The larvae remain in the eggs during the winter. The eggs hatch the following spring.

—*Forest Insect & Disease Leaflet 162*, US Department of Agriculture Forest Service, 1989

46.

Jules

He was twelve. A few years younger than Brooks. His father had dragged him ten stops on the bus out to Cherryville. There were no cherries there; Jules had known that because even the toughest kids on his block, like Fireman Timmy's son, Clive, called Cherryville the ghetto, and when neighborhood moms stopped to chat on one another's stoops, they talked about the C-ville gang wars. He knew it was a bad place where bad shit happened because when his pops talked about *Them*, he meant the blacks who lived in Cherryville.

His pops said there were two kinds. Those trying to make a life for their families. And *Them*. Them let their kids run around in dirty diapers and too-small shoes. Them were late with bills and got their heat turned off midwinter but leased shiny cars with neon tubes lighting up the undercarriage and stereos that boomed bass so it made your stomach roll. Them let their dogs crap on the sidewalk, counting on the rain to wash it away. Them dumped old furniture, stoves, cracked sinks, and stained toilets on the sidewalk without calling sanitation for a pickup so the garbage sat for weeks.

It was his view, his pops said. Jules's too.

Now his dad was dumping Jules *there* with *them* to teach him a lesson.

Get off the damn bus, his pops ordered.

The tired passengers turned to stare. They were all brown-skinned like him and his dad but felt foreign. Jules was in his fancy school uniform and the gray cashmere overcoat his mother had taken on extra mending work to pay for, wanting him to fit right in at school. The faces on the bus were slack, uninterested, and years later, he'd understand that they'd practiced that look of not caring to protect themselves from all the shitty things they had and would witness.

His pops's eyes had been rolling mad since he'd picked Jules up from Mrs. Lee's corner convenience store, where Jules worked a few hours after school twice a week. Mr. Lee had gone through Jules's backpack and found the pack of baseball cards he'd swiped. Mr. Lee called his pops. Who was throwing Jules into the dark streets of C-ville, among the gangs of murderous thugs his dad had warned him about—spinning stories rich with guns and beheadings and heroin and man-rape and dirty switch-blades, stories darker than any Grimm fairy tale. A skinny motherfucker in a private school blazer. A crybaby. 'Cause he *was* crying, whispering through his tears and snot. *Never again, Pops. Never. I swear.*

He huddled inside the bus shelter—the tips of his school shoes, polished by his mom every night, shining in the streetlight. He sweated through his clothes and when the bus came back on the opposite route twenty minutes later and he climbed on and sat next to his father, his pops's nose wrinkled from Jules's stink.

His father's hand reached between Jules's legs and pinched the soft inner skin of his thigh.

Hope you learned your lesson, son. Fear is your best friend. You stay scared. Hear me?

Jules heard him now.

His father visited. In the hour Jules walked the prison yard watching, waiting, for someone—a relative of the boy or a hit man hired by the boy's family—to kill him. Stab him in the liver with a jail-made knife, break his neck with a finely placed grip-squeeze-twist. He spoke with his father in the yard, figuring it didn't hurt that he looked crazy arguing with himself. Hell, maybe he was crazy. Not crazy enough, his lawyer had told him after the psychiatrist from court visited.

His lawyer, Stan—a jittery twentysomething in thick, black-framed glasses—had asked so many questions. About Jules's parents, his grandparents, stretching way back when, to great-great grandparents he'd only seen in yellowed photos in his mom's albums. Stan was digging, Jules realized, for a story. An offering for the judge. Stan asked Jules if anything bad had happened to anyone in his family, any victims of racially incited crime. Jules had almost laughed. Shit, what black man didn't have a bucket-load of stories to tell?

They had meeting after meeting. Jules recounting stories his mother and father had told him years ago, or he'd overheard as a kid at his great-aunt's dining-room table. Jules ate half-cooked Hot Pockets and cherry Coca-Cola Stan bought from the vend-ing machines in the visitors' area, and the small gray meeting room filled with ghosts. His father's. His mother's. His great-aunt Eunice, who'd been raped by a gang of white men at the hotel she'd cleaned uptown. The further back, the bloodier the stories, the happier the lawyer seemed—nodding as he took pages of notes on yellow legal pads. More, Stan demanded, more. Jules's grandfather Samuel had lost three fingers in a machinery acci-dent at a lumber mill down in North Carolina. His grandmother Laverne's daughter Susanna had drowned in the Ashepoo River floods when she was four, Eva's age. And there was Grandpa John, his pops's father, a sad old man with a crooked back who Jules remembered visiting when he was a boy. He'd had a cane top made from the hoof of a deer, the fur blond and silky.

Sad how? Stan asked, and Jules felt the lawyer lean forward in his chair. Hungry for a story.

He told how Grandpa John's shop—a general store that sold packets of seeds and dry goods and other sundries to the blacks of Beaver Falls, Pennsylvania—was burned down to its posts one night by a group of men Jules's dad claimed were KKK. The lawyer pumped a sleek suited arm in the air. Like they'd bet on the right horse. PTSD, his lawyer explained. Handed down through generations. Trauma so powerful it changes a man's DNA.

Jules wanted this to be true, and when he visited with Stan each week, the man's enthusiasm when he spun that tale (Jules knew the story no longer belonged to him, not to Grandpa John either) almost made Jules believe he hadn't known what he'd been doing when he grabbed the rifle from the glass case in the Castle entry hall, pointed, and fired.

He should have known it would be loaded. What gun on that island wasn't? He should've seen it coming, starting with the *Cattleya labiate*. The fragile orchid bobbing up and down on that cow's bosom at the fair. The demented Colonel asking Jules if he was the admiral's *man* in the tower as the cold stone floor vibrated with the bell's tolling. *Should've, should've, should've* circled Jules's head like those bluebirds did Tom the cartoon cat's head after he got bonked by the teeny mouse who looked like he couldn't hurt a fly.

Jules lived for his talks with Pops, who seemed to enjoy them too. Some led to spats, insults, silent grudges that lasted two or three days—Jules sitting on the cold floor of his cell wishing for his father to return.

Julius. He felt his father shaking his balding head.

"You told me to follow the rules. I did that. And look where it got me."

His father laughed. *You call moving to an island thick with white people playing by the rules? Son, you strutted right into the lion's den.*

It was her, Jules thought. Scheherazade. Leslie had led him. He wouldn't admit to it in front of his father—give him the pleasure of saying, again, *I told you so.*

"What good are the rules," Jules asked, "the laws, moral this and that, when you can't follow them *and* protect your family at the same time?"

His father's voice was slow and dreamy, like he was half asleep. Or was it Jules who was falling asleep? *Oh, is that what it was? Self-defense? I told you,* he began.

Jules threw a plastic cup against the wall. Someone—a guard, an inmate—shouted *Shut the fuck up* down the cell block.

Tell me what I said. His father's voice was stern. Disappointed. Had his father seen Leslie wail when she visited, the social worker dragging her from the visiting room so as not to upset the other families? Did he know about Brooks refusing to talk to Jules even over the phone? And Eva's tiny voice telling him she loved him just before the pay phone timer cut out so he couldn't say it back.

What did I tell you?

"Get off the island," Jules mumbled.

Every night, in the garden, as Jules had picked the caterpillars until his blisters wept. Every night, as he'd scraped the furred egg clusters off his chestnut tree. His pops had whispered the same command.

Get off that island. Grab your son and get gone. Go. Go now.

He should've known when he saw that tar-faced lawn jockey the night of the traveling dinner party, tucked among the crimson *Spigelia marilandica* blooms. When he listened to Veronica make excuses, prattling on about George Washington's devoted servant who'd given his life for his master. He tried to imagine what Jocko would've seen if he hadn't perished, hadn't frozen to death with the reins of Washington's horses in his hands. The praise, the hurrahs. All those white men acting as if, for a moment, he was their equal. How beautiful Jocko's reflection would've seemed staring back at him, mirrored in those white men's eyes.

Jules sat crosslegged in his cell (*crisscross applesauce,* he heard little Eva say) and recited the Latin names of plants. *Digitalis grandiflora* (yellow foxglove), *lonicera caprifolium* (honeysuckle), *myosotis sylvatica* (forget-me-not). Named two thousand years ago by Carl Linnaeus, a God-fearing man who believed in a divine plan, and whose rigid classification system—Kingdom, Phylum, Class, Order . . . had always made Jules feel safe. More now than ever.

He closed his eyes and imagined a cell within his cell but one whose walls were living, breathing, growing. Blooming. Vines and tendrils stretched across the scarred cement—pink twining clematis and Heavenly Blue morning glory. His mind was a magic wand. One flick and fiery *vitis coignetiae*'s heart-shaped leaves striped a wall; another draped with fragrant starry jasmine.

He smelled the boxwood's oily leaves heating in the sun, heard the rustle of fern fronds. He was in the secret garden, the room at the heart of the maze. The buttery forsythia was in bloom, the peonies bursting and spotted with ladybugs. Plenty of time to replant. Grow from seed. Heal. He dug his naked fingers into the soil, past the blind earthworms and pill bugs and even a scuttling millipede. Deeper, deeper, he hit sand and silt, and, deeper still, cool damp clay. He dug until he himself was buried—his mouth and nose filled with a dark earthy odor. When he opened his eyes, he felt spent, his muscles aching, as if he'd worked his land all day.

Many species of birds have been observed feeding on gypsy moth larvae or adults. Nuthatches, chickadees, towhees, vireos, northern orioles, catbirds, robins, and blue jays are probably more important in sparse gypsy moth populations. Cuckoos and flocking species such as starlings, grackles, red-winged blackbirds, and crows may be attracted to areas where the gypsy moth exists in large numbers.

Some mammalian predators of the gypsy moth include the white-footed mouse, shrews, chipmunks, voles, and squirrels. Shrews, which are often mistaken for mice, are voracious insect feeders that consume their own weight in prey each day.

—"The Homeowner and the Gypsy Moth: Guidelines for Control," United States Department of Agriculture, *Home and Garden Bulletin*, No. 227 (1979)

47.

Dom

Today, he was Hermes, right-hand man of Zeus. Winged messenger. A god so cunning he was still in diapers when he stole his big brother Apollo's prized cattle.

Hermes was Dom's favorite. He was one of those sticky gods, no saint but not one hundred percent sinner. He stole, cheated, lied, and even killed when his mission demanded, but he did it with style.

Dom had memorized all of Hermes's roles. He was the deliverer of dreams, the world's first Sandman—choosing which men slept in peace and which tossed and turned. He was the escort of the newly dead to the Underworld and the protector of youths. He was the patron of sports, especially fighters like Dom's WWF wrestlers. Worshipped by shepherds and travelers, merchants and gamblers, and even military men like the Colonel. Dom had read about ancient generals, on the night before battle, sacrificing lambs, honey, pigs, incense, and cake at the feet of mighty statues carved in Hermes's likeness—each topped with his winged hat.

Dom had combed the beach and found two white-and-gray seagull feathers. They weren't the same size but good enough. He'd cut a hole on each side of the soft gray brimmed hat he'd found in his grandfather's closet. The feather ends fit perfectly—one on each side of Dom's head.

As he tramped through the woods, he saw the webs thick as Halloween decorations in the crooks and bends of branches. The moths were dead. Now their eggs sat, waiting for spring. He waved away clouds of no-see-ums shuddering in the still and wet August heat, trying not to smudge the makeup he'd spread over his face—a tube of mercury-colored lipstick Maddie had worn one Halloween when she went as the Tin Man. Sweat beaded over the greasy cream and his hair was already soaked under the too-big hat. But he told himself to man up—he bet Hermes hadn't ever complained about any of *his* missions.

By the time Dom reached the Castle, his T-shirt was stuck to his sweating back and he could already feel the itch of the mosquito bites swelling up and down his legs. His left foot stung where Maddie's sandals, a size too big, had rubbed. He'd used silver model-plane paint to transform the sandals into a sterling Arcadian pair fit for the god of trickery. It was magical sandals that had saved Hermes from Apollo's wrath over the stolen herd, Dom remembered, hiding Hermes's footprints, and his identity.

Maddie's journal mentioned two codes to get through the maze, and Dom had memorized both, but now he couldn't remember which code went to the center and which to the cottage. He stepped into the maze—the scent of fresh-cut wood reminding him of the first day he met Jules and how gently the man had wiped Dom's clay-covered face.

He was lost after only a few turns. Was it left, left, right, left? He tried to circle back to the entrance. Start over. After two rights, a left, and another right, he was still lost.

More turns and he found the hedge-walled room at the center. He imagined he could see the impression in the grass where Maddie and Brooks had lain.

It seemed a hundred lefts and rights later he was still trapped. He fell against the leafy wall and hugged his knees to his chest. He'd have to yell for help. Hope that Brooks found him. If it came to that, he'd abort his mission and go back home. Dig out the bottle of vodka he'd hidden behind the Drāno and crap-caked toilet plunger in the bathroom upstairs and drink it all. Maybe chase the vodka with the Drāno.

His father was right. And those scumbags at school, MJ and Victor, all of them had been right when they called him names, told him just go ahead and kill yourself, why don'tcha? He was blubbering like a goddamn baby now and the greasy lip paint came off on his fingers, got in his eyes and stung, made the tears come faster. He knew what the Colonel would say. *Shape up or ship out.* Don't be soft. That was the problem with the world today. The world in peacetime. People got comfortable, started feeling safe, and instead of worrying about life and death, they worried about how much everyone liked them, and whether they were pretty, and what if they weren't special.

He stood. He'd give himself one more try and surrender if he failed, shout for help like a child lost in a supermarket. *Mommy! Mommy!* He held his breath and listened. The jingling call of a dark-eyed junco overhead. Or was it a pine warbler? He never could tell the difference. Something scampered in the woods. A crow cawed. He blew snot from his nose and it landed in a glob on the trampled grass. Then he heard the long rip of what sounded like packing tape. Like a sign, it lured him forward. Showed him the way. Left, right—no, that wasn't it—the sound of the tape ripping, cardboard scraping told him so. Left, right, left, and the sounds grew louder and he knew he was moving in the right direction. He was Hermes again, returned to his mission. He saw the light of the cottage burning through the last hedged wall, heard the music playing, picked out the saxophone wail, the hum of the upright bass.

He was the god of games and omens, of diplomacy and guard dogs. He was the protector of homes. He remembered what the Colonel had said: *Sometimes, you're the mouth. Sometimes, you're the meal.* Dom didn't want to be the meal—never again.

48.

Maddie

She was in the cottage packing the rest of her things. Once Brooks had finished boxing up his family's stuff at the Castle and was back in the city with his mother and Eva, she would go to him.

Sun trickled through the tree canopy outside. Some of the leaves had grown back.

A crack sounded through the woods. Then two more. She heard the airy flapping of startled birds.

She was out the door, running toward the Castle. Running without seeing, without her bare feet touching the muddy path, without feeling the bramble thorns tearing at her naked legs.

Brooks was on his stomach, his face pressed into the overgrown lawn. Like he'd felt tired and laid down, the lush grass a pillow. A box had tumbled onto its side next to him. Eva's brightly colored plastic blocks scattered.

She rolled him over. A yellow buttercup stuck to his cheek. His face fell back into the grass, and she whispered, *Oh I'm sorry*, although she knew he was gone, gone, gone. She stood, slipped on the blood-smeared grass and fell back, the air knocked from her lungs. He needs to be fixed, she thought as she crawled back to him, through the warm pool of his blood. He is broken. And needs to be fixed. Just like Penny was fixed.

She was screaming *Fix him! Fix him! Fix him!* when the shots came from White Eagle.

49.

Veronica

She had considered blaming Bob.

Finally, she had taken responsibility for the mess herself.

She sat next to her husband of more than fifty years. He was splayed out on the sofa, the back of his shattered skull tipped back like a broken marionette, blood and brain staining the serene pastoral print.

Her ears rang from the two shots she'd fired into his head. Her shoulder ached from the gun's recoil.

He released his last breath and she smelled feces and burnt things. Like when her father branded a new cow back in Palmyra.

She had found her grandson in White Eagle's back garden near Ginny's childhood playhouse with the pink shutters and thatched roof. The boy was on his knees in the grass. Staring out to sea. His costume and his hands splattered with blood. Champ at his side, tail thumping happily as the dog licked her grandson's round boyish face. She'd given the boy orders: hide your clothes in the woods. Burn them tomorrow. Shower quickly. Scrub your wrists and fingers and arms and chest and face. If anyone asked, tell them you'd practiced shooting with the Colonel that morning. Never, ever tell the truth. Never tell Maddie. The greatest gift he could give his sister, Veronica had said, shaking the shocked boy so his greasy black bangs whipped his cheeks, was ignorance.

She would save her family. What did it matter, the ruining of Veronica Pencott's name, when her true self was unknown to anyone on the island. Anyone alive. Lucy Veronica Phelps. Bob's mother had urged her to use Veronica. Elegant enough to hide the stink of cow shit between her toes.

As she slid the gun barrel into her mouth, the metal squeaking against her dentures (she wouldn't be found toothless), she imagined Maddie sitting next to her. Her chiming laugh. Her scent. Like fresh-cut cantaloupe and white soap. Veronica told her to stay naïve, enough to believe in all their affirmations. And make up her own.

She would be leaving something behind after all. Her family. How silly she had been—believing she could erase herself from this world before leaving it.

50.

Dom

He was in his room. Waiting. He had accomplished the missions Veronica assigned him. Wash his hands (check), change his clothes (check), hide his dirty clothes in the woods (check). Never tell the truth. Not even to Maddie. Especially not Maddie.

He dug in his pocket and found the crushed honeysuckle flowers he'd picked. He'd watch her use her front teeth to snip the end of each bud, one after another. Until she smiled, laughed, said her tongue felt fuzzy. Maybe he'd convince her to play a game of Gods versus Mortals. He'd volunteer to play the bad guy, and when they went back in, their mom would be awake and their dad at the stove stirring a pot of sauce. He'd give both his parents hugs, his heart thrumming from the chase through the woods, his thigh muscles twitching, the cool night air wicking the sweat from his arms. All of it an antidote, a magic potion hand-delivered by Zeus himself, to make the creepy-crawlies vanish forever.

Maddie came to him, barefoot and crying. Bloody. He held her. He knew she wouldn't leave him now. She needed him to tell her everything would be all right.

51.

Leslie

The last dead baby had been full term. It was her eighth pregnancy. Eva had just turned two. She'd insisted on giving birth in the city hospital near Our Garden. The delivery nurses had looked at her funny—this white woman laboring among rows of black mothers.

She pushed for six hours. Jules kneaded the knots in her calves with his strong hands. The soil from Our Garden stuck under his nails. He counted her contractions until the numbers blurred.

The doctor who delivered the baby left when he saw it was dead. Leslie would never forget the swish of the swinging doors as the room emptied. The one nurse remaining—*Margaret,* her name tag read—urged them to take a photo with the baby. They may not want to look at it now, she said, but someday . . . The nurse swaddled their baby in a blue hospital blanket and he looked like he was sleeping. Like he'd open his swollen eyelids and blink hello. Crack open his blue lips and howl. They took turns holding him. Leslie asked Jules, *You won't leave me, will you? We can try again, can't we?* Repeated I'm sorry, I'm sorry, I'm sorry until she choked on her tears and snot and threw up in a pan next to the bed.

The nurse finally found the photographer. The same man happy new parents paid to take photos of their sleepy babies. *Baby's first bottle. Baby's first diaper. Baby's trip home from the hospital.* The camera flashed. The baby—they had planned to name him Linnaeus after Jules's beloved botanist—was taken away.

Epilogue

When the sun begins to sink into the gold-tipped waves, their mothers call them for dinner. The children leave their plastic buckets on the sandbar, filled with flailing hermit crabs, sea snails, and the honey-colored shells worn thin by tumbling waves so they are gnarled like toenails. That's what the children call them. Toenail shells.

Sandy arms and legs are toweled off and dressed in long-sleeve shirts to protect from the bite of green bottle flies. As the clouds turn the color of bruises, each family finds their table on the beach, the red-white-and-blue tablecloth weighed down with rocks gathered by the children. They settle down to eat as the sun sets on this last day of summer.

A summer they call unforgettable. *What a summer.* They talk about the caterpillars instead of the unspeakable things that happened at the Castle.

They pass plates of steaming shellfish—crab, lobster, mussels, and cherrystones—and roasted corn on the cob, red potatoes, and sweet sausage, all of it wrapped in seaweed and burlap and buried deep in the sand with fire-hot stones.

The fathers are proud of the feast. Cooked right there on shore, steps from where the shellfish were harvested, in the way of the Shinnecock tribes of long ago who lived only on what the island offered up. The infinite bounty of the sea. The men roll up their sleeves and flex the muscles they've earned at the factory. They paint lines under their sun- and beer-reddened eyes with shards of pink clay their children find on the beach. They whoop like the Indians they watched in spaghetti westerns as kids—white men in face paint. They slap their palms against open mouths until one of the mothers tells them to sit down and eat.

There are no exclamations—*Oh, how gorgeous* or *Look at*

that color or *It's like the sky is on fire*—because all the comparisons were made long ago when they first moved to the island. Or, they were born on the island, and watching the sun rise from and sink into the sea has always been routine. The beauty is their inheritance.

Thanks to the Colonel, the Grudder men think, not that they would mention his name aloud. Not yet. The island needs time to recover. The scant leaves left after the caterpillars' feast will soon turn color and fall to the ground. The island will go into hibernation, a much-needed respite to recoup its strength. On the third of November, Bill Clinton will win the presidential election with forty-three percent of the vote. Sheriff Stroh and his men will have a hellish week. Seven DUIs. One hostage situation at the Wildcat Café on the west side. A Grudder executive will hang himself in his private cabana at the Oyster Cove Country Club clubhouse. The hanged man will mention, in his suicide note, his disapproval of the first lady, Hillary Clinton, being given an office in the West Wing. He'll call it "unnatural and perverse."

Most of the furred gypsy moth eggs lovingly insulated by their long-dead mothers' body hair will perish during that unusually cold winter, and in the spring, the leaves will return. More plentiful than before. By that time, Julius Simmons will have served nine months for the shooting, in self-defense, of Vinny LaRosa. Vinny will wheel his chair into the courtroom to protest Julius's pardon and release. The courtroom will echo with islanders' outraged cries when the two-to-four-year prison sentence (attempted manslaughter and criminal possession of a weapon) is overturned. Judge Harvey Matthews will mention the tragic death of Brooks Marshall Simmons in his final statement, and some of those present, Enzo LaRosa for one, will think of that old biblical saying. An eye for an eye.

But for now, let the people of Avalon Island enjoy the last night of that eventful summer of '92. The whistling song of Singing Beach calls hundreds of islanders to the shore, sparklers and cold beers in hand, ready to sing "God Bless America" as fireworks light up the sea and a trail of paper lanterns dots the horizon like a ribbon aflame.

Let the girl (almost a woman) with the sun-kissed shoulders

run across the smooth wet sand, take her brother by the hand, pull him toward the woods for one more game before night falls. *You can play the hero*, she promises.

Let the men and women of Avalon Island, East and West, play make-believe—pretend they control life and death, war and peace, their kings and queens and workers and servants and country, and the warbirds they bring to life with aluminum and steel, baptized by fire. Let them believe—for one last night—they are immortal.

Acknowledgments

My earliest notes for *The Gypsy Moth Summer* are decades old.

One of my first creative writing assignments in college—back when I thought I'd deliver on my parents' wish for me to become a lawyer—resulted in a character sketch of the Colonel. That sketch turned into a story, then a novella, then an opening chapter that I revised once every year or so. I rewrote that first chapter from the Colonel's point of view, from Dom's, from Maddie's, and, once (I am ashamed to admit) from the perspective of the gypsy moth caterpillars, whose *cack-cacking* drone seemed to call to me. It was a story and world I could not forget.

Thank you to Elizabeth Beier, my editor, my mentor, guide, and friend, for bringing *The Gypsy Moth Summer* to life, and for accepting both the beauty and tragedy of Avalon Island, and my own perspective. Your positivity is an incredible gift and has taught me so much these past five years.

To Maria Massie, my agent and endlessly supportive friend, I would be lost without your strength, wisdom, and wit. Thank you for always making me laugh, even in the toughest times.

To the hardworking team at St. Martin's Press—Nicole Williams, Brittani Hilles, Courtney Reed, and Brant Janeway, and publishers, Sally Richardson and Jennifer Enderlin—thank you for your faith in me.

Deep gratitude to my earliest readers, writers Amy Bloom, Francine Prose, Caroline Leavitt, Joanna Rakoff, Matthew Thomas, Kaitlyn Greenidge, Scott Blackwood, Sophie Mc-Manus, and Rick Sayre; and independent bookstore owners and sellers Mary Cotton (Newtonville Books), Christine Onorati (WORD Bookstores), Mia Wigmore (Diesel Brentwood), and Andrew Unger (Kepler Books). To all the bookstores that have hosted me and supported my books, thank you. You make our world a better place.

To my children, Luca and Cecilia, your imagination and big-heartedness is the purest form of inspiration I've known. You've had to sacrifice so much for mommy's books. Someday, I hope you will understand why I couldn't play LEGOs with you all those hours I spent working. You taught me to love, and to *be* loved—a knowledge that enhances every word I write. Special thanks to Luca, whose love of Greek mythology inspired so much of this book, especially the ending. Never stop reading and sharing your brilliant stories.

Mille grazie to the Sackett Street writers who taught me how to write.

Thank you to the literary communities of NYC and Los Angeles, and to the bookish community online. My friends on social media, I heard every one of your cheers and they helped me bash on.

Long Island, my home island, thank you for your beautiful beaches and forests, which supplied endless atmospheric inspiration.

Special thanks to friends (and brilliant artists) Miranda Beverly-Whittemore, Amy Shearn, Kris Widger, Lisa Desimini, and Matt Mahurin, who were there when I needed them most.

Thank you to my two families—the Fierros and the Feinsteins. *Grazie* to *mio padre* Salvatore Fierro for the gypsy moth caterpillar illustration at the beginning of the book. And special thanks to Howie, who read the earliest versions of *The Gypsy Moth Summer* and reminded me again and again that it was a story that needed to be told.

To my literary kindred spirit, my best friend and forever reader, Caeli Wolfson Widger, thank you.

To Justin Feinstein, a partner in the truest sense—*ti amo*. Every word I write is dedicated to you and exists because of you. You are my everything.